sedan

an entertainment the **part** **one**

phil **cosker**

LAUGHING HORSE

Laughing Horse Books
Heighwood House
Timms Lane
Waddington, Lincolnshire
England LN5 9RQ

E-mail: philcosker@fsmail.net

ISBN 0 9547429 0 7

British Library Cataloguing in Publication Data.
A catalogue record of this book is available from the British Library.

> **Disclaimer**
> The characters portayed in this literary work are
> entirely fictitious and are not based on any person,
> or persons, living or dead.

In the case of quotations used in this literary work that are not in the public
domain the author has made every effort to secure permission for their use.

Edited by Jules Sewell
Cover Illustration by Allison Read
Cover design by Optima
Project managed by Richard Joseph Publishers Ltd, PO Box 15, Torrington,
Devon EX38 8ZJ.

Printed by Creative Print & Design (Wales) Ltd, Ebbw Vale

I dedicate this book to my family and friends.
Thank you for your love and support without
which this would not have been written.

The author acknowledges, with appreciation, the permission from Cécile Eluard Boaretto to reproduce Paul Eluard's (1895-1952) poem *Liberty*.

Introduction

This story is about the people of England in the future, after the 'big war' that no one won, and after the slump. The fossil fuels had run out. But people still had to get about. Money had to be made. (After all capitalism wasn't something that was ever going to go away.) Life went on.

The new transportation system was green, based on people, for the movement of people. The Sedan chair was the vehicle of choice (actually the only vehicle allowed or possible). Vehicles ranged in size from the two person single seater Sedan through to the Sedanathon (a large lightweight container) carried by a century of Legits (pronounced 'leg its') and commanded by a Legiturion. So far as the private traveller was concerned there was a range of vehicle types from the standard Plebsedan through to the luxury Aristosedan. The good thing about Legits was that they were living proof of equality of opportunity in action; both men and women of all races and creeds were allowed to carry their betters. This right had been enshrined in statute.

The newly elected Prime Minister (John Green) and his New Lablair Party had recently been elected to its 11th consecutive term as the government of His/Her Androgynous Majesty, the monarch known as HAM. Green's Cabinet had been busy ensuring that the "new national network of privatised sedan companies integrate their routes in such a way that the unemployed underclass are strategically exhausted on a regional, and sub regional, basis" (Hamish Hume, Minister of State for the Regions and Nations, *Hansard* on a wet Friday afternoon). Terry Travers (Minister of State for Transportation) had put it more simply: "It's bums on seats that count", "and feet in clogs" added Colin Cartage (the Regulator of ONLEG, The Office of National Legit Governance). The first franchises had been awarded to: Harlot Sedan; East Coast Sedan; Terminal Sedan (an economy line); South Con Sedan; Slog Sedan; and Imperial Sedan.

Each hamlet, village, town and city had its own sedan centre, or Sedantory as they were officially known. This method of transportation was only available to those who could afford to use it: after all England wasn't a meritocracy.

Significant members of the propertied class had their own garages of sedans and a stable of their very own indentured Legits. There had been some concern over illicit breeding between Legits but Betty Bekkes (Minister of State for Birth Control and Selective Breeding) had quipped, "No, I'm not worried. If you clip off the right balls you don't get many surprise pregnancies."

Members of the upper propertied class, and what remained of the aristocracy, were allowed to breed their own Legits to ensure continuity and the creation of Legits that were 'fit for purpose' (at this early period of development the prime benefit of using the underclass as Legits was that it reduced their numbers and kept them on the streets but not rioting). The State police used well fed, and highly trained Legits to carry their famous red and white Jamsedans to the scenes of crimes and protest (oh yes, there were still protests).

Legits were drawn primarily, though not exclusively, from the underclass comprised of single parents, the homeless, the long term unemployed, the educationally sub normal, the feckless, and a specially genetically engineered strain of super long-distance Legits. For certain short routes Legits were drawn from day care centres and homes for the old, senile and bewildered (where these still existed).

The criminal classes (whilst in prison) were not involved in the transportation of Sedanists (those entitled to travel by sedan) but rather in the construction and maintenance of the vehicles themselves. The futile attempt to privatise the prison service had been replaced by custodial factories within which those interred received the necessary training in transferable skills associated with sedan manufacture. The notion of life long learning (a long cherished aspiration of New Lablair) was supported through a skills enhancement programme that enabled inmates to move from the manufacture of basic standard class sedans through to luxury class. For those who successfully met their quotas there was the opportunity for parole to the Legit service proper: in the first instance focusing on the rubbing down and greasing of Legit limbs, thence to foot blister services, moving on to the care of the vehicles, the compounds in which they were kept, and ultimately to the freedom of the open road (that's what it said in the leaflet).

Investment in the road network had ceased. However, the motorways were busy with the movements of Sedanathons and the massive Sedanteknikons (carried by teams of 500 Legits) nicknamed 'Nikons'. Road maintenance had largely been abandoned and what little needed to be done was undertaken by children (from the underclass but who were not yet old enough to carry) who were deemed to be failing for one reason or another. Young Legits didn't go to school; there was no point.

There was an extensive and comprehensive range of ex-motorway service station compounds for the feeding and watering of Sedanists (those who were carried) and the maintenance and recycling of Legits. Normally those carrying Sedanathons and Sedanteknikons were replaced every eighteen to twenty miles. They then rested until the next big load trundled in across the tarmac, clogs clogging in true Legit-like unison. These stations provided a full range of services including: Chapels of Rest; infirmaries; mortuaries; crematoria; Fornicons; immense sexually segregated barracks or dormitories; and clog repair shops.

The average expected working life of an adult Legit was calculated as being between 6 and 10 years (depending on the geographical area and its terrain). This had radically affected investment in the welfare system and had reduced the necessity for the state to provide statutory benefits in illness, old age or retirement. There weren't retired Legits only those who had given their lives in service.

Legits wore clogs. This was for two main reasons: the trade treaty, with (what used to be called) the Netherlands, meant that England had acquired sole (no pun intended) rights to the Dutch Clog Mountain; the other reason was noise. Sedans had no electrics and no horns. The sound of clogged feet ensured a lack of collisions and accidents. Though it does have to be said that the sound of a Sedanathon, that's 200 clogs powering down the outside lane, could be a bit scary (particularly in wet weather!). I know someone who suffered permanent hearing loss after a Sedanteknikon had to make an emergency stop.

But now it's time to tell the story, of how England would be forever changed by my Mum, Una Uevera, and the Sedanistas.

It was Spring in England. There were no animals in the fields and where once there had been crops were now great swathes of weeds and nettles. (Of course there's nothing wrong with nettles; they make fine tea.) It was one of those days when you really wanted to be cosied up next to a good campfire, preferably out of the wind. No such luck for Una as the wind and rain howled across a deserted road deep in deepest Lincolnshire (and that's deep).

Una, and her Sedanistas, had found shelter in a wood near the road, at the brow of a hill, where they hid and waited. She was apart from her warriors and she smiled as she watched a spider roam across the palm of her hand and between her fingers. Her hair hung loose around her shoulders, and framed a face that could have launched a thousand ships (I read that once). Her skin, weathered by the sun and rain, glowed with the health of freedom. Her eyes, sharp blue, saw what many others missed.

As she stood and waited, her thoughts drifted to her long lost father, "Dearest Anvil, if only you'd been my Dad, instead of that bastard, Orb, who deserted us all those years ago."

The Sedanistas were a mixed bunch of militants. Unlike the Legits, whom they sought to liberate, they wore no clogs upon their feet, but rather cloth bound with leather thongs. Their clothes were fashioned from sacks and recycled woven wool, their belts from woven reeds and grasses. On the backs of their tunics were stitched the letters 'SOD' (Sedanistas Overthrow Despots). In their hands they carried stout staves, upon some of which were mounted size 16 –18 wooden clogs.

"How long we gonna wait, Una?" a young female Sod asked.

"Not long now," she replied as she parted the green leaves of the beech hedge to scan the adjacent road.

Una cocked her head to one side and listened intently as the wind brought the sound of clogs clacking on the broken asphalt of the road. She stared at the brow of the hill. The noise of clogs grew louder.

Four Legits, carrying an Aristosedan, came over the brow of the hill and dumped the chair upon the ill kept road.

"I'm knackered," one said.

"Fucked!" another added.

A male voice, from within the chair, shouted, "Come on, you Legits. I'm late for dinner!"

"Fat bastard," a third Legit replied.

At that moment Una and the Sedanistas burst forth from the wood and surrounded the chair. Staves waved threateningly in the air. The rain continued to lash down. Birds scattered in fright.

"Stand and deliver!" Una shouted.

The passenger climbed from the chair, and enquired, "Isn't that a bit hackneyed?"

A Sedanista poked him with a stave, "Don't get bloody clever with us, mate."

"I doubt that I'm your mate. Who the hell are you anyway?"

"It's them!" a Legit whispered.

"Una Uevera, and these are Sedanistas."

"Sods we is," a bedraggled Sedanista added.

"You've never heard of us?" Una asked.

"No," the passenger replied.

"These," indicating the throng, "are liberated Legits."

"All Legits are free men and women," the Passenger stated.

"Bollocks," a Legit responded.

"Join us, join the revolution," a Sod shouted.

"Pyres of clogs will burn across England; they will light the night sky; the cries of the liberated will be as the roaring of the west wind; the mighty will fall; the weak will rise up, knowing that they are at last strong, the. . ." added a be-spectacled Sod.

"Steady, Wesley, steady now," Una interrupted the developing peroration. Turning to the passenger Una instructed, "Empty your pockets."

Grudgingly the man did as he was told. His wallet was passed to Una. Inside there was a wad of bright crisp notes: Hamsters, as they were known. (You won't know of course, but the English Euro was replaced with the new currency absolutely ages ago.

10

The notes actually said 'Ham Sterling', but everyone called them Hamsters.)

Una was pleased with her haul. She turned to the four Legits and said, "It's a good life on the wild side. Join us?"

The Legits were uncertain, but then, one of their number moved away from the other three towards the Sods. "I'm up for it," he said. They moved off leaving the three Legits and the passenger standing in the rain. The logic of logistics hit. "How do you carry a sedan with only three Legits?"

Answer; "You can't."

"What am I supposed to do now?" the passenger shouted as the Sods disappeared back into the wood.

The skies cleared as Una and her Sods walked through green lanes. Wesley walked next to Una.

"Aren't you pleased?" Wesley asked.

For a moment Una didn't reply. "Stealing wallets is not what this is about."

"We need the money, for the war chest."

"Maybe, but what will we buy with it? There's nothing we need that we can't steal or grow."

"You buy people with money, Una," Wesley replied.

"I'd forgotten that you were once a banker."

"People have a price, and when the time comes we will need all the Hamsters we can lay our hands on."

"You're right, but it doesn't seem right. There's so far to go, and we're still so few," Una responded.

"But we grow every day. It's not like you to be downhearted."

"Time passes so fast and the people suffer."

"Most know no better now."

"Isn't that the point, Wesley?"

Later that day, as evening fell, the Sedanistas made camp on the trek back to their base. A secure spot was chosen, where guards could be mounted, and where the smoke from the campfire would be lost amongst the plantation trees. The evening meal was rudimentary, even by the standards of troops on the move. Vegetable and herb soup was served with small helpings of unleavened bread. At least one could now drink from streams; the demise of industrial farming had cleared the waterways of phosphates and all the other

11

crap they previously used.

Una and Wesley sat by the fire. Una was lost in thought. After some time Wesley plucked up the courage to speak. He had been surprised that Una had stopped his speech earlier in the day; his flights of rhetoric usually received a more than positive response.

"How did you come to this?" he asked.

"I don't talk about the past, Wesley."

"Why be thee so low?"

"Some other time."

"You're our leader. We respect you, but that doesn't mean you can't share. . ."

Una cut him off, "When I want to share my life with you or anybody else I'll let you know."

"I didn't mean to pry."

"I know, but the past is sometimes too painful to remember. I can't afford to be weak."

"Talking isn't weakness."

"Wesley, my friend, I know you mean well, but right now talk must have a purpose for me and the riddle of my past is nowhere near as important as the task we have at hand. How are we to win? Come on; let's get some sleep. We'll be on the move before dawn."

2

In London it was a bright sunny day. Despite all that had happened over the last many years Number 10 Downing Street was still home to the Prime Ministers of England – in this case, John Green. A small crowd of people had gathered behind the barriers waiting for something to happen. Well, they would, wouldn't they? After all this was the day that New Lablair had been returned to their eleventh consecutive term of office as the government of England. Soon Green would return here from his audience with Ham at Hampton Court.

You are probably wondering what happened to Buckingham Palace. It's still there but has not been used by the monarchy since, I think, about 'ABW five' (After the Big War, year five). It's deserted now. The Mayor of London and his thousands of sycophantic bureaucrats took it over as accommodation when his new building collapsed after the explosions. He reckoned that there was nowhere else to go, and the then heir to the throne was a bit touched, went around hugging trees and blabbering on about grey goo taking over the world – how wrong can you be? So, Red Ken, as he was known, moved in with the Monarch's blessing. Then it became obvious that there was no point in having regional government of any sort. There wasn't much to manage and there were no resources left – except people, of course.

Where was I? Downing Street.

Some of the crowd started to cheer as a large stately sedan carried by twelve liveried Legits entered the street. These were very well fed and drilled Legits; their polished wooden clogs marched in perfect harmony until they gently placed the sedan on the red carpet outside Number 10. Green alighted from the chair and the crowd cheered.

Green could really only be described as 'sharp'. He was a lean man of average height whose eyes were piercing blue even if the left one did not quite line up with its pair. His hairpiece was of the best quality: in fact, so good that none of the public realised that his gorgeous, well-trimmed locks were false. Not that it mattered, of course: it's what you did that counted, not what you looked like. But on the other hand appearances had to be maintained, especially if you had to wear hand-me-down suits. One of the criteria for becoming Prime Minister was that you could fit into the suits of the previous incumbent(s) (Saville Row went out of business when the sheep ran out and, as for synthetic fibres, as they were known, there was now nothing to make them with), thus the old phrase 'one size fits all' had taken on quite a new meaning. There had been big talk of trying to re-establish sheep as a species, but the square-riggers bringing new stock in from Australia had never arrived. Even if they had, it would have been very hard to breed them for their wool, as there would have been great pressure for legs of lamb and mint sauce.

A happy crowd, and a happy scene, were suddenly disrupted as a clog was hurled with great force from the rear of the crowd towards the PM.

A voice cried out, "Power to the Sods. Burn the clogs."

It was a bloody good shot as it struck Green hard on the side of his head, knocking his hairpiece slightly cock-eyed. The crowd scattered as footmen hurriedly pushed the staggering Green inside the safety of the house.

A young female Legit (the clog thrower) sought to make her escape as the crowd cowered in the face of uniformed Swabs. She was soon over-powered, her cries of liberation rapidly ended by several well-judged punches to the face and stomach. The crowd stood and stared. Swab whistles were blown and within moments a Jamsedan, carried by eight Legits, ran up. The crowd stood and watched as the young woman was given a good kicking and then bundled inside the vehicle. The crowd were silent as the Jamsedan moved off.

A well-dressed woman whispered, "You'd think they'd be glad of a job for life."

Another replied, "That's what she'll get, life."

Inside Number 10, in the Prime Ministerial bathroom, an apothecary administered a cold wet flannel to the side of Green's bruised head.

"Is that the best you can do?" Green asked.

"I'm sorry, Prime Minister, but this will help. I've sent for your acupuncturist."

"Not more bloody needles."

"In a world without synthetic drugs it's best to use the good old tried and tested ways."

"I've got Cabinet in an hour, and then our victory party. Bandage me up," Green instructed.

The apothecary removed a long white bandage from his bag whilst Green adjusted his hairpiece. He was soon swathed in a majestic turban like structure.

"I look like some bloody wog," Green observed as he inspected the construction in the bathroom mirror.

"You're too pale for that, Prime Minister, and you are a prime minister," the apothecary replied.

3

Colin Cartage, (The Regulator, ONLEG) stood, surrounded by his minions, on a bridge over the old M25 motorway, surveying the scene.

No motor vehicles of any sort moved on the ten lanes of the motorway. Abandoned cars, vans and lorries rusted away in piles on the hard shoulders, the embankments, and on the carriageways themselves. These derelict vehicles had not been moved since each finally ran out of fuel. One lane was clear even though it wasn't in a straight line. A Sedanteknikon carried by 500 Legits made good progress northwards up the vacant lane. The thousand wooden clogs made a fearful noise. In the opposite direction a Sedanathon carried by one hundred Legits was positively rushing along. A boy drummer trotted in front of it beating out the trotting rhythm for the carrying Legits. Who can tell what would have happened without the rhythm of the drum, (such music was still important to the English)?

Cartage, turning to one of his secretariat, observed, "It fills me with immense pride to know that I have kept the wheels of commerce moving."

"Wheels, Sir?"

"It's a figure of speech, young man, and if I were you, and had any desire to advance through ONLEG, then I would suggest that you respond to the spirit of what is being said rather than to the exact meaning of the words themselves," Cartage replied.

"Will we ever clear the carriageways, Sir?" an earnest young woman asked.

"Perhaps one day."

The ONLEG party crossed the bridge to observe the traffic flow in the opposite direction. There was a pile up as a Legit carrying an Aristosedan collapsed with exhaustion causing a number of Plebsedans, who were travelling too close, to crash into the fallen chair. There was much commotion as passengers tumbled from their chairs and Legits stumbled and fell.

I should point out that great care had been expended on the

organisation of the Legit force. Along each side of the nation's main transportation arteries there are Sedantorys (the old disused motorway service stations) where spare Legits were housed and fed. The really clever thing had been to put in small compounds every mile where a few emergency Legits were housed. In the circumstance of a collapse or accident, a replacement Legit could be fitted within a few minutes.

"Should we do anything?" the young woman asked.

"No. Time the change over. We have a standard requirement of a replacement within six minutes. Start counting."

A young man started to count, "One potato, two potatoes, three potatoes, four. . ."

A spare Legit was 'fitted' to the Chair.

"Two hundred and twenty five potatoes, two hundred and twenty six. . ."

"How long was that?" Cartage asked.

"Four hundred and twenty three potatoes, I mean beats sir," the young man replied.

"In minutes, man."

"Seven minutes and twenty three seconds, Sir."

"Not good enough. Make a note of the number. There's a fine due for this."

The vehicles once more moved off.

The exhausted Legit, who had caused the problem, was left unattended on the hard shoulder.

"What will happen to him?" the young woman asked.

"Shall we take a look?" Cartage suggested.

Slowly they made their way down the embankment to where he lay. The young woman knelt by the Legit's side and felt for a pulse in his dirty scrawny neck.

"He's dead, Sir," she said, "What happens now?"

"I'd forgotten you'd just started with us. Wait and see."

They returned to their position on the bridge. Within fifteen minutes they saw a large, entirely black, windowless sedan, coming towards the dead man.

"There it is now," Cartage observed, "there's one every fifteen to twenty minutes at peak periods: the good old Hearsedan."

"Or the Stiffsedan as it's commonly known," the young man said with a smirk.

"I would have thought you might have got the message by now. You have subversive tendencies," Cartage replied.

"What happens to the body?" the young woman asked.

"It goes in the burner at the next Sedantory."

"I never imagined that it was this well organised," she said.

"ONLEG is a model for all public services. What's your name by the way?"

"Diane Ami."

"You'll go far, especially as you're bright and pretty. I'm going to a party later. Would you like to come?" Cartage asked as his hand gently rested upon her left buttock.

4

Night had fallen. In the middle of nowhere, in the countryside, a long and very dilapidated high-speed train rested on the track exactly where it had stopped when the electricity was all used up. It was almost invisible within its culvert where trees and bushes now flourished. Candles flickered in some of the carriage windows. Smoke billowed from the metal chimneystacks that poked through the roofs of some of the carriages. You could smell the fragrance of beech and rowan upon the gentle night breeze.

This train was home and HQ to Una and the Sedanistas. It was quite extraordinary to realise that only the old at the encampment had ever seen a train in motion. For the young who lived within the comparative safety of the train, it was only a long thin metal house, and as such was much more comfortable than rough shelters in the woods, or the barrack beds in the Sedantorys. When Una had stumbled upon it three years earlier she had thought, at first, that it was deserted. It wasn't. It had a sitting tenant, one Anvil Ammer. He'd taken a bit of persuading that Una was a 'suitable' fellow tenant, and even more persuading as others arrived to join the struggle. But by then

Anvil had become the 'wise man' of the Sods.

It was something of a mystery how he came to be there at all. According to his story, he had been transporting his laboratory from Cambridge to Lindum when the train came to its final resting place. There was too much to move and no way to move it, so while the other passengers trudged off across the fields in search of civilisation, he stayed put. By trade, if that's the right word for it, he was an embryologist, but he now described himself as an alchemist.

Anvil was an old codger of some eighty years though still bright as a button for most of the time. He was inside his carriage. A brazier burnt brightly in the darkness, most of the smoke going up the thin chimney pipe. He was dressed in an incredibly dirty, once white lab coat. He sat by the brazier, his cat, Sickle, upon his lap. The cat purred as Anvil stroked her. Anvil was not alone. A young male, ex-Legit child, called Lump, cowered, afraid, just inside the door.

"Please Mr Ammer, what's that thing?" Lump asked.

"Doctor Anvil Ammer to you, boy. It's a cat."

"What's a cat?"

Anvil sighed in sorrow and replied, "It's the last cat left alive in England. They ate them all after the Big War: not enough meat."

"What with all that black fur on 'em?"

"They skinned them first."

"'Orrid!"

"I agree, but for some people the prospect of life without meat was impossible."

"We eats birds now and then."

"What's your name, boy? And come out here where I can see you."

"Lump, Doctor."

"Lump?"

"That's me, Doctor. What you goin' to do with it?

"With what?"

"The cat."

"I'm going to make another cat, if I'm very lucky."

"Why're you goin' to do that?" Lump asked.

"I like cats. I shall give it to Una."

"That's why I come here. Citizen Una asked me to give you a message."

"Which was?"

"Can you pop round tonight?"

Further along the train Una was reading by candlelight. Her text for that night was a very battered copy of Marx and Engels' 'Manifesto of the Communist Party'. At the table her second-in-command, Roque Forte, was sharpening a hunting knife on a whetstone. Roque was a tall powerfully built Asian man in his late twenties. He drank dandelion tea from a chipped GNER cup.

"Is it any good?" he asked.

"What?" Una asked.

"The book."

"It's hard to follow; it was written so long ago. But they could be writing about us."

"Why?"

"The first sentence says it all: 'The history of all hitherto existing society is the history of class struggles'."

"That's a bit different to what they used to teach in my school, before they took me off."

"The myth of, what do they call it?" Una asked.

"Consensual Civil Society. But I don't reckon being a Legit is very consensual." He paused for a moment, shook his head and said, "I'd better get to bed. Got a big day tomorrow."

"A battle to fight."

There was a rapping on the carriage door. Una said, "Come in," and Anvil walked in.

"Good evening, Una, Roque."

"Anvil, my wise friend, don't be offended but I must go; I need to rest. Good night," Roque said.

"Sleep tight and don't let the bugs bite," Una responded.

"I haven't heard that in a long while. But what's up with him?" Anvil said with a smile.

"My grandmother used to say it; it just came into my head."

"It was always a strange saying."

"But very appropriate in our circumstances," Una Laughed.

"And Roque?" Anvil asked.

"You know Roque, he wants to to be valued, to impress."

"I wonder why?"

"Anvil!"

"You sent Lump to get me?"

"This book you leant me."

"The Manifesto?"

"Yes, it's fascinating but I find some of it hard to apply," Una replied with a frown.

"The most important thing to remember that Marx ever wrote, goes something like this: 'The philosophers have only interpreted the world. The problem, however, is to change it'."

"But we have to know why."

"That's obvious, Una. The question is how the hell are we going to do it?"

5

At the same time, at the very centre of government, the Cabinet Room at Number 10, a 'knees-up' was taking place. Some things hadn't changed. The great and the good, the Cabinet and their non-elected officials, were celebrating yet another term of unfettered power in the service of the few, to the detriment of the many.

Parliamentary democracy had moved on, or maybe back. In the old days, so I am told, there was usually some doubt as to which party might be elected. Not any more. You qualified to vote if you owned property, even if it was a grass verge the size of a pewter plate. All you had to do to register was to show your deed of ownership and you were on the roll. Given that Legits, Land Labourers and other menials within the underclass owned nothing, then the whole process was both quicker and more effective in maintaining continuity of government. It worked pretty well in the urban areas (where the Townies lived) but in the countryside you had squires and their families voting themselves into the Commons. Thanks be to Ham that they were heavily outnumbered by the

Townies. Not only that, but it seemed that a degree of inbreeding had exacerbated their congenital stupidity. What could be more bizarre than seeing them out hunting: no dogs, no horses, no foxes, just a bunch of nutters dressed in red, blowing their horns and chasing indentured Legits across the barren fields? Still, freedom of expression was still regarded as a right for those of property.

John Green was leading the celebrations, his head still swathed in his ornate bandage. At least Mrs Green had had the sense to tuck a little English flag in its front. The cross of St George looked just right with an image of Ham in its centre. It was one hell of a party. It was a shame that the English climate couldn't support a wine industry but then again it prevented the adulteration of Englishness with foreign practices. The alcoholic drink of the night (and every night) was gin. It was the sort of product that could be easily made at home for domestic consumption. Not that the Prime Minister was expected to make his own. No, that was the responsibility of the Head of the Cabinet Office, the Right Honourable Fiona Floodgate (or Ruin as she was know to her intimates). Ruin was in the process of dispensing generous libations when Green held up his hand for silence.

"Please be upstanding. I have a toast," he drunkenly gurgled, "To us, the Government, The Androgynous Majesty and," suddenly searching for his words, "and, and. . ."

"England, England and St George!" shouted Betty Bekkes from the corner of the room where she had been playing darts.

There were merry drunken shouts of "England and St George!" from the assembled statesmen and women.

The Cabinet Room was much as it had always been with buxom serving wenches moving about with jugs of gin and silver salvers bearing canapés. Green's favourite was a mixture of wild garlic and thrushes' eggs. The big difference in the room was the enormous portrait of their founder, Tony Blair, who smiled benignly down upon his successors. (It's worth noting that Green wore the very same suit worn by Blair in the portrait, though it has to be said that it was now beginning to look a little tatty round the edges.) Whoever had once suggested that he would not find a suitable place in history had been proved very wrong, very wrong indeed. There he was forever, hanging, albeit on the wall.

TerryTravers (Minister of State forTransportation or Moving People About) was vying for the attention of Diane Ami with Colin Cartage who, though not elected by anyone at all, was an important member of the Cabinet (another traditional vestige of the past).

Suddenly the electric lights flickered, dimmed, and the room descended into darkness. There were many shrieks and giggles as the serving wenches came under attack from the drunken men who ruled England. Candles were lighted. Not such a good idea as it turned out as Cartage was seen to be in the process of trying to mountTravers whom he had mistaken for Ami in the dark. Such is the power of gin to distort the sensibilities of 'normal' men. Travers punched Cartage on the nose as Ami descended into a case of drunken hysterics.

Green had taken charge. "Travers, go and see what's happened. They must be changing shifts in the treadmill."

"Aye, Aye, Prime Minister," Travers replied.

"And as for you, Cartage, get a grip. Take your floosie upstairs if you wish," Green admonished the Regulator.

"I'm no floosie, I'm an under secretary."

"Don't you like it on top?" Bekkes asked with a twinkle in her eye and a giggle in her voice.

On entering the cellar, which was lighted and warmed by large candles,Travers came upon a sad sight.

The great treadmill that drove the generator that powered the lights, but little else, had come to a complete standstill.

"What the hell's going on?" he asked.

"That," said the foreman Legit pointing to a body half in and half out of the wheel with its leg trapped in the main driving cog. The injured Legit made not a sound. The other nine Legits had vacated the wheel and were standing staring at the still body.

"Can't you get him out? We're trying to have a party upstairs," Travers asked.

"It's difficult, Sir," the foreman replied.

"Don't be daft, man. Just rotate the wheel backwards and he'll fall free."

"These wheels only go forwards, Sir, no reversing, no going back. It's a principle of your government."

"Ah, I see. Well, forwards it must be then."

"I'll just see how he is, Sir," the foreman said.

The foreman walked to the wheel to inspect the supine Legit. The foreman shook his head.

"Back in the wheel, you lot. Forward it'll be."

"What about Smike?" a Legit asked.

"Smike is no more," he solemnly replied.

The wheel started to turn. Travers recoiled as the cogs bit into Smike's legs. The bones cracked in a most disturbing manner as the body fell free. Travers gagged at the noise.

He returned to the Cabinet Room and sank a large gin as the chandeliers flickered back into life.

"All well?" Green asked.

6

Day to day life progressed as normal. At the Hypertension Market parking lot snow was in the air. The full range of Sedans from Plebsedans to Aristosedans were parked in neat ordered rows whilst their passengers experienced the delights of shopping inside the vast concrete box that housed the limited, but expanding (slightly) range of products available to the monied class. Outside, Legits shuffled about in a vain attempt to keep warm as the first flurries began to fall. At the edge of the lot were stationed some twenty Jamsedans; their Legits trotted up and down on the spot under the lazy supervision of attendant Swabs.

Sedans came and went, their occupants unaware, or uninterested in the efforts of those that made their shopping therapy possible. At the rear of the Market, out of view of the shoppers, stood the Generator House. It was an incredible scene. One thousand athlete Legits were riding one thousand exercise cycles that had been lovingly preserved and constantly serviced by mechanics. These athletes worked in three-hour shifts before being replaced by another batch of the cream of the fit underclass. A day's operation of the market required the services of three thousand men and women. Beyond the Generator House lay the athletes' village. This had been salvaged from the failed bid to host the Olympic Games that had not taken place on the cusp of the BW. It is probably worth noting, in passing, that the daft idea that sport could produce world harmony had been blown to pieces, as well as many other things, in the Big War. At least the village was at last proving useful.

I suppose I ought to give you a bit more info on what a Hypertension Market was. In the period of austerity and extreme rationing that took place immediately following hostilities the large Supermarkets of yore all went bust. There was nothing much to sell and even less money to buy it with. The Government of the day was faced with a big question, 'What is to be Done?'.

Simply told, although the process was very drawn out and fraught, the State took over all commercial retail (leaving aside the black-market of course) and created vast Hypertension markets in each of the English sub-regions. I don't know what you think about shopping but it seems to me that there were always two basic types of shoppers: those that loved it and those that hated it. I have been told that both types found the experience 'tense', particularly when there wasn't enough stuff to go around. The point was that the Government was worried that shopping could be a health risk. No, really. So what did they do? They got it wrong, or at least I think they did.

There were two criteria for entry to the Market. The first was that the shopper had to have a 'Passport' that showed that: they owned property and had liquid assets (as they were called: plastic cards had gone, there being no technology to support their use); and that they were healthy. Now the first of those criteria might have been described as 'reasonable', the second was, well, difficult to define. The solution had been to subject each potential shopper to an ECG test before they were granted entry. When this started the idea had been that those suffering from hypertension (high blood pressure, in case you don't know) would be denied entry until their blood pressure had been reduced. It soon became apparent that on this basis the markets would have very few customers. What would you have done? Given up? That's what I would have done, but Government Departments and their bureaucracies don't work like that. It was probably just the passage of time, and it seemed to be working okay, so they just let it be. The situation changed so that you could not gain entry unless you had high blood pressure.

Shoppers queued to enter the little ECG cubicles. There were never enough of these, and people were unsure whether that was because of a shortage of such devices (they were antiques after all) or because waiting for ages in a long queue really wound people up.

"Do you know who I am?" asked a fat woman in furs.

No one took any notice.

"I said, do you know who I am?" she shouted.

"A fat furry dollop of lard," a young Legit servant sniggered to another young servant.

The fat woman in furs hit the boy across the head and said, "I heard that, you little git!" She hit him again and shouted, "Git!"

The woman entered a cubicle to the amused stares of the queuing shoppers. The young Legit pissed in the handbag she had left outside the door of the cubicle.

Inside another cubicle an ECG test was being applied to a large man, his chest bare, and already wired up.

"I'm sorry, but you can't go in," the ECG technician said, scrutinising the blank screen (some no longer worked but could still be used as the person being tested wasn't allowed to see the screen).

"Don't be bloody ridiculous. She's sent me down for the aubergine. There haven't been any for years," the man said.

"You're not tense enough," the technician replied.

"Bloody ridiculous!"

"It's going up. What's an aubergine thing?"

"You stupid oaf, you mindless. . .technician!"

"Ah, that's better, a good reading. You can go in now. Sorry for the delay. Next!"

"What's an aubergine indeed? Whatever happened to education?" the man mused.

Outside in the cold and snow everything seemed as normal as it ever was.

In a nearby wood fifty Sedanistas made their way slowly and carefully toward the perimeter of the parking lot. They moved in silence, Roque Forte at their head. Soon they were spread out into two lines waiting for Roque's command.

On the parking lot Sedans settled, rose, arrived and departed. Legits and their passengers went about their normal mundane business.

Roque raised his hand; it fell and the first wave of Sods rushed forward. The attack had begun. They waved their sticks and clogged staves in the air. They did not shout; they just ran at the Swabs. The latter were surprised, unused as they were to organised attack. Hurriedly they rushed to their Jamsedans to retrieve their weapons.

As they were doing this Roque used his tinderbox to ignite first his own flare and then those of the remaining thirty Sods. They rushed forth letting out bloodcurdling roars and screams.

Roque shouted, "Burn the chairs!"

The Sods took up the cry.

As the Swabs engaged in hand-to-hand combat with the Sods the second wave began to hurl their flares into the wooden vehicles that immediately burst into flames.

The fighting was vicious with no quarter given on either side. The first wave of Sods put up a brave show, but though outnumbering the Swabs, they were no match in terms of weaponry; wooden staves were virtually useless against the ancient weapons that had been removed from the Royal Armouries as they weighed in with pikes, broadswords and axes. The Swabs showed no mercy. Within minutes the first wave of Sods lay bloodied and dead upon the tarmac.

Rogue's second wave had used up their flares and now joined battle with the advancing enemy. Roque's strength and ability with the stave laid several Swabs low but then he picked up a discarded sword and set about his foes. Sods kept falling around him, dead and wounded. Roque found himself taking on five Swabs. They came at him hard, slow, measured and determined.

"What a sod," he thought, but struggled on. A Swab lunged at him with a pike. Roque tried to parry the blow, but too late; it made a deep gash in his left shoulder. They closed in for the kill. Suddenly he was joined by an immense Legit who stood well over six foot nine and a half inches. This unexpected ally picked up a double-handed broad sword and set about Roque's attackers.

Down they went. Roque got a new lease of life. The two men fought. Swabs fell, and for a fraction of a moment the remainder of the foe fell back.

"Come on man, we ain't winning. Let's get out of here!" the massive Legit roared.

"The others?" Roque shouted back.

"Too late, out of here!"

Roque saw that he was right. They turned and ran, faster and faster, off across the lot between the burning chairs and the bloody remains of the Sedanistas. The Swabs gave chase, but they'd lost heart. Beating up people who had no means of defence was okay but this had been another matter; the bastards could actually fight.

As they ran blood poured from Roque's wound, he slowed, and then fell unconscious to the ground. The Legit lifted him as if he weighed no more than a bunch of Hamsters, draped him over one shoulder and made off through the woods. The shouts of the Swabs died away. As he trotted his great mane of hair and long black beard flowed in the breeze.

Back at the parking lot Legits stood and marvelled at the devastation, whilst shoppers wondered how the hell they were going to get home.

"I don't know," one shopper remarked, "we seem to live right on the edge these days."

"Trouble is one doesn't know whom to blame," another well-dressed woman replied.

"Well I do!" came the swift reply.

"Who?"

"Foreigners, that's what!"

"There aren't any."

"Well, there were!"

Which just goes to show what a loss the demise of the mass communications industry had been. There was State radio (or HAM radio as it was known) of course, but that just carried old music and the occasional government announcement; hardly enough to generate and sustain well held prejudices. One wit had described this England as "an open society, in the big tent, following the third way."

7

Later that same day, as evening approached, Una was warming her hands over one of the communal campfires that burnt alongside 'The Lord John Prescott' (that was what the train was called. It said so, in once red letters upon its side). No one knew who this bloke was but they figured he must have been something to do with trains.

Sods were cooking their evening meal; there were potatoes, roast chestnuts and big cast iron pans filled with a broth made from herbs, greens and dried pulses from the previous year. Those of a carnivorous bent roasted small birds they had caught in rudimentary nets in the woods. There was much smoke and laughter as young Sods played their favourite game, football. This latter object was a lifeless ball of rags stitched around with thick woven twine. It was quite heavy for young feet and had absolutely no bounce at all. Still, it was keeping the old English tradition of football going – something no longer permitted in civil society. The kids were divided into two teams of as many who wanted to play and they bashed the ball about until it finally came to land in one of the goals. These were wicker baskets laying at the two extreme ends of the train. A match could take hours and was extremely useful in developing a whole range of what used to be 'life skills' but were now thought of as good training for the punch ups to come.

Una stared into the fire, stood and then paced up and down, anxiously looking down the track. Anvil joined her.

"You look worried," he said.

"They should have been back hours ago."

"You care about Roque, don't you?" Anvil asked.

"I care about all of them. They are some of our best."

"I know, but I mean 'care'."

She stopped pacing, looked at Anvil, and blushed.

"You know exactly what I mean," Anvil added.

"There's no room for emotions like that."

"If there's no room for feelings, personal feelings, then what's the point, Una?"

"They take your mind off the things that need to be done."

"If they make us feel like that then we'll never win."

A voice shouted in the distance.

"There's someone coming," Anvil said.

"Strangers!" another voice shouted, followed by another.

"Strangers!" shouted Una, "Take up your positions."

Sods hurriedly took up their staves and clubs and disappeared between carriages and up the sides of the culvert into the bushes and undergrowth.

"Who goes there?" another voice shouted.

The massive Legit carried Roque into view.

"Friend! Friend coming in!" he shouted.

Sods gathered round as Roque was carried through the crowd to a nearby fire. The Legit sank to the ground in complete exhaustion as he lay the man down. The crowd murmured as they saw the badly injured Roque.

"He's one of yours, a good man," the Legit said.

"What happened?" Una asked.

"We lost the battle."

"Where is everyone else?"

"Dead, all dead," the Legit replied.

"That can't be true! You're lying," Una cried is disbelief.

"I wish I was. We two fought through and against the odds just managed to survive."

"I don't know you. You're not one of us."

"I think he is now," Anvil said. "Get Roque to my carriage. He looks in a bad way."

Later, Una stroked Roque's head, as he lay unconscious upon a mattress on the floor. "Will he make it?" she asked Anvil.

Anvil finished dressing the wound. "Yes, I think we got to him just in time. Lift his head, please.

Una raised Roque's head and Anvil poured a phial of liquid into the man's mouth.

"Those weapons they use are dirty, old and dangerous," Anvil said. "Leave him to me now. You've talking to do."

Una stepped outside and found the Legit sitting by the fire eating a baked potato skewered on a stick. The Sods kept well away. Una watched him eat and then moved toward him and sat down next to him.

"Thank you," she said.

"He's brave. Any man, or woman, would be proud to call him comrade," the Legit replied.

"You saved his life. Why? Who are you? What's your name? What do you want?"

"You've got a lot of questions. You must be Una Uevera."

"How did you find us?"

"He told me the way, in those few moments when he could speak. Is he going to recover?"

"Anvil thinks so. I just hope he's right."

"He's a man of will. My name is Marx. I want to join you."

"Why?"

"I saw them fight. I couldn't stand by, done too much of that of late. Those men and women of yours didn't stand a chance; they were butchered."

"They'll never be replaced."

"No, they won't, but others will come to fill their places."

"They were my family."

"All the more reason to avenge them."

"Are you a Legit?" Una asked.

"I used to be Ham's bodyguard. I told someone I thought I could trust that Ham was a fat pig who cared for nothing except excess. I was betrayed."

30

"So they made you a Legit?"

"They castrated me first."

"Made you an eunuch? For that?"

"They thought it would weaken me, but they were wrong."

"I don't know what to say."

"Well, at least they haven't brought back the death penalty."

Anvil joined them at the fire. "Philosophising?" he asked.

"No," Marx replied, "philosophers only interpret the world. The purpose, however, is to change it."

"Marx said that."

"I just did," Marx replied.

"No, I mean the real one."

Marx laughed, "Ham had a good library, used to be called the British Library, I think. I read a lot, found Marx, liked what he wrote, and decided that I'd use his name."

"So your first name's not Karl?" Anvil enquired.

"No, just the one name."

"Look, this is a crisis. We've just lost fifty Sods, Roque's wounded, and you two are droning on about bloody names!" Una interrupted.

"Sorry," they both said.

"What I need to know is how to run a guerrilla war," Una said.

"Strike often and fast, hit targets that will frighten and weaken the enemy, but most of all get the oppressed on our side," Marx replied.

"We need weapons and we need to find an advantage."

"There's the Legits; there's more of them than anyone else, that's an advantage," Marx said.

"That's always been true, but they need to be persuaded," Anvil added with a sigh.

"They need to see that it's possible," Una said.

"We still need something special that they don't have."

"Like what?" Una asked.

"Wheels would come in handy," Anvil answered.

"There aren't any," Una pointed out.

"You might be wrong about that," Marx said.

"What do you mean?"

"Listen, I'm done for. I need some sleep, to think, to remember. Where do I go?"

"There's plenty of room now," Una said.

"I'll show you," Anvil offered.

8

The next morning Green and Cartage surveyed the scene at the Hypertension Market Parking Lot. The only bodies left were those of the Sods lying exactly where they had fallen. Their blood had dried into sticky black pools amidst the charred remains of burnt out Sedans. The dead and injured Swabs had been removed from the scene. Trade was quiet for a Saturday morning.

"I'll get this lot cleared up," Cartage said.

"You'll do no such thing," Green replied.

"They'll stink; in fact they stink already – it's much warmer today. It's revolting."

"So?" Green asked.

"It'll be bad for business."

"They've nowhere else to shop, have they? No. Leave them where they are to rot."

"Will this send this right message to the electorate?"

"Fuck the electorate. I'm going to put a stop to this revolutionary nonsense,' Green said.

"How?"

"They want a war? Well, they can bloody have a war; they're a threat to democracy with their weapons of mass destruction."

"Sticks aren't weapons of mass destruction."

"They are, if they're enough of them."

"I see. Well, I guess you know what you're doing. You're the politician after all."

"Correct. I need to get back to the House; there are things that need to be said. Where's my chair?"

Cartage blew a shrill whistle and the regal chair rose up from the corner of the lot and trotted towards them. As he was carried away a plan formed in his mind. "I need to put all the pieces in place. Yes, a secret war, for now," he mused.

32

The moon cast a benign light upon the Sedantory. The single storey wooden dormitories looked calm and still. Within the female dormitory the majority of women were asleep, some with their children tucked up with them in the many rows of wooden bunks. In a far corner a small group of young women talked, smoked and drank in the glow of candlelight. The bottle was passed round.

"Where you get that then?" one of the women asked.

"Some old geezer left it in the chair; he was pissed as a rat."

"What is it?" another asked as she placed the neck of the bottle to her lips.

"Dunno, can't read it in this light."

"Can't bloody read more like. Giss us here. Glenmorangie," she slowly read, "Glen moran gee."

"What's that then?"

"Whisky, innit?"

Another drank from the bottle. "Shit!" she said, "that's something that is."

"It'll 'ave been smuggled in 'cross border."

"It's got to be better in Scotland."

"How's that then?"

"Kilts."

"Kilts?"

"Frees up the tackle."

"Don't you ever think of nothing else?"

They stopped talking as they heard tapping at the window.

"That'll be the men," one said.

"Best let 'em in then," said another as she smiled.

Soon the women, and their two male companions, were quite drunk, unused as they were to drinking single malt whisky.

"Those two have been a long time," said one of the men.

"I don't know how he does it. I'm too bloody knackered to get it up these days," the other replied.

"Bit limp are we, me ducks?" a woman giggled in response.

"Come on then and we'll find out, eh?"

"Just don't make too much noise, or we'll all be in it," a woman remarked as the couple walked off through the dark dormitory.

The communal toilets were very dark. There were groans and giggles. Backs and buttocks banged on closed cubicle doors as men and women coupled in the passion and pleasures of illicit, and illegal, sex.

Sorry to interrupt what's probably the most exciting bit so far, but I thought you might be wondering about that word 'illegal'. There was no point in having a 'Ministry for Birth Control and Selective Breeding' unless you gave it some teeth, some real penalties to back up the legislation (which had got to the statute book with a colossal majority in one week flat). What was deemed necessary was strong Legits, of either sex, of any race, or combination thereof, who weren't terribly bright; this could only be done by careful selection, and management. I know there used to be arguments about nature or nurture but it didn't really matter; you bred strong thick Legits, gave them an awful environment, denied them education, and bingo you had the ideal workforce. Well, that was the idea anyway.

The entrance doors to the toilets burst open and three male and three female Legiturions marched in. Heavy truncheons were banged on cubicle doors and three acts of coitus interruptus were simultaneously performed.

A male voice cried, "Oh shit!"

"We're fucked now," another added.

"Too fucking true! Out!" a female Legiturion shouted.

Three men and three women emerged from their cubicles pulling their ragged clothes back over their unwashed bodies.

The six Legits looked at each other; one gave a nod, and all rushed the Legiturions in a bid to escape their law. The Legiturions wore ancient black plastic police riot body armour. They weren't very mobile, but in close combat, and armed with their bloody great truncheons, they were just about invincible. The fight was short. The malefactors were marched to the emergency exit.

"You're going to the cage," a Legiturion said.

"Give us a break. It's only natural," a Legit pleaded.

"It's illegal."

34

The emergency exit opened. The Cage Manager stood waiting; he held sets of crude wooden manacles, within which the Legits' wrists were soon imprisoned. The Legits struggled as they were dragged toward the great cage. It was covered in very rusty razor wire. A sign read 'G-Bay detention services'.

As they had reached the door, one of the Legits, a tall young Afro-Caribbean man, broke free and ran off at great speed. Two of the Legiturions set off after him but their cumbersome armour slowed them down and they soon gave up the chase. The young Legit disappeared into the night as the remaining Legits were locked up.

"He'll not last long in the Wilderness," a puffing Legiturion observed. "No time at all."

10

The next morning was bright and clear at Navenby Hall. Serene Id, a beautifully faded white woman in her late seventies, whistled as she moved amongst the many cycles in the main hall that had once been the National Cycle Museum. She dusted the bikes with a large feather duster that had seen better days. Sunlight streamed through the windows and many motes of dust floated in the air. The cycles were clean and shiny; all else was covered in dust and cobwebs.

"You'd look sweet upon the seat of a bicycle made for two. Daisy, Daisy, give me your answer do, I'm half crazy," she sang, and then said, "That's true, no one came in the old days either. Did they? They've forgotten us, haven't they? Yes, they have. I'm telling you. They have. Forgotten."

The large clock that advertised 'Raleigh Cycles' interrupted her as it struck eight. "Time to feed the chickens," she announced to the 'Claude Butler' that she was polishing.

As she emerged onto the top terrace she stood to admire the view of the great plain below the ridge upon which the Hall stood. The early morning light was clear and bright. On such a day the derelict cooling towers of the five power stations could be clearly seen. The glistening ribbon of the Trent gave movement to a landscape in which very little moved.

She sighed, "It could be a painting, a still life. But there is life: creatures are alive out there, while I'm here, waiting. Come on, Serene!" she told herself, "Jobs to be done, jobs to be done."

11

Meanwhile Anvil searched his carriage. He was looking for something special amidst his many test tubes and boxes of scientific paraphernalia.

"Now where did I put it? All the labels have come off. It must be here somewhere," he mused.

"Mr Anvil, Sir?" Lump asked as he stroked Sickle. "What was that funny word you said you once was, umpiresologist?"

"Embryologist, boy," Anvil laughed.

"And you made babies in them test-tubes?"

"No I didn't, not in these. It was a strange time, so many chances to do good, so many decisions that were bad, wrong or downright dangerous. Human beings are precious, Lump."

"Why's that?" Lump asked.

"That's a big question, boy."

"You'll tell me though?"

"Over the years you'll see why. I'll give you a start and then it'll be up to you."

"No one thinks us is precious, does they?"

"I do and you should. The big 'they' out there are wrong."

"What was wrong back then?" Lump asked

"Just like now, Lump, not everything, but rather a lot. But we're going to have to change all that, aren't we?"

"Do you think Commander Una can do it?"

Anvil continued his search. Clouds of dust rose from the lids of long unopened boxes.

After some time Anvil announced, "Ah! Here it is at last," and after a pause added, "I think."

12

His/Her Androgynous Majesty, Ham, sat upon the throne in the Throne Room (which is where the throne was kept at Hampton Court Palace) dressed in the customary purple silk pyjamas (being overweight the Royal 'jamas were ever so comfortable allowing belly, buttocks and thighs ample room for wobbly movements). A little golden crown glistened amidst the golden curls upon the Majesty's head. Ham's face was blessed with dark piercing eyes, though these were offset by a rosy flushed fatness garnered through a lifetime of self-indulgence. Wasn't that to be expected of the Monarch?

At Ham's side stood the Majesty's chief advisor and fixer, Axel Whiskerbot. Rumour had it that Axel had once been a pretty canny computer whiz-kid (in his long past youth) who had worked on the sensory capabilities of rodents, for whom the mystacial vibrissae (facial whiskers) provide a rich tactile description of local surface shapes and textures. He had apparently developed an artificial whisker array for a robotic rat before moving on to games design (it was he who had designed 'Rat Pak' and 'Run the maze or Die') with the Worldshitonem Computer Corporation in Seattle. He had managed to get back home just before the war and now found himself as Ham's chief flunky, with not a computer in sight.

Ham watched a troop of Morris Dancers perform to the accompaniment of a squeezeboxist. Truth be told, the sound of the rhythmic beating of their brightly painted clogs almost drowned out the music. They curled, weaved, clanked their sticks, rang their bells and waved their little hankies.

Royal Courtiers stood about watching the ancient ritual dance. Some seemed bemused; others had fingers in their ears, whilst others had pained expressions (though one could not tell whether this was because of the event taking place or because they were of high birth, and had been bred to look perpetually in disdain).

Ham, on the other hand, was in seventh heaven; the Royal

face bore a broad, perhaps even cherubic smile whilst little chubby fingers beat out the rhythm of the dance upon ample thighs. As the dancers finished and bowed Ham clapped ecstatically. Courtiers followed the lead and rhythmic clapping filled the room.

"That was lovely, really lovely. So good to know that the old traditions so central to our nation are alive and strong. Wonderful," Ham pronounced.

"Would your Hamness like more?" Whiskerbot asked.

"No, not now. Perhaps tomorrow. Yes, ask them to come back tomorrow. Oh look at that, it's almost time for my news."

Whiskerbot turned to the dancers, thanked them, told them to go and return on the morrow (despite the fact that they had heard everything Ham had said).

"I say, Whiskerbot," Ham called, and then added in a whisper, "You see that rather pretty boy and girl, those at the end? Have them sent to my chamber this afternoon, about four, for my tea."

"As you wish, your Majesty," Axel replied as he moved across to speak to the two young dancers.

"Bring me my radio!" Ham shouted.

Whiskerbot returned and stood next to Ham as a footman brought forth a wind-up clockwork radio that sat on a pink velvet cushion.

"Wind it up, wind it up! I haven't got all day." Ham said.

The footman placed the radio on the table that sat next to the throne and turned the handle. The radio crackled into life; the reception was bad and intermittent.

"Silence! Silence for Ham's News!" Whiskerbot shouted.

You could have heard a feather flop as the announcer said, "And here is the news at Radio Ham. Today is Tuesday March the tenth ABW thirty seven."

"I know that. Get on with it, man!" Ham grumbled, as if the poor bloke was actually inside the radio.

"Here is the Prime Minister, the Honourable John Green," the announcer said.

"Oh god, not him again," Ham complained.

"I have an important announcement," Green said.

"Odious man," Ham said.

"Last night in Parliament the Government of the Imperial Hamness passed important legislation that will make our country safe again. Safe from all those who threaten democracy. Safe from those who engage in the mass destruction of our long cherished liberties and freedoms. Safe from those who dissent beyond the limits of the toleration so beloved of our society and who seek to bring change and terror into every respectable person's home. Safe from those who would return us to the dark ages. Safe from ideologies that threaten the rule of natural justice and law in this England. Your England."

"God, doesn't he blather on?" Ham asked.

"Indeed," Whiskerbot replied.

"It was rhetorical," added Ham.

Green continued, "The death penalty will be introduced for those committing crimes against the state, and as defined on the piece of parchment that I am looking at right now."

"What?" Ham shouted.

"This legislation will come into immediate effect as soon as the Imperial Majesty has signed the statute later today," Green continued.

"Oh, will I indeed?" Ham shouted, "I think not. Turn that damn thing off. Go and get Green. I want to talk to him. Now!" Ham said and stamped the Royal foot.

"I would suspect that he'll be on his way in the very near future," Whiskerbot replied.

"Don't argue, Bot. Just do it."

"I shall send the pigeon immediately, your Majesty," Whiskerbot replied as he left the room.

The mood at the Motorway Service Station's Magistrates' Court was subdued. The three female and two male Legits, who had been caught 'up to no good' in the toilets the night before, stood in the dock. On the 'bench' (which was actually two antique white plastic garden chairs and picnic table) sat an ancient woman and man.

"I shall sentence the women first," the male Magistrate said. "Having considered the evidence, it is the judgement of this court that you are young and pretty enough to be sentenced to service in the nearest Fornicon. You will serve five years, or less, if you are found to be unattractive, and then you will be transferred to a factory penitentiary."

"Do you have anything to say?" the female Magistrate asked with a disparaging sniff.

"Please, Miss, what's a Fornicon?"

"I'm a Mam, not a Miss, young woman. A Fornicon is a brothel."

"What's a brothel, Mam?"

"A place where men and women pay to have sex with you," she replied with a shake of her head and a look of utter contempt. She turned to her colleague and whispered, "I can't abide the uneducated."

"Do we get to keep the Hamsters?" the woman asked.

"Of course not," the male Magistrate replied. "This is punishment. Your earnings will go towards your upkeep; whatever profit is left will go to the State. Take them down."

"Thank you, your honours," another female Legit said.

"Why are you thanking us?" the male Magistrate enquired.

"I like shagging, Sir," she replied.

"Disgusting!" the female Magistrate observed.

"I'll tell you what, my girl," the male Magistrate said, "after five years of servicing the likes of me you might just change your mind. Eh?"

"What, blokes like you?" the woman asked and then added, "fucking Aida, that's a thought that'll keep yer knees together and that's for certain. "

The male magistrate smiled.

"I shall sentence the men," the female Magistrate said. "It is the judgement of this court that you shall be made eunuchs and shall then continue to serve the state, and your betters, as unencumbered Legits."

"You fucking old cow, you can't do that!" one of the male prisoners screamed.

"What do they do?" the other asked.

"They cut your balls off," the other prisoner replied in tears.

40

"What, for having a fuck?"

"The law is clear. There are notices. You were told."

"I'll get you, I'll find you, I'll kill you! I'll fucking tear yours off with me teeth."

"The sentence is to be implemented with immediate effect. Take them down," the male Magistrate concluded.

"Or rather 'take them off'," the female Magistrate laughed.

"Next case," he replied.

14

Back at the train Roque was sitting up in bed.

"I'm glad you're so much better," Una said as she squeezed his hand.

"Thanks to Anvil's potion," he replied.

"What was in it?" Una asked Anvil.

"A mixture of Feverfew, and, never you mind," Anvil replied with a wicked smile.

"You're a secretive man, Anvil," she said.

"I'm sorry, habit of a lifetime. If I died tomorrow the lore would die with me. Not a good idea. So I've decided that Lump will be my apprentice; he can learn."

There was a knock on the door. Anvil opened it and Marx came in. Soon they were engaged in a discussion of tactics. They all agreed that one of their first tasks was to recruit more Sods, not just in one place, but all over the country. Una found this disheartening, as it would take months, even years, to send recruiting officers the length and breadth of the land on foot. They fell into silence.

"When you brought Roque back you said you had to think about wheels," Una asked.

"I did," Marx replied.

"Well?"

"Ham has many old coaches from the past," Marx said.

"But no horses," Anvil pointed out.

"We could pull them," Roque suggested.

41

"I'm sorry Roque, but well, what good would that do us? And anyway we'd never get in the palace."

"There's ways to do that, secret ways. Remember I was his body guard," Marx replied. "No, I was thinking of something else, other wheels. I saw them once when Ham was on one of the Royal visitations to the countryside. When the bloody Hamness. . ."

"Saw what, Marx?" Una interrupted.

"Bicycles. It was a museum full of bicycles."

"What's a bicycle?" Roque asked.

"Trouble is, I can't remember where it was," Marx said.

15

Ham and Green were in the throne room, locked in conversation. Whiskerbot sat to one side at a little desk with parchment and dip pen quill.

"I will not sign this bill," Ham said.

"Don't be ridiculous," Green retorted.

"Don't you dare speak to me like that. I am your Majesty."

Whiskerbot scratched away making his meeting note.

"You're nothing, just an expensive figurehead. And you, Botty," he said pointing at Whiskerbot, "you can stop taking notes. This is off the record."

"Call the guards! Arrest this man, this is treason."

"I would advise caution, your Majesty. He does have a point," Whiskerbot advised.

"Which is?" Ham asked.

"You're their excuse, and a very important excuse, for keeping control," Whiskerbot answered.

"Of what?"

"Everything – the Legits, the propertied class, money, everything."

"Well, I don't like it," Ham stated.

"Tough cheese, your Hamness," Green replied.

"You can use my quill," Whiskerbot said.

The parchment was presented and duly signed. Whiskerbot lit a wooden spill with his flint box and melted wax ready for the royal seal that Ham wore upon the Royal finger.

"You may go now," Ham said as he pushed the ring into the hot wax, "I've had enough for today. I have people for tea."

"I'm not done yet," Green replied.

"I think the Majesty indicated that your audience was over," Whiskerbot suggested.

"We have a problem," Green replied.

"That's all you ever come about, problems."

"This is serious. Can you get rid of arse hair, or whatever his name is?" Green asked.

"You know his name perfectly well."

"This is private."

"Whiskerbot is my trusted advisor. We have no secrets."

Whiskerbot imagined Green trapped at the end of a large maze, an immense rat poised to rip his neck apart. He worked hard at the image, but the loathsome man was still there when he opened his eyes.

"Do you have to sit on that bloody throne?" Green asked.

"It's a symbol of power."

"Bollocks!" Green responded. "I want to talk to you. Come and sit by the fire."

Ham grudgingly climbed down from the throne and sat opposite Green by the log-fire. It was not hard to believe that one had returned to the age of Chivalry except, of course, for the behaviour of the Prime Minister and the Monarch. Whiskerbot stood behind Ham as the conversation continued.

"How old are you?" Green asked.

"Forty six. Why?"

"There is no heir to the throne."

"I thought you didn't approve of the monarchy?"

"I don't. But, as has been explained by your trusty arse-licker, you're useful for the exercise of my power."

"Have you no sense of etiquette?" Whiskerbot asked.

"England needs an heir, or heiress. I don't much care which, in fact I wouldn't give a toss."

"Why now?" Ham asked anxiously.

"In case it has passed your immense intelligence and powers of observation, things are a bit tricky in the country at the moment. A marriage, followed by a child, would make a very worthwhile diversion for your subjects."

"And take the attention away from you and the other imbeciles who are ruining Albion," Whiskerbot asserted.

"I'll have you for that, you ancient nerd," Green responded.

"You seem to have forgotten that I'm androgynous, i.e. I've got both sets of equipment," Ham replied.

"I shall try and be simple so that your Majesty may understand. It seems to me that you've got three choices. Fuck yourself. Be fucked. Or fuck someone else, preferably a woman."

"Shall I have this crude oaf removed, your Hamness?" Whiskerbot rather boldly asked.

"Merely stating the bald facts. So what's it to be? One, two or three?" Green asked.

"I can't fuck myself," Ham answered.

"Not long enough?" Green asked.

"What an extraordinary remark. Of course it's long enough," Whiskerbot replied.

"Yes, the royal bum boy would know all about that wouldn't he, arse hair?"

"You miss the point, Prime Minister. Our family is too inbred anyway; to impregnate myself would be far too risky."

"Then be fucked. I'll find some good stud, with decent lineage, and then we can disappear him, a tragic accident," Green suggested with a smile.

"Don't be disgusting. I am not having a baby, and that's final."

"Then the matter's settled. I shall find you a suitable bride. Any preferences?"

"I'm really not sure about this, Green."

"The deal is simple: you do as you're told, and you can continue to live your life of unfettered debauchery. The alternative is abdication or an accidental death by drowning. I'm sure your sister wouldn't mind."

"She'd adore it," Ham said.

"The people will love you for it, producing a successor; a very mature and responsible act from a monarch who has been distant from the people for far too long."

"Do you think so?"

"You ought to sleep on it, your Majesty," Whiskerbot advised.

"You sleep on it, arse hair, like you normally do. So any preferences, your Highness?" Green enquired.

"Well, good family, no nutters in the line, not too bright, young, big tits and a really nice arse," Ham replied.

"Pretty face?"

"Wouldn't hurt, would it?"

"Yes, I've heard that you're not worried about the mantelpieces when you're. . ."

"That is quite far enough, Prime Minister," Whiskerbot interjected angrily.

"I think I have the very person in mind," Green replied. "Don't worry, I'll see myself out. I'm sure you both have much to discuss. I'll be in touch."

16

As you know the Criminal Justice System had been reformed. Distinctions had been drawn between: crimes against the state; crimes against property; crimes against people of property (up to, and including murder); and lesser crimes committed by, to, and between those without property (up to and including murder).

Back in the days Before the Big War (BBW) such simplicity was impossible. It has been argued that this was largely because almost all the MPs were barristers; a circumstance where endless, fruitless, disputes about law were endemic. There was, I have read, even an organisation that called itself 'Liberty'. Their prime purpose was to throw up every conceivable objection to potential infringements of what they called 'human rights'. This included the rights of those foreigners who sought 'asylum' in England. Such difficult issues had been somewhat reduced and resolved by the Government closing all the borders; there was no immigration, and thus no one needed asylum any more.

Ham's Lord Chief Justice, Judge Hangedogge, summed it up thus, "English Law is based upon statutes, and those statutes are designed to preserve and protect those that make England great. Anyone who does not want to make England great, or who thinks that England is not great, shall have good cause to fear the law. I would add that I am very pleased that the statute reintroducing the death penalty, for crimes against the State, has received Royal Assent. It is the final piece in the jigsaw that will see our land preserved from change for a thousand years."

But you shouldn't think that Hangedogge lacked imagination, or humour, for it was he who had coined the name 'Legit'.

Custodial sentences were endured within the HPFs (Ham's Penal Factories), and it really wasn't such a bad life. Indeed some Legits thought that it was a cushier number than a life upon the open road. You'll have to make your own mind up.

In the Lindum HPF male prisoners worked on the production line that constructed Aristosedans. (Plebsedans were made in places like Hull and Hackney.) Wood was cut by hand, holes drilled with ancient 'braces and bits', frames were assembled using hand carved wooden 'dowels' hammered into the holes to make the joints. As the prisoners sought to meet their quota a large vat of glue bubbled and spluttered on an immense brazier.

"We're running low on the glue," a prisoner observed.

"Not your problem, git," the trustee foreman replied, "and anyway there's a rigger coming in with a boat load of horses' hoofs from Spain."

"They got horses there then?" another asked.

"Must have, wouldn't be hoofs otherwise would there, you thick bastard?" the foreman said.

"If they brought the horses in there wouldn't be no need for these fucking chairs, would there?" the prisoner asked.

"Do you want to go in solitary?"

"Just wondering."

"Don't wonder. Work. It's what we make in this country, Sedans. Now get on with it," he concluded as he walked off down the line toward the paint shop where the chairs would receive their first coat of grey undercoat that went beneath the grey topcoat before being customised with the livery of the franchisee or individual owner at the point of delivery.

"If there was horses then what would the likes of us do then?" a prisoner asked.

"Good point," came the perplexed reply.

Elsewhere in the HPF female prisoners were upholstering sedans. Dry straw, grass and weeds (mostly straw in the case of Aristosedans) were being stuffed into cushions that were nailed to the interiors of the passenger cabins.

A factory bell tolled and the women stopped work. Many were exhausted from the long shift. The bell tolled once more; they formed themselves into an orderly line, and passed through a doorway into the mess hall where they collected their lumpy gruel and pieces of mouldy bread from the servery. They moved to the rough wooden benches and tables and stood waiting.

The Governor appeared on the dais at the end of the hall. "We will now say Grace. Repeat after me."

"Here we bloody go again," a woman whispered, only to receive a clout on the ear from a passing screw.

"Thank you Ham for feeding and watering me," the Governor piously intoned.

The women chanted the line.

"For I have sinned and there is no good in me."

The women repeated the words.

"I seek redemption through work. I ask for forgiveness. Long live England. Long life to Ham. Amen."

"Amen," came the mass reply.

The women sat and ate their main meal of the day.

"So you've been rehabitated then, have you?" a woman asked her companion.

"That's what they said, paroled."

"How'd you get that then?"

"Me? God, this food is shite. Shagged the foreman."

"We can't all shag the foreman."

"Well, not at once anyway," the woman laughed. "I'm off Legiting tomorrow."

"I can't stand it in here, locked up."

"How long you got to do?"

"Another eleven."

"Months?"

"Years."

"What did you do?"

"They said I was a vagrant. I was selling ciggies to get by."

"What real ciggies, black market ones?"

"Nah, beech leaves and wild herbs."

"That's not serious."

"I had no licence, no fixed place of abode, and them trading standards said as how I was diseased and breaking the state monopoly on tobacco."

"I'd shag the foreman if I was you," the woman advised.

17

Anvil and Lump were at work in Anvil's carriage.

"Now you listen, Lump, there's a lot for you to learn, starting with reading and writing."

"It's hard, Mr 'ammer, Sir."

"Now that you're my official apprentice you can call me Mr Anvil. Now where's that flask?"

"Here, Sir."

"Mr Anvil."

"Mr Anvil," Lump repeated.

"Is Sickle still nicely asleep?"

"Purring nice and easy."

"Good."

"What's in the flask, Mr Anvil?"

"Good boy! It's cat sperm, Lump. Or at least I think it is; the label's come off."

"What's sperm?"

"Dried cat's sperm, actually. It needs to be reactivated: I need to find the liquid. It must be here somewhere."

"But what's sperm?"

"Sperm makes babies, well, partly anyway. In this case, cat babies."

"What you going to do with it?"

"Ah, here it is," Anvil said as he found the phial of pink liquid. "Put it in Sickle, then she'll have kittens, then there will be cats again."

"Just like that?"

"It's a bit more complicated than that, but if we get very lucky, and everything is just right, then, yes."

"Where did you get it?"

"What?"

"The sperm stuff."

"You don't need to know that, Lump," Anvil said as he added the phial of liquid to the contents of the flask, which he then shook vigorously. "Let's see to Sickle before the hemlock wears off and she wakes up."

They went to where Sickle lay on a little whitish sheet on the table between various twisted tubes and jars.

"Who's a nice pussy then," Anvil observed.

Outside, in the fresh air, Roque punched an old mailbag that hung from the branch of a large rowan tree. He grunted as he laid into the bag that was steadied by Wesley. Wesley was in full flight. Una watched the two men from a distance.

"There is a green hill far away." Thump. "Without a city wall." Thump. "Does that mean it didn't have a wall?" Thump. "Or does it mean that it had a wall?" Thump. "That's a good one." Thump. "We may not know, we cannot tell." Thump. "What pains we'll have to bear." Thump. "But we believe it is for us." Thump. "That we struggle here." Thump. "Harder!" Thump. "We only can unleash the faith." Thump. "That freedom will be there." Thump. "It doesn't work does it?" Thump. "There are no others good enough." Thump. "To bring us freedom fair." Thump. "Better!"

After having watched the two men at their labours Una went closer, a broad smile upon her face and said, "You're looking good."

Roque smiled back and continued his workout, whilst Wesley became silent: a condition that never lasted for long.

"That's it. You've done enough for today, comrade," Wesley

said with rye smile as he glanced at Una.

Roque did as he was told and rubbed the muscles around his shoulder wound. "It's almost back to normal," he said, "Wes? You got any of that embrocation that Anvil made up?"

"Right here," Wesley replied, holding up an old glass jar on which a label read 'Dr Nelson's improved Horse Liniment FOR EXTERNAL USE ONLY'.

Una took the jar from him, pulled out the cork stopper and recoiled at the smell. "What in god's name did he put in this?"

"It works a treat," Roque said. "I'll rub it in."

"No," Una replied, "I'll just wait until my eyes have stopped streaming. Sit down there."

Roque sat on a log and Una rubbed the embrocation into his shoulders and back, "You wouldn't want to be wearing this on a raid. They'd smell you coming from miles away."

Wesley watched as Una worked on Roque's muscles. "I think I'll leave you to it," he said as he walked away. They didn't seem to notice.

"You've got lovely hands," Roque said.

"And you have a wonderful body."

She stopped rubbing. She bent her head towards him and kissed him lightly on the cheek. He stood and turned toward her. They embraced and were about to kiss when Marx trotted up to where they stood.

"I've remembered. It's all come back!" he shouted, "Oh sorry," he added.

"Just as well, I suppose," Una replied as Roque released her from his arms.

"What have you remembered?" she asked.

"The museum, the cycle museum. I know where it is, or was anyway. Navenby Hall, in a place called Lincolnshire."

"Those old counties don't exist anymore," she replied.

"But they'll be on the old maps," Roque said, "and Anvil has those. I've seen them."

They made their way along the culvert to Anvil's carriage and Roque knocked on the door. Anvil opened it and said, "Greetings citizens, do come in. Lump and I have just finished our little experiment."

"What have you been up to?" Una asked.

"It's a surprise. What can I do for you?"

"We need to look at your old maps. Marx has remembered where the cycle museum was," Roque said.

"Do you know where they are?" Marx enquired.

"Good question. They'll be in here somewhere. Which county were you looking for?"

"Lincolnshire."

"Lump and I will search for them now," Anvil replied. "Do you want to wait?"

"No, it's okay Anvil, we'll wait outside. You could hardly swing a cat in here," Roque observed, and saw the sleeping Sickle curled up in a chair. "Sorry, no offence to Sickle."

They left as Anvil and Lump began their search.

"They should be in the library," Anvil said.

The next compartment was entirely given over to shelves containing books and boxes of papers. It was very untidy. They coughed as dust floated from shelves that had never been dusted. After some time Anvil spied the rolls of maps on the topmost shelf. Lump climbed up to get them down.

Later, the map of Lincolnshire was spread out on the ground held down by stones.

"This is Lincolnshire?" Roque asked.

"Yes, we're in Lincolnshire already. Extraordinary isn't it?" Anvil replied.

"Why did they call it Middle East England then?" Una asked.

"So nobody would know where they were," Marx responded.

"Bastards!" Roque commented.

"A classic means of alienating the people from their historical roots," Marx said.

"There it is," Una interrupted. "And you reckon we're about here, Anvil?" she asked placing her finger on the map.

"Yes I think so."

"So how far is it?" she asked.

Anvil removed a long piece of string from his tattered trouser pocket and measured the distance on the map.

"Um," he said, "as the crow flies, it's about eighty five miles."

"What's that in kilometres?" Roque asked.

"Haven't a clue," Anvil replied. "I was too old to get the hang of kilometres."

"But we won't be able to go in a straight line," Una said.

"No. Looking at this I reckon it's about one hundred and twenty miles," Anvil replied.

"That's a good five days march," Una said.

"More," Roque said, "especially if we have to travel by night."

"The Roman soldiers used to be able to do forty, even fifty, miles a day on a forced march," Marx observed.

"Our Sods aren't Romans, more's the pity," Una said.

"There'll be many hazards along the way," Anvil said. "You don't know what you'll find out there."

"We'll get there. Let's allow six days there and six days back," Una answered.

"I just hope it's still there," Marx said.

"It'll be there," Anvil said. "I can feel it in my bones."

18

In the Capital, the Prime Minister had broken with tradition. He had left his sedan back in the Sedantory behind 'Number 10'. What he was doing was secret and extraordinary: he was walking. In his hand he carried a velum bound London 'A to Z'. This he consulted as he walked through streets he hadn't seen in years. Though there were now no newspapers, and thus no photographs of the great and the good, he had been concerned that someone might recognise him as he went on his mission. Given this worry he had adopted a disguise. He was dressed as a priest and upon his head he wore the standard headgear of a member of the State clergy, a black balaclava on which was embroidered (in white) the insignia of His Holiness the Bishop of England.

After a good hour's walk, that left him both breathless and tired, he arrived at his destination; a once charming mews with its once charming houses. The cobbled sets had not been tended in years, rampent weeds grew between them and buddleia had run riot along the walls. Nevertheless, the house he sought, number five, still had something about it – perhaps it was the crossed swords above the front door next to the integral side garage. He approached the front door and rattled the knocker that was fashioned as a small automatic pistol. He knocked more firmly and waited. There was no reply. The garage doors were slightly ajar and so he went towards them.

He stood and listened. He was perplexed as he was sure he could hear the sounds of a man making noises that, if his memory was not wrong, reproduced the roaring of a motor car engine as its gears were changed and acceleration made. Very slowly he pushed open one of the doors and went inside.

A white man, in his fifties, sat behind the wheel of a very old, beautifully polished, British Racing Green, Aston Martin DB4 sports car. This man wore a Paisley cravat and a rather old double-breasted blue blazer with shiny gold buttons. He seemed lost in memories as he gripped the wheel, changed gear, and roared his impersonation of the high-powered car. His moustache twitched with pleasure.

"Mr Gilt?" Green asked, trying to make himself heard.

Gilt continued to roar.

"Mr Gilt!" Green shouted as he advanced toward the car.

Gilt continued to roar. Green knocked on the windscreen. Gilt stopped roaring and got out of the car.

"Who the hell are you?" he asked.

"I'm," Green started to reply.

"A bloody vicar," Gilt interrupted, "I don't do the religion thing, old man."

"I'm not a vicar," Green responded. "I'm the Prime Minister of England."

Gilt burst into hysterical laughter. "Oh yes? And I'm the Imperial Hamness."

"I'm in disguise."

"You're a nutter."

Green pulled off his black balaclava and asked, "Now do you

recognise me?"

"Never seen you before in my life. Are you one of the bewildered? You know, care in the . . ."

"Community. No, we lock them up nowadays. I am the Prime Minister."

"Look," Gilt said, becoming suddenly stern. "Piss off before I break your bloody legs for you."

"If you touch me you'll be in trouble," Green responded as he moved away from Gilt. "I can prove it."

"You'd better be quick about it."

Green was frightened but he managed to get his hand underneath his cassock to his suit jacket. He pulled out his ID card on which was engraved his likeness and his title. This he handed to Gilt.

"Could be a fake," Gilt observed.

"But it isn't, and nor is this," Green said as he passed Gilt an envelope. "Open it."

Gilt did as he was told and withdrew a letter that carried the Royal Seal and Ham's signature. Gilt read the letter, returned it to Green and said, "It would seem that you are the Prime Minister. What can I do for you?"

"Are you Gilt?"

"As charged, Sir," he laughed. "Agent PP2 at your service. Shall we go into the house?"

"What exactly were you doing out here in that car?"

"No petrol. Just taking it for a spin. No harm in that."

"Right. Yes, well, perhaps we'd better go in," Green said arching an eyebrow.

Green and Gilt sat opposite each other at the table in Gilt's dining room. They drank brandy from large Napoleon glasses.

"I haven't had a brandy in years," Green said.

"Enjoy."

"How did you come by this?"

"Ah well, built up a good cellar. Good contacts, you know."

"It seems ironic that the Prime Minister doesn't have a supply whilst a secret agent does."

"So what's the service called these days?"

"The Androgynous Majesty's Secret Service."

"Bit of a mouthful that," Gilt observed.

"SS for short."

"Rather unpleasant historical connotations, don't you think? MI5 had a better ring to it."

"I'm not here to discuss bloody names, Gilt."

"I was forgetting my place, Sir."

"I don't trust any of them."

"Who's them, Sir?"

"My so called colleagues, of course – the cabinet, dross all of them," Green replied and then asked, "When was the last time you killed anyone?"

"Be about fifteen years ago. Some royal fella, bit of a cock up really; had to take out his kids as well."

"That's why I'm here. You have the craft. You are ruthless."

"Well thank you, Sir."

"I want you to find someone for me."

"I thought no one would ever ask, thought I'd been forgotten, left on the shelf."

"You're a dinosaur, Gilt, but I need you."

"Who's the target?"

"She's not a target. I want her brought back alive."

"No killing?"

"Anyone else you need to, but not her."

"Be better to kill her surely?"

"We will kill her. She will be tried for treason, and she'll hang. I want the people to see what happens to terrorists."

"You're the Prime Minister."

"We think she's called Una Uevera. English, but with dago ancestors, if we've got the right one. She leads a band of terrorists."

"The Sedanistas?"

"You know of them?"

"One still maintains some of the old networks. Nasty bunch by all accounts."

"Do you still have a gun?"

"That's classified."

"Don't be bloody stupid, man. I'm your commander in chief."

"And two clips of bullets."

Green stood up and took off his cassock. From around his waist he removed a well-filled money belt that he pushed across the table to Gilt. "There should be more than enough there. I will double the sum when you deliver her to me, alive."

"It may take some time you know."

"Just do it. I want her alive, and remember, you're on your own in this. You don't exist anymore and I never came here today. Understand?"

"Just a vicar looking for free hand-outs."

"Precisely."

Green disguised himself once more and slid out into the gathering dusk.

19

In Lincolnshire the long march to Navenby had begun. Una, Roque and ten Sods travelled by night. Marx had stayed behind to lead the remaining Sods and to ensure the safety of the insurgents.

They were on a bridge above what had been the A1M motorway. There were no lights to be seen and clouds obscured the moon. It felt like rain. There was no traffic on the carriageways beneath where they hid. Private and transport sedans didn't travel by night as they had no illumination with which to see either derelict vehicles or other sedans that might have come to a halt.

The Sods lay very still. At the end of the bridge there was a barrier and a guardhouse. Two Swabs were on night duty. They stood talking as they rested, their hands on their double-handed broadswords.

In the distance could be heard the sounds of two hundred trotting clogged feet. (The one vehicle to move at night was the Sedanathon 'Night Mail', or S'n'M as it was known.) The noise rose as the vehicle approached. Roque and Una nodded at each other. She took a catapult from her belt and fired a heavy round pebble at one of the Swabs. It hit him straight between the eyes. He fell to the ground unconscious. The noise of the clogs beneath them was deafening. Roque rushed forward, and before the remaining Swab had a chance to work out what was going on, Roque was upon him. He grabbed the man and in one movement hurled him over the edge of the bridge to the carriageway below.

None of the Sods heard the body hit the ground (just missing the end of the Night Mail) as they cleared the bridge and ran off into the night. Roque, however, went back and collected the two broadswords. They kept going until the first light of day.

As they entered a small clearing within the wood through which they had struggled for a good part of the night Una raised her hand and said, "Halt! Enough for one night. We're all exhausted."

The Sods immediately sat down upon the mossy ground and leaves beneath the broad-leafed trees.

"Make camp. No fires. Roque, set guards," she commanded.

"This place is safe," he replied.

"Nowhere is safe; nothing in this England they've made is safe."

"You two, Wesley and Hornet, check the wood. See if there are any houses near by," Roque said.

The two Sods did as they were told, whilst the others sat and received the rations that Roque doled out. All was quiet for a few moments; they sat and listened to the birds' early calls.

Wesley rushed out from the undergrowth, "You need to see this."

They followed him deeper into the dark wood. They found Hornet standing over the unconscious body of a young black Legit. His hands were locked within crude manacles. His beard had grown and he looked gaunt, his closed eyes sunk deep in his face.

Roque knelt down beside him and felt for the pulse in his neck, "Still alive, just."

"Get those evil things off his wrists," Una said.

Roque broke open the heavy metal locking clips with a stout thick bladed knife. They lifted him carefully from the ground and carried him back to their encampment. Having wrapped him in their cloaks they fed him drops of water. Slowly he regained consciousness.

Wesley and Hornet continued to care for the man whilst Roque and Una stood at the edge of the clearing.

"What shall we do with him?" Roque asked.

"We can't take him with us. He's too weak, and we don't know who he is."

"He's an escaped Legit; he was manacled."

"That's what it looks like."

"I don't understand," Roque said.

"They'll come after us, soon. Maybe they've already started."

"And you think that poor lad could be a threat to us?" Roque asked.

"He might be."

"Una, I'm sure you're right: they will come looking, but not like this, surely."

"It's just me. Let's go and see if he's up to talking. But in any case he stays put. We'll leave Hornet with him."

Wesley fed the man a dry biscuit.

"More, more please. I'm starved. I've only had berries in days," the man said.

"Steady now. There's food. What's your name, friend?" Roque asked.

The man mumbled a reply though a mouth full of unleavened bread.

"Say again," Roque said.

"Spencer," Spencer replied.

"Okay, Spencer, why were you manacled and where did you come from?"

"We was caught having sex. It's illegal; they was going to castrate us, but I escaped."

"Where from?"

"How would I know? I just carry Sedanathons up and down the Sedanway."

"We'll need to talk to you some more about all this, when you're up to it." Una said.

"Who are you?"

58

"Sedanistas, Sods, we're going to overthrow the state."

"Like get rid of the chairs?"

"Yes. Do you want to join us?"

"I'd have died if it wasn't for you."

"Get some sleep."

"I'd rather eat if you don't mind."

"Then eat. You can rest here with Hornet while we complete our mission," Una said.

20

The nation was at work, at least some of it was (even though it was a Sunday). Much consideration had been given to the structure of the working week. As you probably know Sunday had been traditionally regarded as a 'day of rest'. But the word 'rest' had caused problems for the creators of the New Lablair England. Take the situation of the Legits. Their function was to work: that was what they were for. This is hard to explain. In previous millennia there had been no distinction between work and leisure, there was simply 'life'. Leisure was something that came from industrialisation, or so I've read, and the amount of 'leisure' you acquired was determined by your status in society. If you were a member of the ruling class then you had 99.9% of leisure, whereas if you were a coal miner you had 99.99% of work, give or take a few percentage points. So, in ABW post industrial society, there was once again work and for those that worked that was it. I'll have to come back to this as I haven't really come to grips with some of the logic here. Simply put, Legits didn't get days off, whereas the majority of those that got carried around did, lots of them, nearly all the time.

One hundred Legits came to a weary halt and lowered their Sedanathon onto the broken tarmac of the immense motorway service station parking lot.

"Right, that's your eighteen miles for today. Time for R and R.

In yer beds early, it's another long day tomorrow," their Legiturion commanded.

Amidst the groans and murmurs of disapproval several
Legits fell to the ground exhausted. Others tried to help their
fallen comrades. A number were beyond help. The
Legiturion kicked an inert body with the toe of his steel clad
clog. It didn't move.

"Get this one out of the bleeding way, I've got work to do,"
the Legiturion said.

Legits dragged the body out of the way as a fresh Century
marched toward their load, commanded by their own
Legiturion who said, "To your places!"

"Drum!" the Legiturion said to his drummer boy who began
the slow beat. The Legits marched in time upon the spot.

"On three lift! One. Two. Three. Lift!"

The Sedanathon was raised.

"On three move out. One. Two. Three."

The Sedanathon started to pull away.

"Up the beat! One and two and three."

They picked up speed as only a fresh Century could as it
moved forwards on its eighteen-mile stage.

Gilt had always taken great pride in his work, and though this
mission was less exciting than many he had undertaken, there
was the opportunity to cause much mayhem and alarm along
the way. His preparations had been meticulous. He had begun the task of disguising himself as a middle-aged Legit. He
was happy in his work, singing, "Hey Ho, Hey Ho, it's off to
work we go," as he stopped to consider himself in the ornate
gold mirror. He had been sad to loose the moustache but in
the service of the state no sacrifices were too great.

He wore ragged and torn trousers (known in the trade as

'tressells') made from sacking that he'd found in the back of the garage. Around his waist he had a wide belt with many pouches in which he had placed: a short dagger (in a scabbard, so he wouldn't harm himself); a Swiss army knife; a gun; and two clips of bullets. He took a very large roll of Hamsters and placed it in one of the pockets. He then pulled on various other layers of clothing including a disgustingly dirty shirt. He looked quite tubby by the time he had finished.

Finally he applied earth from a dish to his hands, face and hair which he turned into a crumpled mess, "And who said the days of the secret agent were over," he murmured as he admired himself in the mirror, knowing that this would be the last opportunity he would have for some time to enjoy his own reflection.

22

Orb was ready for business. The church bells peeled their invitation to the faithful, and the faithless, to indulge in the rituals of inclusion offered by the State's official religion. A crowd of inquisitive Sedanists, property owners, and landless serfs gathered around the stone cross that sat in the centre of the ancient market square, waiting for Orb to begin.

Orb smiled and waved at the crowd. Years on the road had taught him that trying to talk over the sound of bells, fights, lynchings and childbirth was not a good idea. So he stood there, with his long star-spangled cloak blowing in the wind, and his tall pointed red, white and blue hat glistening in the sun. He stood on the steps of the cross on which was propped a large hand-printed (it was nicely done) sign that carried the single word 'PARDON'.

"My name is Orb," he began. "I have come. . ."

"You ain't from round here," a serf shouted.

"Yes, where are you from, old man?" a Sedanist enquired.

"I came from the mainland, as we used to say, from Spain

many years ago," Orb replied.

"You're a foreigner then," another serf observed.

"I am an English citizen and I have the papers to prove it."

"Why don't you get on with it?" a Sedanist shouted.

Orb was used to this. He waited.

"What's a bloody pardon when it's at home?" a serf asked.

"It's what you say when you've done a fart," another replied.

"Belch, don't you mean?" a sedanist replied.

"Ignorant oaf!" another added.

"Who you calling ignorant?"

"You. Want to make something of it?

"Shut up will you? Let's listen to this here Orb," another serf suggested.

Orb studied the crowd as it quietened. "Good. I shall begin," he said, in what was, despite all his years in England, still a discernible Catalonian melodic drawl.

"I bring you the Pardon. Pardons are the most wonderful things that money can buy."

"I haven't got any money," a serf shouted.

"I bring you a special offer. A very special offer indeed. Normally the Imperial Hamness issues pardons after you've done something wrong. Whatever it is, little or big, it matters not, you pay accordingly."

"If you have the Hamsters," another serf interjected.

"I don't think he's speaking to you," a sedanist interposed.

"This new offer is sensational, and will result in a future from which worry will have been erased."

Serfs wandered off, whilst sedanists and property owners moved in closer.

"These new improved pardons can be bought in advance! It can't be, so you might think, but it's true. In advance. Sooo! If you're going to do something naughty or bad, even if you don't know what it might be, you can spread the payments over a period before you do the deed. What's more, when you need to use the pardon you don't need to start again. This pardon lasts forever; it's an everlasting pardon! Isn't that wonderful? Sooo! You do not have to be good. You do not have to walk on your knees for a hundred miles through the desert, repenting. You only have to let the soft animal of your body love what it loves, and pay for it in advance."

"How much are they?"

"Pricing is a matter between you, the client, and myself as a registered representative of the Pardons Services Agency, or PSA as it is known. I have my diary and am happy to make appointments now. I shall be here for the next two days."

"Where?"

"In the front room of the 'Lick and Spittle', just over there."

"Do these pardons cover everything?"

"Only that which is not illegal," Orb replied.

"What's the point in that then?"

"To remove guilt from your life my friend."

"I don't feel guilty."

"Then you are not living life to the full, not exploiting the opportunities that being a person of property affords."

Seeing as we have been talking about money a few words on the economy might be useful. There was, of course, no longer a Chancellor of the Exchequer to bang on about tests and frugality. But you would be wrong to think that England had become an entirely service based economy with the manufacture of sedans as its only industry. There were Hamsters. They had to be made. I will come to that in a moment, but first you should understand the principles involved.

The propertied class were issued with an annual income based upon the value of their property. This value was determined every five years or so by Ham's Office of Monetary Evaluations, Guarantees, Urban, Agricultural, and Rural Distribution Services, (you can work out the acronym for yourselves) but to be honest there was little point in doing this as property seldom exchanged hands. Nevertheless, members of this Government Department spent a lot of time defending the property values of England. The only circumstance that led to a transfer of property rights was when a member of the propertied class was found guilty of a crime that resulted in either incarceration, being reduced to a Legit, or, after the new legislation, death. The annual income was delivered in notes, by sedan, in twelve instalments, subject to a forty percent overhead and handling fee charged by the state. This income could be used to purchase goods and services from the State owned operations such as Hypertension Markets, Hostelries, Pardons and Fornicons. In this way the circulation of the currency was actually truly circular within and between those entitled to it. The so-called 'black market' was another matter.

The manufacture of Hamsters took place at Ham's Royal Mint that had been relocated to the ancient Principality of Birmingham. The entire city had been given over to the manufacture of Hamsters (there was no coinage as there was no metal left) where thousand upon thousand of Minters were employed. It was a complicated process: paper had to be made, cut up, printing plates engraved, ink manufactured, printing presses operated, notes bundled up, and all by hand. It was an extraordinary operation.

The issue of new notes was strictly regulated though they were, of course, in constant production. New notes were distributed when the ink on the old ones had faded beyond an acceptable level and thus had to be withdrawn as no one could be certain that they were worth the paper they were written on. In addition new notes were issued to celebrate important national events such as Ham's birthday, the anniversary of the end of Big War, St George's Day, and when everyone in government was feeling a bit short of the readies.

24

Gilt had begun his quest and had progressed as far as West Byfleet near the M25. He had decided that he needed to get into trouble. He entered a private road, Blackwood Close, and approached a man at number 11 who was tending his lawn with a scythe whilst he smoked a cigarette.

"Sorry to bother you, guv, but is the old motorway far off?" Gilt asked.

"Bugger off! You shouldn't be here. Dammit, you're a Legit," the man replied.

"That I am, but I'm lost, well lost. That's a ciggie you're smoking, ain't it?"

"What of it?"

"I haven't had one in years and years. Haven't got one to spare have you, guv?"

"No, I most certainly do not. On your way."

"Go on, give us a ciggie."

The lady of the house observed the scene from an upstairs window where she was darning her net curtains.

"This is private property," the man said.

Gilt lunged at the man's gardening jacket pocket and cried, "Come on, you bastard, give us a ciggie!"

The lady of the house leant out of the window and began to toll the rope that rang the large alarm bell mounted on the front of the house.

Gilt and the man struggled. (It wasn't much of a struggle as Gilt wasn't really trying. If he had been the man would have been dead already.) They fell to the ground where Gilt allowed himself to be held down.

Within a few moments the Jamsedan arrived and two Swabs jumped out whilst their Legits watched the scene unfold.

"Hello, hello, what's going on here then?" the fatter of the two Swabs asked as he and his thin friend grabbed Gilt and dragged him to his feet.

"First he asks the way and then he tries to steal a cigarette."

"Did he indeed, Sir? We'll deal with it now, Sir. Sorry you've been bothered, Sir," the fat Swab replied.

"Do I need to press charges?" the man asked.

"Not any more, Sir," the thin Swab said. "We do it for you. Quicker that way, no paperwork, on the spot arrests."

"Zero tolerance?" the man asked.

"It's the only way, Sir."

The lady of the house joined the man and started to brush the grass from his jacket.

"Right my, lad," the thin Swab said to Gilt, "you're in trouble."

"Where you from? You shouldn't be here." the fat Swab asked.

"I don't know, boss. Me memory's gone."

"Oh has it indeed?" the Swabs asked in unison, as they pushed Gilt into the waiting Jamsedan.

"Well, we'll just have to try and help you get it back, won't we," the thin Swab said poking Gilt in the stomach.

25

Gilt's quarry was some distance away, in fact one hundred and eighty-nine miles away. Una, Roque and the Sods had made good time. It had taken them five and a half days to reach Navenby. They found the ornate gates to the Hall's drive well and truly locked with rusty chains and padlocks when they arrived in afternoon sunshine. The old road was deserted and they soon scaled the high stonewall to reach the grounds within. They moved slowly and carefully through thick banks of rhododendrons that ran parallel to the drive. After struggling through the undergrowth for a couple of hundred yards Una decided to use the drive itself, whilst the others remained hidden.

She stood and listened in silence as an old woman appeared round a corner of the drive riding a tri-cycle. Una was as surprised to see the woman, as the latter was to see Una. The woman braked and stopped. "Who are you?" she asked, a broad smile upon her face.

"My name is Una. Is this the National Cycle Museum?"

"It most certainly is, my dear."

"We've come to see it," Una said.

"We? There's only one of you I think, though my eyes are not what they were."

"Come out now," Una called.

Her compatriots emerged from cover and joined Una and the old woman on the drive.

"Oh! There are lots of you. Lovely, visitors at last. You walk on up to the house and I'll get the front doors open. Oh visitors! People to talk to! Oh wonderful," she chuckled. "Oh, by the way, I'm Serene, Serene Id," she said, as she cycled off.

"Thank you," Una called, "we'll follow you."

Within the hour Una and her fellow Sedanistas had almost completed their first look at the collection. They were gob-smacked as they had never seen anything like it. It was a big collection ranging from Penny-Farthings through to the splendid BBW titanium and carbon road racing bikes. Serene had done a splendid job over the years keeping everything clean and well oiled. She watched with pleasure as Wesley looked, open-mouthed, at the vast range of bi-cycles.

"The one you were on earlier had three wheels, but these only have two." Wesley stated.

"Have these all got wheels missing?" another Sod asked.

"No, young man, they are a different design to mine; these are meant to only have two."

"Then what do you do?"

"You learn to ride. You balance and turn the pedals."

"And steer at the same time?" Wesley asked again.

Una and Roque were lost in thought. Una looked at Roque who returned her gaze. They both nodded. The penny had dropped but they said nothing.

"Is it hard to learn to ride?" Wesley continued.

"You'll fall off a lot at first."

"Can we try?" Wesley asked as he grabbed a particularly splendid silver and black machine.

"Don't touch that! It's an exhibit. These aren't for riding; they're only for looking at," Serene admonished.

"It's alright, Miss Id, he meant no harm, did you, Wesley?" Una intervened.

"Oh no, no harm," Wesley smiled at Serene. "They're beautiful," he added.

"Well, that's alright then," Serene said, but her high delight with visitors had disappeared now that her life's work seemed to be threatened.

"It would be great to learn to ride a bike though," Una said as she smiled broadly at the old lady.

Serene studied her for a few moments and then said, "I've some old ones in the barn, that I got for spares but never used. You could learn on those if you like."

"That would be wonderful," Una replied, her enthusiasm genuine. "Thank you."

"Great! Bring me my wheels of whirring gold, bring me bow of burning. . .," Wesley added.

"Wesley!" Una stopped him with a smile.

"Come on then. Follow me," Serene said.

"Would you mind if we just stayed and had a look for a little bit longer?" Una asked.

"No, that'll be alright, what was it? Una?"

"That's right, Miss Id."

"You can call me Serene," she said as she led the Sods away.

Una and Roque waited for them to leave before speaking.

"You know what this means, don't you?" Roque asked.

"I most certainly do."

"How far could you go on one of these in a day?"

"A very long way."

"You know what Marx has done. He's found us our wheels. The world will change."

"It certainly gives us an edge."

"And what an edge! He'll go down in history for this, will comrade Marx."

"I don't think Serene will be very happy to let these go," Roque warned.

"You leave Serene to me."

"We could just take them, you know."

"We could not," Una angrily replied. "They will only go with her permission."

"And if she won't say yes?"

"Let's go and join the others and find out how it's done."

They found the Sods learning to ride on a grassy slope at the rear of the Hall. They rode on somewhat dilapidated bikes of various shapes and sizes. Serene was very much in charge.

The first lesson consisted of a Sod being balanced on a bike at the top of the slope supported by two others. At Serene's command the Sod on the bike was pushed away by a third Sod. As the bike and its rider rolled down the hill Serene shouted, "Pedal! Pedal! Pedal like hell!"

There was much laughter, and even more crashes, as they tried to master the art of cycling. Some did better than others. Wesley soon had the hang of it but learnt the hard way that brakes were useful when he hit the wall to the vegetable gardens. But there was no harm done.

Serene turned to Una and said, "Come on you. You're not getting away with it that easily."

Una did as she was told and mounted a cycle that Wesley held for her. On Serene's command he released his grip and Una rolled down the slope. She pedalled. She wobbled. She rode. She turned the handlebars and disappeared from sight.

"A natural!" Serene shouted in pleasure.

Within a few moments Una returned to their view and cycled back up the rise to where they all waited. The Sods cheered and Serene smiled at their joy.

It was nearly dusk when Serene said, "That's enough for today. Are you hungry?"

They ate a meal of root vegetables accompanied by an immense omelette that Serene had made with fresh eggs. The mere eating of such food raised all sorts of possibilities in the Sods' minds. "We could do this," they thought.

At the end of the meal many thanks were given to their elderly hostess. The Sods were in for another new experience as Serene led them to the dusty bedrooms within which they would sleep alone in proper beds. Una waited for Serene to return, "Can we talk?" she asked.

"Shall we go outside?" Serene replied, "I haven't had a walk and talk in the dark for years."

It was a clear night in the late Spring. Stars twinkled above them as they walked along the shingle path towards the walled garden. The air was filled with the scent of broom.

"What a wonderful smell," Una said.

They walked on in silence; their feet crunching like they do at the sea side.

"I have a special place when it all gets too much," Serene said. "Would you like to see it?"

"If that's alright."

They wound their way through the well-kept vegetable patches toward a small wooden potting shed at the far end of the garden. As they entered the building Serene said, "This belongs to me. I bought it for myself, fifty years ago. The rest, well I just keep it; I'm just a curator."

The smell of earth and creosote was deliciously intense. Serene lit a small vegetable oil lamp with a cigarette lighter and two wicker garden chairs came into sight.

"What's that?" Una asked.

"A lighter, we had thousands of them. They've got the name of the museum on the side, see," she said passing it to Una.

"I've never seen one before."

"I've hundreds left. You can have some if you like."

"Only if you can spare them," Una replied, unable to disguise her excitement at the prospect.

"Please sit down," Serene invited.

"This shed, it smells of something strange," Una said as she sniffed the air. "I'm not sure of what."

"Of the past, like me."

"It's a good smell. When was the last time you saw anybody?" Una asked.

"I've lost count of the years."

"You've never been outside?"

"Beyond the gates? No. Not since the end of the BigWar. The planes never came back, you know."

"All this time."

"I was too afraid, and then, I stayed afraid, and no one came after I locked the gates."

"How have you survived?"

"Kept what was already here, learnt to garden. There were plenty of books and there were the chickens: I've still got chickens."

"You've not been lonely?"

"Oh yes, but I've kept myself busy, and I've always liked my own company. I talk to myself you know." She paused. "Why did you come, Una?"

"It's a long story. Do you know what they've done out there?"

"No, and I'm not sure I want to."

"Can I tell you?"

"I fear you must. Go on, my dear," she sighed.

It was nearly dawn by the time Una had finished her tale of the world and the place of the Sedanistas within it. Both women were tired. Serene rose from her chair and extinguished the lamp.

"Time for breakfast," Serene said as she opened the door.

Una remained in her seat, "I'm sorry," she said.

"Come on, back to the house. You'll soon be missed."

"Could we use your bikes?" Una asked.

"I don't know. I need to think," Serene replied. "Let's get you to a bed while I cook breakfast for your troops."

"I wouldn't be able to sleep, but I'd love to eat," Una smiled.

26

As Una and Serene made their way back to the kitchen, and the Aga (that the Sods found to be the most miraculous of cooking machines), Gilt was cleaning his toenails with one of his knives in the holding cell at the Swab Station where he had spent the night.

"Bloody clogs," he grumbled, "make a real mess of your feet."

In the Station Day Room the two Swabs approached the

end of their twenty-four hour shift.

"Have you searched him?" their Sergeant asked.

"Have you smelt him?" the thin Swab replied.

"He reeks, that's what he does, reeks," the fat Swab added.

"He's still got to be searched."

"Why bother? All we've got to do is hand him in at the service station."

"It's all that'll happen anyhow."

"Go on, Sarge, cut down on the bloody paperwork."

"Is there any ink anyway?"

"Rules is rules," the Sergeant observed, "and no, there isn't any fucking ink, hasn't been none for months."

"Well, there you are then," the fat Swab said.

"I got some backy," his thin companion added.

"What sort? Virginia?" the Sergeant asked.

"Nar. A nice little lid of wacky."

"I suggest you take him down there right now," the Sergeant commanded, "and then we can have a nice relax when you get back."

As you have probably noticed your standard Swab was in no way similar to the highly trained and motivated PC Plod BBW. Swabs, for the most part, were comprised of the remnants of the armed forces, and as lower ranks they had never been regarded as much more than cannon fodder.

The rain poured down as Gilt was unceremoniously kicked out of the Jamsedan on the service station parking lot. A Legiturion who was assembling Legits to carry a massive Sedanteknikon observed his arrival.

Gilt gave the departing Sedan 'two fingers' and shouted, "Fucking morons!"

"Oi! You!" the Legiturion shouted.

"Who? Me?" Gilt replied looking behind him.

"Come here you. What's your name, Legit?"

"Glisten," Gilt replied.

"Glisten, boss."

"Glisten, boss," Gilt repeated.

"That's better. Glisten? What sort of a bloody name is Glisten?"

"It's French, boss."

"A frog eh? Well you'll be a glistening frog in a minute. There's a space for you just there. We was just one short."

"But I'm old and tired, boss."

"What a shame. Get in fucking line," the Legiturion prodded Gilt with his stout truncheon. If he had known what Gilt was thinking he would have been afraid.

Gilt joined the other four hundred and ninety-nine Legits as the drummer boy, dressed in his orange sackcloth and bowler-like hat, began the beating of his drum. As they waited to lift the vehicle Gilt asked the Legit in front of him, "How do we get round corners?"

"You don't, mate. Everything's straight forward here. Well mostly, otherwise it's a lot of shuffling about."

"Oh."

"You new to this?"

"To something this size."

"Well, it's knackering."

27

The words had proved to be prophetic for Gilt who was now fast asleep in the great cold dormitory surrounded by over a thousand noisily snoring Legits. Warm breath condensed in the cold air to produce a microclimate of fog.

Though indeed knackered, he had gone to sleep contented, if not happy, knowing that he was now in the territory of opportunity; which was more than could be said for the men that surrounded him.

As he lay asleep on his floor level bunk, a Legit moved furtively and silently between the rows of wooden bunks. From time to time the man stopped and searched through people's possessions, slight as they were, for objects of value. He found nothing.

He arrived at Gilt's side and began to insert his hand carefully into Gilt's greatcoat.

As you will know, the training that a secret agent receives prepares him for such events. Years of sleep deprivation and alertness enhancing exercises meant that Gilt had developed a sixth sense, an ability to know when danger was near, even when asleep.

Gilt slowly opened his eyes and watched as the man's fingers gently felt for the inside pocket. A slight smile played upon his lips. With sudden and silent great speed and agility Gilt grabbed the man's windpipe with one hand and covered his mouth with the other. The man struggled for breath. Not a sound could be heard as he was locked in Gilt's deathly embrace. The man struggled. Slowly he lost consciousness, but Gilt held on tight until the body was still. Gilt checked the man's pulse; there was none. He gently lowered the dead body to the floor beside his cot.

Gilt wrapped himself up in his coat and went back to sleep.

Early the next day Anvil and Lump were eating their breakfast when the evidently pregnant Sickle raised herself from her bed and struggled to walk towards them for a tit-bit from their table.

"There's something wrong with that cat," Anvil observed.

"You said she'd swell up like when she was preggers," Lump replied.

"But not like that. She's huge."

"Perhaps she's 'aving two?"

"I was worried about that sperm."

"What you stuck in her?"

"I wouldn't have put it quite like that, Lump, but yes."

"You put the wrong one in, didn't you?"

"I'm beginning to think I did. So many tubes, so many missing labels," Anvil mused.

"What will happen, Mr Anvil?"

"I don't really know, Lump. Nature will just have to take her course."

Sickle was unimpressed with the piece of unleavened bread that Anvil offered her. She meowed quite fiercely.

"She's hungry," Lump observed.

"I can see that, boy," Anvil replied.

"She's too fat to hunt her own birds and mice."

"Then you'd better get out there and find her something she will eat."

"Like what Mr Anvil?"

"Anything. Preferably dead, if you're bringing it in here."

At Navenby Hall the Sods had spent the previous day honing their cycling skills and now sat eating a splendid breakfast of fried eggs and potatoes that Serene had prepared for them for the second day running.

As they tucked into their meal Serene stood and watched. She was happier than she had been for a very long time.

She rapped a wooden spoon on one of the highly polished Aga ring covers until the Sods quietened.

"I have an announcement to make," she said.

Una shot a glance at Roque who raised his shoulders in a gesture that said, "I don't know."

"I have spent the last days talking to Una, Roque, and the rest of you, and I've done a lot of hard thinking. I want to join you, become a Sedanista, but I refuse to be called an old Sod," she laughed.

The Sods whooped with joy and banged their cutlery on their plates.

Una was quickly on her feet and was soon giving Serene an enormous hug, "Thank you!" she said.

Roque nodded with pleasure and smiled at Una as Serene

raised her hand for silence.

"There are conditions, things I need to work out with Una; good conditions, I think. The bikes are yours, but we need to think about the best way to use them. That's one of the things I need to agree with Una and Roque."

"That's just fine, Serene. We need to do that anyway," Roque replied.

"We'll beat the bastards now," Wesley shouted. "The meek will be meek no more. The lamb will be a lion. There will be eggs for breakfast, and the sun will shine. Be afraid, bastards! We are fit for war."

"Mind your language, Wesley," Serene said.

"Sorry, Serene," Wesley smiled back.

"Now finish up and go and do some more training on your bikes. You'll be no use forever falling off."

"The old ones, or those made for the glory of the open road, the highways and bye ways of this once glorious land?" Wesley asked.

"The old ones, for now. After lunch we'll start selecting the best models for the jobs to be done," Serene replied.

30

Things had not been quite as jolly in the Legit Dormitory. Gilt had awakened to find the dead body exactly where he had laid it during the night. The cadaver was not a pretty sight; its swollen terrified eyes stared from yellow skin.

Gilt started to scream hysterically, "Oh Ham! Oh shit! There's a stiff!"

Men woke and some began to move toward the apparently hysterical Gilt and the corpse.

"A stiff, a stiff, I say! A stiff!" he continued to shout.

Gilt trembled and gibbered in mock shock and horror.

"Ain't you seen one before?" a legit asked.

Gilt shook his head.

"Well, you will round 'ere," another observed as he closed

the dead man's eyes.

Soon a small indifferent crowd had gathered. "I'll go and get the boss," one said and left them staring at both Gilt and the body.

"What do we do now?" Gilt asked in a tremulous voice.

"Nothing. They'll see to it," one of the crowd said, boredom apparent in his tone.

The crowd soon returned to the business of getting ready for another carrying day.

Within a few moments the Legiturion arrived. "What's going on here," he asked.

"He's been screaming; shit himself I wouldn't wonder," one of the remaining Legits commented, indicating Gilt with a jerk of his thumb.

"What, the bleeding frog?" the Legiturion asked, recognising Gilt.

"I just woke up and he was just lying there like that, staring eyes and all," Gilt said.

"Listen, Glisten. Shut it, alright?" the Legiturion stated.

"Are you going to get the Swabs?" Gilt asked.

"I'm the law here. You nervous or summut?" the Legiturion asked.

"No, not me, boss. I just don't like stiffs."

"Well, you're going to have a chance to get better acquainted. Get him out of here. He's a health and safety risk, that's what he is."

"Me, boss?"

"Yeah, you and your three mates there. Move it!"

Gilt and the three Legits carried the corpse out into the fresh air and across the great parking lot where transport sedans were parked.

"Where are we going?" Gilt asked.

"You'll see."

"Is it far?" Gilt asked. "This bloke's heavy."

As they walked to the perimeter of the site a large black wooden compound came into view.

"What's that?" Gilt asked.

"The crem, you daft git."

Inside they found a man feeding a wood fuelled cremator.

"Where you want this, mate?" one of Legits shouted above the roaring of the flames.

"On the chute, up there," the man replied pointing to steps that led to a large chute that fed into the top of the cremator.

As they carried the body up the steps one of the Legits asked, "Got many in?"

"Usual, after a cold night," he replied.

They placed the body on the chute and watched as the man pulled a lever that shot the corpse into the leaping flames below. The fire roared, flames soared, and black smoke spiralled up from the chimney-less burner.

"What a job," Gilt said.

"Better 'n carrying," a Legit replied.

"But the smell, it's, it's disgusting," Gilt replied as he retched, and almost vomited. It was the first genuine thing he'd said so far that day.

31

Betty Bekkes and Green took the afternoon off as, "A break from the awesome burdens of government," as Green had put it. They went to Kew Gardens to pay homage to the foresight of their predecessors. I'd best explain.

After the Big War the importation of tobacco into England had ceased. The absence of cigarettes, cigars and pipes looked set to cause untold damage to the mental stability of the propertied class; in fact the entire fabric of England seemed at risk. Why you may ask, when BBW every effort had been made to stop people smoking (voluntarily of course)? It seems that it was something to do with 'pleasure'.

It had always been said that one should take pleasure in the little things in life, the ordinary normal things, like a beautiful sunset or the glance of a gorgeous human. ABW there was little that was normal nor was there a great deal of pleasure to be found. People took up smoking again: it was something they could do; it seemed to take the tensions out of life, and make things better, even if for a few moments. People wrote prose poems about it, like this by Kathleen Partridge:

> Slim little lady out of a box. Little white pinafore, little brown socks. Trimmed with a crest in letters of gold, with an affection slim fingers take hold. Isn't it wicked to set you alight, to wreath you in smoke for a moment's delight. Blue misty clouds caressing your waist, blacken the white of your pinafore chaste.
>
> Your life is so short, but every full minute is filled with the pleasure you have put in it. Perhaps you are proud that your presence is blessed by toil-wearied minds with a moment to rest. Seduction there is in your vivid red head, and perfume still lingers although you are dead.

Luckily the government of the day realised that supplies were running out before the warehouses were completely empty. They acted swiftly and strict rationing was introduced. They knew that this wasn't going to solve the problem; it merely put the evil day off when tobacco would be no more.

But England had always been blessed with many great gardens. These often contained enormous elegant greenhouses within which were housed the treasures of the natural world that had been 'rescued' by the explorers of old. The most notable of these were the many glasshouses of Kew. These houses, and others around the country, were immediately given over to the cultivation of tobacco plants. The first crops were harvested, cured and dried just as the old stocks ran out. Unfortunately there still had to be rationing, as there wasn't enough to go around. But at least the consumption of tobacco, with all its proven benefits, had not disappeared from England's cultural life.

A politician of the period said, "I resonate with this strategy!" (I'm not sure what he meant but I've seen the quote.)

Green and Bekkes wandered between aisles of plants smoking cigars.

"These are lovely," Bekkes said as she inhaled deeply. "Whose idea was it?"

"Darling," Green replied.

"Oh John, how sweet," she replied taking his hand.

"Darling, Betty. That was his name."

"Oh," she said, somewhat crestfallen.

"He was health at the time. But it could be darling if you wanted it to be Betty?"

"I thought you said it was Darling?"

"It was Darling, but you could be darling too," Green said.

"Oh John," she said, "Kiss me!"

"Let's find a quiet spot," he said as their lips finally parted.

They quickly made their way through the great hall of glass until they reached one of the many drying sheds to its rear. Once inside the darkened room, Green bolted the door. The smell of tobacco was intense.

"Wouldn't want anyone to come. . ." he said.

"Oh, I wouldn't say that, John," she giggled as she interrupted him. "Come here," she added as she started to unbutton his shirt.

Within a few moments they lay naked upon a vast bed of warm tobacco leaves engaged in the act that usually used to precede a cigarette. As their bodies moved in pleasure the leaves softly moved and rustled as the drying out process was accelerated. Their exertions were noisy and drew the attention of the passing Head Gardener as he went about his business as Ham's Tobacco Master Laureate (HTML).

He found one of his many wooden ladders and climbed to the ventilation windowpane in the roof of the drying room. The noises within became more intense as he reached the top of the ladder and looked in. He could not believe his eyes. First Betty's ample buttocks ground down on the Prime Minister, only to be followed by Green's energetic exertions to her welcoming body. He scampered down the ladder and gathered a few of his trusted staff to him. Soon their ladders enabled them to watch the antics of the copulating pair. The workers struggled to stifle their guffaws and hoots of delight as they watched Green's pockmarked arse bounce as he plumbed the depths of Bekke's infinitely accommodating private parts.

After half an hour Green and Bekkes lay back, sated, their flesh slightly tanned by their exertions upon the bed of steaming leaves.

"Well, that was a first for me," Bekkes said.

"Surely not, Betty?" Green asked.

"With the Prime Minister, on a bed of baccy leaves, yes I think so." she laughed.

"And very good it was too," he cooed back.

"Do you think it's safe to smoke in here?" she asked.

"Oh, I don't know, wouldn't want to go up with this lot."

"We'd better find somewhere that's less of a fire hazard the next time."

"Next time?" he asked

"Oh yes, please."

"We'd better keep this between ourselves," he said as he pulled on his underpants.

"What are you doing?" she asked.

"Getting dressed."

"If I can't have a cigarette then. . .what about a bit more tobacco rolling?"

"Oh," he said as he took his pants off, "Ooh yes, why not? We're not due back to the House until six."

HTML, and his three subordinates, watched as the couple renewed their passionate endeavours. He, of course, being HTML had a pretty good idea who these shaggers were. A wicked thought formed in his mind as he saw the red briefcase, embossed with the Royal Arms, that Green had left lying next to his clothes; that it contained sandwiches was irrelevant.

Una, Roque and Serene had spent some time in the potting shed before they had worked out what should be done and how it could be achieved. This is what they agreed.

Una, Wesley and two Sods would return, on 'mountain' bikes, to Hornet and Spencer and thence back to the train.

Roque and the remaining Sods would remain at Navenby Hall to protect Serene and the bikes.

Over the coming months there would be a regular transfer of selected Sods from the train to Navenby for training as a cycle strike force. Eventually this strike force would be based at Navenby and would be under Roque's command. The Hall would become the strategic headquarters for the war against the State, as it was connected to a road network of sorts.

Young children would be transferred from the train to the Hall where they would be schooled (by Serene) and properly fed (by Sods whom Serene had trained in culinary arts).

Marx would be placed in charge of armed (recycling the weapons garnered from their various skirmishes with the Swabs) and unarmed combat training back at the train.

The building of the force, and the recruitment of further Sods, would be incremental; many small steps rather than a great leap. Una had found this hard to stomach but realised that ultimate victory was more important than winning individual battles.

The protection of their secret weapon was paramount; to this end Roque would create a specialist cadre of bike guards.

They would move Anvil's maps from the train to Navenby and a set of strategic targets would be established along with an outline 'time-line' (Serene's phrase) for the conduct of the insurrection. Serene had insisted strongly that their ad hoc attacks had to be replaced with a plan. This latter would be posted on the war room wall that was to be located in the cellar of the Hall.

Una would remain as peripatetic Commander in Chief. She would always travel by bike and would never travel alone.

This might not sound a lot but it represented an enormous change in thinking for Una and Roque.

33

Meanwhile, the arrangements for the Royal Wedding had moved apace. On the 'special day' the large open space in front of St Paul's Cathedral was jam packed with a cheering crowd held in check by a continuous line of Swabs, their old plastic riot shields gleaming in the sun. It was said that over three hundred and twenty seven thousand people were there that day, which wasn't at all bad considering there were only about two hundred thousand of the propertied class living in the Capital. Many of the crowd waved English flags as they cheered the arrival of each of the procession of sedans that halted at the foot of the steps to deposit yet another Grandee.

Eventually Ham's enormous, ornate, gold sedan arrived to tumultuous applause. As the Majesty stepped forth there were gasps and cheers in admiration of the royal clothing. Having decided upon the inevitability of marriage Ham had decided to make the best of it and had thus had a special bridal suit manufactured (to the royal design) by the team of seamstresses normally employed to repair the increasingly dillapidated fabrics of the Palace.

Its kaleidoscopic appearance had not been accidental but had been a necessity, using as it did, fabrics and materials pillaged from the vast collection of clothes that had been handed down from generation to generation. Pieces of linen, cambric, mohair, flannel, muslin, gingham, seersucker, chintz, Holland, silk, foulard, damask, satin, sateen, taffeta, tussore, chiffon, tulle, lace and chenille, all of many colours, had been carefully assembled into the shimmering outfit that the Majesty so proudly wore.

Ham had decided that male attire would be best in the circumstances and thus wore a multi-coloured doublet and knickerbockers set off by the Majesty's last pair of white silk stockings and black patent leather shoes. The Royal head had been carefully prepared to carry the burden of the gold and be-jewelled crown. Rouge adorned chubby cheeks whilst dark eyeliner allowed the sparkle of the Monarch's eyes to be clearly seen (if you were close enough).

A stir of admiration ran through the congregation as Ham processed to the altar where the two Royal Marriage Thrones waited.

After due delay the organ struck up 'Here comes the Bride' as the latter walked towards her 'husband' to be. She was dressed in a long white dress attached to which was a train twenty feet in length carried by pageboys and girls dressed in their own liveries. Her face was veiled from sight.

Ham stood as she joined the Majesty at the altar.

His Holiness the Bishop of England began, "Dearly beloved, we are gathered together. . ."

The really important bit came when she had to take her vows. The Bishop asked, "Wilt thou, Camellia Bic-Croquet, have this person to thy wedded, umm, husband, to live together after God's ordinance in the holy estate of matrimony?"

"I will," she said.

"Wilt thou obey, um, the person, and serve, love, honour, and keep the person in sickness and health?"

"I will."

"And forsaking all other, keep thee only unto the person, so long as ye both shall live?"

"I will."

"Then I pronounce you Ham and wife."

Rings were placed upon fingers and the Bishop said, "You may kiss the bride."

Ham raised the veil to see the Royal bride's face for the very first time. She was a round faced, rosy-cheeked young woman of eighteen years, a descendant of the noble Bic-Croquet dynasty. They had been just plain Croquet until increasing poverty had required marriage into the pen and razor manufacturing company some years before the outbreak of the Big War. The Croquet's principle claim to historical fame was their invention of what was still one of the two English national games.

Ham leant forward, embraced her, and kissed her passionately on her lush red lips. Ham went on kissing her until the

Bishop was forced to whisper, "I think that will do for now, your Imperial Hamness."

As they disengaged their lips smacked, such had been the power of the suction between them. Ham stood back licking the Royal lips.

34

Out in the Hamdom of England the Royal wedding meant nothing to the Legits that carried the vast Nikon (an abbreviation to identify a Sedanteknikon) up the incline of the motorway exit slip road. In fact they didn't know or need to know anything about it.

The constant beating of the drum had not helped Gilt's humour; he was fed up and tired, and it showed.

The Legiturion walked along the ranks of the plodding Legits. As he did so he poked those who were slacking with his long heavy truncheon. He walked beside Gilt and poked him hard with the truncheon and said, "Come on, frog! Keep those cloggies moving." He poked Gilt again. Gilt glowered.

A new plan formed in his mind: he concluded that the carrying game was not for him and that it was very unlikely that he would find the Sedanistas and Una using his current strategy.

Eventually they arrived at the Hypertension Market and after much difficulty and shuffling about they finally placed the rear doors of the Nikon at the entrance to the loading bay. As it came to rest exhausted Legits collapsed to the ground. Gilt, however, stood and stared at the Legiturion who moved to where he waited, a smile upon his face.

"Who you smiling at, frog bastard?" the Legiturion asked.

"You. You piece of shit!" Gilt replied.

The Legiturion rushed at Gilt brandishing his truncheon. Gilt was too fast. As the truncheon began its arc towards his head Gilt cut his opponent's throat, from ear to ear, with one clean sweep of his razor sharp dagger. Blood gushed and spurted everywhere. For a moment it seemed as if his head might fall from his shoulders. It hadn't by the time the dead body hit the ground. Legits cheered as many Swabs and other Legiturions ran to the affray.

With great speed Gilt removed one of his thick rolls of Hamsters from where it had been hidden in his secret belt and hurled them into the air. The breeze blew them towards the Legits, Swabs and Legiturions, none of whom had ever seen so much dosh. The shower of money fell and swirled as the throng crashed and bumped into one another as they fought for the notes, struggling to garner riches beyond their wildest dreams. It was pandemonium.

Gilt smiled as he quickly and easily made his escape. As he disappeared over the security fence and ran off into the countryside one of the Legits detached himself from the still struggling mob and followed Gilt. This Legit was called Tracker.

As the day passed Tracker followed Gilt along back roads, green lanes, across open fields even, and through woods. He was good; he remained at a safe distance but never lost sight of the man he followed.

Gilt was surprised that there were so few animals in the fields. He saw land labourers, serfs, tending their crops using their primitive hand tools. In one field four large men dragged a plough through the hard soil. Gilt was shocked and shook his head in disbelief as he stood and watched their labours.

Quizzically he suddenly sniffed the air and swirled round sensing that he was being followed. The long and winding lane was empty. "You're getting jumpy, old man, but at least you're now a wanted man," Gilt said to himself.

35

Evening had fallen as Una, Wesley and the others rode along the track alongside the railway line that led to the train. Hornet was perched on Wesley's cross bar whilst Spencer happily jogged at the cyclists' side. Their welcome was ecstatic; they had been absent for some time. Marx had been worried that something had gone wrong but had, of course, kept his thoughts to himself.

The Sods at first found the bikes a bit frightening but as Wesley demonstrated his prowess their fears dwindled and there was soon a queue for lessons that he organised deep into the night.

Una didn't feel the need to have a mass meeting right then and there. Her first task was to explain to Marx and Anvil what had happened and to see what they thought of the plan. This she did, at some length, and in some detail.

Anvil seemed distracted throughout her account of their mission to Navenby Hall. Marx on the other hand could not have been more attentive or excited. The prospect of taking the battle to the enemy filled him with new hopes and ambitions for their collective struggle.

Late in the evening Una asked Anvil, "What's the matter, dear friend? You don't seem your normal self. Aren't you pleased to see us back, with our wheels for the cause?"

"Oh, more than delighted on all counts," he replied, "but I am both worried and perplexed, if that's the right word for it," he continued.

"Do you want me to go?" Marx asked.

"Would you mind?" Anvil replied.

"What is it then?" Una asked.

"Well, it's silly. I wanted to give you a surprise, a special present, but I don't think I can now."

"What was it?" Una asked, "I haven't had a present since all this began."

"A kitten," Anvil replied.

"What, a baby cat?" Una asked.

"Yes."

"But there is only Sickle left."

"There was only Sickle. You've probably forgotten but I used to be a scientist, something of an expert on animal reproduction. Well, I had some specimens, so I made her pregnant, and soon she will give birth."

"But that's wonderful," Una responded.

"I fear it's all gone wrong. She's enormous. I should have stuck to my guns: don't meddle with nature."

"Perhaps it'll be alright."

"I doubt it."

"What else, Anvil?" Una asked, realising that Sickle's strange pregnancy wasn't the only thing on his mind.

"Serene Id," he replied.

"What of her?" Una enquired. She's wonderful."

"She always was," Anvil replied and then paused before adding, "we used to be, umm, I find this slightly embarrassing . . . well, we used to be lovers, before the BigWar. I thought she had died."

"Are you sure it's her?" Una asked.

"From what you've said, yes. And, let's face it, there aren't many Serene Ids around these days, are there?"

Una was lost for words.

Suddenly there was a sharp rapping upon the door.

"Mr Anvil, Sir," Lump cried. "It's begun!"

Anvil and Lump watched as Sickle struggled to deliver her kitten. She meowed in pain. Anvil knelt beside her and stroked her head. Lump stayed where he was.

"Come on, Sickle, you can do it," Anvil said.

Sickle strained and pushed. A head appeared.

"Urggh! It's horrible!" Lump cried.

The body soon followed the head. The kitten, the creature, was large, almost the same size as its mother.

"What is it?" Lump asked in awe.

"It's not a moggie and that's for sure," Anvil replied.

It had a huge head, small body, and abnormally long legs. From its mouth protruded large sabre-like teeth. Its body was covered in short fur that was bright orange with many small purple patches. Anvil went as if to touch it, and though its eyes were not yet open, it lunged at Anvil and caught his hand with a glancing swipe of its teeth.

Anvil recoiled as blood spurted from the wound, "Ow! That hurt," he cried.

Lump shouted, "There's another coming!"

He was right. Soon the creature's sibling was born. It was identical in form except that its fur was bright purple and the patches were bright orange.

"Poor Sickle," Anvil said, "not quite what I had in mind."

Both beasts immediately suckled at the exhausted cat. Anvil and Lump could do nothing but stand and stare.

"She'd better mind them teeth," Lump observed.

They had been so lost in their amazement that they had not heard Una enter the carriage. "How are the kittens?" she asked trying to see what was going on.

"Eatin'," Lump replied.

Una moved past Anvil and his apprentice to see the new arrivals. Her mouth fell open, and for a moment she was silent, "What are they?" she then asked.

"I don't really know," Anvil replied.

"You wouldn't really want to come across them on a dark night would you," Una said.

"They'll train. All animals are capable of being trained," Anvil somewhat optimistically observed.

"Become domesticated?" Una asked.

"What's dosmessiticated?" Lump enquired.

"Tame," Anvil replied.

The two kittens finished their first meal as Sickle quietly snored. Her offspring were not asleep and made a constant, low, almost growling, sound.

"Tame's an interesting idea," Una said.

"What'll you call 'em, Mr Anvil?" Lump asked.

Anvil thought for a few moments and then said, "Well, they're a new species. I shall call them Anvil's Bloomers, since it was my mistake."

"Bloomers is good," Lump said, "but what about their own names?"

"That'll need thinking about," Anvil replied, "when we've found out what sex they are, and that'll be best done whilst they're asleep."

36

The soft toned sandstone walls of the thatched cottages glowed in the evening sun as Gilt walked along the main street of the village. He had not realised that such places still existed. The contrast between this tranquil world and that of the Legits was profound. For a moment he almost felt moved, but the feeling soon passed. He was not a man much given to sentimentality.

Gilt was somewhat conspicuous amidst the villagers as they made their way home from the fields, dressed as they were in dirty smocks, overalls and baggy trousers.

"Evening, stranger," a villager said.

"Evening," Gilt replied.

"You bin a Legit, bin thee?" the villager continued.

"An ex Legit actually."

"You talk funny, you do," the villager observed.

"It's a good thing that we aren't all the same, isn't it?"

"You take ye the good care now," the villager said as he started to move away.

"Hang on," Gilt said. "What is this place?"

"What, here? This place? You don't know much, do thee?"

"No."

"This be 'The Set'," the villager replied.

"The Set?" Gilt repeated.

"Aye."

"What's it mean?"

"It's what it's called. You ever heard of filums?"

"Filums? You mean films?"

"That's what I just said, dint I? Well they made 'em here, before my time, mind thee."

"This is a film set? And you all live in it?"

"What else would thee do with it?" the villager asked, adding, "Have thee a nice day," as he walked off.

At the end of the street Gilt came to 'Tess's Welcoming Arms' (The Set's only Inn) and went inside.

Candles lighted the public bar. Dead fruit machines stood

idle, covered in a thick layer of dust. Gilt nodded to the scattering of regulars and received quiet stares in return. A single Hogshead of ale was mounted on a sturdy plinth behind the bar counter. Gilt watched as the buxom barmaid drew a pint directly from the barrel.

At the bar he asked, "Is that beer?"

"It is that, my dear," she replied.

"A pint please," he said. "Do you do food?"

"Starling pie."

"Starlings?"

"It's good it is. They're fresh, like the beer," she said as she handed him a pewter tankard filled to the brim with flat cloudy beer.

He sank it in one and smacked his lips in pleasure, "I haven't had a pint like that in years. Another please, wench," he said handing her a Hamster.

"It's the way I pulls 'em, " she said as she gave Gilt a long wink, "You got to 'old the little knob just right to get the best out of it."

"And you know how to do that, I bet."

"You need a bed for the night then?"

"Is there room?" he asked.

He did not see Tracker enter the bar.

She leant forward across the bar, pushing his pint to one side, revealing yet more of her ample breasts. "I've got a real nice warm cranny just for you, my dear," she whispered in his eager ear.

"Sounds like the place to be," Gilt replied as Tracker tapped him on his shoulder.

Gilt whirled round, but remembered that a violent response might put Tess off (he assumed that was her name, wrongly as it happened). "Who the hell are you?" he asked.

"I need to talk to you," Tracker replied, "In private."

"In the corner," the barmaid suggested, "I'll bring your grub over," and added with another theatrical wink, "Don't you go worrying now; I'll keep it warm."

The two men made their way to the dark corner and sat opposite each other at the small round table.

"Do I know you, Legit?" Gilt asked.

"No. But I know you."

"Do you now. So who am I then?"

"I don't know your name, but I saw what you done."

"And what am I supposed to have done?" Gilt asked.

"Killed that bastard Legiturion, that's what."

"And you followed me here?"

Before Tracker could reply, Gilt's hand flashed under the table and grabbed Tracker's testicles in a fearsome grip.

"Pardon? I didn't quite get that?" Gilt asked.

"Yes," Tracker squeaked in immense pain.

"If you ever want to use these again," Gilt said as he squeezed even harder, "you'd better explain."

"Oh shit man! Ease off!" Tracker begged.

"Talk."

Tracker could hardly get his words out, "I'm not a Legit. I'm a Sedanista. A Sod."

"So why were you carrying that fucking Nikon?"

"Recruiting," Tracker almost screamed as the word came out.

"Undercover, eh?"

"Yes," Tracker replied in a feeble whisper.

Gilt released Tracker's balls and sat back smiling as Tracker frantically massaged his severely bruised equipment.

"Fancy a pint then?" Gilt asked.

At the bar the barmaid asked, "What happened to your friend?"

"Got his balls caught in the wrong place."

"Ooh nasty."

"But mine are fine," Gilt smiled.

She smiled as Gilt returned to the table with the tankards of ale.

"What's your name?" Gilt asked.

"Tracker."

"That's original."

"Sorry?"

"So why follow me all this way?"

"It was the way you did him; it was vicious."

"And that's good, is it?" Gilt asked.

"It is when we're at war."

"What do you want?"

"For you to join us — become a Sod."

The bar had emptied of regulars and the barmaid waved at Gilt. He waved back as he stood up and said, "I think I've always been a sod at heart."

"Where did you get all them Hamsters?" Tracker asked.

"Stole them."

"Even better," Tracker said as Gilt moved toward the bar and its beguiling maid.

37

As Gilt and Shirley (he never did find out that she wasn't called Tess) mounted the stairs to her little attic room Ham and Camellia were in the far more regal surroundings of the Royal Chamber at Hampton Court.

It had been a long evening for their Highnesses shaking hands with people who Ham never wanted to see ever again (like her bloody awful parents). But that was in the past, as the Majesty now lay in bed ogling Camellia as she undressed.

"Do we have to have all these candles on?" Camellia asked.

"Of course. This is our wedding night, our nuptials; I want to see what I've married."

"I'm shy," she said as she continued to undress.

"Green and Whiskerbot did a good job," Ham thought as the Majesty studied her now naked body. "I shall call you Cammy, it's softer," Ham continued as she moved to the bed, trying to shield her breasts and pudendum from Ham's eyes.

"Um, very nice," Ham said as she slipped beneath the covers. In a flash Ham threw back the silken sheets to reveal the royal nakedness and a very erect penis.

"Ooh!" she gasped, "It's ever so big!"

"All the better to roger you with," Ham chuckled.

The Majesty lay very still as Camellia stared at the erection.

After a moment of awestruck silence she asked in a trembling voice, "What's that?"

"It's known as a Prince Albert, family tradition."

"Does it stay in all the time, even when we. . ."

"Keeps me pert, my dear."

"Doesn't it hurt?"

"No. Do you want a closer look?"

"Can I?"

"As close as you like," Ham replied.

She moved down the bed until she was level with the penis and then recoiled, crying out, "You've got a, a, "

"Vagina," Ham helped her find the word.

"But you can't possibly have both!"

"I can and I do. Royal prerogative, runs in the family. Didn't you know?"

She jumped from the bed.

"No, no. I didn't know. Oh!"

"Everyone knows."

"I didn't," Camellia replied.

"Where have you been?"

"In a nunnery."

"So they didn't lie; you're a virgin."

"Yes."

"How very charming. Now, get back into bed at once, and that's an order."

Her cheeks flushed as she climbed back into bed.

It is best to draw a veil over the rest of the proceedings.

38

The week following the Royal Wedding was declared a National Holiday (for those who lived in London, it would have been too difficult to organise in the great 'out-there'), except for those who carried non-commercial Sedans, and even these were restricted to essential journeys. These latter primarily consisted in getting the propertied class to and from 'THE GAMES'. This gesture of governmental magnanimity was not without a certain amount of political adroitness.

In the period that had led up to the Big War sport had remained an essential ingredient in maintaining a collective sense of national pride and purpose. Green had spent some time thinking and working with Baron Cobalt of White City (the only hereditary black Baron) on a plan. The week's holiday would be filled with sport. The Games would take place at what had once been Lord's Cricket Ground.

This ancient venue had been used right up until the time when the Australian Eleven had won the Ashes for the umpteenth time but on this occasion in so comprehensive a manner that the Old Ham had insisted on drastic action.

"Stuff the Ashes! Impale the bastards on the bloody stumps," the Monarch had pronounced.

Indeed, they were bloody stumps, as the English Eleven (and the twelfth man) had been dispatched to greener pastures. After that the ground, hardly surprisingly, had fallen into disuse and disrepair.

When Green and Cobalt had gone to inspect Lords they found it in a very sorry condition. The once green sward was now a wild pasture; nettles and bindweed fought with rye grasses and massive umbellifers for dominance. Initially Cobalt had been concerned that they would not be able to adequately prepare the pitch. But Green had correctly pointed out that it would be as flat and bare as a pancake by the time the Games had finished.

You're probably wondering what they had planned. It was 'Blind Man's Buff', on a scale never before seen (or even played) ABW. The rules had been changed to make the spectacle more entertaining and more in keeping with the times. All contestants started blindfolded. The object was to remove the blindfolds of others whilst keeping one's own blindfold in place. The last person who remained blindfolded was the winner.

Their Plan went like this.

The contestants would be Legits who would be walked in from all around the metropolis and kept in the empty hospitals and apartment blocks of Shepherd's Bush.

The crowd would comprise of members of the propertied class who would pay ten Hamsters each to view the spectacle. This income would be used to provide prize money for the victors and the Supreme Champion.

Over the five days of the tournament there would be ten heats, one in the morning and one in the evening. Five thousand Legits would take part in each heat, with the one that remained blindfolded the victor. In addition to the Hamsters each victor would win, there was also a title deed to a small portion of trampled ground that would be taken away at the end of the Games. This ownership of property would mean that the victorious Legit would be a Legit no more, but someone with property and cash (though given the size of the piece of land not very much cash).

On the Saturday and Sunday the Grand Final would take place (it was expected that ten blindfolded people might take some time to find one another). In the final, the ten heat victors would compete against each other for the title of Supreme Champion. The prize for this achievement was to become a member of Ham's household with the honorary title of Ham's Bluffer, and thus do nothing of note for the rest of their lives (except of course to play the same game with Ham when required). A prize indeed!

The success of the event surpassed their wildest dreams.

On the first morning the five thousand Legits had been securely blindfolded as they entered the circle and when they were all assembled a quiet hush had fallen upon the expectant competitors and excited crowd.

It had seemed right that Ham should open the Games and this the Majesty did by blowing upon an ancient 'Acme Thunderer'. As the first shrill note issued from the whistle the contest began.

How the crowd cheered and how the Legits fought; no quarter was given or taken. At first it was easy for the contestants, jam-packed as they were one against each other. As those who could see, or who lay injured upon the floor, were immediately removed by squads of Swabs, it became more and more exciting.

The crowd roared encouragement, "Over there! Here! Behind you! Watch out!" they shouted. None of which was much use at first, the battling Legits being unaware of where 'here' and 'there' were.

After some time there were twelve sightless contestants left in the game. As the numbers of combatants had dwindled a circle of Swabs hemmed them ever more tightly in (there did have to be two heats a day). Soon there were four, and then the final two, a man and a woman. These last two found themselves in a square of Swabs no larger than a boxing ring. The contest was vicious; they struggled and clawed, kicked and scratched, butted and punched.

The crowd hadn't had so much fun in years and there was not a soul in the ground who didn't believe that they had spent their money wisely. Green, Cobalt and the Cabinet glowed with self-satisfaction.

As they approached the point of exhaustion (they had been at it for nearly four hours from the start) the woman tore the blindfold from the man's face.

The crowd roared their approval as she did a lap of honour waving her winning blindfold in the air. She was then guided through the little wicket gate (through which only winners passed) and into the Long Room where Ham presented her with her title deed and forty-nine thousand Hamsters (ticket sales had reached one hundred and twenty thousand Hamsters on that first morning but the balance had been used to cover overheads).

By the weekend not a ticket could be had except from Touts (who were actually working on commission for Green and Cobalt).

When the Grand Final began the ten contestants were surrounded by a circle of Swabs at the perimeter of the field of play. None of the grass and foliage had been removed but had been left as both a hindrance and a help to the players. Over the week the crowd had come to realise that their silence was needed if the blindfolded Victors were to find one another. The tension was extreme, a game of cat and mouse as the players tiptoed through the foliage, listened, tripped and suddenly ran in the direction of a noise. By the end of Saturday there were still eight combatants left, and the crowd were getting bored.

Green and Cobalt needed to think of something, otherwise all the hard work and success of the previous days would come to nothing. By the next morning they had found a suitable and innovative solution.

The size of the playing surface was reduced and each of the contestants was fitted with Morris Dancer's bells upon their legs. In addition each had been issued with a stave. The whistle blew at ten o'clock sharp and the battle commenced, for battle was what it had become.

The crowd looked on in awed silence as the players whirled their sticks and listened, every nerve alert, every sense (except sight) active as they sought the ultimate victory.

The first to go down was a man who was felled with what was a lucky blow. As the opponent knelt to pull off the blindfold another fell upon him, and then another, soon they were all involved in a fabulous brawl. This was not what Green and Cobalt had predicted. Swabs pulled away those that could see whilst these in turn fought back and tried to get at their fellow players. The crowd, however, seemed to love it.

After twenty minutes there was a bloodied and bruised Supreme Champion. It was the woman who had won the first heat.

As a sedan carried her away to Hampton Court, Green turned to Cobalt and said, "We've a lot to learn, Cobalt, old chap, but I think we're onto a winner here. I think we'll make it an annual event."

"We should think of a better name than just 'The Games'," Cobalt mused.

"We shall call it the Opportunity Games," Green replied.

"The criers could promote it with the right slogan, I know, 'It could be you!'"

"Brilliant!" Green replied as the two men entered his sedan. There would be plenty of time to count their profits or 'overheads' as they were called.

39

The next weeks proved tedious for the Sods. Even with the bikes, things went slowly. They were faced with the challenge of adapting to the use of new technology and fully comprehending the opportunities that wheels would provide. It was all very well for the Leadership to explain and explain, but the endless preparations were a daily drag on morale. Back and forth they went between the train and Navenby, and all under the cover of darkness. They grumbled and moaned as the Leadership seemed to do nothing but sit around and talk. Little did they realise that a 'master' plan was being forged.

They were now ready to begin the campaign, though the assembled force of Sods at Navenby did not know this. Una was confident that they were now well trained and that surprise was on their side.

Amidst the intellectual struggles that Anvil faced in ensuring that there weren't any loose ends, he also faced a personal and emotional dilemma: what was he going to do about Serene? Una had said nothing but he thought that she now looked upon him in a different way; not a bad way, but different. He guessed that it was difficult for her to imagine how a senile old git like him could ever have been filled with lust and passion, and that those feelings were still there, although probably now permanently inert. He was wise enough to realise that this was a mistake that the young had always made.

As a man of action he decided that something had to be done, so he went for a walk. As he reached the end of the path beside the train he came upon Lump taking the Bloomers for a walk accompanied by Una. From where Anvil stood and watched it looked more like they were taking him for a trot, attached as he was to the ropes tied to their collars. The two Bloomers were now quite large: they measured three feet to the ridge of their brightly coloured backs; whilst their huge heads added another two feet; their bodies were still small and round. From a distance they appeared as two spheres balanced on poles. Their sabre like teeth had been secured within primitive, but effective, muzzles.

As Lump tried not to break into a canter, Una strode beside him. "How old are they now?" she asked.

"Eight weeks."

"You'd better hope they don't grow any more."

"They was this size after a week. Mr Anvil, he says as how they won't grow no more."

"They got names yet?"

"Yeah," Lump replied, "The girl, that's the orangey one, is called Maggie. The boy, he's called Ronnie."

"Why?" Una asked.

"Don't know. But Mr Anvil, he couldn't stop laughing when he gave 'em them names."

At that moment a rare pigeon settled some distance from the Bloomers. Ronnie saw it and rushed off after it dragging Lump with him. "They're always hungry!" Lump shouted as the two Bloomers raced toward the bird that flew in Anvil's direction.

As the two animals reached their creator, Anvil stood very still and shouted, "Sit!"

Una was amazed as the two creatures immediately stopped and sat, as Lump crashed into them.

Anvil smiled and said, "I knew they'd train."

Not only were the Sods fed up, Una and Anvil had begun to get the same way, and so, that night, they decided to have a game of chess together. As they sat and played the two Bloomers, without their muzzles, lay contentedly at their feet making their strange growling snores. Maggie raised her head and lent it against Una's thigh. She in turn stroked its ear as she considered her next move and mused, "Domesticated, who would ever have thought it?" Anvil did not reply but moved his Bishop to King's Pawn two.

Ronnie stood up, stretched, moved toward Maggie and began sniffing at her rear end. Maggie stood and moved off a little way from the chess players who were lost in their game. Ronnie mounted Maggie and the two creatures, programmed as they were to procreate, did what they knew best: they mated.

Suddenly Una and Anvil became aware of the increasingly loud howls of pleasure that came from the two animals.

"Oh bloody hell!" Anvil observed.

"Can't you stop them?" Una pleaded.

"Sit!" Anvil commanded.

Ronnie growled.

"I don't think I'd like to try right now," Anvil continued.

Una and Anvil watched until Ronnie dismounted, a strange smile of pleasure upon his face.

"But they're brother and sister," Una said.

"Perhaps I should have called them Anvil's Bogies."

In The Set, morning had broken to find Tracker asleep on the floor in the corner of the bar. Gilt entered wearing only a pair of bedraggled underpants, observed the sleeping man, shook his head and poured himself a pint of ale from the Hogshead.

"God knows when I'll get another of these," he thought as he sipped his pint with great pleasure, and as he looked up at the ceiling added, "Or some more of that," as he licked his lips.

He walked over to the sleeping Tracker and gently woke him with the toes of his right foot by placing it just beneath Tracker's snoring nostrils. The man awoke in some degree of distress and gasped for clean air.

"Wakey! Wakey!" Gilt called, "Time for breakfast."

Shirley (aka Tess) joined them in the bar; she wore a calico shift that left nothing to Tracker's imagination but added considerably to his envy and admiration of Gilt.

"Eggs sunny side up be it, rasher of badger, side order of sautéed potatoes?" she asked.

"Eggs?" Tracker gasped.

In respect of love Gilt was not a bad man; he had left Tess

(aka Shirley) with enough Hamsters to keep herself to herself until he returned, which he had assured her he would, one day.

As they walked the two men talked. Gilt had tried to find out if this recruiting officer had any direct link to his quarry.

"I've never met her," Tracker had insisted.

"Shame, I've heard such a lot about her," Gilt had replied.

"But I think my Commander will know where HQ is," Tracker replied.

"What's he called?"

"Turpentine," Tracker responded.

"As in Dick Turpentine?" Gilt laughed.

"Her name's Mary."

"A woman?" Gilt asked.

"There's still a lot of 'em about you know we're democratic," Tracker responded.

They walked all day, passing through ghost villages where they saw not another soul, and they became tired, hungry and irritable. You don't need to know the sort of language they used.

As evening fell they eventually came upon the village of Leadenham. There were people; there was an Inn; there was a market cross, and there was Orb, setting up his sign at the foot of the cross.

41

Green had had a bloody good few weeks after The Games. What had particularly pleased him was that he was now re-cognised by significant numbers of the Propertied Class as he walked about his Capital. He had invented something he called 'Walkabout'. This consisted of taking the air, say along 'The Strand', at a pace that was almost funereal (have you noticed that people who think they're important have always done this) so that passers by (few in number) and Sedanists (larger in numbers) could stop and compliment him upon his efforts in restoring England to her previous reputation (amongst its old and bewildered population) as a 'World Leader' (whatever that then meant).

He was tired as he reached the front door of Number 10. It was with great effort that he climbed the stairs toward the Cabinet Office and opened the door. The room was dark. He took his tinderbox from his pocket and lit the candle that always stood on the little shelf inside the door.

He almost jumped out of his skin as a voice said, "I'm hungry John, hungry!"

He knew that voice. It was Bekkes. He turned and the lighted candle illuminated the almost naked form of his Cabinet mistress lying on top of the great desk. He groaned with desire. She was drunk. She wore a basque that, to be very honest, struggled to cope with the trembling volume of her voluptuousness.

"I've been on walkabout," he somewhat pointlessly said.

"John," she moaned.

"Do you think this is wise?" he prevaricated.

"Wise?" she screeched, "I want you, John, now!"

"I want you too, but not here. It isn't safe."

As she struggled to sit up the laces holding the straining front of the basque together split apart rendering her completely naked. This proved too much for the Prime Minister and he fell upon her, burying his face in her breasts whilst she frantically tried to undo his trousers. She pulled at the zip with drunken, but determined fingers, until there was a great tearing sound. She hadn't undone his trousers; she had torn them apart. As she finally exposed the member, there came a knocking at the door.

"I'm sorry, Prime Minister," a voice said, "but I have some people here to see you, and they won't go away."

Bekkes frantically tried to dress herself whilst Green attempted to fix his trousers using antique bulldog clips, as he said, "I'm involved with matters of state security in here!"

"I'm sorry, Sir, but they won't go away."

"Who are they?"

"It's HTML; it's about the tobacco."

"Surely that can wait until tomorrow?"

"They say there's a crisis that only you can solve."

Bekkes had by this time managed to get her clothes back on and stuff the ripped basque into her red briefcase. Green shrugged as he left her behind and wondered what the hell was going on.

He soon found out.

HTML (Ham's Tobacco Master Laureate) and his three assistants were seated in the ante room as Green entered and asked, somewhat tersely, hoping that the bulldog clips weren't too conspicuous and that they would do their job, "HTML, what is the crisis?" and added, "I was involved with affairs of state," and suddenly felt stupid for saying that.

"We understand, Prime Minister," HTML responded as he stood and held out a wooden cigar box. "This is for you," he continued as he offered the box to Green.

As Green took the box he appeared perplexed, "Cigars?" he asked.

"The finest, Sir," HTML replied.

"It's very kind, I'm sure, but I do have a more than adequate supply already."

"But not like these, Sir," HTML replied as his assistants sat smiling on the dilapidated pink chairs and sofa.

As Green opened the box he said, "They look perfectly normal to me. English cigars."

"These were hand rolled from unique leaves," HTML replied.

"Unique leaves, how so?"

HTML cleared his throat and said, "Why don't we sit down, Prime Minister?"

A terrible thought was beginning to form in Green's mind. Indeed an overwhelming sense of panic seized him as a red flush spread up his neck to his face.

"We would want to be discrete about this, Sir," HTML said.

"Discrete? About what, for God's sake, man?" he demanded, hoping that attack was the best form of defence.

"A meeting between the Prime Minister and a female member of his Cabinet in a tobacco curing house at Kew, Sir."

"Oh!" Green said. The terrible thought had taken on real and compelling form.

"You were observed," HTML said as he indicated the other members of his team, "by us."

"Oh!" Green said looking up at the ceiling. "There were roof lights," he thought.

"These cigars were made from the, um," HTML cleared his throat, "from the leaves upon which the, um, meeting took place. We thought you might like them as a memento."

"Oh," Green said as he looked at the cigars in quite a different way.

They all remained silent for a few moments.

"What do you want?" Green asked. "Money I suppose?"

"That would be appreciated, Sir," one of the assistants replied with a broad smile.

"You can't prove a thing. No one will believe you."

"Won't they?" HTML asked.

"I'm the Prime Minister, and you're just. . ."

"A nobody by comparison," HTML completed the sentence.

"Rumour has it that you made a handsome profit from The Games," another assistant suggested.

"But not officially," another added.

"No one will believe you," Green said for the second time.

"Word of mouth is a wonderful thing," HTML said.

"No smoke without fire," an assistant added.

"There's nothing like a good rumour," said the third assistant.

"How much?" Green asked.

"Lots," HTML replied.

Later that night Bekkes and Green didn't quite feel up to continuing where they had left off. Their conversation had been fraught. Neither had the slightest desire for their respective spouses to become aware of the cigars. Eventually Bekkes calmed down when Green said, "If they don't keep their mouths shut, then it's Legitude for them, and that's a promise."

42

Though Una had said nothing to Anvil she had noticed that he was troubled and she knew it wasn't their plan that concerned him. One morning she arrived back at the train with her two bodyguards on their cycles, with a fourth Sod riding a tricycle.

As usual Anvil was up early. He was completing his 'Ba Duan Jin Qigong' exercises when Una arrived and said, "Anvil, I have something for you."

He didn't seem to hear her as he completed his Tan Tien breathing exercises.

"Sorry," Una said, "I didn't know you hadn't finished."

Anvil exhaled, fully opened his eyes, saw Una and broke into a broad smile, "Una my dear, how good to see you. I didn't know you would come back today," he said. "Is there a problem?"

"No, no problem. I've brought you something," she replied. "Look," she said, turning and pointing at the tricycle, "you said you could never ride a bike and you were too old to learn. Well, now you don't have to."

"Why now?" he asked.

"It's about to begin and we need you with us. We need your mind. Your wisdom."

"It was agreed that I would stay here."

"None of us thought that was such a good idea. Marx will command the train settlement and we will leave good strong men and women to protect the rest."

"I don't know," Anvil replied.

"We want you with us, Anvil. We need you."

"What about. . ."

"Serene?" Una replied finishing his question for him.

"Yes, Serene. She knows about me?"

Una nodded and smiled.

"What did she say?" Anvil asked.

"She wants to see you. Will you come?"

"Let's go and find Lump," he replied, "I want to see how the Bloomers are doing."

Una and Anvil walked to the end of the train where a sturdy, rough wood compound had been built against the side of one of the train's carriages.

As they made their way Anvil asked, "And how is our esteemed comrade Roque?"

Una blushed slightly as she replied, "Anvil, you are sometimes a wicked wise man. He's fine; he's essential. . . to the struggle."

"And to you?"

She stopped and looked Anvil in the eyes and said, "To me."

"Does he know?"

"I don't know," she answered as they neared the compound.

Anvil laid his hand upon Una's shoulder and said, "Best find out, or you'll end up like Serene and me."

They found Marx and Lump talking next to the compound that contained the Bloomers – all eight of them.

"They breed like rabbits," Anvil said.

"That would be fine if they weren't so savage," Marx replied. "There's not enough meat on 'em to eat," he continued.

"You couldn't eat Mr Anvil's Bloomers. That wouldn't be right," said the outraged Lump.

"What shall we do with them?" Una asked.

"I been thinking," Lump replied, "but you'll say I'm just a lad and stupid with it."

"You are a lad, but you are not stupid. Go on," Anvil stated.

"We trained Maggie and Ronnie. Why don't we train the rest?"

"To do what?" Marx asked.

"To be fighting cats, Bloomers, I mean. They could fight the enemy, scare the shit out of 'em."

"Cats of war!" Marx exclaimed.

"What a crazy idea! I like it. Well done Lump," Una said.

"Who'll do it?" Anvil asked.

"Me, Mr Anvil, me. I can do it."

"Yes, you can, but you'll need help," Anvil said.

"I think we've got just the person for this; we found her the other day," Marx announced. "Let's go and find her."

"Hang on a minute, will you," Anvil said, "I need a few words with my friend Lump here."

"Would you like us to go?" Una asked.

"No. Listen, Lump. Una has asked me to go to Navenby to help the struggle from there. You are to stay here with Marx."

Lump looked completely devastated at the news. He and the old man had become very fond of each other over the months that the boy had grown from a frightened kid into an 'almost' young man and faithful apprentice.

Lump fought back a tear and said, "Please can I go with you, Mr Anvil, please?"

"I'll come back for you, I promise. It's not forever."

Suddenly Lump threw his arms around the old man, lost for words and full of tears.

Anvil hugged him tight and said, "Tell you what, if you can train my Bloomers up into fighting cats, then we'll be invincible, think of that." Lump looked up into the old man's eyes as Anvil said, "That's your job. I shall be proud of you when it's done."

"Come on, let's go find our helper," Marx said as he put an arm around Lump's shoulders.

Lump nodded and said, "You will come and see me before you go, won't you?"

"I will," Anvil replied.

When Marx and Lump were well out of earshot Una said, "You may be wise, but I suspect that you have never realised the love you inspire."

Anvil stared at her open-mouthed. It was not a sight Una had ever seen before.

At the opposite end of the train from the Bloomer compound Marx and Lump found an old woman sitting on the ground fettling arrows. Though she was old, she looked wiry and strong. Marx guessed that she had once been very pretty. She wore the usual habit of the Sods but also sported a rather worn and tattered bright red cape upon which had been sewn many stars of many colours.

"Hail, Citizen!" Marx said.

She looked back up at him with piercing grey eyes and raised an eyebrow.

"Baby Whiteknight?" Marx continued undaunted.

"Who's askin'," she replied in a Texan drawl.

"I am comrade Marx. I am in charge of the train."

"A train guard, gee, I'm impressed," she replied.

"Are you Baby Whiteknight?" Marx asked again, not just a little put out.

"We needs your help, Mrs Whiteknight," Lump said.

Baby smiled in reply and said, "And who might you be, young fella?"

"I'm Lump."

"Lump? That's a helluva name," she said.

"You talk funny," Lump replied.

"That's cos I'm from the good old US of A, boy. Why do you need my help?"

"To train the Bloomers," Marx replied.

"What the hell's a Bloomer?"

"They're scary," Lump answered.

"I seen scary, kid," Baby replied.

"You used to work in a thing called a circus?" Lump asked.

"Indeed I did. Uncle Sam's World, it was called, long ago, before the Big War."

"Marx said as how you used to work the Lions and Tigers. Were them fierce?" Lump asked.

Baby pulled up the sleeve of her right arm to reveal long livid white scars, "You're too young to see the rest," she said pointing at her arse.

"Cor!" Lump said.

"Training the Bloomers would be more exciting than making arrows," Marx said.

"I've had enough excitement for one life," she replied.

"Please, Mrs Whiteknight?" Lump pleaded.

"What you gonna train these here Bloomers for?"

"To fight the enemy," Lump replied.

She rose to her feet and said, "Best take a look then."

Baby stood and looked through the gaps in the compound wall as Ronnie, Maggie and their offspring growled in their special way.

"Now, that's what I call awesome, truly awesome. Shit man,

scare a soldier straight out of his fatigues," Baby said, "Count me, in guys," she added. Turning to Lump she said, "You can call me Baby, son."

43

In the Burton Lazars Arms Gilt, Tracker and Orb had finished their evening meal (it couldn't have been described as 'dinner' as there were no starters or desserts).

Though a violent, and, when necessary ruthless man, Gilt was also a skilled interrogator. On a whim, as Tracker's company was not very exciting, he had decided that he would find out all about Orb and his trade in Indulgences and Pardons.

At first Orb had been reticent and secretive but as the evening wore on he became more loquacious, ale being a marvellous lubricant. After nearly two hours Gilt reckoned that he knew everything there was to know about being a con artist, not, of course, that selling Ham's Indulgences could be regarded as a con. The range of products all carried the handwritten label 'On the instructions of the Imperial Majesty Ham this indulgence guarantees to the holder of said indulgence immunity and absolution of any guilt associated with any sin, or other act that could be regarded as sinful, such as is printed out on the dotted line below'. In fact only a very few Indulgences were licensed by Ham. Those that Orb had invented included: 'the indulgence in advance' (which you already know about); 'craving the body of an indentured Legit'; 'not saying the Ham's Prayer'; 'saying alternative and scurrilous versions of Ham's Prayer'; 'playing with oneself in the dark'; 'being pompous'; 'not washing on every third Friday as decreed'; 'pretending to be more important than you are by walking very slowly'; 'walking at all when there is a sedan readily available'; 'imagining that the world will change for the better'; 'believing that everything is for the best in this the

110

best of all possible worlds'; 'thinking that the exploitation of the underclass is a bad thing' (that one was very expensive); and 'beating a Legit into unconsciousness for jolting the chair through stumbling' (this was the cheapest of the lot as Orb had decided that with this one he would go for profit through volume rather than exclusivity). The list went on and could easily be extended if the customer thought of something new to say to Orb whilst they were sitting in the little portable folding confessional.

By the time that Gilt had acquired all this knowledgeTracker was fast asleep having taken too much beer. Gilt returned to his seat with two more tankards and sat quietly near to Orb.

Out of the blue Orb asked, "Are you a married man?"

"No, I'm a bachelor boy through and through."

"I was married once, a long time ago," Orb said, as tears welled up in his eyes.

"Not to worry, old man," Gilt comforted. "You aren't now."

"I feel guilty," Orb replied.

"Then sell yourself an Indulgence," Gilt joked to no avail.

"No, not about the wife, about the child."

Gilt tried to change the subject; family sob stories were not his cup of camomile tea. "Orb can't be your real name, so what are you really called?"

"Ernesto," Orb replied.

"Ernesto?"

"Ernesto Uevera," Orb drunkenly replied.

Gilt almost fell off the wooden bench, "Sorry, missed that, must have dropped off. What did you say?"

"Ernesto Uevera."

"What an unusual name," Gilt said as he stared at his companion. "You were saying something about a child?"

"My little girl, my Una," he cried (literally into his beer).

Gilt fixed Orb with a steely grin and thought, "God moves in mysterious ways, but then again women always do." What he said was, "Una Uevera. That's an unusual name. Any idea where she is or what she's doing now."

"Not a clue. Lost to me, forever," Orb wailed as regulars stared at the strange man in the pointed hat.

Gilt put his arm round Orb's shoulders and said, "Not to

worry, old man, I've just had the most wonderful idea."

Tracker snored on. Gilt looked at him and shook his head.

"What's that, then?" Orb asked, just managing to stay awake.

"I'll tell you in the morning," Gilt replied. "Time for bed now, methinks, eh?"

Orb started to snore. Gilt gently awakened him, got him to his feet, up the rickety stairs into one of the bedrooms that had been taken by Orb and Gilt respectively. Once inside the room he carefully undressed the sleeping man and popped him into the bed and then drew the covers over him. It had suddenly become a cold night.

When Gilt returned to the bar Tracker was still fast asleep, though he had stopped his dreadful snoring.

The Landlord said, "If he's with you then you'd better move him; he can't stay there all night."

Gilt smiled and said, "Not to worry, I'll see to him."

Now matter how hard he tried he couldn't wake Tracker and so, placing one hand under each armpit, he dragged him from the public bar.

"There's a disused stables out back," the Landlord called as Tracker's heels bounced along the floor.

"Cheers," Gilt said. "That'll do nicely."

When Gilt emerged the night was dark and the village street deserted. He pulled Tracker across the Green to the edge of the birdless duck pond and gently lowered Tracker's face into the murky waters. Pressing down he helped the awakening man into a breathless death beneath the water.

It was deep into the night before the pub was finally silent. Gilt tiptoed along the short landing and into Orb's room. The man was fast asleep. Gilt removed all of Orb's clothes, trappings and box of indulgences to his own room. This task completed, he returned to Orb, placed a pillow over his face, and suffocated the man who was still so drunk that he put up no hint of a struggle. Gilt then carried Orb to his own room and quickly dressed him in his own clothes (avoiding the inevitable stiffening up). Everything was fine.

As he drifted off to sleep, in what had been Orb's bed, he said, "Una, my Darling, Daddy's coming."

44

The months had passed and Her Highness Camellia had commenced her labour; a successor was to be born. She had suffered a long and painful (there were no synthetic drugs and though copious amounts of mugwort had been burnt they had had little effect and had simply made the room very foggy) nine hours. To cut a long story short she eventually gave birth.

"It's a girl," the Doctor said, "Call them in."

Ham, Green, Whiskerbot, courtiers and various other hangers-on duly arrived.

"Well?" Ham asked.

"They'll both be fine," the Doctor replied.

"What is it?" Green asked.

"A healthy baby girl," the Doctor said.

"A what?" Ham asked.

"A girl, your Hamness," the Doctor responded.

"You mean a girl-boy like me, of course?" Ham asked.

"No, I mean a girl, an ordinary girl."

"Oh no!" Ham shouted. "It cannot be. My genes have regressed. It's the end of the dynasty!"

"Or the beginning of a new one," Green tactlessly observed.

"You can try for more," Whiskerbot suggested.

Hangers-on murmured in a distraught manner.

"I shall be succeeded by a Queen," Ham bellowed.

Camellia looked stern. She was fed up.

"At least now we know what we've got now," Green said to the doctor.

"I heard that," Ham raged, and pointed a chubby finger at the Doctor and shouted, "It's all your fault! You quack! You've done something wrong."

"Don't be ridiculous!" the Doctor replied.

Ham looked even more taken aback when Camellia shouted, "Shut up! All of you, shut up! My daughter and I wish to be alone."

"I don't think that. . ." Whiskerbot ventured.

"Shut it, Botty!" Camellia interrupted.

Whiskerbot looked distraught whilst Green was on the point of complete hysterics.

"Out! Now!" Camellia shouted.

Rather strangely, they all obeyed her command.

Outside the door Green turned to Ham and said, "The announcement needs to be made; the people are waiting."

"Stuff the people!" Ham shouted and stormed off.

"I shall instruct the Criers," Whiskerbot responded.

45

As you know BBW there had been mass communications and such things as newspapers were printed every day, sometimes more than once. ABW there were two types of communication for official announcements and proclamations; the carefully hand lettered 'Big Sheets' (as they were known) prepared by Government Monks housed in the vast scriptorium that was Westminster Hall and the Royal State Criers (or RSC for short). The problem with the former was that it was so slow, whereas the latter provided an instant and effective means of communication with the people. The Crier would walk about crying for a couple of days to get the message across, and then word of mouth would do the rest. Several weeks later Big Sheets would be put up and this would re-establish the facts of the first message that had obviously become distorted and changed as the message moved from person to person. This was fine for those that could read and could be bothered to stand in the pouring rain deciphering all that fancy pen-work, but for the rest?

It was raining, as was usual for June, when the fifty or so RSCs left Hampton Court to walk across the City along their designated routes. RSCs never rode; they always walked, and as they walked, they cried. The role of 'Crier' was hereditary and was passed down to the eldest male child along with the rather splendid costume, hat and bell; there had been a brief period just BBW when consideration had been given to legislation making access to the role available to the first born, irrespective of sex, but it was not a popular idea.

On this important day in the history of England they cried as they tolled their hand bells, "Oh Yeah! Oh Yeah! Now hear ye this! There was born this day in the City of London a child unto the House of Ham, a girl child! Oh Yeah! Oh Yeah! A child is born! Praise be to Ham! A child is born!"

Sedans halted and settled, walkers stopped dumfounded and many a RSC was asked, "Did you say it was a girl?"

There was a remarkable similarity in the conversations between members of the Propertied Class. Most went like this.

"Well that's it, then."

"The end of the line."

"No more AC DC monarchs then."

"A girl, who would have believed it?"

"A Queen to succeed."

"When Ham pops the clogs, you mean."

"Ham doesn't wear clogs."

"Just a manner of speaking."

"It won't be the same."

"How do you mean?"

"The Highness won't be any different to the rest of us."

"Just a normal human being."

"Probably not normal."

"You'd be right about that."

"Not one apart."

"Not different in every way."

"Not much point in having them then, is there?"

"You've got a point there."

"Things'll never be the same."

"I don't know."

"Who would have thought it would have come to this."

And so on.

46

A few days later a select band of 'the important' (as they thought of themselves) gathered for the baptism of the heir to the throne in the Imperial Chapel at Hampton Court. Camellia held the baby, which was just as well because Ham was drunk. This private baptism would be followed by the public state baptism conducted by His Holiness the Bishop of England at a later date, or so it was thought at the time.

You will probably find it hard to comprehend but ABW the rituals associated with royalty, religion and government had not withered away; in fact quite the reverse. The pageantry that had been so successful in maintaining the financial credibility of England BBW had been deepened and extended, despite the fact that there were no tourists to see it. The panoply of the state represented and given form through the three inextricably linked institutions of Monarchy, Church and Government was of paramount importance in maintaining the self image of the members of those institutions. It was also believed that the various rituals and practices used enabled the Propertied Class to feel integrated into the central values of English society.

This was, of course, bollocks. Only those who lived in London were even aware of all this tripe. For the majority of the Propertied Class such events as Royal Baptisms were merely interludes in ongoing boredom. The Underclass apart from Legits carrying chairs weren't invited.

The priest, nearing the end of the ceremony intoned, "Through Jesus Christ our Lord. Amen."

"Amen."

Camellia passed the child to the priest who said , looking up, "Name this child."

Two godparents moved forward wearing the approved godparent costumes; the male noble wore a black doublet and britches and beneath the latter white socks upon which were emblazoned Masonic emblems, whilst the female noble was dressed in a purple gown upon which there were further arithmetical dividers and stars. They both looked as if they had nothing between their ears other than rice pudding as they said, "Gloriana Beatrice Ham."

The priest said, "I baptise thee, Gloriana Beatrice Ham, In the Name of the Father, and of the Son, and of the Holy Ghost. Amen.

"Amen."

Green thought, "Or GBH for short."

47

After the ceremony Green excused himself on the grounds that he had to attend a meeting at Number 10 that might prove useful to England. For once he hadn't lied.

On entering the anteroom to his office he found an incredibly small man sitting frantically fiddling with his immense beard; this was Professor Gordon Gilberdyke of Ham State University. England still had one university, a proper university; there were no students, every member of faculty was a professor, and the focus was on thinking about 'things' (or research as it had once been called). Gilberdyke was Professor of Transport Logistics; his particular area of specialism was 'thinking outside the box'. It had taken him fifteen years, but he had finally made it 'out of the box' and that was why he was so excited, and why he had finally managed to get an appointment with the Prime Minister.

The two men shook hands and went inside to Green's private office, the Professor carrying two immense suitcases. A factotum (Civil Servant) offered to come in to take notes but Green made him wait outside.

Once suitably comfortable in the ornate armchairs, Green asked, "Well, Professor, what can I do for you?"

"Water, Prime Minister," Gilberdyke responded with great enthusiasm.

"Water?"

"Water!"

"You want a glass of water? Never touch the stuff myself; fish shit in it!" he laughed, in a vain attempt to demonstrate his wit to this incredibly erudite Prof.

"Indeed. No, thank you, I don't want a glass of water."

"Then what do you want?"

"Canals."

"Canals?" Green seemed stupefied.

"I have discovered that hundreds of years ago England was covered with canals. These were man made waterways and upon them barges, a sort of flat boat. . ."

"I know what a barge is. Ham has a state barge that is moored on the river."

"But they used to move," Gilberdyke replied.

"There's no fuel, remember. I thought you were a professor?"

"Yes, I know all about that, and barges on canals wouldn't work with sails. No, the point is this: barges were pulled by horses, and before you say it, Prime Minister, yes, I do know that there are no longer horses. They could be pulled by Legits."

"What would these barges do?"

"Carry goods, open up the country to faster transport than sedans can supply."

"Where are these canals then?"

"I have old maps. They were all over the country, absolutely everywhere. Trouble is, they're all filled up with rubbish, weeds and debris; absolutely useless."

Green sat in silence staring in disbelief. He eventually framed his question in a pleasant way, "Then why are you telling me this, Professor?"

"I have had an idea."

"Then perhaps you would be kind enough to share it with me. I have another meeting to attend," Green said, thinking of Bekkes with whom he would shortly have a cigar (as they had come to call the physical exploration of each others' bodies).

"We set up a company, we sell shares, we clear the canals, we offer services, we sell those services, we carry goods, people. We employ, I use the term loosely, the Legits, or whatever we have to call them if they're pulling barges. We offer holidays, we make lots of money," Gilberdyke blurted out.

"Money? Holidays?" Green mulled the matter over and said, "This needs thinking about."

Gilberdyke pointed to the suitcases and said, "I've brought it all with me: the maps, the business plan, everything. I can leave it with you so that you can read it all and decide on how to move forward."

"Most kind, most kind, Professor."

"When shall I come back?" Gilberdyke asked.

"Same time next week?" Green suggested.

"That would be fine, Prime Minister. You'll make sure my plans stay safe?"

"This is Number 10."

"Forgive me. Thank you, Prime Minister."

Within moments he was gone and Green had the first of the cases open upon the floor.

I can guess what you're thinking, "I don't think I'd have done that if I was Gilberdyke." Right? No, I wouldn't have either but then if you just spent your entire time sitting around thinking then you never know what you might be foolish enough to do.

By the time Green and Bekkes had finished their 'cigar', Cartage had arrived at Number 10. By the time dawn broke, he and Green had been through the suitcases and had laid everything out on the Cabinet room table. Though tired and dishevelled the two men were euphoric.

"You do realise that these concepts are revolutionary?" Cartage asked.

"And very profitable."

"We may change society for ever," Cartage chuckled.

"Legislation will be needed to do this."

"Well, you can sort that, John, no problem. What are you going to do about the Professor? Give him a share?"

"He's too small to be a Legit, but I'll think of something," Green smiled.

48

It had taken longer than expected for Una and Anvil to complete their ride to Navenby. There were three reasons: the weight of the immense box of tricks that he had insisted was strapped on the rear of his trike; trikes couldn't go cross country; he was old and found it hard going. As the Security Sod stationed at the gate had let them in Anvil had been seized with a severe panic attack at the prospect of meeting Serene again. Una had thought it was a heart attack and had made him lie down on the drive. She had been terrified, as she had come to think of him as the father she wished she hadn't lost but whom she had never really known. Anvil had lain very still and breathed deeply until his heart rate became stable. His heart had settled down, but his emotions hadn't; he kept seeing Serene as she had been; worse than that, how he had once been.

As he rose to his feet he embraced Una and thanked her. She in turn scolded him for giving her such a fright. As they neared the doors Una rang her bike bell and within moments Serene stood on the steps looking down at them. Roque joined her.

"Is that you, Anvil?" Serene asked.

"Serene?" he replied.

They did not embrace but kissed each other lightly upon each cheek (as was the custom amongst Francophiles and those who worked in something that used to be called 'the creative industries' [sic]) and then simply stood and looked each other up and down and round about.

After a few moments Roque took Una by the arm and said, "Fancy a cup of nettle tea?"

As they walked away, tall, young, strong and proud, they were a stark contrast to the oldsters, in appearance anyway.

Later that night, after the plans for the next days had been finally agreed, Anvil and Serene sat talking in her shed at the end of the garden. Neither quite knew how to proceed, and so potted life histories had been exchanged and then the inevitable had happened; they reminisced about 'old times'.

"I brought some things," Anvil said, as he pointed at the large leather satchel that had been hidden within his immense box of tricks.

"Is that the same satchel I bought you that Christmas?" Serene asked.

"It surely is," he said as he scrabbled within its vast interior. He seemed to change his mind, stood, removed some flower pots from inside an old wooden crate, up-ended it, and placed it between their chairs to act as a small table. "That's better," he said.

"Mr Organisation," she smiled, "everything in its place and just so."

"It takes one to know one," he teased back. "I don't know if this'll be any good," he said, as he placed two metal containers, sealed with old dried out sticky tape, on the crate, "but we could give it a try."

Within a few minutes Serene had constructed an immense spliff from the materials contained in his boxes (he had never been very good at rolling, even using the big red Rizla papers). To their immense surprise and pleasure, neither the tobacco nor the marijuana had totally dried out despite its considerable age. Soon the shed was filled with the delicious mixture of 'shed' and 'grass'.

"Umm," she sighed, "this is mellow, man."

"Man?" he queried as he laughed, "Man? We'll be saying cool soon."

"Far out," she giggled.

They passed the spliff back and forth and smoked in silence for a while until Serene asked, "Why did we split up, Anvil?"

"You liked opera, I didn't, he did," Anvil replied.

"Ridiculous," she said.

"I thought so."

"So do I, but it doesn't matter now," dragging the last smoke from the exhausted joint. "What else have you got in that bag of tricks?"

"Surprises," he teased.

"You wait here. I've got something to show you, but it's up at the house," she said as she stood up. She was just a little wobbly on her feet.

By the time she returned Anvil had "just closed my eyes for

a moment" as he claimed when Serene woke him by kissing him on the forehead.

In her hand she held a sheet on paper on which were typewritten words.

"What's that?" he asked.

"I'll read it to you," she said, and read,

> Love is like breakfast in bed,
> Brown bread toast crumbs stuck in your pyjamas,
> Sometimes it catches you the wrong way,
> But most of the time it gives you that well-fed feeling.

"Bloody hell!" Anvil said.

"You wrote that for me," Serene softly replied.

"It's dreadful."

"It's lovely," she said quite firmly.

"It's a dreadful poem," Anvil insisted.

"So what?" she asked, "You weren't a poet, just a young man in love."

At that he smiled and fished in his satchel and brought out a small brown paper parcel.

"What's that?" she asked.

"You left it behind when you left," he said as he handed her the parcel that she began to undo. "It was under the bed."

In her hands she held her old battered copy of 'Kaddish'.

She looked up from the book and into his eyes. He smiled.

"I love you," she said.

"I love you too," he replied.

49

The Sods had not been idle in their weeks at Navenby while their forces were amassed for the battles ahead. Not only had there been riding and fitness training but also construction. The idea had come to Roque when he had found a contraption that was pulled behind a bike in order to transport a child or even the shopping. It had two wheels and a tow bar that fixed to the back of the bikist's bike; so Serene had explained. At first she had not been keen on his idea but had come to see that it would be of real benefit in the struggles to come. Una had thought it brilliant but had not told Anvil as she had wanted to keep it as a surprise. It had come as something of a shock to Una that not only was Roque 'drop-dead-gorgeous' but in addition, very bright.

The next morning Serene took Anvil to the old stable-yard and told him to close his eyes. When all was in place Una told him to open them. He gasped and said, "Carts!"

"What are carts?" Una asked.

"They were a bit like those; horses pulled them," he said as he pointed at the four vehicles that stood in the bright sun-light of the yard.

The 'carts' had been constructed from bike parts and some old scaffold poles Roque had found in one of the barns. They consisted of a rectangular frame (about six foot by three foot) with two wheels on each side. Carpets had been removed from the hall (Serene had drawn the line at the tapestries) and firmly secured across the frame to provide a lightweight, but effective, carrying surface. The frame was in turn con-nected, by poles, to two mountain bikes that had been fixed together in such a way as to allow two bikists to sit side by side and pedal the 'cart' along. In other words an eight-wheel vehicle that was capable of carrying at least two passengers, goods and weapons.

"Whose idea was this?" Anvil asked, "they're stupendous!"

"Roque's," Una replied.

Anvil went to Roque and gave him a massive thump on the chest and said, "Well done my boy, well done! Shake my hand!" Roque blushed as Una felt a warm glow of pleasure at his success.

"You can't call them carts," Serene said; "too pre-industrial."

"You're right," Anvil replied.

"It doesn't matter what we call them," Una said. "It's what they'll do that matters."

"Of course that's true, but it's important what we call things," Anvil observed.

"What about trolley-bus," Serene suggested.

"A bit too long maybe?" Anvil replied.

"How about Sodsters?" Roque suggested.

For a moment there was silence until Una, Serene and Anvil, almost all at once, said, "That's it!"

The Sodster had been created.

50

That night the first of the Sodsters went into action accompanied by ten outriders led by Roque.

The Bishop of Lindum, the Right Reverend Petrus Hamondi, had been preparing a young boy chorister for his confirmation for some hours (well that's what he told them later) when there came a sharp knocking on the vestry door.

"Go away. I'm doing god's will," he shouted at the closed door.

The boy raised himself up from the kneeling position in which he had been placed and adjusted his cassock. The door was knocked again.

"I'm coming!" the Bishop cried.

After a few moments he opened the door to find his verger holding a lighted candle accompanied by a tall Asian man dressed in rags. The chorister pushed past them and disappeared into the great vast darkness of the Cathedral.

"Yes, my son?" the Bishop asked.

"Bishop Hamondi?" Roque politely enquired.

"Yes, my son."

"I want you to come with me," Roque said.

"No, my son."

"I thought I'd ask nicely," Roque said.

"I'm going to my palace. Make way! Lead on, verger," the Bishop commanded as he pushed past Roque, crook in hand.

It was no contest. Two Sods came from the shadows and grabbed the Bishop, whilst two others restrained the verger, bound and gagged him with vestments and locked him in a cupboard.

"Where do you keep the valuables?" Roque asked.

"None of your business, you heathen yokel," Hamondi replied with perhaps misplaced bravado.

"I don't want to hurt you, but I will, if you're stupid," Roque calmly stated.

"Shall I slap him?" one of the Sods asked.

"You wouldn't dare," Hamondi said.

Roque nodded at the Sod who had posed the question. The Bishop didn't like the broad-handed slap that landed on his left cheek. When he had stopped whimpering and rubbing his injury he said, "In the treasury."

"Please take us there, Bishop," Roque commanded.

They made their way through the great dark space until they reached a black oak door that was locked.

"Open it, please," Roque said.

The Bishop fumbled beneath his vestments until he eventually withdrew a bunch of keys that hung from a gold chain about his neck.

Once inside it took a few moments for their eyes to get used to the light. Upon the many shelves sat a large collection of gold and silver ecclesiastical utensils of various sizes and shapes.

"Blimey!" one of the Sods observed, "this lot must be worth a fortune."

"Not any more," Roque replied, "Who would we sell them to? No-one. Okay Bishop, where do you keep the cash?"

"What cash?" the Bishop answered.

"The tithe money, the Hamsters that you extract for the protection of the people from the state and the church," Roque stated.

"That is for the upkeep of the fabric of the cathedral," Hamondi pleaded.

"Pull the other one," Roque responded. "Where is it?"

Reluctantly Hamondi unlocked a further inner door that stood between the rows of shelves. Inside there were five stout wooden chests. Once opened they discovered that they were stuffed full with Hamsters.

"Okay," Roque instructed the money laden Sods, "let's get this lot out of here."

The Bishop's hands were tied behind his back and the surplice, dropped by the chorister, was used to blindfold the protesting cleric. Within minutes they were under the great canopy above the South Door. They placed the Bishop on the Sodster, where two Sods held him still. After a few minutes more, the chests of money were safely stowed around the Bishop. The Sods' bikes were nowhere to be seen. They waited in silence in the dark. They heard footsteps and saw the light from a lantern carried on a high pole. Two Cathedral Swabs came into sight. The Sods made no sound.

Roque merely nodded as the two Swabs came parallel to where they were hidden. Four Sods were upon them before they knew what had hit them (which were actually good solid wooden clubs). The unconscious men were pulled into the dark corner of the canopy and tied hand and foot but otherwise left unharmed. (There was still a degree of superstition about killing people on hallowed ground.)

The Sods gathered their bikes whilst the Bishop and the money were securely lashed to the Sodster. They made their way down the great hill and out into the countryside. Their passage was fast and silent except for the sound of rubber on road and it only took them just over an hour and forty minutes to make the return journey to the Hall.

Few saw them pass, and those that did thought they must have seen ghosts or monsters; such was the strangeness of their being.

Once back at the Hall, Bishop Hamondi was not very pleased to discover that Sedanistas had kidnapped him.

"Do you know who I am?" he asked Una. "I am the Right Reverend Petrus Hamondi, Bishop of Lindum."

"I know," Una quietly replied. "That's why you're here."

"But do you really know who I am?" he persisted.

"Yes, you are Ham's cousin by birth, not marriage. That is why you are here," Una responded.

"Oh, you know that, do you? But why do you want me?"

"I'll explain, but in the morning. I hear you've had a busy evening," Una said as she locked the door to the small bedroom, "Sleep tight, don't let the bugs bite." He heard external bolts as they were pushed into place.

He pulled back the extremely dusty drapes to find that the window was barred, "Oh shit!" he thought. A cloud of dust rose from the bed as he sat upon it. He began to cough as he removed his vestments and thought that he had better check the mattress for bugs. He didn't know what he would do if he found any as he didn't have a damp bar of carbolic soap to stick them to. There were no bugs but Hamondi fell into a state of gloom. He could not understand why these beastly uncouth people would have wanted to kidnap him. What was the purpose? Though he was related to Ham, and he was a bishop (because as the second son of the Earl Yamborough there was nothing he could legitimately do except be a cleric without being an immense drain on the family's diminished fortunes) and was of no importance to the great scheme of things. If they thought they would get a ransom, he knew them to be mistaken. He was dispensable; there were plenty more where he came from. Had he had faith (as it was known) he would have prayed; instead he eventually subsided into a tearful sleep.

That same night Una placed the message that Anvil had written, in the capable hands of the fittest Sod there was, (who had acquired the nickname of Rocket due to his great road speed) and said, "Be careful Rocket, hide your racer somewhere near the palace, and when you get to Hampton Court just hand this in at the gate, and get the hell out of there as fast as you can."

Rocket looked at the envelope and said, "What does it say?"

"Ham. The Times they are a-changing," she replied.

"I'll be back in four days," Rocket said as he raced off into the night.

When he had gone Anvil said, "I'm not sure about this. What benefit is there in having this bloody bishop locked up?"

"It shows we have power. They will be afraid," Roque replied.

"I'm not sure about that," Anvil observed.

"They will come looking for us. They'll want to know what we have," Roque asserted.

"It just might be," Una said, "that if we take the battles to them, we are on their territory and, they have strength. Here we can prepare, acquire arms, be ready and claim a victory."

"It's a risky strategy," Anvil replied, "it's not what we had planned, but I won't dissent. We'll just have to be very careful from now on."

It was only after this business was completed that Roque and Wesley began the long task of counting the money. Things were looking up: they had wheels and now a war chest that could in time grease eager and grasping hands.

51

Gilt had found that his role as Orb was not hard to execute, far from it in fact. When he had finally emerged from the Inn, after a hearty breakfast, he saw that Orb's sedan was exactly where it had been left the night before. All that remained to be done was to walk down to the Sedantory and pick up a fresh pair of Legits and he could be on his way. It had been fortuitous that he was just about the same size as Orb, perhaps a little shorter, and so the Pardoner's costume had fitted pretty well, even if it was somewhat hot, what with the cape and all.

Things had been a little trickier earlier that morning as it was quite unusual for there to be two deaths, albeit strangers, and Legits to boot, in the village in one night. The landlord had found Tracker face down in the pond and the chambermaid (landlady) had found Orb when she went in to empty the piss pot. It had probably been her hysterics that had got the landlord going so that he had been in quite a state by the time the village Swabby had arrived. The latter was as thin as a rake and seemed to be of a highly excitable nature.

So before breakfast Gilt had endured an 'interrogation' as the Swabby rather pompously called it.

Yes, he had been drinking with the dead men the night before.

Yes, they were both pissed as a flea on heat (the Swabby

had raised an eyebrow at that).

No, he didn't know the man in the pond having only met him on the road the previous day.

No, he didn't know the dead Legit who had bought him his food and drink the night before.

Yes, he had presumed that the dead Legit was after a cheap pardon, bribery being common currency in the trade.

Yes, he had a licence (he'd had to show it).

Matters had finally been resolved when Gilt had asked in a very confidential tone, "When did you stop beating the wife?"

The Swabby looked shocked; he blushed.

"Well?" Gilt asked.

"She asked for it; she always does," the Swabby replied.

Gilt reached into Orb's bag and pulled out a pardon and said, "You need one of these."

"What's that then?" he asked as Gilt wrote in 'wife-beating' in the offence box.

"Absolution," Gilt replied.

"Can't afford it, got no money."

"On the house, old chap," Gilt said, "Can't have the local Swabbary feeling guilty, can we?"

The skinny shit Swabby bastard (sorry) was delighted, but would have been less so had he realised that in other circumstances Gilt might have treated him somewhat differently. Even secret agents had some sense of decency, 'Eat it!" might have been the admonition.

Gilt was then faced with a choice: which way should he instruct the Legits to walk? Instinct told him to go north to Melton Mowbray, probably for two good reasons: there was a signpost with 'Melton Mowbray' written on it (and nothing else) and he had once had a pork pie when he was a boy.

As he made his way toward Melton he sensed that he was definitely going in the right direction. He had always believed that top secret agents, like his dear self, were possessed of a sixth sense; something akin to the lodestone in a pigeon's forehead. A sense of direction, of purpose, like putting your nose into the wind and smelling the charcoal burner's fires many miles off and beyond sight.

His Legits made slow progress across the wolds and by the

time they reached Croxton Kerrial they were done for and came to a halt outside the ornate gates of a large brick house. It was the sort of house that had been built by rich farmers or merchants just BBW. The gates themselves gave the game away, or rather the adornment of the gateposts, upon which were seated two gigantic concrete (he assumed) Eagle/ Griffin 'things'. Only someone with lots of dosh, and no taste whatsoever, would have been crass enough to stick those things up for all the world to wonder at.

He told the Legits to wait whilst he went and explored. The gates creaked as he pushed the right one open, but at least it hadn't been locked. The house itself was immense and made from red bricks. The front façade was two storeys and filled with many windows. The front door was reached through a 'Georgian' portico. Gilt walked to the door, tapped the pillars, and ascertained they weren't of stone. He rang the door bell but it didn't work, so he rapped at the door but no one answered, though he thought that he heard a sound somewhere deep inside the house.

At the rear of the property he found four garages, with little ornate wooden turrets, but the garage doors were firmly locked. As he turned and looked back at the house he was sure that he saw something move in an upstairs window.

He tried the back door, and, surprisingly finding it unlocked, went inside. He moved through what must have been a utility room and into an enormous kitchen. As you know, he was a man of some experience, and some of it, well, had been shocking. Nevertheless he was ill prepared for what he saw. The room was filled with two vast shire horses; their heads bent forward as their backs touched the ceiling. They stood very still, which was not surprising as they were stuffed, though Gilt had not initially realised this. There was no way round the horses so he crouched, a little, and passed beneath them towards what he thought must be the dining room. On the way under his tall pointed hat was dislodged. As he retrieved it he had looked up in surprise not realising how big a stallion's undercarriage was, particularly when stuffed. A cold sweat formed upon his brow and spread to his back.

He hesitated as he opened the door; there was no furniture,

but there was a flock of stuffed sheep, so life-like that he expected them to move and bleat at any moment. To be frank, he was unnerved, but intrigued. He clambered over the sheep (those that he knocked over he felt obliged to reinstate) toward the lounge. He wondered what he would find next as he passed through the archway. Once again there was no furniture but there was a bull (with a ring in its nose) and twelve cows (he didn't know what sort). The floor was bare except for the imitation cowpats that had been fashioned from something he wasn't sure of, and was not inclined to find out.

He stood and stared for what must have been minutes until he heard movement upstairs. In the entrance hall there were stuffed chickens, some in nests sitting upon marble eggs. He climbed the curving stairs and went along the landing. The master bedroom was full of pigs; its en-suite contained geese.

At this point his sense of humour returned and he started to laugh. It was a proper laugh; he couldn't control it, and he was soon back on the landing leaning on the balustrade wracked with uncontrollable hysterics.

"What you laughing at?" a voice said.

"Nothing. Nothing," he giggled as he saw the owner of the voice. It was a bedraggled man, of uncertain age, dressed in tweed plus fours with a deerstalker upon his head. More worryingly he held a double-barrelled shotgun in his hands.

"You think it's funny, do you?" the man asked.

"No, not at all," Gilt soberly replied, eyeing the gun, "Is that loaded?" he continued.

"Might be."

"Did you, er, stuff all these yourself?"

"They were mine, all mine; ruined, ruined now. I loved them. Why you dressed like that?" the man asked.

"I sell pardons, indulgences. My name is Orb."

"There's no one left, just me."

"What happened?" Gilt asked.

"We ate 'em all, and when we'd eaten 'em, I stuffed 'em."

"We? The other people?" Gilt enquired.

"We drew lots; there was no food; nothing."

"You ate?"

"Aye, each other," the man replied as he raised the gun and pointed it at Gilt's chest, "I could do with some meat."

Gilt's laughter echoed through the house. The man looked dumfounded as Gilt simply walked up to him and took the gun from his trembling fingers. On opening the breach he found it empty.

"Don't leave me this way!" the man begged.

"Pull yourself together, man!" Gilt impatiently replied, "We've all got problems."

"I'm so lonely," the man said as tears rolled down his grimy face.

"Should of thought of that a bit earlier, old chap."

"Take me with you," the man implored.

"Get lost!" Gilt replied.

When he returned downstairs with the mad man following, he found his two Legits standing in the kitchen staring wide-eyed at the horses.

"What's they?" one asked.

"Horses. Come, lads. Time to move on," Gilt replied.

"That's Longfellow and that's Enid," the man said pointing at each horse in turn.

"Is there more?" the other Legit asked.

"Take a look," Gilt rather wickedly replied, "I'll wait outside in the chair."

He had not waited long when the two Legits ran from the house chased by the man, now wielding a knife. They picked up the chair, and, with considerable energy, rushed the Sedan away from Croxton Kerrial. After a mile, the man appeared to give up. He stopped, stood in the middle of the road and looked about. At least he'd made it out of the house. He didn't try to catch the disappearing Sedan but he didn't turn back the way he had come.

"This could only happen in England," Gilt mused as the clogs rattled upon the broken road.

52

His Holiness the Bishop of England had been in quite a state when he had arrived at Hampton Court for an urgent audience with the Monarch. It wasn't everyday that a pigeon arrived carrying a message that read 'One of your Bishops is missing. See me immediately. Ham.'

He had been astounded when Whiskerbot had attempted to prevent his entry to the throne room but a hard crack upon Whiskerbot's head from his Holiness's ornate Crook had resolved the matter.

BBW Bishops tried to look like ordinary people; just a bit of purple, the odd cross and a suit. Not any more. Bishops wore their finest robes all the time and were never seen without their Crooks (crooks being curvy staves that you held in your hand, and not possessed by the entourage of fawning sub deans looking for handouts and the opportunity to pinch boy's and girl's arses). In England, a world of scarcity, status was all. Bishops, to put it simply, now strutted their stuff. His Holiness had become something of a role model for all clerics that aspired to a life of service and easy living.

The scene that greeted His Holiness as he entered the throne room was not a happy one. A 'domestic' (as I believe they were called) was underway. Ham was curled up in the throne, royal hands covering royal ears, as Camellia repeatedly clouted the Monarch with her black handbag.

"You unspeakable, loathsome, bag of pigeon droppings!" she screamed.

"It was only fun," Ham blubbered.

"Fun! Fun!" she cried as she beat Ham about the head.

His Holiness looked on aghast.

"You pustule!"

Whack!

"You pimple!"

Whack!

"Your Highness?" His Holiness enquired.

"On the face of England!" she continued.

Whack!

"Your Highness?" His Holiness tried again.

"It was a joke," Ham whimpered.

"A joke!" she repeated as she clobbered the Monarch again. "Well, I don't think it was funny!"

Whiskerbot staggered into the room holding his head as His Holiness pounded his Crosier upon the wooden floor, "Desist!" he shouted. "I command thee, desist!"

Camellia turned and looked at the Primate, "Command? Did you say command?" she said as she came down the steps from the throne and advanced toward the ornate Cleric.

"Your Highness, I only . . ."

"You only what? You listen to me, Bish. I've had it up to here," she said holding her hand above her head. "I've put up with this royal scumbag's infidelities, in the plural, infidelities yes, with all and sundry, men and women alike, Morris Dancers even, but I've turned a blind eye. I've done my duty, there is an heir. But now it's gone too far. I shall not share my bed again with this, this, this haemorrhoid!"

His Holiness winced as Camellia swept past him and out of the room.

The Majesty unfurled itself from the throne, brushed itself down and said, "Your Holiness, thank you for coming."

"Is there something you need to confess, your Majesty?" His Holiness asked.

"No thank you," Ham replied. "The pigeon arrived then?"

"I am your spiritual father my, um, Highness," the cleric tried again.

"What's the matter with you, Whiskers?" Ham asked noticing his advisor's condition.

"He hit me with his crook," Whiskerbot replied.

"He wouldn't let me in," His Holiness responded.

"And now you know why you thug, you religious bully!" Whiskerbot said.

"I'm sorry, my son, I was over rough."

"Rough? Hitting someone with that bloody thing is more than rough!"

"Now, now, boys, there are important matters to be discussed," Ham intervened, "Kiss and make up."

With some reluctance Whiskerbot kissed the Primate's extended hand.

"Good," Ham said. "Now let's all sit down and have a cup of tea. Whiskers, will you do the honours, please?"

"Yes, your Majesty," he said as he left the room.

"I have sent for the Prime Minister," Ham said.

"Please explain," His Holiness asked.

"Hamondi has been kidnapped."

"It can't be so! He's your cousin!" His Holiness responded in mock horror, as he couldn't stand the man.

"Read this," Ham said removing the letter from the top pocket of the Royal silk pyjamas.

His Holiness read the note penned by Anvil, signed by Una and delivered by Rocket.

'The Bishop, your cousin, is now in our safekeeping. He will not be harmed. He is merely the first to be taken. Others including you will follow him into the arms of the Sedanistas. Be afraid! Ham, the times they are a-changing. The War of Liberation has begun.'

As His Holiness was about to ask what it all meant Whiskerbot rushed back into the room (without the tea trolley). He held up a pigeon message and shouted, "This just came!" Green followed him in.

"What is it?" Ham asked.

"A message from Lindum, saying that Hamondi has been taken prisoner."

"We know that already, Whiskerbot!" Ham replied.

"No, you don't understand. This message is dated two days ago, but the letter was delivered this morning."

"So what?" asked Ham.

"God, you're thick," Green observed.

"You should not speak to the Hamness in that way," His Holiness said.

"The letter was delivered before the pigeon arrived," Green said very slowly.

Ham and His Holiness looked perplexed.

"How can a letter, presumably from Lindum, arrive before the pigeon post from Lindum?" Whiskerbot asked.

"Precisely," Green said.

"That's impossible," Ham said.

"Clearly not," Green replied. "I think we have a problem."

"What will you do?" asked Whiskerbot.

"Establish a war cabinet; make ready for war, strike before we are struck." Green replied.

"Not again, please," Ham said.

"This will be a different war. Hardly anyone will know it's happening," Green replied. "I'm going back to Number 10."

"I'll see you out," Whiskerbot responded.

"I should go and pray for Bishop Hamondi," His Holiness said, "but before I go there's just one thing: what was Her Highness so cross about?"

Ham smiled and said, "You'll never know."

"Oh, go on!" His Holiness pleaded.

"She refused to have what you would call 'relations', with me."

"To 'know her' is the correct biblical term."

"Whatever," Ham replied, "so I put a slow-worm in her knickers draw."

"Not a wise move," His Holiness rather obviously observed.

53

As Green was carried back across London he tried to think it through. If it hadn't been for those three words 'Una Uevera' and 'Sedanistas' he would have thought it was a clever trick or hoax. There had been so much to do and now there was the legislation to set up 'Barge England' that he had almost forgotten about the Sedanistas and Gilt's mission to bring her back alive.

"If there was ever a time for the Secret Service to deliver it is now," he thought. He was actually pretty fed up, as all he wanted to do was make himself a pile of money from the barges and then retire. Now he would have to spend some of his own time chasing bloody revolutionaries. What made it worse was that he'd spent weeks bribing people to support his new enterprise; the Hamsters had flown through his fingers like water. By the time he reached Downing Street he was in a rotten mood.

The war cabinet that was comprised of Green, Bekkes, Cartage, Terry Travers (Minister of State for Transportation), and Jock Robinson (the Head of Counter Insurgency Services) had been in session for almost two hours. These people were 'doers', not thinkers, and had thus found it very hard to solve the conundrum 'how had the letter beaten the pigeon post?' I won't bore you with the details of their deliberations, as they were pretty poor. Simply put, they hadn't a clue. In the circumstances Green needed a thinker, someone who knew something about transport and thus Professor Gordon Gilberdyke was saved from his potential new career as doorman at the South Hampstead Fornicon.

After Gilberdyke had signed the Official Secrets Act he was brought into the cabinet room and the situation was explained to him. The speed with which he reached a conclusion was astonishing.

"There are three possibilities: this is a hoax; they either have very fast runners, or, and this is a more extraordinary proposition, they have wheels," Gilberdyke said.

Cartage broke the stunned silence when he said, "Wheels? You must be mad Professor. There aren't any."

"You cannot be certain that in the whole of England that there aren't any," Gilberdyke replied.

"Those that weren't lost in the Big War were destroyed when we moved over to Sedan production," Cartage stated.

"Their use was made illegal," Green said, "their existence would have undermined the new national industry."

"There's no fuel, anyway," Bekkes joined in.

"Self powered wheels," the Professor said.

"Self powered? What does that mean?" Green asked.

"A bicycle," Gilberdyke replied.

The proposition took a few moments to sink in until finally Green asked, "Are you suggesting that they have found a bicycle and that is how they beat the pigeon?"

"It's possible," the Professor replied "and the pigeon also probably got lost, they often do, but that does not in itself invalidate my thesis."

"My god!" Cartage said, "Bicycles."

"It's only a theory," Gilberdyke replied.

"But what if you're right," Green pondered.

"Then we're in trouble," Travers coolly stated, and turning to Robinson said, "Jock, I think we've got work to do."

54

Lump missed Anvil most dreadfully but had stuck to his allotted task with great determination. The Bloomers would be trained, he had promised!

The first thing that Baby Whiteknight suggested was that they build a stout wattle and daub compound away from the train and the distractions caused by Sods going about their daily business of hunting, gathering and being taught to fight by Marx. The training compound was duly constructed in a small clearing about half a mile from the encampment and for nine hours a day (including tea breaks and lunch), seven days a week Lump and Baby worked.

The matriarch Maggie and patriarch Ronnie now had great, great, great, great, great grandbloomers; there were nearly thirty in all and their numbers kept growing. Maggie and Ronnie now seemed almost mild by comparison with the generations that had followed them. Each new pair of Bloomers (they were always pairs, and there was always one of each sex) was fiercer than that which preceded them. What was also interesting was that though they were fiercer they were also perversely more biddable. Once the training process got under way the parents of the latest twosome would nip their offspring if they stepped out of line.

This is not to say that it was easy because it wasn't. Let me give you an example of what was involved.

Bloomers were always hungry and you couldn't train them

by calling "Here pussy, pussy!" and then giving them a pat on the head and a tickle of their tummies. They needed 'treats'. Treats consisted of assorted dead vermin that were dished out from a large tub. How many vermin can you get through in a day training up to four Bloomers at a time? I can tell you, a lot! Given that Lump and Baby were training the whole time a large group of young Sods were given the full-time task of garnering the vermin from the surrounding fields. At least vermin bred quickly and were plentiful, there being no nasty pesticides and stuff like that.

Each time the trainee Bloomer correctly responded to a command such as "Walk. Sit. Heel. Good cat, come, good cat." it was rewarded with, for example, a vole or a harvest mouse. This was but the first part of training; as the trainee progressed there were more significant tasks to perform.

The 'graduation prom' (as Baby insisted on calling it, though Lump hadn't a clue why) went as follows. Human-like dummies were placed on the far side of the compound. A Bloomer would be led, on a lead, to the dummies and the command "Friend" would be given. At this command the Bloomer would lie at the dummy's 'feet' and would receive a dormouse. Next, the same Bloomer would be taken to the next dummy and the command "Foe" would be given. At this, if the Bloomer growled savagely and tried to bite the dummy it received yet another portion of vermin, say half a rat. The ultimate part of the graduation prom was when they obeyed the command without receiving a reward.

Marx was a man who liked to keep things in the right place and so had pretty much left Lump and Baby to get on with their work while he did his. But eventually a change in circumstances caused him to visit the compound. As was usual Lump and Baby were busy when he arrived.

Max stood outside the gate and called, "Hello, it's me. How's it going in there?"

"Great," Lump called back.

"Can I come in?" he asked.

"For sure," Baby replied.

Baby had mellowed now that she had an important role in life; not outgoing exactly, but not downright hostile anymore to everyone except Lump.

"Come right on in," she said as she let Marx through the gate.

The Bloomer stationed at the gate started to make very unpleasant growling sounds at the sight of Marx.

"Friend!" Baby commanded, and the Bloomer lay down and the growl subsided to the normal background rumbling noise Bloomers always made.

"Hello, Mr Marx," Lump said as he ran up followed by a Bloomer kitten.

That particular day there were eight Bloomers in the compound all at Prom stage.

"Would you like to see 'em at it?" Lump asked.

"If that's okay," Marx replied.

"Sure is," Baby drawled. "Shall we show comrade Marx the mass attack?" she asked Lump.

"Is they ready, Baby?" Lump responded.

"They sure are. You wanna give the command, Lump?"

"No, Baby. You taught 'em the best."

"You sweet boy," she said as she ruffled his hair. Lump looked embarrassed. "Comrade Marx, you stand very still, and I mean very still, by the gate."

He did as he was told as Baby and Lump lined up the eight Bloomers across the compound from the row of dummies.

Baby pointed at the dummies and said, "Foe!"

The Bloomers snarled, growled and strained at their leashes.

"Foe!" she said again as she nodded at Lump and shouted "GO!" as she and Lump released the leads.

Baby and Lump shouted as one, "Attack!"

The Bloomers raced across the compound and were soon upon the dummies. Within a few frantic moments they were totally destroyed.

"Bloody hell!" Marx said.

"Friend! Home!" Baby and Lump called as the Bloomers trotted back to be fed with two pieces of vermin each. They had been good Bloomers.

"The cats of war!" Marx chortled. "Well done you two, well done."

"I thinks we got us some fine weapons of mass destruction

there, comrade," Baby calmly observed.

"Are they all trained now?" Marx asked.

"Until the next litter arrives," Lump answered.

"Good. I have important news; we have had a command from Una. We are to leave here and travel to a safer place," Marx said.

The pleasure of success drained from Lump's face. "This is my home," he said.

"I know, Lump, but the Bloomers, well you didn't train them for fun, did you?" Marx replied.

"Time to grow up, Lump," Baby said with a kindly smile and a pat on his back.

"We need to begin to make ourselves ready," Marx said. "Things are beginning to move out there and we need to be part of it. It'll be slow going and we've a long way to go. Will you be able to manage all the Bloomers?" he asked.

"We'll need helpers," Lump replied.

"Then helpers you shall have."

55

At Number 10 the war cabinet had finished its business but Green asked Robinson and Travers to stay behind. As he returned from a quick 'cigar' he had found them playing 'paper, stone, scissors'.

"Stone! Scissors!" they simultaneously cried.

At least they had the courtesy to stop as the Prime Minister took his seat at the end of the table beneath the portrait of his illustrious predecessor.

"There is something you don't know," Green said, "something secret. Come nearer."

They rose and moved closer to their leader, all ears.

"I have a secret agent out there," Green continued.

"There aren't any, Prime Minister," Robinson stated.

"There is the one, the last of the few, of the brave."

"Who?" Travers asked.

"PP2," Green answered.

"PP2?" Travers repeated.

"Gilt?" Robinson asked.

"Indeed, Gilt," Green said.

"Gilt is no more," Robinson insisted, "he was put down after that, er, rather nasty mistake."

"No, that's what you were all supposed to think. My predecessor had the presence of mind to falsify the reports of his death. He was given a new identity and hidden away."

"By Ham, I should have known this!" Robinson objected.

"Some things are only in the gift of a Prime Minister. On taking office one is handed a number of items. One of mine was an envelope on which was written 'Only open if the state of England is in the greatest peril!' I opened the envelope."

"But why?" Travers asked.

"Sedanistas," Robinson stated.

"Exactly," Green said.

"And you knew that they were an urgent and compelling danger?" Travers asked.

"Of course. I am the Prime Minister."

"And now that bloody professor thinks they've got bikes," Robinson rather unnecessarily reminded them.

"Gilt has been tasked to bring Una Uevera back alive," Green explained.

"Clever," Robinson observed.

"Thank you," Green smiled, "But time is not on our side. We must move quickly to remove the threat. We are at war, even if war has not been declared. We are faced with a threat, the horror of which we can barely understand, the like of which we have never known. Word must not get out."

"We worked out a plan while you were having your cigar," Travers said with a wry smile.

"You were playing that silly game," Green said.

"That was after we'd done the plan," Travers responded.

"And?"

"As Head of Counter Insurgency Services I have also been preparing," Robinson rather pompously declared, "I have trained troops, trained in intelligence, trained in counter insurgency, in terror, in war."

"I didn't know that," Green said with great annoyance.

"Nor did I, not until earlier," Travers sympathised.

"Need to know basis," Robinson calmly stated.

"Who knows about this?" Green asked.

"The three of us, my field commanders and of course the troops, my CISTS."

"The what?" Green asked again, bemused that someone whom he controlled was doing things he knew nothing about (nothing new there then!).

"Counter Insurgency Services Troops, or Cists for short."

"Sounds unpleasant," Travers said.

"Believe me they are, they most certainly are, and foaming at the mouth to get into action," Robinson chortled.

"They're armed?" Green asked.

"The usual weaponry, but with a few little extras."

"Like?"

"Blowpipes," Robinson responded.

"Blowpipes? You are joking of course?"

"No, Prime Minister, they are no joke. Our best snipers can kill a Legit at fifty paces; the very best further than that."

"They've undergone field trials?"

"Rigorously."

"How many Cists do you have," Green winced as he uttered the word.

"A thousand, give or take a few."

"What do they fire?" Travers queried, feeling a bit left out of the conversation.

"Darts, sharp darts."

"What good are bloody darts?" Travers asked.

"Poisoned darts."

"Oh, yes?"

"Well, they've killed everyone we stuck them in."

"How quickly?" Green asked.

"It can take as long as two minutes, but normally it's instantaneous, especially if the victim's thin. In either case it's not a pretty sight," Robinson replied.

"I expect not. What's the plan?" Green enquired.

"Five groups of one hundred Cists, each under the leadership of a Cisturion, under the overall management of Legates, will be sent north and east, two further groups will go south; the rest will remain in the Capital to protect Ham."

"And the government," Green added. "But why north and east?"

"That's where Lindum, is Prime Minister," Robinson replied, with a distinct air of superiority.

"So, between the Cists and Gilt. . ."

"We will be victorious," Robinson asserted.

"And there are thousands and thousands of Swabs," Travers rather forlornly added.

"Well done, Jock!" Green said as he patted him on the back, and thought," I'd better find out what the poison is. Could come in useful."

56

Gilt found Melton Mowbray disappointing: not only were there no pork pies, but it had become a ghost town. Piles of ancient and rancid litter blew about the streets and there was absolutely nowhere to eat or drink. By the time they travelled the fifteen miles to Grantham the Legits were on their last legs and Gilt was hungry and not a little worried.

The incident at the house with the 'mad stuffer' (as he thought of him) had actually rather thrown him. There were so many of these strange little villages, and now he wasn't sure what he might find in them. He also couldn't understand how a town as big as Melton Mowbray could be entirely deserted. He put his anxiety down to the fact that he was an urban being and as such had been blessed with the certainties of city life BBW; food in shops, booze in bottles, snooker at the club, whores at street corners, chocolate; but out here in the rural wilderness?

It was quite a relief when they reached Grantham; not only was it populated but its square was graced with a stone statue. The 'creation' was more than life size; it was entirely white and was of a headless woman who carried a large handbag. The plinth on which it sat bore the legend 'LadyThatcher, Grosser of England'. I think this was a mistake on the carver's part; the correct word, I believe, was 'Grocer', but then again it might have been correct.

There was a time when 'groceries' and the trade of 'grocering', undertaken by a grocer, were at the very centre of English life. The principles of grocering were really very simple; 'success is built on commonsense and perseverance'. As I understand it there were High Grocers and Low Grocers, the former believed in something called 'free trade' whilst the latter believed in 'free trade with a human face'. High Grocers believed in hanging, Low Grocers believed in life sentences that lasted for life. High Grocers believed that anyone who wasn't pure white was an inferior being and could be treated as such; Low Grocers believed that you shouldn't say that out loud. High Grocers believed that they had the right to the pursuit of life, liberty, and happiness whilst everyone else could get stuffed; Low Grocers were 'wet' and thought that they had to do something for the 'respectable, deserving poor' (do any of you know what that means?). High Grocers were homophobic; Low Grocers had token 'gays' (as they were called, god knows why, it couldn't have been much fun) in their ranks.

The trade itself consisted in supplying provisions, comestibles, food even, through retail outlets where the personal relationship between the customer and the grocer was of paramount importance. The knowledge and care that could be given to the customer because of the grocer's knowledge of the customer's most intimate needs enabled not only food transactions to be undertaken but also personal and deep relationships to be forged. It was believed that 'going to the grocers' was a life enhancing and deeply satisfying experience. Because of this the professional grocer was able to charge significantly more for the product as the customer was getting so much more than the packet of ginger nuts in their wicker shopping bag. I summarise: profit for the grocer, profit for the customer.

It was on these simple principles that the English State was run for nearly two hundred years, possibly longer.

There was also a pub in Grantham, The Gatherers Arms, or the 'Gatherers' as it was known to those few who could afford to eat and drink there. Before dining, Gilt set up his stall in the lounge bar. This was achieved through the donation of a 'future' pardon to the Landlord. Trade was good, and by the time Gilt sat down to eat the steaming pudding of squirrel with a side order of sautéed turnips and hazelnuts (they knew how to live in Grantham), his bag of Hamsters was even fuller.

Though blessed with the constitution of an ox (male cow) he had subsequently suffered from indigestion and had decided to take the benefit of the night air. He found himself on the old towpath beside the river Witham watching the wind caress the water and the banks of rushes and wished he could have had a nice fat redheaded duck rather than a squirrel. "But at least," he thought, "it was meat."

As this thought began to subside he heard a noise. It was coming nearer. It grew louder. He knew that noise; rubber whirring on the path. Keenly alert, he waited. The noise grew louder and then out of the darkness a bike rushed forth. Gilt moved slightly to the side as the racing Rocket, head down, approached. Too late Rocket saw the danger. With a mighty punch Gilt thumped Rocket from the saddle of his bike and he crashed awkwardly to the ground. Gilt smiled.

As Rocket regained consciousness he found himself tied hand and foot and lying head down on the short steep bank that lead to the lapping water. Gilt sat holding his feet.

"Good evening," Gilt said. "Nice evening for a bike ride?"

"Fuck off!" Rocket replied.

"Tut, tut," Gilt said as he let Rocket's head slip beneath the water. After a few moments he pulled the spluttering man back up and out.

"Shall we start again?" Gilt asked. "Your name?"

"Get stuffed!" Rocket replied.

Gilt lowered his head beneath the water.

It didn't take long for Gilt to break the brave Rocket. Within the hour he discovered all he needed to know; Una and the Sedanistas were less than twenty miles away at Navenby, and they had bikes.

Rocket drowned with dignity as Gilt undid the quick-releases on the wheels of the bike and carried these with the frame back to his Sedan at the rear of the pub. These he carefully secreted beneath the various sheets and bags used by Pardoners to secure their trade. As was normal in the circumstances he slept the sleep of an innocent.

57

The day before the night of the 'big move' had not begun well. Comrade Marx had struggled to see the strategic advantage in kidnapping the Bishop; taking the money was very sensible, but bringing the Bishop was quite another matter. All night he lay upon his narrow bed and rehearsed every argument, but to no avail. By first light he was in a strop, and by the time he was seated at the kitchen table with a cup of camomile tea, he was struggling to contain his irritation. This he did until the business of the meeting had been completed (he put it down to the tea).

The previous day Una, Marx, Roque, Anvil and Serene had gathered to review the situation. Rocket had not returned and they had begun to worry about his safety. They decided to give it a few days and then send out two search cyclists. When Marx had learned of the abduction of the Bishop and the means whereby he had been brought to Navenby he had been worried. When he had learnt that they had despatched a speed cyclist to London to deliver the message to Ham, he had been aghast. It was then that he had realised that these dear people were either young enthusiasts or old wise ones, none of whom had any real sense of what was going to be involved in the overthrow of the state. They just hadn't thought it through. Green and his mobsters were not stupid and would probably work out that they had wheels. As you know he was absolutely correct in this assumption.

Marx believed that it was essential that they leave Navenby as it was no longer safe. The argument had raged for hours but in the end it had been Serene who brought it to a close. She had sat and listened and said very little, anxious at the developing conflict between her new friends. She held up her hand and when they wouldn't listen, banged it hard upon the kitchen table.

"Stop this at once," she said. "I have something to say. Marx is right. We should leave here as soon as possible."

There was silence, and then, as their objections began she continued, "No individual is more important than our struggle. I'm an old lady, a very old lady. This place has been my solitary home for more years than some of you put together. I love this place, every dusty nook and cranny, my garden, my plants, my chickens, my shed. I loved my bicycles, but when I knew what was out there I gave them up; I gave them to you. I had learnt to live with solitude, thought I had come to know myself. Then you arrived, Una, and now all of you are here, and my world has been turned upside down. Anvil opened new hopes and old wounds. If you don't want to leave here it is for the wrong reasons; if I don't, it's for a good reason. This is my home; you are visitors. But I shall leave and you will leave with me. I will not risk what we have to do and nor should you. So there!" she said with a final embarrassed smile.

Una rose from her seat and crouched down beside Serene, "I'm sorry," she said, "Pride isn't very useful. I'm sorry."

Serene patted her head and said, "Go on; there's things to plan – much to do."

Roque looked sullen but nodded his agreement.

The question they then faced was where to go. Wesley, who was now in charge of scouting the immediate area for security and opportunity, was called to the meeting. The situation was explained and his advice sought. After several minutes of thoughtful pacing up and down he said, "Somerton Castle, it look's strong."

"Where is it?" Una asked.

" 'Tis nearby, just down over the cliff road; 'tis hidden amidst the trees and it has water all about."

"A moat?" Anvil asked.

"If that's what thee callest it," Wesley replied. "There be big mounds of earth, and high walls, and tower things."

"I know the place," Serene said. "It's old, mediaeval earthworks and indeed a moat."

"Have you been inside?" Marx asked. "Is it empty?"

"There was no one there when I went in but there were lots of big rooms, most empty, but one big room with hundreds of things in it," Wesley replied.

"What things?" Una asked.

"They were strange."

"Describe them," Marx instructed.

"Well, they was wooden, and they was curvy; some had holes in their middles and they had wires, I think they was wires, but some weren't like wires, that went up this straight bit to another bit with knobs on it. When you touched 'em they made a noise. They was all stood up on sort of prop things."

"They're guitars!" Anvil laughed.

"They would be," Serene said with a smile. "I had quite forgotten. Do you remember, Anvil, we went to one of his concerts?"

"I'm struggling, Serene," Una said.

"Aidonis F. Carter."

"Aidonis F. Carter! My god, he was good!"

"Sorry to interrupt, but what are you two talking about?" Una asked.

"There used to be things called rock concerts; Aidonis was poetry rock, and when he went electric there was one hell of a storm," Serene replied.

"Oh Serene, do you remember that open air gig in the park?" Anvil enthused.

"Oh, that night!" Serene responded.

"Please?" Una pleaded.

"Sorry, Una. Aidonis was a brilliant guitarist. He bought Somerton Castle just before the war, and I suppose he's been living down the road all these years. It's strange to think I knew nothing about it." Serene replied.

"Were these guitar things covered in dust?" Marx enquired.

"No, they was beautiful; they was clean," Wesley replied.

"Then the castle is not deserted," Marx observed.

"He was a good guy. He'd be on our side," Anvil said.

"We should go there. It will be safer than here, easier to

defend," Serene said.

"Perhaps it would be wise if we let him know we're coming," Una suggested. "Wesley, take me there. I'll talk with him."

53

So that morning as Marx sat sipping his tea he was pleased that they were moving out but was still enraged about the bishop when Roque came into the kitchen.

"Morning, Comrade," Roque said.

"Morning," Marx grumpily replied.

Roque made himself some tea and put an egg on to boil. Marx continued to drum his fingers on the table. When Roque finally sat down opposite Marx he said, "What's up with you this morning? You got your way: we're leaving."

"Why did you take the bishop?"

"It seemed like a good idea at the time."

"Well it wasn't. We don't need bloody hostages; we need weapons, arms, people."

"I wanted to show 'em that we had the power."

"And ruin our surprise advantage?"

"It won't ruin anything. They haven't got wheels."

"But they have got people, lots of them, and they'll all be armed and probably looking for us."

Roque was silent for a few moments and then said, "I wanted to impress Una. I wanted to show her that my Sodsters worked, that I could do something brave, not like the hypertension market."

"Impress her?"

"That's right. You're wiser than me, Anvil's wise, Serene's wise, I'm just, just. . ." Roque's words trailed off.

Marx mused on this for a few moments, "Are you jealous of me, Roque?"

"Maybe."

"Comrade, I am an eunuch; you have nothing to fear from the likes of me."

"It's not sex, it's respect!" Roque replied.

"You have her respect, all our respect."

Roque and Marx stared at each other.

"Why don't you tell her you love her?" Marx asked.

"I'm afraid," Roque said as he bowed his head.

Marx stood and walked to where Roque sat, "Stand up," he commanded. As Roque stood Marx embraced him and was embraced in return, "Tell her, my friend, tell her. Now eat your bloody breakfast."

Roque sat down as Marx moved to the door, "Oh, and by the way," he said over his shoulder, a big smile upon his bearded face, "just tell me what we're going to do with the bishop."

The 'Leaving of Navenby', as it became known, was difficult and emotional. For most of the Sods who had been billeted there for many months, they were leaving the first stone and brick building in which they had ever lived. It was little things, like being able to go up three flights of stairs (even if one didn't sleep up there), having proper food, being taught to read and write (though Anvil could be a tad impatient) in the library, children learning to ride bikes, laughter, and hope. They were mostly little things, but important all the same.

59

Una and Wesley left early that same morning to reconnoitre the Castle. They pushed their way down disused bridle paths and down the great green lane that zig zagged down the escarpment. The morning was bright with shimmering light after a night of light rain. When space allowed they rode next to one another. It brought out the best in Wesley and he found himself unable to endure Una's reflective silence.

"And there will be peace in the land, the west wind bearing gentle sounds of summer, and war no more. We will have risen up; we will have seen the light of freedom. We will have embraced the chalice of dignity. Ah! But the road is long and narrow, you say, but it is sure," Wesley intoned, "We are on the way."

Una took a sideways glance at him and grinned as the sunlight glinted upon his pre BBW specs (Anvil had lots in a box). "Is it far?" she asked.

"No, my lady," he replied.

"Pardon?"

"The Queen and her knight rode forth to the castle gate and rapped thereon. Within they trembled at the power of her majesty, the wiseness of her. . ."

"Wesley," Una said as she stopped and pointed at the castle hidden beneath the bank of broadleaf trees in the valley less than a mile away, "Is that the castle?"

"It is, my queen."

"Wesley!"

"Just having fun, Una. There's got to be fun, or there isn't any point is there?"

"No, my good knight," she replied, "Now, how did you get in?"

The castle was very much as Wesley had described, and for once he had underestimated its antiquity, dereliction and size. They passed through the earthworks, avoiding the great banks of nettles, across the drawbridge (under which they left their bikes), over the fetid water, around the base of the castle wall to the small door through which Wesley had previously secured entry. It was locked.

"What do we do now?" he whispered.

They continued around the wall until they reached the drawbridge once more.

"Well, think that answers your question," Una finally replied.

They climbed back up the grassy slope dragging their cycles with them and leant them against the castle wall.

Una rapped on the great studded castle door.

"I said you'd do that," Wesley observed.

Una gave him a stern look and rapped once more using the hilt of her broad sword that had been tied to the bike's crossbar.

Nothing; not a sound was heard from within.

Una rapped harder.

At last they heard movement within and a muffled voice (the door was very thick) asked, "Who goes there?"

"Una Uevera, Commander of the Sedanistas."

"What you say?"

"Aidonis F Carter!" she shouted, "We need your help!"

"He don't see no visitors," came the gruff reply.

"We must see him; we need his help. We're fans," Una lied.

"Like fuck you are. Piss off!"

"Please, it's very important," Una pleaded.

After a long pause the voice said, "You wait there. I'll ask him, but it'll be no."

They waited for what seemed like an eternity until they heard the click of locks and bolts being withdrawn, and then the small door within the great door creaked open.

"He says he'll see you. Beats me why," the man said.

He was in his mid sixties and was dressed in battered black jeans, black T-shirt and black cowboy boots; he was unshaven and his long greasy grey hair fell untidily about his shoulders. "Just follow me," he instructed.

They walked through the darkness to the door that led to the inner castle. The man opened the door and for a moment their eyes were blinded with light and their ears were assaulted by noise. Una and Wesley blinked in the bright light. Before them was the black silhouette of a large man.

"Aidonis F Carter?" Una asked.

"You know me?" came the surprised reply.

"Your fame lives on!"

"Come on in," Aidonis said.

"Thank you," Una said.

Aidonis pointed at the man and said, "This is Clem. Clem Atkins, my friend and guitar technician, most everything else these days."

"Good to meet you, Clem," Una said as she extended her hand in greeting, which Clem reluctantly shook. Wesley followed suit.

"And these," he said, "are my family."

Una and Wesley stared, drop-jawed, at the animals. Pigs, cows, an ox, sheep, chickens, turkeys, goats and geese milled about in what had been turned into a farmyard. They turned to look at Aidonis. They beheld a tall man of some girth in his early sixties (successful rock musicians had always been younger than their older fans imagined, not that Una or Wesley had ever seen a rock star) who wore very long hair, a beard, a be-jewelled kaftan coat, blue jeans and sandals.

He smiled at their astounded silence and said, "This is my ark. What you think?"

Una was the first to speak, "Do you know what's happened out there?"

"That is why they are here," Aidonis replied.

"What you mothers want?" Clem asked.

Aidonis smiled and said, "Don't take no notice. Clem's been a-taking care of me for too long, it's okay."

"And the animals were in their byres, and there was food upon the table, and the goat lay down with the ox, and the people were happy, and there was peace in the land, and we saw it, and it was good, and," Wesley pronounced.

"Wesley!" Una admonished.

"Hey, brother, what's your name?" Aidonis asked.

"Wesley."

"Gimme five," Aidonis said holding out his right hand.

"What?" Wesley said as he backed away from the big man.

"No problem, man, I'll show you later," Aidonis said and turning to Una asked, "What was your name again and why do you need my help?"

"Una Uevera, and it's a long story," Una replied.

"Hit me," Aidonis said.

"What?" Una asked.

"Hit me with it, dig?"

Perplexed as she was, Una punched Aidonis in the stomach who doubled up in what she assumed was pain. She soon realised that it was not pain, but laughter, that rocked his frame. He un-doubled, still roaring with laughter.

"Ways to go lady, ways to go! Come on in," he chortled as the two Sods followed him toward the castle Keep. "Come on, Clem, let's make these guys welcome. We ain't had no goddam visitors in years."

"We ain't never had any visitors, man, not ever," Clem

rather bleakly replied.

"Well, we have now," Aidonis replied, "so let's go in!"

Aidonis and Una had taken each of Wesley's arms to get him through the many animals; he was simply terrified.

"You do know how important these creatures are, don't you?" Una asked, perhaps unnecessarily.

"I've been waiting, maybe the time has come," Aidonis replied as he nodded his head.

Clem did not look pleased with the intrusion into his world.

Later that night as Aidonis and Clem were about to go to their separate beds, Clem said, "Listen Aid, I don't go for this. We're safe here, no hassles. We got all we need."

"Oh yeah?" Aidonis replied.

"Yeah, we're safe. What they're wanting's gonna get us in deep shit man, deeeep shit. It's too big an ask."

"I've made up my mind, Clem, I'm gonna help 'em just like I said I would."

"But why?"

"I liked her, and they wanna do the right thing."

"You just hungry for some pussy, man."

"Leave it out Clem, okay? It's not that."

"What then?"

"It's all them Sods. They need to be somewhere."

"People, who needs fucking people?" Clem asked.

"I do; it's been lonely."

"Ah gee thanks. Grateful son of a bitch, ain't you?"

"Come on, Clem, don't take it that way. You know what I mean, yeah?

"I guess, but I don't like it. It'll bring us nothing but heartache," Clem answered.

"Hey, come here, man, giss us a hug," Aidonis said opening his arms wide.

The two men hugged and Aidonis said, "It'll be exciting, doing something, yeah?"

"I guess," Clem reluctantly replied.

60

The throne room had been deserted when His Holiness arrived. Whiskerbot entered and said, "Yes?" rather gruffly.

Whiskerbot led him through the corridors to Ham's wing and to the door on which was printed 'Royal Absolution'. Inside, His Holiness found Ham already seated on the left of the two-person cubicle that sat against the far wall of the room. His Holiness climbed in the other side.

"Any news of your cousin?" His Holiness asked.

"Hamondi? No, probably dead by now; good riddance quite frankly."

"Your majesty!"

"Well, I ask you."

"Not in here."

"This is a Catholic ritual. Why do we do it?"

"One nation, one state, one religion; it's far more inclusive," His Holiness advised.

"Why would I want to be included? I am the monarch."

"Regard it as a form of counselling, of therapy even."

"Go on, then," Ham sighed and closed the little curtain that hung between them.

"How's things?"

"Bloody awful, actually."

"The burdens of state?" His Holiness asked.

"Come off it, Bish, I don't have any burdens of state; that little Green snot bag pox of a politician does all that. I'm not allowed. I'm merely the Monarch."

"So what's it all about, my child?"

"Camellia."

"The slow-worm?"

"Stupid cow. She said it was the final straw."

"Go on. You have something to confess?"

"I have nothing to confess. I am the monarch for god's sake. There was a time when I was happy, free, and then that bastard Green made me get married."

"And how is the princess, your majesty?"

"I thought you were supposed to listen? I could have what I wanted when I wanted it."

"Food, drink, sport?"

"Stop interrupting, Your Holiness. Sex, I'm talking about sex. It's not easy carrying the burden of androgynous monarchy, not easy I can tell you. Two sets of desires fighting for satisfaction on a daily basis. It was so simple. There I'd be sitting on my throne and the Morris Dancers would be clogging away and I'd think 'ooh that's a pretty boy', or 'that's a pretty girl'. I would mention it to Whiskers, and there, low and behold, there they would be, at their sovereign's command. Then there were the courtiers; I used to hand pick them. Most of the old lot have gone, hardly a tasty morsel in sight. I'm starved of the sustenance of life!"

"Camellia has taken charge?"

"Charge? Charge is not the word for it. She is no longer 'known' to me and never will be so far as I can see and she's taken the princess."

"So, after the slow-worm joke she took the princess, what's her name?"

Ham paused for a moment deep in thought, "That's it! Gloriana Beatrice Ham. Well, I thought, bugger it, so Whiskers found me a couple, a nice lad and a lass. There wasn't time for one at a time so I went for a 'two on one', gorgeous. It was all going very nicely when the door opens and there she is. Bloody woman has come home early, obviously taken pity on me as she's wearing, well, nothing actually."

"Oh dear."

"Well that was it; she was incandescent."

"Where is her Highness now?"

"That's the problem, I don't know. I don't know what she might do."

"You're worried about the safety of the child?"

"No. I'm worried about my safety. It's not a kind world out there you know, what with the Sedanistas. Who knows what might happen?"

"I see," His Holiness inanely observed.

"Well, go on then, say it!" Ham commanded.

"I absolve you from your sins."

Having left the cubicle Ham stretched and said, "God, I could do with a good fuck!"

"So could I," His Holiness replied. "I hate Lent," he added.

"There's a new Fornicon in the village, so Whiskers says," Ham suggested.

"We can't go there, not during Lent."

"I know, but they've got a new service: 'takeaways'," Ham grinned, "I'll get Whiskers right on it. What would you like, Your Holiness?"

Jock Robinson had despatched the CISTS as soon as he had returned to the barracks that was housed in what was once (according to the faded signage) 'Tate Modern'. The thousand massed troops had stood in the generator hall and waited for their instructions. They were indeed a force to be feared.

Unlike their down-market comrades, the Swabs, they were well equipped for their function, which was destruction. Jock's staff had spent many months scouring and searching for the necessary elements, and then there had been the additional problem of finding a suitable design for their costumes and accoutrements.

Underpants had been the first problem. Expert advice suggested that constriction of the testicles inhibited the ability to fight. Though unproven, this had been accepted in the desire to ensure total capability. Jock had suggested that the troops' genitals could hang free, but had accepted the argument that for some of the better-hung this could be a handicap and an impediment in battle. Weeks had passed, with little success, until a consignment of jock straps had been found in a previously unnoticed cricket wholesaler's warehouse in Barking. There were over two thousand straps, which meant that each CIST could be wearing one, whilst the other was 'in the wash' (an unlikely event). This was the moment of revelation for Jock: he knew that this was an omen. They would be invincible, and how could they be otherwise with the manhood of the CISTS comfortably nestling in a contraption that bore his own name? They gave up on vests.

Two of everything else proved to be impossible. A detachment was sent to Portsmouth to see if anything could be found in the naval dockyard warehouses (there being no navy of course). Eventually a pigeon had arrived at Tate Modern with the message, 'Sir, necessaries secured. Please send Sedanathon asap'.

There had been great excitement as the sound of the two hundred clogs arrived in the concourse. Inside they found boxes containing over one thousand blue naval rating's shirts and green lightweight flack jackets. That was wonderful but was to be surpassed by the four hundred and fifty camouflaged battle helmets (they probably had a proper name but no one could remember it). It was clear that four hundred and fifty helmets were not enough for a thousand CISTS so a system had been devised. Naturally, the commander of each unit of one hundred CISTS (a Cisturion) would receive a helmet that he could personalise in some way. Each CIST unit would receive forty-five helmets and each day lots would be drawn from the Cisturion's helmet to determine twenty-four hour ownership. Jock had been concerned that this posed a health risk and thus conducted an analysis to secure the avoidance of risk. The solution: each CIST would have a shaven head. That may sound simple to you but the number of cutthroat razors still around was limited. Further weeks passed whilst one hundred such razors were found, and then there was the strop on which to sharpen them. This in turn produced an additional rank in each unit, that of the 'close shaver', known as the 'Cist-cropper'.

Much anxiety and effort had been expended on the vexed question of trousers. A thousand of the same design could not be found. A consignment of jodhpurs had been discovered but there weren't enough and the idea of a forced march wearing them was easily dismissed.

One of the reasons that Jock had risen to a position of authority was that he was able to think laterally (the other reasons were many, and included ruthlessness, dissemblance, ingratiation and a keen sense of self-preservation). As you will probably have guessed, Jock was of Scottish extraction, his parents having taken English citizenship BBW, and so it was perhaps no surprise that the idea of kilts sprang to mind. This had not been warmly received by his senior officers and the Cisturions, but his soliloquy on the roman solder's attire had carried the day. The search for kilts then began. Jock was reasonable in his request; the clan tartan was not a problem, any old kilt would do. But there were no kilts, other than in Scotland, and there was no way of getting those without a war.

It was a crisis; the CISTS couldn't run about in just their jock straps. Jock called a summit and asked the team that had gone down to Portsmouth what else was left there under lock and key. He wasn't pleased that they didn't know and so decided to make the long trek south to see what he could find.

The once great naval dockyards contained many vast warehouses that were now largely empty and what they did contain was useless for his or any other purpose, e.g. truck tyres. His gloom had deepened as the exploration of the buildings continued. At last they came upon a warehouse that bore the legend 'Fleet Air Arm'. Inside, all that remained were many wooden crates on which the word 'parachutes' was stencilled. The hairs on the back of Jock's neck stood up in excitement.

The final part of the uniform was thus secured, and as the CISTS stood in the turbine room waiting for his command he was proud. The parachutes had been cut up to make triple layer tie-around skirts and they looked spectacular in the grey light of the hall. They were a perfect solution, light, quick drying, and only slightly transparent (in parts). You are probably worrying about what they wore on their feet. The answer was nothing. Months of stamping on the ground and kicking at wooden doors and concrete posts had turned their feet into not only their means of transport, but also an effective weapon. So you can now imagine them standing there in serried rows, fully costumed, medieval weapons in their hands, bamboo blowpipes across their back and quivers of blow-darts tied at their waists.

"CISTS!" Jock began, "We shall go on to the end; we shall fight in the regions; we will fight on the fields and the roads; we shall fight with growing confidence and growing strength with your darts through the air; we shall defend our England, whatever the cost may be. We shall fight them in the villages; we shall fight them in the towns; we shall fight them in the lanes, and in the forests; we shall fight in the hills; we shall never surrender!"

The CISTS cheered.

"Let us therefore brace ourselves for our duties and so bear ourselves that if England last a thousand years men will say, 'This was their finest hour'."

The CISTS roared.

A senior officer turned to another and said, "Now if that isn't the speech of a future prime minister, then I don't know what is." (The officer in question was not, of course, the owner of a battered copy of 'The Oxford Library of Words and Phrases', whereas Jock was.)

And so the CISTS set forth to war.

The 'Leaving of Navenby' had not been easy to organise. It had been decided that the great majority of the four hundred and eighty nine Sods would make their way to Somerton Castle on foot. The Sodsters would run back and forth between the two places carrying goods, chattels, the very young, those that were ill, and the few oldsters. The 'Leaving' would take place under the cover of darkness and would enable the Sods to arrive as dawn broke.

As night fell Marx and Roque led the blindfolded Bishop Hamondi of Lindum up onto the old Lindum Road.

"What are you going to do to me?" the Bishop wailed.

"Nothing, nothing at all," Marx replied.

"Can you find your way home?" Roque asked.

"I'm hopeless with directions," the cleric responded.

"We'll help you on your way," Marx said helpfully.

"Can I ask you something?" the Bishop enquired.

"Of course," Marx answered.

"Why did you kidnap me?"

Marx turned to Roque with a smile, "I think that one's yours."

"To prove that it could be done," Roque answered.

"To show the power of wheels?" the Bishop continued.

"Yes."

"They, the authorities, will be disturbed."

"Yes."

A Sodster pulled up beside them and the Bishop was securely tied to the carrying area. He was driven away and released, still blindfolded, at the deserted tower at Temple Bruer. The two peddling Sods paid no attention to his cries of despair as they peddled off into the night.

As the sun had set the convoy was ready to move out. Baby and the Bloomers would lead the way followed by Marx and the walking Sods; Anvil and Serene were to be the last, followed as rear guard by Lump, Maggie and Ronnie. Roque was to follow on at the very last when all had safely departed. As they moved off into the night there was no sign of Serene. Anvil dismounted from his trike and went to Serene's shed, knowing she would be inside.

He found her sobbing, her head in her hands. She looked up as he entered. He sat beside her and put his arm around her shoulders. "There, there," he said, "please don't cry."

She could not stop her tears and dragged down great gulps of air that made it sound much worse in the small space. Anvil held her tight and after sometime she quietened.

"I can't go, Anvil, I just can't; for all my brave words, I can't," she sobbed.

"It's not safe to stay."

"I know, but I can't go; it's all I've had for years, this place."

162

"Then we shall both stay."

"That's not possible. You have to go. I want you safe, and Una needs your wise old head," Serene said as her tears dried.

"No. If you're not going nor am I."

"Anvil Ammer, you are needed elsewhere!"

"And so are you, my dear. What wise female council can Una get from anyone except you?

"Anvil!"

"So are we going to camp out here in your shed or our bedroom in the hall?"

"I'm not staying in the shed."

"I'm too old for this, Serene. I could never work it round so that you came to the right conclusion."

"Like opera, you mean?"

"Yes, like that. Come on, my love. We don't want to be too far behind the others."

As she stood, they kissed, "You win, you demented old sod, in the old sense that is."

"Tell you what," Anvil said as he closed the shed door behind them, "when this settles down we can either come back, or at the least come back and get your shed."

"You're very sweet. Let's go; adventure calls."

As they reached the brow of the hill she looked back and blew the hall a kiss. Lump was quite touched as he thought it was for him. He smiled as he watched the two old cyclists slowly peddle away, their panniers laden down with their most precious personal possessions and Sickle sat atop Anvil's pile.

As Lump, with his two Bloomers, followed in the dark he wondered about all that had happened over the last year or more. "Was it really that long?" he mused. "Here I be a boy of going on sixteen summers, so they tell me, but I ain't just a boy; I'm Keeper of the Bloomers. I'm important, but I'm still a boy. Una and the others they like me, and Mr Anvil, he's the best. I was just a snotty runt when he took me in and I be still his apprentice. What more does I have to learn, I wonders? Stop pulling, Ronnie," he said out loud. "Will there be something special like as I has to do that none else could do? I could be a hero like Roque, or grow up wise like Miss Serene. What if we looses? But we won't, will we Maggie?" he asked as he tickled her ears. She looked up at him and made her special friendly growly rumbly grumbly growl. "You's a good 'un, you are," he concluded.

Roque stood and waited till there was silence in the valley below. As he waited, he remembered the first day he had learnt to ride a bike and the day he had invented the Sodster. The gates to the drive had already been locked so he too followed the track that led from the hall and into the green lane beyond. It was a night for introspection. He looked up at the new moon and said, so the world could hear, "When we get there, I shall tell her I love her. I shall say 'Una, I love you! Let's be together forever." As the words came out of his mouth he felt truly embarrassed but his stride lengthened now that his decision was finally made.

63

As Ham and the Bishop of England enjoyed the pleasures of the Fornicon takeaway service Camellia was more productively employed. Whilst Green was working, sorting out the last details of the legislation that would bring into being the first public private investment opportunity since the BigWar.

"Yes!" he said as the door to his study was knocked for the umpteenth time in half an hour. "What is it?" he spat at the Cabinet Secretary who had the temerity to interrupt his plans for a personal fortune.

"It's the Highness Ham, Prime Minister."

"What's the Monarch doing here?"

"No, not the Androgynous Majesty sir, but Her Highness Camellia Ham, sir."

He stood up in shock and said, "Oh! What in Ham's name does she want?"

"She wouldn't say; she said she must see you, on a matter of great importance to the State of England."

"Then," he said putting the papers away, "you had better show her in."

"Your Majesty, it is my honour and pleasure to welcome you to the seat of English democratic government," he said offering his hand as she entered the room. At the same time he had thought, "Oooh! You'd make a cracking shag!"

She declined his outstretched hand and said, "Cut the crap, Green, we've got business to do." At the same time she was thinking, being a woman of some perception, "This ambitious prick would do anything to get inside my pants."

Green was a little take aback by her attitude but didn't let it show; he was after all Prime Minister. "Would you like a gin, your Majesty?" he asked, "It's distilled at Number 11 and is of the finest quality."

"Yes," she said, "why not?"

Once they had settled themselves comfortably in their armchairs, Green thought it proper to propose a toast, "To Ham," he said.

At which, Camellia scowled and said, "To Ham's end!"

Green sat in stunned silence for three mintes before Camellia spok again.

"Let's cut to the chase, Prime Minister," she said leaning forward conspiratorially. "You and I want one thing, power."

"Power?"

"Am I right in thinking that you chaired the 'search committee' that chose me as the Royal consort?"

"Yes, I had that privilege."

"It wasn't, and isn't a privilege."

"You are now the Queen, well, in effect."

"I am not a queen. I am the mother of the Queen to be."

"That's pretty good isn't it?"

"No, it's not! Get me another gin, please."

Green did as he was told.

"I was selected, I presume, because I came from an old noble family. I was 'attractive'," she continued as Green handed her the gin, "and I was believed to be a virgin, and fecund."

"Fecund?" Green asked.

"Fruitful, fertile, as in a plant or an animal," she replied. After all, she had been educated in a nunnery.

"Of course."

"Of course, nothing! I have been fertile, but I am not a plant or an animal."

"I don't understand, your Majesty."

"You can call me Camellia."

"I don't understand, Camellia."

"You're a very literal man, aren't you, John? The sex mad buffoon that you selected me to breed with is not only disgusting but useless."

"In bed?" Green rather stupidly asked.

"It's a pity men's cocks aren't in their heads; we might then get a bit more cerebral activity."

"Please go on," Green said as the colour rose above his collar and into his neck.

"Ham is no more of a monarch than you are trustworthy, John."

"You can't speak to me like that. I run this country!"

"Precisely. That is why I am here."

"You want me to do something for you?"

"Not exactly, John. It was more reciprocal than that," Camellia said as she smiled. "Do you believe in the monarchy?"

"Of course. The English State needs a monarch, a figurehead, that can give the people, er, a, sense of continuity, of purpose even, in a period of great change and many privations," Green replied.

"In other words, no."

"The time is not right for a republic," Green said, more than a little taken aback.

"I agree. What we need to do, John, is to sort out the interim arrangements."

"Get to the point, Camellia," Green said, feeling the need to reassert himself in this extremely strange conversation.

"Gloriana Beatrice will be Queen and I will be Regent. You and I will then work out what needs to be done."

Green pondered this for a moment and then said, "Look, to be honest, Ham's a nuisance, but I can pretty much do what I want anyway; Ham has no real power."

"No, in some ways that's true, but everything still must receive the royal assent. How much easier would it be if that assent was guaranteed; how much easier would it be if we were in agreement; how much easier if all the very difficult decisions could be laid at the door of the monarch? I take it that you haven't forgotten that the new written constitution enables the monarch to enact laws by royal proclamation."

"Yes, but that was just a device to keep Ham's predecessor happy. We knew it would never be used," Green replied.

"But what if it was?"

"There is one little fly in this ointment of yours: Ham," Green observed.

"Ham has to go."

"Oh, just like that? I don't think so. We've got a potential revolution on our hands, remember," Green objected.

"Couldn't that be useful?"

"The Sedanistas are after me, not Ham. They want to liberate the Legits," Green stated.

"But Ham could get caught up in it?"

"We're going to defeat them. Actions are underway."

"I'm sure you will, but perhaps a few might get through, get into the palace. Things happen like that, blame can be assigned." Camellia suggested.

"Interesting," Green said.

"It would need careful planning, and Whiskerbot would have to be dealt with."

"Bum Fluff's no problem but I don't see what you'd get out of it," Green asked.

"I hate him."

"The monarchy?"

"It would still be a monarchy by name, but a republic beneath the sheets, so to speak," she replied "and it could be ours, John. No parliament, a state of emergency, royal proclamations, written by you, signed by me as Regent. What do you think?"

"We would need to be very careful."

"Of course."

"I need to think about this, Camellia."

"Forgive me for saying so, John, but isn't Bekkes a little on the old side for a man of your energies?" she asked.

"I beg your pardon?" he said going bright red but with an increasing sense of arousal.

"I seem to have heard something about tobacco. Was it at Kew? My memory fails me."

Green cleared his throat uneasily and wished he could disappear into the ground.

"There's no need to be shy, prime minister. Word has it that you are rather good," Camellia said.

"I don't know what to say."

"Say nothing, John, just go and lock the door."

The Bishop had spent an uncomfortable night on the stone floor within the ancient tower of the KnightsTemplar. On awakening two things had struck him: his back was in spasm and he was ravenously hungry. This was immediately followed by a third thought, "I need to get back to civilisation". He used his crook to lever himself from the floor and emerged from the door, down the steps and into the morning light. The nearby cottages were derelict and empty; there was not a person in sight. He had, of course, lied to the Sods as he had a perfect sense of direction and knew that if he went first north and then due west he should arrive back at Navenby and from there the road to Lindum was straight. As the sun rose his vestments became increasingly heavy and he became increasingly hot and dry. Nevertheless he persevered, comforting himself with the thought of his Lord in the wilderness, and the desire for revenge upon the disrespectful Sods. He had little difficulty in finding the way, as the tracks left by the Sodster were clear in the grass of the green lane.

Gilt had an altogether better start to his day. He was a happy man. He believed that two of the indispensable elements that led to the status of a top-notch secret agent were fate and luck, and luck was the most important. This, it seemed to him, he had in abundance. What, he wondered had been the odds of him taking a night walk along a towpath and running into the only night cyclist in England? Still his was not to reason why; someone, somewhere meant it to happen.

When they left Grantham he had hoped that they would make Navenby by nightfall, but it was not to be. He had been unable to get replacement Legits and his two were in need of more than a night's rest particularly after they struggled up the escarpment along which they had to travel. As they reached Caythorp he realised that they must rest, and this they did; he in the College Arms, and his Legits in an outhouse, though he did ensure that they were well fed and watered. He did not sleep well as he spent the night rehearsing the role he was about to play.

Gilt's sleep might have been even worse had he known of the Mad Stuffer's developing obsession. For reasons that remain obscure he had decided that Gilt was the cause of his liberation from his taxidermist's nightmare and thus he would follow him until the time came for him to be of service to his benefactor. He had soon worked out that you didn't need to stay in close touch with a sedan as the sound of the clogs made it easy to follow at some considerable distance, particularly when there were no other vehicles on the road. The Mad Stuffer also felt a deep sense of guilt, and this, he believed, he could assuage through 'good' acts particularly as he had mistaken Gilt, in Orb's costume, for some sort of religious person. As he walked he thought back about what had happened. He could not understand how he, a respectable English farmer, albeit with a hobby of stuffing dead animals (better than live ones, he supposed) could have had recourse to eat first his serfs and then his family. Like all cannibals he now felt that he possessed their collective minds and strength and as such he would prove to be invincible if ever there was the need for active strife. He had been surprised when Gilt had tortured and drowned the cyclist but had assumed that it was a form of nocturnal baptism that had gone wrong. If the act had been evil he was sure that Gilt would not have seemed such a happy man as he had gone about his business before leaving Grantham. He had been hungry but provided himself with something of a feast by scavenging in the wicker waste bin at the rear of the College Arms.

65

Una sent Wesley back to Navenby with the message that the castle was occupied but that the Sods were more than welcome. She had been surprised at how easy it had been to persuade Aidonis that the castle, his home, could be used as the new headquarters for her revolution. One doesn't wish to be cynical but Aidonis had been a high priest of rock and as such had benefited from what I am told were described as 'groupies', and he hadn't seen a woman in twenty years and most certainly had not seen one as beautiful as Una for forty. To be kinder, he had been outraged at the excesses of the state, and had immediate sympathy with the desire to establish England as a free and open society for all. Una realised that Clem was hardly enthusiastic about their imminent arrival but reasoned that Aidonis would bring him around and that he would get used to the idea.

All through the night the Sods walked to the castle. Aidonis and Una stood at the drawbridge and welcomed them. Aidonis insisted on clapping them in as if it were some sort of 'happening'. Nevertheless his joy at seeing so many people was genuine. His only real moment of anxiety had been at the very first arrivals, Baby and the Bloomers.

To be honest their arrival had nearly scuppered the whole thing. The Bloomers could smell the animals and the latter most certainly could smell the Bloomers; they ran about, hid, screeched and made the most dreadful noise. The cacophony was painful. It was all Baby and her helpers could do to keep the Bloomers in check. Aidonis turned to Una and said, "They ain't going in there, lady. I ain't been keeping this ark of mine for all these goddam years for a bunch of, what the hell are they anyway, critters to come in here and eat 'em all up."

Una took his point and explained, "They are our fighting cats; we will need them in the battles ahead. Is there somewhere we can keep them, please?"

Aidonis thought for a few minutes and said, "The church! You get back outside and I'll get the keys." He returned with the keys and asked Clem if he would help guide the Bloomers into their new sanctuary. Though terrified, Clem did as he was asked.

The castle's church, that had been a late addition to the estate in the nineteenth century, was outside the walls and situated half a mile away within what had become an overgrown wood. Baby took the Bloomers to the church where they were locked inside. They didn't like it, but being well trained animals, they settled in, particularly when they were watered and fed with left over offal from pigs that had been recently butchered. Disaster had been averted.

The Sodsters had gone the long way round so as to avoid those on foot and so by dawn had done a brilliant job in moving people and things to the castle. As the castle grounds reached capacity, it was decided that the Sodsters would be hidden in the woodland that abutted the northern perimeter of the earthworks.

At the very end of the cavalcade Anvil and Serene arrived followed by Lump, Ronnie and Maggie.

Anvil dismounted, walked up to Aidonis and said, "Aidonis F Carter! Man, what a gas!" as they shook hands.

Serene said, "We are fans."

"Fans?" Aidonis enquired.

"Once a fan always a fan," she replied.

"We saw you for the last time in Leeds on the Hill. Do you remember?" Anvil asked.

"I remember the Hill man, it was awesome, but I don't remember you," he laughed.

"There were forty two thousand other folks that night," Serene laughed back.

"It's real good to see ya; you'll be welcome here."

It was then that he noticed Lump and the cats. "Sorry, young fella. They can't come in here: the animals, you know."

Lump hadn't heard a word. He stared open mouthed at creatures he had never seen before. "What's them things?" he asked pointing at the pigs.

"They're animals, boy; they won't hurt you none," Aidonis said. "But it's not safe to bring your beasts in here right now."

"They ain't beasts, they're Bloomers; this one's Maggie and this one's Ronnie," Lump replied.

At that point Aidonis started to giggle, then he laughed and finally gasped, "Jesus! Someone's got a sense of humour."

"Mr Anvil, that's 'im there, he gave them their names," Lump replied. "What's so funny?"

"Are they safe?" Aidonis asked Anvil.

"They're safe; they won't leave Lump's side," Anvil replied.

"Okay," Aidonis said, "but any trouble and they're out, okay?"

"Yes sir," Lump replied.

"Maggie and Ronnie! Well, hell, if they ain't the best names for them funny looking things," Aidonis laughed.

Lump looked cross.

"It's okay, Lump. Aidonis here knows what the originals were like, that's all; he means no harm," Serene said.

Roque had taken some time to arrive as he had been attempting to disguise their trail in case anyone should follow them. When he eventually arrived Una gave him a big friendly hug and then took him to be introduced to their host. The two men, generations apart, got on like a house on fire. Clem retired to his quarters, feeling that it was worse than he had expected.

It took them the best part of the day to organise who and what was going where. Aidonis could not have been a better host; he opened the entire castle, even those rooms where the stars shone through the broken roofs.

As the day drew to a close Roque decided to explore and found himself in the room that contained the guitars. He stood and looked, trying to imagine what all these things did. He moved forward and ran his fingers across the strings of a particularly nice 'Fender'.

"It's out of tune," Aidonis said.

Roque turned to find that the musician had been watching

him, "I'm sorry," he said.

"Not a problem. You play?"

"Me? No, no-one plays."

"You guys don't listen to music?" Aidonis asked.

"I heard a squeeze box once with the Morris Dancers. Was that music?"

"Yeah, that's music, but it ain't my sort of music."

"The old people sometimes hum things."

"Doesn't anyone sing?" Aidonis asked looking even more depressed and perplexed.

"Not that I've heard," Roque replied.

"I want you to help me do something, Roque. Can you come back here in a couple of hours?"

"Sure," Roque replied as he walked off, Una on his mind.

He found her as she went from person to person, family to family, throughout the castle making sure that every Sod, old and young, was comfortable and that they understood that though this seemed idyllic there were harder times to come. It might be argued that this 'reality check' was not a wise management move, but then again Una wasn't a manager. Her people would know all that she knew (well almost) and in that way they would be able to think forward and protect themselves. You probably know better, but it seemed to her that one of the reasons there had been a Big War at all was that the 'people' believed what they were told by their 'leaders', and that the 'facts', or even the various 'truths', were so disguised, embroidered and moulded to the need of the moment that acceptance and acquiescence followed. It was as if there was no realisation of even the possibility of saying, "No, we don't think that's a very good idea: stop now." I know it's not as simple as that, but one has to start somewhere. If those that have gone before us had said no, then we wouldn't be where we are today, would we? Sorry.

I've just thought about that, and I'm not sorry. I realise that as the storyteller I'm supposed to let the events and the characters speak for themselves so that you, the reader, can make your own judgements, but that's tricky. What I'm going on is based on tales and stories told long after the events described here took place. After all I wasn't even born at this point. There are some written records, such as Anvil's diary, but a lot of the information is partial, and possibly partisan; Mum and Dad weren't likely to be objective. What I'm getting at is that the BigWar was unnecessary and only took place to benefit the rulers and their cronies in the weapons industries. I was forgetting about oil; some said it was all about the stuff. What a waste of time, as there's none left, so far as anyone can tell. But I bet someone way back then made a heap of their equivalent of Hamsters. There has been only one real benefit; England might be isolated, be barely self sufficient, be a lousy corrupt and downright oppressive place to live (unless you have property) but at least it's free from the 'benign' supervision of what used to be the United States of America.

"Una?" Roque asked, "can we talk?"

"Of course we can talk. Why do you look so serious?"

"I need to tell you something."

"Is it serious?"

"It's important to me," he replied.

"Then it's important to me. Where shall we go?"

"Outside the walls. We could check that the Sodsters are well hidden."

They walked out of the castle past the guards to where the Sodsters rested. They found them almost buried beneath shrub and fallen branches from the un-coppiced wood. "I'm not happy with this," Roque said, "if we needed to we'd never get them out of here in a hurry."

"Roque?"

"I'll get these better set up in the morning. What do you think?"

"I think we didn't come out here, nice as it is, to talk about your wonderful Sodsters."

"No, we didn't."

Spying the fallen trunk of a beech, Una said, "Why don't we sit down and then you can tell me what it is."

They sat together in silence listening to the birds in the trees and the wind in the leaves.

"It's beautiful here," Una said.

Roque cleared his throat and began, "Hear me out. When I escaped from the prison and you found me wandering, stealing, living as I could, I was lost. You took me in; the Sods cared for me, and gave me shelter. You explained the world in ways I'd never thought of before. I learnt and grew strong again."

"To become the fine warrior you are," Una interrupted.

"I idolised you; you were Una Uevera, our leader, and I had so much to learn and do. And then that day, that seems so long ago now, do you remember when you rubbed that evil smelling stuff that Anvil made into my shoulders?"

"I remember."

"It was then I wanted you, and I wondered, oh how I wondered, if you wanted me."

"Couldn't you tell?"

"Well, then I thought that's just lust, and so I thought better of it. You didn't need to be bothered with all that. And then funny things started to happen. I became jealous when you listened to others. I knew they had good ideas, better than mine. I felt so foolish. That kidnapping of the Bishop was stupid, pointless, but I wanted to prove that I was worthy."

"Worthy?"

"Yes," he paused, "worthy of your love. I love you, Una. There I've said it."

She moved close to him and took his great dark face in her hands and kissed him full upon the lips. They embraced.

Lifting her lips from his she said, "Love isn't about being worthy, my love; it's about love, that's all."

They kissed again and then sat for a moment until Una said, "Be clear: never ever misunderstand again, no matter what. I love you and I always will."

They embraced and kissed once more but quickly disengaged at the sound of feet running toward them through the undergrowth. It was Lump with Ronnie and Maggie on their leads.

"Comrades, it's Mister Aidonis! He's getting everyone into the big hall," Lump shouted. "I don't know what he's up to."

"I was supposed to help," Roque observed.

"You had better things to do. What's our rock star up to?" Una asked with a warm smile.

"I don't know for sure, but we'll find out soon enough."

Hand in hand they followed Lump back over the draw-bridge and into the castle.

Jock had revised his plan to send the CISTS to all angles of the compass in the light of discussions with Green about the pigeon messages from the north and the pattern of Sedanista actions over the last year. Three hundred had been sent due north; three hundred northeast, and the remaining four hundred would defend the capital, the monarch and the government (with a particular emphasis upon the latter).

Jock's superficial knowledge of the procedures of the Roman army had led him to conclude that if Roman Legionnaires could manage forty miles a day on a forced march then his CISTS could manage at least fifty. After all, it was over two thousand years later and the human body had evolved to a higher and more superior form. (You can make your own judgement about that.) He had thus calculated that at least one unit of CISTS could reach Lindum within five days; six if the weather was bad and there were leaves on the broken roads.

At first the six hundred going north had run as one. As they passed up what had once been the A1(M) they carried all before them; Sedanathons and Nikons pulled out of the way as the CISTS rushed past, their diaphanous white skirts billowing around them. The first part of their journey proved uneventful except for an unfortunate incident at the Watford Gap service station. They had run in off the hard shoulder in search of food and water (as a mobile unit they had no quartermaster and thus had to provision themselves en route) and just managed to hit a Legit transfer period and feeding moment. Pushing the Legits, Legiturions and Swabs aside they had rapidly consumed all the provisions allocated for the already starving Legits. It didn't go down well and the Legits became uncontrollable due to the anger of the Legiturions and Swabs; after all, their jobs would be impossible with angry, blood sugar awry, Legits. A brawl developed but soon ended when a Cisturion called a retreat. The Legits stood and cheered; they had won. As the first wave of CISTS withdrew a further wave loaded their blowpipes. At the command they blew and the poisoned darts flew straight and true into the standing Legits. Over one hundred fell injured and about to die, and, whilst the remainder made for the cover of the dormitories, a CIST dart collector gathered darts from the fallen bodies. One thing had been certain; word of the new danger would spread and fear would precede the CISTS wherever they went.

So it was that they made their way north. Once off the old motorway they passed through towns and villages. They bivouacked where they chose; they took what they liked; they left the people bare of their hard won necessities, and exemplified the values of a new emerging state. Worst of all, they sought to gather intelligence. In itself a reasonable enough motive given their circumstances, it was their methods that caused fear and alarm. They had the power, and the right, (or so the Cisturions asserted and who was going to argue?) to interrogate anyone whom they thought might know anything about the Sedanistas and their leader. Hardly any did, and needlessly died under 'investigation.'

That night the six hundred slept at Peterborough; they were making good time.

It had been tight fit but all the Sods had managed to squeeze into the castle's great hall. Most of the roof had collapsed years earlier but the end under which a makeshift stage had been constructed was still covered by its original wooden beams and slates. As Una and Roque, followed by Lump and the Bloomers squeezed into the back, Wesley had already begun his introduction.

"Sedanistas, Sods!" he shouted.

The crowd roared and clapped. He held up his hand to quieten them.

"Sods, dear Sods, we have done many things, and we have suffered many hardships; we have seen new ways of living and, we are the new way for England. We have come here to this castle on our journey to victory. Tonight, something very special is going to happen, something we have never seen or been part of before, all except Mr Anvil and Miss Serene, of course: a concert, a rock concert. A celebration of our struggle, a night of pleasure in the war against the evil state."

The crowd roared.

"I've been told not to take too long. So listen up, comrades. Tonight we will hear music, live music, from two great musicians, men from before the Big War. First we have a man who is reputed to be the greatest bass player still alive, a man who in his prime laid down the beat that drove the great Aidonis F Carter Band, the enigma: Clem Atkins!"

Clem emerged onto the stage to the acclaim of the Sods, acknowledged their support, and sat, unsmiling, upon a stool at the rear of the stage.

"And now!" Wesley continued, "A man who has stood up for freedom, and expressed it through his music. I give you the great, the exciting, the extraordinary, the greatest musician alive in England, the man who has sold twenty five millions albums, whatever they are: the completely unplugged Aidonis F Carter!"

The crowd cheered as Aidonis walked onto stage, bowed to his audience, and sat on the stool at the front surrounded by many acoustic guitars. His feet were bare. He was dressed in blue jeans, a white floppy shirt and a black waistcoat. The crowd sighed in awe, as they had never seen such fine clothes. His long locks were held back in a ponytail.

"Sods!" he shouted, "Welcome to the castle, welcome. Tonight I'm gonna sing you some songs that I ain't sung to an audience since before the Big Fucking Totally Fucking Useless Fucking War!"

The Sods cheered and clapped. Una squeezed Roque's hand and he squeezed back. Lump had climbed up onto a ruined wall and he sat there open mouthed with Maggie and Ronnie at each side. He suddenly realised that they were totally silent, and that had never happened before.

"Okay, here we go!" Aidonis shouted and the crowd gradually quietened.

"The lyrics, the words for this, are based upon a poem written by a guy called Thomas Hood, hundreds of years back, it's called 'The Song of the Shirt'."

In his version of Ernest Jones' 'The Song of the Low', he even managed to get the Sods to join in the chorus.

> We're low we're low we're very low,
> As low as low can be;
> The rich are high
> We make them so
> A miserable lot are we!
> We're low, we're low
> Our place we know,
> But not too low,
> To kill the foe, to kill the foe,
> We're free, we're free, we're free!

Aidonis continued through his repertoire for a further three hours. As he walked off stage with Clem, the Sods cheered and stood and cheered and cheered and cheered. When he didn't immediately return, they began to sigh and give up. At that moment Anvil and Serene climbed up onto the stage and with their encouragement the uproar began again.

Aidonis and Clem returned to the stage and devoted the entire encore to Paul Éluard's 'Liberty'. The last two of the twenty-one stanzas he sang were,

> On health returned
> On the risk disappeared
> On hope without memory
> I write your name
>
> And the power of a word
> I start my life again
> I was born to know you
> To name you
> Liberty.

The beauty of his playing and the mystery of the words made them all silent, rapt, held and moved by the singer's broken baritone passion. As the last note faded he looked down at their faces and smiled. There was total silence. Then the Sods broke into the chant they had so recently been taught by Anvil and Serene.

"More! More! More!" and so it went until he raised his hand and said, "OK guys, just one more for the road. I wish I'd written this, but I didn't, and there ain't a word to touch or alter; it's from the greatest of them all, Bob Dylan: 'The times they are a-changing'."

They, of course, had never heard of Bob Dylan, but then again they knew their times were surely changing. Una looked at Anvil; they smiled. He had used the very same words as part of his message to Ham.

Aidonis asked Una, Roque, Marx, Serene and Anvil back to his own rooms after his concert and they sat and talked of the music of that night and what it meant. Clem was with them but he seemed withdrawn and exhausted by his playing.

"You guys are real nice, thanks," Aidonis said as he finally called a halt to their stream of compliments.

"Do you know how important this was?" Una asked. "Well, let me tell you. These people have had faith that we could overturn this world of servitude. But it was only faith, what would lie beyond? They had no concept of that because it was all just a promise that things would be better. But to do what? You showed them beauty and passion; you gave them music. Now they know that at the end of all this are things that are good, fun, and full of feeling and happiness, not just a lingering sadness."

"Thank you," Aidonis replied.

"Thank you!" Anvil and Serene said as one.

"Am I still okay then?" Aidonis asked.

"Better than ever, man!" Anvil replied, offering his hand for a 'high-five to which Aidonis responded; they completed a '3-stage high'.

68

After downing a modest breakfast at the College Arms, Gilt went to find his two Legits. He wanted to be on his way to Navenby as soon as possible. On entering the outhouse he found them to be in disrepair; one was throwing up and the other appeared to have severe stomach pains.

"What the hell's the matter with you two?" Gilt asked.

They groaned in response.

"What's your name?" he asked the one who was holding his stomach, which was making the most extraordinary gurgling sounds.

"Lance," he replied, and then rapidly rising to his feet, added in a panic stricken croak, "Oh Christ I need a shit!"

"Outside!" Gilt shouted as Lance seemed to be about to evacuate his bowels exactly where he stood.

Lance rushed through the door as Gilt asked, "And you?"

"Wot," he replied, as he wiped his mouth and chin with the hem of his ragged sack shirt.

"No, I asked the question; what are you called?"

"That's it, Wot, w, o. . ."

As he was about to complete the spelling of his name they heard the disturbing and dramatic noises of Lance's explosively liquid crap, immediately followed by a smell that could have been used as war gas. Wot immediately threw up, whilst Gilt covered his mouth and nose with his hand as he made a speedy exit. Outside, Lance was preparing for his innards to burst forth once more. As Gilt hurriedly moved away, he heard that the preparations had been completed.

By the time Gilt found the Landlord, he had lost any sense of good will toward the human race.

"What did you feed my Legits last night?" Gilt asked.

"We had some leftovers from the last few days."

"Leftovers?" Gilt asked, trying to repress the desire to crush the man to pulp.

"They seemed happy enough with it; never had food like

that before, they said."

"Listen, let's get a couple of things straight shall we? I paid you for their food, for decent food, not leftovers."

"They're only bloody Legits, int they?"

"You're a moron, do you know that? They do not need to be well fed, but they do need to be properly fed, otherwise how the hell are they to work?"

"I've never fed Legits before," the Landlord replied, by way of excuse.

"I'm in a hurry and they can't move; one's throwing up everywhere and the other is attempting to pass his entire insides."

"I hope they're not making a mess of my outhouse," the Landlord observed, seemingly unaware of the gravity of his situation.

"By now I would expect it to be at least three feet deep in faeces of a liquidness never before produced by a human being. So where can I find replacement Legits?" Gilt asked.

"There's none here; those that are belong to someone and are in use."

"So there's no Sedantory or Legit fitting station?"

"No. Like I said, I hope they're not making a mess in my outhouse."

It was too much for Gilt.

If you put your thumb inside your mouth between your top teeth and the inside of your lip you'll find this sort of stiff membrane that links the top inside of the lip to the gum. Got it? Right, now place your first and second fingers on the outside of the lip, and press, not too hard, this is merely a demonstration. Hurts doesn't it? Imagine how it would feel if the hand that executed the act was filled with power and anger. That is what Gilt did.

He led the squeaking Landlord by his upper lip to the outhouse where the condition of Lance and Wot seemed to be getting worse.

"Now I'm going to tell you what you're going to do. You're going to give me my money back; you're going to put Lance and Wot in one of your two bedrooms, and you are going to find a herbalist who can fix them up. One more thing: you had better pray to whatever or whoever you pray to that they make a rapid recovery, or you, my Hamster pinching bastard, are in real trouble," he advised, and giving one last even more powerful squeeze, asked, "Got it?"

The tears rolled down the Landlord's face as he nodded his complete and utter agreement.

"Then get on with it!" Gilt instructed. "You two," he said to Lance and Wot, "don't try any lead swinging, I want you better and on the road. Understand!"

They nodded in grateful assent. Gilt would have been surprised at the developing feelings of loyalty to Orb that were forming in Lance and Wot's preoccupied minds.

It took nearly thirty-six hours for the two Legits to be in a condition to carry Gilt to his destination at Navenby.

69

The CISTS had continued their relentless forced march north. It was late in the afternoon when they had reached Lindum, Cathedral City, and home to a thriving community of clerics and elderly retired academics from the once thriving university. Though an administrative centre, it had no discernible government beyond that provided by the Bishop, the Dean and Chapter. In the absence of Hamondi no one was very clear who was in charge, not that it was terribly clear even when he was. The church seemed to be like that, and certainly the academics preferred it that way; someone had once said that managing academics was like herding cats (obviously being ignorant of the Bloomers).

Through the millennia Lindum had always been a settlement of two parts, 'uphill' and 'downhill'. Uphill was, unsurprisingly, on the top of the high escarpment whereas downhill was on the flat plain beneath. Fairly obviously, the Cathedral and its population of the propertied class was high and the underclass were low. Those that lived on the hill were largely ignorant of the lives of those who lived beneath them, whereas those who lived below had a clear knowledge of the behaviours of their betters. This was to be expected as they performed the essential functions of carrying, cleaning and labouring to keep the propertied as comfortable as was possible. Those on high would have been surprised to know that those below were not entirely happy with their lot. In fact, they were really pissed off, not only with having to climb a bloody great hill to work each day, but also with the drudgery of their daily lives. But there was no spark to lead them; what protests there were, and to be honest they were few and far between, consisted in trivial acts of vandalism. Some were more amusing than others: dropping a dead rat into the hogshead of ale in the Wig and Mitre certainly got to one or two digestive tracts before the addition was noticed but was a bit sad really; whereas the secretion of dead flea ridden hedgehogs into the vestry was both elegant and compellingly funny. It was obligatory, albeit not a legal requirement, that the propertied class attended communion on a Sunday morning (more than once was regarded as eccentric). Once the fleas had moved from the vestments to the clerics, there was but a short journey to the communicants. Soon there had been a flea epidemic uphill.

The first passage of this prank must have been amusing, seeing the clerics and the rest frantically scratching and smacking themselves to try and kill the little beasts. But it was inevitable that the fleas would also transfer to the underclass. Lindum became flea ridden and for the first time in its history it was as one; a great collective itch. It is said that this only came to an end after a particularly bitter winter but the preceding summer and autumn had been unendurable despite the establishment of a flea killing task force that sought out and killed fleas and searched for the eggs of the next generation. This process of extermination was difficult amongst the propertied but impossible within the underclass. This had been realised early on during the epidemic and thus flea 'road checks' had been established; no member of the underclass was allowed to enter the uphill enclave until they had been searched, cleansed, and had been issued with special work clothes into which they changed on entry and returned at the end of an extended day of labour. Their costumes had been fabricated from what was probably the largest store of cassocks in England (Lindum had once been the national centre for cassock manufacture). It was felt necessary that clear identification of those that were clean was made, and thus the Cathedral's embroiders had been required to sew the initials 'WWF' (worker without fleas) upon the back of every cassock whereas clerics wore the initials 'CWF'.

This time was long past when the CISTS arrived that afternoon. They had passed along the long and derelict High Street (that started downhill), past the rows of terraced houses where the underclass 'lived', on up past Stonebow, up Steep Hill until they reached the square; on their left stood the castle and to their right the Cathedral. They were greeted by the Dean, the Sub-Dean, Viscount Horl (pronounced 'all') of Spital in the Street (it still exists), the Precentor, the choristers, sundry clerics and uphill residents that were not a little concerned at the ingress of low life (albeit in the employ of the English State).

As the weary CISTS halted, the choir, on the direction of the Precentor, the Reverend Barabus Defnute, broke into song with a heart-felt rendition of 'For those in Peril on the Sea' (no one knew why). When this had finished the Dean welcomed the troops as he was handed Ham's Royal Warrant and a letter from the Prime Minister. The gist of these documents was that the CISTS were to be quartered within the castle and that all possible support should be given to the 'defenders of the state'. Viscount Horl, the Keeper of the Keys (to the Castle), was not all pleased at the prospect of five hundred starving and unruly men invading his well-kept historic pile. There was, of course, no choice in the matter and he went about the task of requisitioning supplies from wherever he could find them. A course of action that confirmed that these men were in reality an occupying force.

The Cisturions immediately placed guards at all entry points to the uphill City. No one would now come or go without scrutiny and interrogation. In the old days one presumes that a 'State of Emergency' would have been formally declared but not then. Presumably if the government thought there was one they did what they saw fit and that was the end of it; no questions asked or replies received.

The Dean and Sub Dean sought to gain clarity from the Cisturions as to the nature and purpose of their mission. "Is it to do with the kidnapping of the Bishop?" they asked. This was pointless as the Cisturions had never heard of the Bishop, and all they would say was that they were "acting under orders" and that they could ask the Legates when they arrived in a few days time (Sedans were slower than CISTS). By the time night fell the CISTS were comfortably bedded down whilst the good people of uphill were shitting themselves.

70

The morning after Aidonis' concert began slowly. The Sods were not used to staying up late; their pattern was 'early to bed, early to rise', so to have stayed up until the early hours, clapping, laughing and having fun had meant weary heads. As the morning finally got under way, it became clear that something had changed. Sods, excellent citizens though they were, had not previously possessed a cheery ethos; in fact most of the time they walked round with hunched shoulders and with frowns upon their faces. The struggle 'against the odds' was a serious business, and most certainly not fun. The bicycles had cheered them enormously and the laughter of learner bike riders had been joyous and an inspiration to all concerned. But this morning they displayed not temporary pleasure but something more enduring. They walked just that little bit straighter, taller even, and there was more zest in their steps as they moved through the cycle of their chores and between the many animals in the courtyards. They didn't have broad grins upon their faces, which would have been somewhat worrying, but more a sense of deep-seated pleasure. I have been told that they looked 'confident' in a quiet and certain way. Una had made sure that none were under any illusions about what they faced, but instead of looking downright miserable about it, they now looked like people who believed in themselves.

It is no doubt foolish to believe that a concert could have acted as such a catalyst, but sometimes something simple and beautiful can break the mould of expectation and open new perspectives for the self, particularly if that experience is collectively shared. It is hard to realise that these people had no experience of art in any of its forms; the war and the State had reduced the human spirit to the functional, what needed to be done to survive, what needed to be done to control, what needed to be done to endure, what needed to be done to escape the tyranny of the equality of oppression. Aidonis had opened a door that could lead to another condition; freedom of course, but to more than freedom. Perhaps they saw the potential for celebration through music, the celebration of themselves, and perhaps they even saw that just by singing along they were somehow different, their lives enhanced. Whatever the explanation, they looked different, as Una, Aidonis, Marx, Anvil and Serene, stood upon the battlements and watched the Sods below. Clem slept in.

Outside Lump made his way toward the church where his Bloomers were kennelled. As he entered the porch with Maggie and Ronnie in tow he found Baby asleep on one of the wooden benches that sat each side of the porch. From inside the church came the low rumbling growl of hungry cats. Lump turned to the three young Sods who had come with him and asked if they would put down their panniers of offal, bones and discarded meat by the door. As they departed he tried to wake Baby, but she was deeply asleep and not for waking. Lump watched her as her eyes began to move beneath their lids; she was dreaming. He suddenly found himself thinking what she must have been like when she was young; he imagined that she had been really beautiful before the Tiger got her. He blushed; he suddenly saw her as a young woman and he was kissing her. Though no one knew it, and he was not sure, he suddenly became a young man and not a child, albeit one who could train savage animals. As he was

187

dealing with this revelation Baby began to sing in her sleep.

"Nelly the elephant packed her trunk and ran away to the circus, trumpetty trump, trumpetty trump, trump, trump, trump, and all the king's horses and all the king's men couldn't put Nelly together again in the sky with diamonds, diamonds in the soles of her feet and they called it puppy love, oh they called it puppy love, never a tear must fall," she sang.

"Baby, are you okay," Lump quietly asked.

Baby stopped singing and opened her eyes, "Hey Lump! How's ya doin?" she said rather blearily.

"What's an elephant?" Lump asked.

As Baby began her explanation, Una, Roque and several Sods started the task of re-positioning the Sodsters. There was no logical reason why Una needed to have joined Roque in this enterprise, but then again logic isn't everything.

Roque's initial purpose was to ensure that: a) the Sodsters were well hidden; b) that they could be released into action within moments. Though these were perfectly reasonable aspirations they were not easily attained in un-coppiced woodland. A Sod was despatched to bring back axes, machetes and hunting knives from the hoard at the castle, which it might be noted now had a considerable armoury due to the Sods' successful liberation of arms from the enemy. After several hours of hard labour the desired result was achieved. Each Sodster was hidden within a cunningly fashioned hide, the front of which was made into one quickly removable 'door'. The land in front of each of these hides was cleared so that a direct track led to the wide green lane at the perimeter of the wood. Each of these tracks was camouflaged with panels that gave a very good impression of a normal woodland floor, and which could be removed in a trice as one ran to the Sodster hide. As the final touches were made to the last of the tracks, the Sods were happy, although sweaty and tired from their exertions, Roque thanked them profusely and sent them on their way.

"We ought to get back to make sure all is well," Una said as the Sods ambled away through the wood.

"Thanks for coming," Roque replied.

"It was fun," Una replied with a smile.

Without a further word Roque took Una's hand and led her back to the nearest Sodster hide. Once inside he closed the door and turned to look at her in the dappled darkness of the leafy space. They embraced; they kissed, at first gently and then with greater passion.

As they at last came up for air Una said, "And?"

"And?" Roque uncertainly replied.

"And what now?" she asked.

"I don't know what to do," Roque replied, giving every impression of a small boy lost in an adult's world.

"Oh Roque, you lovely man, come here."

He did as he was told and was soon enveloped in her arms. "First we take our clothes off and then we make love," she said as she undid the knots in the front of his shirt.

"I haven't done this before," he said as he fumbled with the ties in her shirt.

"I haven't either, not for a very long time," she whispered as she kissed his ear.

Soon they were both naked. "Let me look at you," she said. He stood back, somewhat sheepishly, his hands at his sides, and his penis tall and straight above his deliciously large hairy balls. "Oh yes!" she said as her gentle hands encased his swollen cock.

They lay upon the mossy ground, the Sodster above them, and made love; the only words she spoke were, "Go slow, there's no rush."

But of course there was. Then, after he had quickly recovered from his 'rush', they made slow and joyful love beneath the leaves to the sound of birdsong

When they eventually returned to the castle they found Serene, Anvil and Aidonis in the Keep planning the future. Their conversation focussed on the re-introduction of animal husbandry into the countryside and the problems that this would pose – there being a paucity of meat for the oppressed population. As Una and Roque entered the room, Anvil was in full flight on the benefits of selective breeding, a speech which caused Una a wry smile.

Aidonis was the first to notice them, "Hey, guys, how's ya doin'?" he asked.

Una and Roque held hands as Roque said, "Good, very good thank you." While Una added, "We're fine, thank you."

Serene was soon on her feet and hugging first Una and then Roque who looked very embarrassed.

Anvil looked perplexed and asked, "What's going on?"

Aidonis simply smiled as Una said, "We're, we're. . ."

"An item," Serene completed her sentence, "as we used to say in days long gone by."

"Ah, oh good," Anvil responded now that Serene had made it clear for him. "Will you join us?"

"Thanks, but I need something to eat then I'll come back up," Roque said.

"I'm going to take a shower and then I'll come and find you, if that's okay?" Una replied.

You've not heard the word 'shower' used before in this tale because there weren't any at the train or at Navenby, though the latter had been blessed with bathrooms and cold water taps, but no running water. When Aidonis had shown them round his castle he had been very proud of his shower room. The room was of stone and had a flagstone floor with an ancient wrought iron grating in its centre. It was lighted by what had once been a narrow slit through which arrows could be fired. Rainwater was gathered into a great cistern on the roof that in turn fed the tank above the shower room and the actual shower itself. This latter was a large galvanised drum in the bottom of which many round holes had been drilled; over this a sprung metal flap had been fixed. To this was attached a rope, once pulled, the flap opened and water gushed forth. The downpour lasted nearly three minutes. If you wanted more, then you waited until the drum had been filled from the cistern above. It was all immensely civilised and once Una had taken up the offer to use it she had become a daily devotee of the cold shower (though in summer it was tepid).

She undressed and laid her clothes upon the old chair by the oak door that she didn't bother to lock, and then stood beneath the drum and pulled the rope. As the torrent fell upon her she smiled with pleasure and then jumped in alarm as she felt a hand upon her buttocks.

Before she knew it, Clem was upon her. He was fully dressed but didn't seem to care as he grabbed at her breasts and shouted, "I'm gonna fuck you, lady, come what may!" At which Una punched him full in the mouth, but this only stopped him for a moment as the water gushed down. The floor was slippery and as Una moved away from him she slipped and fell to the floor. Clem was soon upon her, and now he held a knife in one hand that he pressed toward her. She struggled and fought, but the sixty year old was tough and wiry. Very soon he had her pinned down, knife at her neck, and his cock emerging from his jeans.

"I ain't had a fuck in years and you's the lucky one."

"You bastard," Una screamed.

"Yeah, now. . ."

Clem didn't finish his sentence as Roque lifted Clem by his hair from the supine Una. He had planned to join Una in the shower and had entered the room unheard as the two fought on the floor.

"Oh Roque!" Una cried but Roque didn't hear.

He held the thrashing man at arms length out of reach of the frantic swings of his knife. As he lowered Clem to the floor, he smashed the knife from his hand and drove his huge right fist into Clem's exposed genitals; an agonised sigh fell from the man's lips.

"Don't kill him!" Una shouted.

Roque drove a massive blow into the man's nose that shattered under the impact. Clem screamed in agony as blood spurted everywhere while Roque clasped his hands around the man's neck and started to squeeze very hard.

"Don't kill him, Roque, don't kill him! Please!" she said as she stood behind him.

"Why not?" Roque eventually asked as Clem's face became ever more purple.

"I don't know, I just, don't kill him. We must have rules, laws."

"This one's mine," Roque replied.

"He's not worth killing, that's all. He's scum," Una said.

Roque released him and Clem collapsed unconscious upon

the floor. Turning to Una he said, "Are you. . .okay. . .he didn't hurt you?"

"No," she said as he wrapped her in his arms and flung his sackcloth shirt about her shoulders. "Why did you come?"

"I wanted to see you, be with you again," Roque replied.

"I'd like to get dressed."

As she did so Clem began to groan as he returned to consciousness. Roque placed his foot on the injured man's chest and said, "You don't know how lucky you are."

It was hard to tell but Roque thought he heard Clem mumble, "Fuck you, cunt!"

71

The information that Rocket had supplied led Gilt to the gates of Navenby Hall. He instructed his Legits to hide the chair, and themselves, amidst the rhododendrons and to wait until he came for them. "There's food and drink in the pannier; don't eat it all or I'll give you a good licking with my belt," he said in a kindly manner. He then placed his Pardoner's hat upon his head and set out down the drive, Pardoner's stave in his right hand. It was time to get back into role. He had expected to find the place crowded with Sedanistas, so when he rapped on the Hall's front door, he was surprised that it swung open. Cautiously he made his way through the now empty cycle hall toward the noise of someone softly singing. In the kitchen he found Bishop Hamondi sitting at the kitchen table eating leftovers as he sang the words of the fourth Psalm. It was not a good sound: not only did the Bishop have no sense of pitch but his mouth was full of food. His mitre wobbled as he masticated and warbled, causing Gilt to smile; at least he could tell what the man did for a living.

"Good morning, Bishop," he said.

Hamondi stopped singing and swallowed a mouthful before asking, "And who might you be?" with as much confidence as he could muster.

"The Pardoner, Orb," Gilt replied with a slight bow of his head. "Do you think you ought to be eating those leftovers. They don't look too good."

"I'm starving. The bastards have taken everything."

"The Sedanistas?"

"Yes, the Sods have gone."

"Where?" Gilt asked.

"Not a clue, but they shouldn't be hard to find. There were enough of them, and bikes leave tracks."

"So, they do have bikes. Why are you here, Bishop?"

"I'm the Bishop Hamondi, Bishop of Lindum and Primate of the East of England. They kidnapped me, abducted me, brought me here and then dumped me at a deserted tower miles away in the middle of nowhere."

"Do you know why?"

"To show that it could be done. No, I know it doesn't make sense, but they looted the treasury as well."

"What? Chalices and stuff like that?" Gilt asked.

"No, just Hamsters, lots of them."

"Lots?"

"Thousands; my tithe money. I want it back."

"And that's why you're here?" Gilt asked.

"Yes, and it was nearer than Lindum," Hamondi replied. "Why are you here? Why do you want to find them, and more to the point who are you?" he asked.

"Ah well, that's a long story," Gilt replied, wondering if he should tell the Bishop the truth.

"Not trying to sell them your bloody useless pardons?" the Bishop enquired.

Before Gilt could reply a bedraggled figure rushed into the kitchen shouting, "Master! Master! I come to serve!" and with that the Mad Stuffer knelt and kissed Gilt's feet.

The Bishop was clearly alarmed at this sudden intrusion whilst Gilt was not exactly delighted to see the hopefully re-formed cannibal.

"What the hell are you doing here?" Gilt asked.

"I come to serve thee," the man replied.

"You said that. For God's sake, stand up, man. What do you

want?" Gilt asked.

"You set me free, released me, let me go, took me out onto the road, into the wide world."

"I did nothing of the sort," Gilt said.

"That's what you think, but you were destiny, my destiny. I heard the words in my head, follow, follow, serve, change your ways."

"You've followed me all this way?" Gilt asked, unused as he was to having a disciple.

"Your powers as a Pardoner seem to be attractive to this creature," the Bishop said with a sneer.

"I'm not a creature!" the man shouted, "Not a creature! Am a man am I, a free man who's left the old ways behind, a man, not a creature. Got it?" he shouted at the Bishop.

"Steady on. The Bishop's not used to the real world," Gilt said with a slight smile.

"I don't like him," the man said pointing at the Bishop. "I'll cut him," he continued pulling a long knife from his belt, "if you wants me to."

"That won't be necessary. Just sit down," Gilt suggested.

"Can't sit while the master stands," the mad man said.

"Alright," Gilt said. "I'll sit, and you sit over there, go on, over there at the end of the table, that's an order!"

The man did as he was told and laid his knife upon the table. The Bishop looked anxious.

"What's your name?" Gilt asked.

This caused the man to stop and think for a few moments. When he did reply, he said, "Seth, my name is Seth, Seth Barnotby, that's it, that's my name."

"Have you changed your ways, Seth? Are you safe?"

"I ain't eatin' people no more, Master," Seth replied.

At this the Bishop crossed himself, something he hadn't done in years, and said, "Is that true?"

"Yes, I think so," Gilt replied.

"You're not going to let him be your servant, are you?" the Bishop asked.

At which Seth picked up his knife and shouted, "I'll cut you!"

"Seth! Put down that knife at once. If you are to be my servant you will do exactly as I say. Understood?" Gilt asked.

"Yes, master," Seth replied.

"Did you come in through the main gates?" Gilt asked.

"Yes, master."

"Did you see my sedan and the my two Legits?"

"No, master."

"Go and find them, ask them to bring the sedan to me here, and you are not to harm them. They serve me, understood?"

"Yes, master."

"Be on your way."

Seth rose, removed his deer-stalker hat, touched his forelock, and left the room.

"You must be mad. He's dangerous," the Bishop observed.

"Yes, he is, but for some reason the poor demented fool thinks I've saved him, so I reckon I'm safe."

"I wouldn't be so sure," the Bishop warned.

"If he steps out of line, I shall kill him," Gilt calmly replied.

"Strong words from a Pardoner."

At this point Gilt made up his mind to explain the nature of his mission to Hamondi.

At first the Bishop was not inclined to believe his story but the signed warrant from the Prime Minister did the trick. Gilt's suggestion that Hamondi should use his Sedan to return to Lindum confirmed that Gilt could be trusted. All that was required of the Bishop was that he seek help and send a pigeon to say that Gilt had found the Sedanistas, which he was sure he was about to do. Gilt also promised that he would retrieve the Bishop's Hamsters as part of the deal. Of course, he had no intention of doing this but that didn't matter so long as Hamondi believed him. Neither he nor the Bishop realised that the CISTS were already in Lindum and waiting for instructions as to what to do next. Had Gilt known this he probably would have bided his time. As it was, he felt that he must carry through his plan to impersonate Orb and find his long lost daughter, Una.

Within fifteen minutes Seth returned with the two Legits and the chair. They then set about removing all of Orb's paraphernalia and Rocket's bike from the chair that they stored in the now empty pantry. This task completed, Gilt instructed his two Legits to take the Bishop back to Lindum and to follow his instructions until Gilt saw them again.

As he waved them off, Seth asked, "Can I have something to eat master?"

As Seth bolted down his food, Gilt explained what they were going to do when night fell.

72

A pigeon had landed in the loft on top of Downing Street bearing the glad tidings that the CISTS had arrived in Lindum and so Green was a relatively happy man as he read the tiny message. His mood changed as Bekkes stormed into his study.

"Okay, you two timing cheating bastard, what's going on?" she demanded.

"Betty, whatever's the matter?"

"You're cheating on me, that's what's the matter!"

"We're both cheating, Betty," Green suggested.

"That's different, cheating husbands and wives; everyone expects that," she replied.

"So what's the problem?" he asked, wondering what she knew.

"You're screwing someone else."

"Why don't you sit down?"

"Why would I want to do that?"

"To take the weight of those beautiful buttocks of yours," he wheedled.

"Something of an expert so I hear," she said as she sat opposite him.

"Come on, Betty love, nothing'll get in the way of us and our cigars."

"So it's true?"

"It's something that I'm doing for the sake of the nation," he pompously announced. "It's not something I want to do, but something that needs to be done."

At this Bekkes burst into a fit of laughter.

"Don't laugh. It's true," Green asserted.

This made her laugh even more. Finally she said, "This has to be the first time that the Prime Minister of England has claimed that he's shagging some tart for the benefit of the nation and not for the benefit of his cock."

"She's not a tart," Green responded.

"So who is she?"

"I can't tell you."

Her amusement disappeared as she said, "John, you're not in a very strong position here. Mabel could be a very unhappy Mrs Green."

"She's always unhappy," Green replied.

"No, I mean, very unhappy."

"You wouldn't?"

"I would."

"But then your husband would know."

"Why would I care? He's bloody useless, and I'm not the PM," she pointed out with some force.

"I assure you," he began.

"John," she interrupted, "your assurances have never been worth the paper they were hardly ever written upon. Who's the slag?"

"How did you find out?" he asked.

"Your first secretary has been trying to chat me up for months, poor little soul. I led him on and he was very forthcoming," she replied.

"You haven't?"

"No, of course not, but he thinks I will. So, who is she?"

"This is an important state secret."

"For god's sake, John, get real," she admonished.

"No, really, you must promise not to tell anyone, anyone at all," Green pleaded.

"Her name."

"Camellia."

"Camellia who?"

"Camellia Bic Croquet Ham," Green quietly replied.

For the first time in his experience, Bekkes was lost for words. She simply stared and then after a few moments asked, "And the purpose of this, apart from the fact that you are old enough to be her father?"

It was clearly the case that to become Prime Minister one needed a range of personal and intellectual attributes. The common view was that John Green had these in abundance. He was: a consummate and convincing liar; a skilled moulder and manipulator of others to his own ends; driven by the lust for perpetual power; aware that his colleagues in government were all (perhaps apart from Bekkes) potential enemies; capable of absolute ruthlessness in fulfilling his personal (and party) ambitions; unable to resist the compulsion to philander; and considerably impressed with his own capabilities.

Nevertheless Bekkes was astounded by the boldness of his plan to become the absolute and unfettered ruler of England through the 'eradication' of Ham and the subjugation of the monarchy to his will before its final and ultimate dissolution.

73

Green and Camellia decided that their plans could only be successfully achieved if she returned to Hampton Court and ostensibly resumed her role as royal consort and principal beneficiary of Ham's considerable and imaginative lust.

Ham welcomed her return as it reduced the necessity for Fornicon 'take-aways' and the hassle of finding willing pliable sexual partners. Whiskerbot was quite a different matter. It wasn't that he suspected that Camellia might be up to no good: he assumed that she was too stupid (coming from an ancient rural aristocratic family) for anything other than a meaningless royal role, but rather that she got in his way. This condition of 'getting in the way' was not about cluttering up the Court but was about the extent to which she undermined his special status and relationship with the Monarch, which had, of course been built over many years of fastidious fawning, procuring and the corrupting of the innocent.

The conspirators understood from the start that if Ham was

to be removed during the course of a Sedanista revolt then Whiskerbot needed to either be brought on board or permantly disposed of. For reasons that remain obscure, Camellia decided that the option of winning him to the cause should be tried first, and it was to this end that she sought him out. As a child, which in her case had not been long ago, she had found that tears worked a treat in getting her own way; even the nuns at the convent had invariably fallen for this rather obvious trick.

Whiskerbot was a creature of habit and it was his custom and pleasure to spend the late morning of a Tuesday in the royal regalia closet polishing the extensive collection of 'Prince Albert' rings that Ham was not currently wearing on, in, through and around the royal member. You and I might find the prospect of such activity somewhat distasteful; Whiskerbot did not. After all, the Monarch could not be expected to maintain the antique collection; all Ham wanted to do was to ask for the velvet lined oak box and choose a ring for that day and know that it had been cleaned and polished and was ready for wear. Whiskerbot saw such personal service as an essential part of his role, though he had drawn the line at attaching the chosen piece of jewellery to Ham's penis.

Camellia composed herself so that when she opened the closet door, tears were streaming down her face. Whiskerbot was more than surprised to see her, "Your Majesty, what is the matter?" he asked without the slightest degree of compassion.

"It's me," she whimpered as she sat down next to him at the polishing table.

"You, your majesty?"

"I've no one to talk to, to confide in," she blubbered.

"You can talk to me," he offered, wondering what he was going to discover from this Royal, but physically attractive, dunderhead.

"You wouldn't understand," she replied.

"I could try," he said in an uncommonly friendly tone.

She stared at him with big wet eyes and eventually said, "Would you?"

"Of course, your majesty."

"It would be easier if you called me Camellia."

"Then Camellia it shall be. What is it?"

"It's me," she said once more.

"Yes?"

"Ham's so demanding. You won't tell the Majesty, will you?"

"It shall be our little secret," he lied as he replaced one of the Alberts in the box.

"Well," she said feigning modesty, "well, Ham uh, since I came back the Majesty wants to have sex all the time."

"I've noticed, but that's normal."

"It's not normal."

"What isn't?" he asked.

"Up my arse; it hurts."

"Always had a liking for buggery."

"How do you know?" she asked.

Whiskerbot raised an eyebrow and offered what he presumed was an enigmatic smile.

"You, you and Ham?" she enquired.

Whiskerbot couldn't resist the temptation to tell the truth and said, "Yes, there was a time when I was privileged to service the majesty's needs."

"What properly?" she said wide-eyed.

"Properly is a strange word in this context. I gave the majesty pleasure up the royal vagina and up the royal arse if that's what you mean, Camellia."

"Good lord," she said.

"And from time to time the majesty felt the need to have the pleasures of my anus, and, yes, it does hurt at first, but you get used to it."

"Did that happen often?" she asked.

"Which one?"

"All of them, I suppose," she said.

"Until you came on the scene, fairly often. Now the majesty seems to prefer younger fresher flesh," he said wishing that he hadn't put it that way.

"Is that why you don't like me?" she asked.

"Who said I don't like you?"

"It's obvious; you're jealous."

At this he laughed and said, "I don't think so. The Majesty's promiscuity is legendary. I got used to being cast aside for a new toy."

"What do you do for um, you know, now?" she asked.

"I'm an older man, getting older by the day. I have abstained of late."

"But I bet you can still get it up."

"When opportunity presents itself, yes."

"Would you. . ." she began to say as Whiskerbot clasped his hand over his mouth. She wondered why he was choking but soon discovered that it was with laughter, wild hysterical, uncontrolled guffaws.

"Why are you laughing," she frostily enquired.

She glared as he took several minutes to calm himself. When he spoke it was with quiet dislike. "You, my dear, are quite the most ridiculous slut I have ever met, so unscrupulous as to make our dearly loved prime minister appear positively saintly, so impressed with your sexual attraction that you think you could break the loyalty between a monarch and servant, so banal in your pathetic political games that I doubt if you could recognise the difference between black and white. In fact, you are a cretin."

She said nothing in reply, but concluded that this was one advisor too many, and if he was not be an ally then he would without question be an enemy who should be disposed of as soon as possible.

74

It had been a hard decision for Aidonis as Clem had been his friend, indeed, his only companion, for so many years, but he felt that he had no choice in the matter. Clem was banished forever from the castle and from the protection of the Sods. Once the sentence had been agreed, it was immediately enforced and Clem found himself wandering through the dark woods, still in great pain from the beating that Roque had delivered, with his old twelve string steel guitar slung across his back atop a backpack that had once travelled the dusty tracks of Nepal.

Gilt and Seth meanwhile had left Navenby Hall as soon as darkness fell and, as they made their way down the lane that led to the castle, they saw Clem's lighted oil lamp glowing in the blackness that surrounded them. Gilt signalled that Seth should be silent and so they waited amidst the thicket as the wobbling light approached them.

The light stopped and Gilt strained to hear the noise that the unseen person was making. After a few moments, he concluded that it was a man whimpering. Clem almost dropped the lamp when Gilt called through the darkness, "What ails thee, friend?" Before he could reply, Gilt and Seth were upon him. He cowered and moaned, "Not more fucking Sods. Please god, no more Sods."

"You'd best come with us," Gilt said as he and Seth lifted Clem from the ground where he had collapsed. So it was that they helped him back to the Hall. Seth was instructed to bring cold water and whatever cloths he could find; with these Gilt proceeded to gently bathe the aspirant rapist's wounds. There was nothing much he could do about the broken nose, but a cold poultice was nevertheless applied. Therafter Clem was fed, though he had trouble chewing with his bloodied and broken teeth and gums. Gilt could only admire the damage that had been done to produce this wreck of a man; he couldn't have done a much better job himself.

After an hour the healing process and the benefits of the food began to take effect and soon Clem relaxed and felt the need to vent his considerable anger and sense of injustice at his treatment. Gilt's sympathetic ear soon provided him with the sort of 'intelligence' that only an insider could supply.

Forward planning was an attribute that had been developed during the period of Gilt's training as a secret agent. This had complemented the skills that he had acquired on his honours degree course in cartography at Cambridge (he got a third [just], as the delineation and description of the female anatomy was considerably more attractive than the construction of the correct cross section of the Hindu Kush, let alone the correct representation of the differences between the actual topography of Gloucester as compared with its illustration within a little known fragment of the Mappa Mundi). Seth found parchment and a box of Bic pens (yes, really) that had been left behind in the museum's shop and with these tools Gilt encouraged Clem to supply the information that enabled him to draw a detailed and comprehensive map of the castle and its immediate hinterland. Gilt referred to this as doing a 'Buchan'; in other words learning the exact topography of the battlefield in which the adventure would unfold.

Once he had completed his maps he instructed Seth to trace his work so that the expected support would understand the lie of the land. Whilst this process was underway Gilt adjourned to bed. Seth did not appear to suffer from any form of tiredness such was his desire to please his self-appointed 'master'. Clem helped with the tracing, as the lack of any sort of painkiller made sleep impossible.

As Gilt prepared for sleep he was a happy man, knowing that death, mayhem, injustice and adventure lay ahead.

The morning after Clem's attempted rape of Una was difficult; it had caused a great deal of anger amongst the Sods whilst Aidonis had quite lost his normal jovial manner. Una tried to make light of the entire incident, saying that nothing had actually happened, but she felt herself more vulnerable than she had done for years. Nevertheless she was more concerned about the welfare and morale of her Sods; nothing should get in the way of the struggle for liberation. Roque had been very angry but had at least had the benefit of punching Clem's lights out. Serene spent some time with Una acting as wise woman and confidant but by 7.30 Una tired of this and suggested that the best thing to do would be to get on with the day and perhaps find Aidonis and cheer him up with reminiscences of the days of poetry rock.

Serene and Anvil followed Una's suggestion and sought him out. The door to his guitar room was ajar and, as they made their way in, they found Aidonis talking with Wesley.

"I know it's hard, but you took the right decision," Wesley said sympathetically.

"That doesn't make it any easier," Aidonis replied.

"Let me tell you a story," Wesley continued, adding. "Hi," as he saw Serene and Anvil.

"Shall we go?" Anvil asked.

"Hell, no, you can hear it as well," Wesley replied.

"Stay, guys. I need the company," Aidonis added.

"BBW I was a banker," Wesley began, as Serene and Anvil sat down. "Now that was a crazy world: venture capitalism it was called. Long back, bankers were wily, wise and wizen, steeped in experience, no flights of fancy, risk averse, dry as dust, and rich as shit. It was an attractive world if you had the right pedigree. Then it all changed. The whole mess of pottage got stirred, mixed, agitated, sieved and thrown down the pan, and I'm happy to say that I played my part. I dipped out of school when I was fourteen, bored as a badger without a set. Mad beasts are badgers. Do you know that they used to make shaving brushes out of their whiskers? I mean what a thing to do to a badger. Leave badgers out Wesley. So I was fourteen and my old man was a senior partner in Stuffem Goode and Longue, big city bank. You probably never heard of them?"

His audience shook their heads.

"We was big, big, big, big. So anyway I was a bright kid and so my old man gave me a job, well more a role than a job, I guess. Oh, and was I prodigal! No I don't mean that, though I guess I was, yes I was a prodigy. So my old man gave me a fund of one hundred thousand euros, which was pocket money to him, and said, 'Okay Wesley, make us some money.' Are you guys bored with this?"

They shook their heads but wondered when he was going to get to the point.

"Yeah, I think you need the condensed version. I made so

much money they asked me to join the board. Can you imagine a kid tycoon banker? Well, that was me. I decided I needed to make changes. Within two years the only old guy on the board was my father, and he was as proud as the nose on my face. I stuffed the board with kids, bright kids who'd dropped out but were sharper than tacks up a bear's arse. Then we got bored. The bank had assets in the order of ten trillion euros, which is a lot of paper to put in your back pocket, believe me, a serious load of dosh. My father pissed me off by then, so as I was now CEO I fired him, and then we blew the entire assets of Stuffem Goode and Longue. I made the worst possible set of decisions; we all did, and we crashed and we brought the whole pack of snivelling dribbling cards down in the biggest crash the world had ever seen."

"You did that?" Aidonis asked, "You were responsible for the big crash?"

"That's why we had a war," Anvil said somewhat frostily.

"That wasn't in the plan. That's why I'm here," Wesley replied. "So if I were you I wouldn't feel too bad about firing Clem. I fired my father, and lost the entire family fortune as well as causing the rest of the rather unfortunate outcomes."

They were lost for words until Aidonis said, "Yeah, well, I guess you got a point there, man."

"You made that up," Serene said with a smile.

"Course I did," Wesley replied with a huge laugh. "Verily, verily, oh how the righteous may be deceived and those that have Hamsters in their pockets may have them easily removed, but I was a banker, of sorts."

"You utter bastard," Aidonis laughed.

"Wesley, you're a tonic," Anvil added.

Marx decided that the best thing would be for him and Roque to do the rounds and make sure that the castle and its immediate environs were secure. Unlike Aidonis he was unsure about the decision to banish Clem, being convinced that this would bring consequences that could be dangerous to them all. The castle had perfectly serviceable dungeons and Clem could have been interred with very little effort. But being disposed to Una's concept of democratic centralism, he had gong along with the decision of the supreme council. It was, for him, almost as stupid as the business with the bloody bishop, who would undoubtedly have by now informed his masters of the danger to their, so-called, democracy that the Sods posed.

So it was that Marx and Roque found themselves outside the castle walls, first checking on the Sodsters and then on Lump, Baby and the Bloomers at the church. They found Lump seated on a gravestone grooming Maggie and Ronnie who had now acquired a majestic demeanour that belied their ultimate danger and savagery.

"Hail, Lump!" Marx greeted Lump.

"Comrades!" he replied seeing the two men.

"Where's Baby?" Roque asked.

"Gone to get the meat. It's lunchtime for the Bloomers," Lump replied, which was really quite obvious given the blood curdling meowing growls and cries that were coming from the church.

"How are they?" Marx asked nodding in the direction of the old church.

"Top cats," Lump replied; "tame as mice."

"Except when needed," Marx added.

"They're at our command," Lump smiled.

"Just as bloody well," Roque commented.

Lump cleared his throat and said, "Comrade Roque, can I as how ask you something?"

"Of course."

"That man, that tried to, err, you know with Comrade Una."

"Yes," Roque answered.

"Why'd you let him go?"

"It was thought best."

"Not by me," Marx murmured under his breath.

"Why do you ask?" Roque asked, ignoring Marx's remark.

"It's not what I'd a done," Lump replied.

"What would you have done?" Marx asked.

"Let him take his chances with Maggie and Ronnie, that's what, see how he'd like have liked that."

"He wouldn't have stood a chance," Roque replied.

"So? Anyone who hurts Comrade Una's, got it coming,"

Lump stated angrily.

Roque smiled and patted Lump on the shoulder, "You're a good one, Lump, but sometimes it's better to show mercy."

"Like hell it is," Baby said as she joined them and put down a great wicker basket full of assorted dead vermin and offal. Behind her were five Sods all carrying similarly full baskets. "It's a full time job feeding these mothers," she moaned.

"I'll help," Lump said standing up.

One of the nave windows had been removed and a wooden chute had been placed through the opening, and to this chute a wooden ladder had been attached. The baskets were taken up the ladder and their contents poured into the church. The Bloomers made quite a fuss but soon there was only the sound of cats chewing.

"They's a bit unruly when they's a want their fodder," Baby smiled. "But who ain't?"

"Speaking of which," Marx observed. "It's time for lunch."

76

Una, Marx, Roque, Anvil, Serene, Wesley, Lump, Maggie, Ronnie, Baby and Aidonis ate lunch together and now that the main meal of the day was concluded they sat and listened to Aidonis sing and play his twelve string steel guitar.

He sang "Long Ago, Far Away" written a hundred years before by Bob Dylan. He was interrupted by a very agitated Sod who stormed into the room shouting, "Comrade Una, stranger at the gate; says as how you knows him; says his name's Orb."

Roque and Anvil stared at Una who had gone ashen white. "What?" she said.

"Bloke in a funny outfit. He's got a bike," the Sod replied.

"A bike?" Marx said getting to his feet.

"It looks like Rocket's," the Sod said.

"I don't believe this," Una said.

"What's this guy, Orb?" Aidonis asked Anvil.

"Orb was the name of her father," Anvil replied, at which everyone, including the cats, looked somewhat confused; they had never thought of Una as someone who had a parent.

Roque rose slowly from his seat and said, "Let's take a look at this Orb."

They found Gilt, dressed in Orb's full paraphernalia, standing on the far side of the moat, a bicycle at his side, the late afternoon sun glinting on the gold (fake) knob at the end of the Pardoner's staff that he held tightly in his left hand.

Una kept in the background as Roque leant over the parapets and called, "What's your name and what do you want?"

"My name is Orb. I come in search of my daughter, Una Uevera," Gilt replied.

Roque asked Una, "What do you want me to do?"

"Ask him where I was born," she replied.

This he did and Gilt replied, "In a tent at Runnymede."

"Ask him my mother's name," Una instructed.

Again Roque did as he was bid and Gilt replied, "Juliana Constantia Evans."

"Why did he abandon us?" Una said.

"I can't ask him that in public like this," Roque replied.

So Una said, "Let the bastard in."

The drawbridge was lowered and Gilt entered, wheeling the bicycle. It only took a brief look to determine that it was indeed Rocket's bike. Sods marched him to the great hall.

Marx and Roque conducted the first part of the interrogation whilst Una sat unseen in the Minstrels' gallery overlooking proceedings.

"Okay, Orb, so tell me again: what happened to Rocket?" Marx asked.

"South of here there's a strange town called Grantham. I'd had the most disgusting evening meal in the pub after a very unsuccessful day of not selling a single pardon. It's not an easy life selling pardons, you know," Gilt replied.

"Look, Orb, I don't give a stuff about your stinking trade. I want to know about Rocket," Roque sternly interrupted.

"I'm just trying to give you the context, that's all. I'd had this awful meal and had the most dreadful stomach ache, so I thought I'd take a stroll down by the river to try and ease it off. That's when and where I found your Rocket. He was barely conscious. I don't know how it happened and nor did he. I think he was cycling fast trying to get back to you. It was dark; the tow path was overgrown. He must have hit something and cata-pulted off his bike, but the odds of him landing on top of a single old iron railing beggars belief."

"Yeah, you might say that," Roque commented.

"It just happens to be true," Gilt continued. "He was impaled on it; it had gone straight through his stomach and out of his back. There was blood everywhere; he was bleeding to death, poor sod."

"What did you do then?" Marx asked.

"I said I'd go and get help. There was no way that I could lift him off that thing myself. I'm too old and he was a big lad, but he wouldn't let me go, said it was too late, that he was going fast. He begged me to help him, get a message to you to say that he'd completed his mission but wouldn't say what it was. He said he was a Sedanista and that I must get the message to Navenby where you all were, take the bike back, and that's when he said the name Una Uevera. I made him repeat it. I couldn't believe it; my daughter was called Una Uevera and it's such an unusual name I knew it must be her, and then I thought that this must be fate, that I should find him, and, and," he hesitated and tears began to form in his eyes, "is she still alive, is she here?"

Marx and Roque looked at each other and Marx raised an eyebrow in doubt.

"Then what happened?" Roque asked.

"I'm sorry," Gilt answered, apparently trying to regain his composure, "I'm sorry, I feel so guilty about Una and her beloved mother."

"Bit late for that I would have thought," Roque observed.

"It's never too late for guilt," he replied. "What happened then was that he died. He just died; his head went down. I tried to comfort him, and then, just as he was going, he said, 'Promise me you'll do it, promise'. I did and then he let out a great gasp and he was gone."

"Do you usually keep your promises?" Marx asked.

Gilt considered his answer for a moment and then said, "No, I don't, but this was different, a promise to a dying man, and there was Una."

"What happened to his body?" Marx asked.

"I went back to the pub, got the landlord and a couple of regulars, and we went back to get him off the railing. It made the most horrible noise as we lifted him off, a sort of sucking squeaky tearing noise."

"We don't need to know that," Roque stated.

"I thought you wanted to know everything," Gilt said in a most apologetic tone.

"Then what?" Marx enquired.

"Next morning we took him to the local crem and he was burnt," Gilt answered.

"Just like that?" Marx said.

"What else was there to do?"

"Nothing, I suppose," Roque said sadly.

"I kept my promise," Gilt said in as humble a tone as he had ever managed.

"So how did you get from Grantham to Navenby?" Marx continued with the questions.

"In my Pardoner's sedan, which is where I had the bike. I took its wheels off."

"Where is it now?"

"The sedan is at the Hall, unless my Legits have run off. It's got all my stuff in it."

"So how did you find us here at the castle?" Roque asked.

"I could see the Hall was deserted, and so I wandered about the grounds and then it was pretty obvious from the tracks which way you'd gone."

"I covered the tracks," Roque said.

"I could see that someone had tried to do that, but it's hard to disguise the passing of so many people, and when I saw the Castle in the valley, I put two and two together, and here I am."

"The tracks weren't that easy to follow," Roque replied.

"I've been about a bit," Gilt said.

"You meet anyone on the way?" Marx asked.

"Not a soul," Gilt replied.

"I think we'll send someone up to the hall, and get your sedan down here," Marx stated.

"That would be most kind," Gilt responded. "I thought it best to walk down with the bike, so that you could see what I was bringing and so that I could explain what had happened and why I was here."

"You're to stay here. We've things to discuss," Roque told Gilt. "Those two Sods over there will keep an eye on you, so stay put."

"As you say. Two things though: is Una here? Could I have something to eat? I'm starving."

"Someone will bring you some food," Marx answered.

"So far, so good," Gilt thought.

Una made her way to her quarters where she was soon joined by Marx and Roque.

"Well what do you think?" Roque asked her.

"Of what? Him or his story about Rocket?"

"Both."

"Let's deal with the story first. He obviously met Rocket and he got directions here, but that's all we really know. It's all so implausible it could be true, but somehow it doesn't feel right," she replied.

"We should send someone to Grantham to find out if his tale is true," Roque said.

"I agree," Una replied.

"Anvil has the maps. I'll go and see how far it is and give you two a bit of solitude; I should think you both need it," Marx said.

"Thanks, Marx. It's been quite a twenty four hours," Una said.

After Marx had gone Roque took Una in his arms and asked, "Are you okay?"

"No, not really," she said as she rested her head on his chest.

"I'm sorry," he said.

She lifted her head and stared into his eyes and said, "Silly man, it's not your fault. You didn't try and rape me; you didn't ask my bastard of a father to turn up here."

"I know, but I am sorry, about both things. I love you."

"I love you, Roque, but it has all been a bit much."

"What can I do?"

"Listen."

"Of course."

"I need to make up my mind."

"About him?"

"Yes, Orb, or rather the man who claims he's Orb, and is therefore my father."

"You have doubts?"

"Female intuition; I'm just not sure."

"Will you talk to him?"

"I don't know if I want to."

"When did you last see him?"

"When I was nearly four."

"A long time ago."

"But somehow I don't remember him this way. He looks right, says the right things, but there's something about his voice; it's, it's lower, harder, not as soft as I remember it."

"If he is your father would it be good for you?"

"That's what worries me. I've never had him as a father when I needed him, so why do I need him now? I have you, my dear friends, the Sedanistas. Why take in some old scheming bastard just because he made my mother pregnant?"

"Were you really born in a tent at Runnymede?"

"Oh, yes. No, I've no choice, have I? I'll have to talk to him. If he's for real then I'll have to deal with it somehow. If he's a fake, then why is he here?"

"If he's a fake, then he's dangerous, because then what is he and what does he want?"

"Just hold me for a minute," Una said. "I just need a little of your strength to rub off."

"You've got more strength in you than me and Marx together. One thing though: until you're sure, I think he ought to be watched and guarded every minute."

"He is; there are two Sods with him."

"No, I mean really guarded."

"By whom?" Una asked.

"I'd thought of Lump and a couple of the older Bloomers."

"Isn't he too young?" Una queried.

"No, Lump's up to it, and he's fiercely loyal to you. If he thought you were in any sort of danger, he'd do anything to protect you."

77

Hamondi had been more than surprised to find Uphill Lindum occupied by the CISTS. In point of fact he was enraged when the CISTS at the gate refused him entry to 'his' cathedral city. He climbed out of the settled sedan and berated the two guards who confronted him. One could, perhaps understand their reticence in allowing access to what appeared to them to be one of the bewildered. He jumped up and down on the spot, shouted, and banged his crook on the ground. What was more his vestments were in a dreadful state: he was unshaven, his golden mitre was muddy, and, quite frankly, his odour was rank. Surprisingly, CISTS were sensitive to unpleasant bodily smells; this may have been because their nether regions were well ventilated beneath their parachute silk skirts. The relationship between Hamondi and the guards deteriorated further when he started to poke at them with the sharp end of his crook, accompanied by a flow of swear words in Latin (not that they spoke the holy language, but even a moronic CIST could recognise abuse). Luckily a sub Dean was passing, and recognising the Bishop, intervened to prevent the two guards from smacking the prelate in the teeth.

Though Gilt had emphasised the urgency of Hamondi's mission in alerting the authorities to the location of the Sods, the Bishop chose to bathe, change into fresh vestments, and eat dinner before searching out the Cisturions who line managed (the word 'command' had fallen from favour) the CISTS.

Hamondi found them, attired only in their jock straps, in the Cathedral's Chapter House in the middle of playing 'Bomb Bomb Barino'. This ancient game of two halves consisted of two teams of equal numbers made up of 'benders' and 'leapers'. The first bender leant against any convenient wall with his (it was only played by men) legs wide enough apart to take the head of the next bender who thus stood in a bent position with a flat back horizontal to the floor. At this point the first leaper entered the game by running to where the bender waited. The leaper would jump as far forward and as high as possible and crash down upon the waiting bender. Now another bender would place his head between the legs of the previous bender and another leaper would jump as far forward as possible. The game continued until the benders collapsed (in which case the leapers had won) or until all the leapers had leapt and the benders had not collapsed (in which case the benders had won that half). In the second half benders became leapers and vice versa; a tally was kept of the number of leapers on benders at the point of collapse for both halves and thus a winner could be calculated (it was very rare for there to be a draw). There was much shouting and sweating as the game progressed and as there weren't enough Cisturions to make for a really good match various well built CISTS (there weren't really any ill built CISTS) had been enlisted to take part. For this tournament there were two teams of thirty.

Hamondi had stood entranced as he had watched the game unfold; he had never seen so many beautifully formed and muscular backsides all in one place all at one time. He was relieved that his vestments clothed his excited lower orders. By the time the second half reached its climax (I say nothing of Hamondi), he felt it necessary to step outside and cool himself down with holy water. When he returned to the Chapter House he found the men involved in much hugging and cheering; the first team of benders had vanquished the first leapers. The Bishop collapsed into his Chair and watched as the men dressed in their uniforms. It was only at this point that one of their number took any notice of him.

"Who are you?" a large and handsome Cisturion asked.

"I am the Right Reverend Petrus Hamondi, Bishop of Lindum," he replied with a twinkle in his eye.

"Pleased to meet you," he said extending his hand, "I'm a Cisturion, name of Alton Turrets."

"Good to meet you, Alton."

"What can I do for you, Bishop?" Alton asked.

"You can only imagine," he thought, but said, "I need to talk to the Cisturions, I have important matters of state security to share with you. It's really quite urgent."

"You should have said earlier. Lads!" he shouted, "Bishop here wants to talk to us. You Cists, out of here. Well played; another match tomorrow."

"Oh good," Hamondi thought.

As the last of the CISTS closed the oak door behind him the Cisturions pulled up Chapter chairs (which Hamondi felt to be inappropriate as they weren't ordained) in front of the Bishop who outlined the events of recent days and the location of Una Uevera and the Sods. At the end of what was rather a protracted tale he had asked, "What are you going to do? When will you set out to capture the terrorists?"

This was a question too far for the Cisturions who found it difficult to reply. They muttered amongst themselves, amidst much shaking of heads.

"Well?" Hamondi asked again.

"Thing is," Alton finally replied, taking on the role of spokesturion, "We got orders. We have to protect Lindum, until we is told otherwise."

"That's ridiculous," Hamondi said. "This is urgent. They'll disappear. They have bicycles!"

"That's as may be, whatever they are, but orders is orders."

"Isn't there someone in command?"

"Flat structure. We're all of equal rank," Alton answered.

"We're waiting for the Cist Legates to arrive. They could tell us what to do," another Cisturion offered.

"Judge Hangedogge is in the judge's chambers," Hamondi suggested. "He could tell you what to do."

"Not part of our line management, Bishop," Alton replied.

"I despair," Hamondi moaned.

"Tell you what we can do, Bishop," Alton said.

"What?"

"We'll send a pigeon off; in fact, we'll send three pigeons off. That should cover it, and then in a few days we'll get a reply."

"I did have something more speedy in mind."

"Best we can do. Any chance you could write down the key points and then get 'em copied for the birds?" Alton asked. "If you've got anyone that can print real small that would help, otherwise the birds keep resting if the message's too heavy."

"I'm sure that can be arranged," Hamondi replied and thought, "Well at least there's another match tomorrow. I wonder if Alton would like a little mature company?"

78

Una kept Gilt waiting for two days. When she finally entered his place of confinement she found him sitting as far away from Lump and the Bloomers as he could possibly manage. For a man of his background Gilt had been surprised, even horrified, that the bloody cats filled him with utter terror; terror not being a condition that he had personally experienced though he had, of course, been happy to develop it in others. The Bloomers themselves, having been well trained by Lump and Baby, had in their turn taken an instant and profound loathing of this strangely dressed man. Lump had struggled to contain them as they seemed intent on ripping the stranger to shreds; this was an assumption on Lump's part based upon the fact that he had to enlist the help of another Sod to hold them back. He had found himself faced with a quandary: this Orb person was supposedly Una's father, but, on the other hand, he sensed there was something wrong about him. This doubt was reinforced by the behaviour of his beloved Bloomers, Maggie and Ronnie. "Surely," Lump thought to himself, "if he really is her father then the Bloomers would know that and treat him well." Though this logic was flawed,

Lump was convinced that the cats understood the difference between friend and foe.

When Una first entered the great hall Gilt was unaware of her presence; she stood silently in a dark corner and observed the creature, Orb. "Could it be him," she wondered, "and if it is, what am I going to do about it?"

Gilt stood up to stretch, at which Ronnie and Maggie began to growl in the most awesome way.

"Keep those damn things away from me, that's all, do you hear me?" Gilt pleaded.

"You do no wrong, Mr Orb, and they'll not be harming you," Lump replied.

"I have no harm in me," Gilt stated flatly.

"Unless, of course, I tells 'em to," Lump teased.

Gilt struggled to keep in role; his desire was to kill this beastly little Sod along with his bloody savage beasts.

Una took a deep breath and walked into the evening light that filtered through the glassless windows of the hall.

Gilt saw her move and said, "Una, Una, is that you? I'm sorry, Una, so sorry."

Unfortunately, at the same time as he said this, he made a rapid movement toward Una. The Bloomers didn't like it, and Lump and his assistant only managed to halt their advance as Maggie's teeth tore into the hem of Gilt's striped robe. Gilt didn't need to act; he was terrified and fled to the farthest corner of the room.

"Sorry, Miss Una," Lump said as he finally managed to get the cats back under control.

"It's alright Lump, they were only trying to protect me. You'd better take them away. I'll never be able to talk to him while they're in the room."

"I can't do that. Roque and Marx said as how he mustn't be left alone with you."

"I know, but I'm going to be fine. I can look after myself."

"They'll kill me if I don't follow their orders," Lump protested.

"No, they won't. I'll tell them it was my command."

"Can we wait outside the door and then, if there's any trouble, you can shout and we'll be there fast as a flea up a cat's whisker?"

"Yes, you can wait outside the door. There's no other way

out, is there?"

"No, just the one big door," Lump replied.

When they left Una said, "Perhaps we ought to sit down?"

"Thank you for sending that boy and his creatures away," Gilt said with genuine relief.

They sat in silence opposite each other in battered Windsor chairs, each apparently lost in thought. Una concentrated on his face to see if there was anything she recognised of her father. Gilt, now that he was finally alone with his quarry had a dilemma: should he continue with his role as Orb, the errant father, or should he simply get on with the business of abducting her and putting into action the plan he had forged with Clem and Seth? He hadn't expected to be kept waiting for two days for an audience with the bloody woman and now that Lump and the Bloomers had left the scene the opportunity might not so easily present itself again. He was also worried that if he left it for too much longer there was the possibility that his two conspirators on the outside might think something had gone wrong and simply clear off. After all, one of them was bitter and twisted whilst the other was a raving lunatic; neither conditions inspired great confidence in the mind of the secret agent.

Una was the first to break the silence. "So you claim to be Orb, my father." she said.

"That is what I have said," Gilt replied.

Una thought that this was a strange reply but said, "Can you prove that you are?"

"No, I can't," Gilt replied, a smile upon his lips.

"Pardon?"

"The time for acting is over," Gilt said, taking his automatic pistol from beneath his robe and pointing it at Una's head, "Una Uevera, I arrest you in the name of the state. You're coming with me."

Una leapt to her feet, ready for a fight, and pointing at the gun said, "That's not real. There are no guns left. It's a fake just like you!"

He released the safety catch and said, "I wouldn't suggest you try to find out. A single shot between your lovely eyes and you're dead."

"You can't escape. There are guards."

"Not the way we're going," he said. "Now put your hands behind your back and we'll be on our way."

"Fuck off!" she replied.

Una was surprised that this man could move so fast, as with one swift movement, he was behind her, the muzzle of the gun pressed hard behind her right ear.

"Your hands, please," Gilt instructed.

As her hands came behind her back, she stamped hard down upon his shin and foot and attempted to reverse butt him in the face, but he saw the latter coming and smacked her across the side of her face with the barrel of the weapon; blood flowed. He pushed her to the ground, holding her flat upon the floor with one foot while he snapped her wrists into a pair of restraints. She offered no resistance as the blow had stunned her. Soon she was once more upon her feet, Gilt behind her, gun at her neck.

"Move!" he commanded as they moved towards the solid oak wainscoted wall.

At the fourth panel from the right, Gilt pressed the wood. Nothing happened. He pressed harder and slowly the panel creaked open.

"A secret passage!" Una said. "How could you know it was there?"

"Clem. Not a wise move to thwart a man as bitter as that," Gilt replied.

They stepped into the darkness and the panel closed behind them. It was pitch dark and Una took advantage of the moment to turn and knee Gilt in the balls. He groaned in agony but didn't go down. He punched Una in the stomach and then knocked her to the ground and fell upon her. The ground stank; it was damp and covered in cobwebs and a hundred years of rat and mouse droppings. Gilt grabbed her hair with one hand and pushed the muzzle of the gun into her mouth.

"Now you fucking listen to me, bitch," he said in his most threatening tone, "normally I would have killed you by now, but I was instructed to bring you back alive, and that is what I am going to do, but being alive doesn't mean in good condition. If you try anything more like that again, I will harm you.

I will disfigure you, maim you. Have you got that bitch?"

Una didn't move.

He pulled her hair harder and forced the gun deeper into her mouth and said, "Just nod if you understand."

She nodded.

"Good. Now lie still until we get used to the dark."

After several minutes they moved off down the passage. Gilt benefited from the fact that Una was in front of him as when she fell he knew there was a hazard and her face was the first to be cloaked in thick cobwebs. They made slow progress but Gilt was confident that his plan would work.

Una's mind raced as she tried to think her way through what should, or could, be done.

Outside the great doors to the hall Lump had been pacing up and down for at least an hour; he was worried. He had listened at the door but could hear nothing.

"What shall we do?" he asked the Bloomers who naturally only uttered their usual low growling sound. "I'm going to get into trouble for this," he continued out loud, and taking a deep breath, turned the handle and opened the door to the now empty hall. His sense of anguish and alarm was immense: it was all his fault; he should never have left her with Orb; his instincts had been right, but where had they gone, and what should he do? He raised the alarm.

79

Alton had not wanted the 'mature company' of the seedy old cleric and had been quite put out that Hamondi had expected access to his body. "That was the trouble with young people these days," the Bishop mused, "no respect for authority."

In these depressing circumstances Hamondi decided to take himself across the cobbled road that led from his palace to the Castle Square to see Judge Hangedogge in his Lodgings. Many years BBW they had first been at public school together and then gone up to Cambridge (as it was then called), he to read geography and the Judge to read media studies. Now, ABW, one had risen to be the Lord Chief Justice of England whilst the other had become the third most important prelate in the English Church. The cynics amongst you might think that it was ever thus; it wasn't what you knew that mattered but where you had been born and to whom you were connected (either by birth or favour). It does have to be said that ABW the law was simpler, more direct, and that the state religion was not blessed with any sense of uncertainty. I have been told that BBW the Anglican Church was riven with conflict over the legitimacy of homosexual acts. It was a relief to Hamondi that those days had long passed; homosexuality was, of course, illegal but was practised with absolute licence and impunity by anyone of real status (after all, it would have been a bit tricky to prosecute Ham).

Hangedogge was pleased to see Hamondi as it had been many years since they had had the opportunity to share a couple of bottles of gin and 'chew the cud' (as they described their long and rambling conversations). Hangedogge hadn't been to Lindum for about eight years and had returned as part of his circuit round the land to put the fear of god into anyone who was handy and, most particularly, the notaries who had taken over the roles of both solicitors and barristers.

Hamondi recounted his recent adventures with some relish, emphasising his part in things in a way that lacked a certain historical accuracy, it didn't matter: it was all good fun. However, when Hamondi explained about the location of the Sedanistas and the response of the Cisturions, Hangedogge's joviality diminished. He rang his bell and when the scribe arrived, dictated a note to the Prime Minister that was immediately pigeoned off. This task completed they opened another bottle of gin and put the world to rights.

"This is damn fine gin, Petrus," Hangedogge said as he sank another big one.

"Thank you, Xavier. I thought you'd like it. I've spent many years getting the best still of any cathedral in England,"

Hamondi replied.

"You know, I think it's fate that I should be here just as they are about to catch these Sedanista fellas."

"They aren't just men, you know. There's lots of women, and they're led by a woman, Una Uevera."

"Any good?"

"Not to my taste," Hamondi replied.

"No of course, dear boy; no offence intended."

"None taken."

"Do you remember that joke you made when you were Bishop of Axholme, I think it was?" Hangedogge asked.

"Remind me."

"You can't have forgotten? I came into your quarters, no pun intended, and you were buggering a chorister."

"How could I have forgotten?" Hamondi said with a slightly embarrassed smile.

"And you said."

"I say could you get them to send me up another choirboy? This one seems to have burst," Hamondi laughed.

It took several minutes for the two men to recover from their laughing fit.

"So, how's life treating you, Xavier?"

"Good. Very good actually, old chap. I like being Lord Chief Justice, jolly good fun, especially now that I have managed to persuade that buffoon of a Prime Minister to reintroduce the death penalty."

"It's progress, isn't it?"

"Most certainly, and I get a real thrill when I put on the black cap."

"Have you done many yet?"

"No, only about ten, I think, but it's early days. Sounds like there could quite a few on the way if they catch these terrorists," Hangedogge said as he rubbed his hands in anticipation.

"Has it been decided what means of execution will be used for different offences?"

"Not fully, but I have some ideas of my own. Have you got any more of that gin of yours?"

Hamondi removed another bottle from his mitre (which

222

can make really good bottle bags) pulled out the cork with his teeth and poured two more tumblers full. "Tell me what you've been thinking," he said.

After having taken a good swig, Hangedogge replied. "There's hanging, naturally, but you can have several versions of that. There's private hanging, public hanging, trapdoor dropping hanging, and just hanging."

"Just hanging?" Hamondi queried.

"Yes, you know, where you just pull them up far enough so their feet don't touch the ground."

"That must be very slow."

"Yes, that's quite an extended form of hanging, very distressing, particularly if it's in public. Then after hanging, as a means of execution, it becomes more controversial. I personally don't favour public stoning."

"What's public stoning?" Hamondi asked, this not being his area of expertise.

"It's quite ancient, actually. You bury the criminal up to their neck in the ground and then invite members of the public, or the family of the victim, if there is a victim, to hurl rocks at the criminal's head until it dies."

"From how far away?"

"Good question. The answer depends on how quick you want the death to be. If it's going to be used, then I think circles should be drawn on the ground around the head that determine how easy it is to hit it, and thus determine how long it takes the criminal to die."

"That's clever," Hamondi said and took another good drink from his glass.

"But what I've really been thinking about is crucifixion."

"Good lord!"

"Yes, bold, isn't it?"

"Sensitive connotations."

"Why?"

"Jesus?"

"No, nothing like that, no nails. Just tie them up there and leave them to perish."

"What crimes would you use that one for?"

"Sedition," Hangedogge replied.

80

The Prime Minister had already started north by the time Hangedogge's pigeon-post landed at Number 10. Robinson and Travers had arrived at Green's official residence in the early hours of the previous morning; each had formed the independent view that Hamondi's 'intelligence' on the location of the Sods was of such importance to national security that their leader should be woken from his sleep.

Green was not asleep when they had arrived. He'd had a busy day dealing with the related affairs of State and the heart (or at least the carnal). Mrs Green, whom one must assume was either very stupid or tolerant, had paid little attention to Green's relationship with Bekkes but felt that his liaison with Camellia was far more personally threatening to her position as the first lady of government (this was a fantasy on her part as everyone knew that she was as informed about matters of State importance as a fly is of the topography of Esher). She had asked her husband for an explanation and had been told in return that it was nothing to do with her as it related to the reconstruction of the English state into a republic; this was probably more than he wanted to say but she had been quite unusually assertive. The argument was bitter and protracted with Mrs Green (her first name is not recorded, but is thought to have been something like Cheryl or Cherub) bringing up her husband's long record of sexual adventures beyond the confines of wedlock. They reached an insuperable impasse at 01.22 hours. When Robinson arrived at 02.48 and Travers at 02.55 they found a line of removal sedans parked outside Number 10 and Mrs Green supervising the loading of her many possessions.

"Useless bloody woman," Green said as they joined him in the Cabinet Room.

"She's leaving you?" Travers asked as Robinson glowered at him.

"No of course she's not; she's taking all her things and half of mine to a bloody sedan boot sale. What do you think?" Green replied.

"I'm sorry," Travers muttered.

"What the hell are you doing here anyway? It's the middle of the night."

They both started to recount the information at the same time but at that moment Mrs Green burst into the room, removed her wedding ring, hurled it at Green and shouted, "And you can keep that, you ungrateful bastard. I hope you get the pox off the royal bitch, and that you all rot in hell," and stormed from the room slamming the door behind her.

Travers and Robinson looked down and maintained a discreet silence until Green said, "Can you please not try and both speak at once. It's been a difficult night. Robinson, you go first."

By the time they had finished the removal sedans on the street outside had been replaced with three lightweight Eccles Sedans (normally used for road racing and named after their inventor) and a troop of thirty-six racing Legits who would speed the three men north.

"Where did you say we were going?" Green asked as he climbed into the lead vehicle.

"Lindum in Lincolnshire, Prime Minister," Travers replied.

It was late afternoon by the time Hamondi felt well enough to venture forth in search of the Cisturions to see if the Legates had arrived. Not for the first time in his life, he had vowed that he would never ever again stay up till the early hours getting as drunk as a nun on god; it always seemed such a good idea at the time.

He dressed in his most ornate vestments in order to make a sufficient impression upon what he assumed would be men of vision and decision. He found the Legates, two in number, inspecting their forces, who were parading in the Castle grounds. He stood and watched as the ceremony came to an end and then approached the two men; one was short and stout and the other tall and thin.

"Good afternoon," Hamondi said. "I am the Bishop of Lindum, Petrus Hamondi."

"Ah, you're the fella, are ya? We been hearing about you," the tall one said. "I'm Legate Blagg."

Hamondi offered a hand to be shaken but the offer was declined.

"I'm Legate Lamont," the other Legate said.

Hamondi did not offer to shake his hand.

"You'd best come with us," Lamont suggested.

"This way," Blagg said as he and Lamont took each of Hamondi's elbows and marched him toward the castle keep.

Hamondi soon found himself seated behind a little table in what was a very small and claustrophobic room, not made better by the fact that Lamont and Blagg smoked as they sat opposite him.

"What have you got to say about all this, then?" Blagg asked.

"I told your Cisturions about the Sedanistas and where they are. Pigeons were sent to the Capital," Hamondi replied.

"We know about all that," Lamont said. "It's the other matter."

"What other matter?"

"Come, come. I think you know what I'm talking about," Lamont said.

"I haven't a clue what you're talking about. You're interrogating me, treating me like a criminal," Hamondi protested.

"If the cap fits, Bishop," Lamont replied, "or should I say the mitre?"

Blagg laughed and then said, "Wouldn't it be better if you just told us the truth and then we could see what we could do to help you? There's always ways, isn't there Lamont?"

"Of course there is, Legate Blagg, of course there is."

"Look. I am an important person. I am related to the monarch. I have important information that will protect the state. I am not a criminal," Hamondi stated with authority.

"But that doesn't make you above the law," Blagg said.

"That isn't actually my experience," Hamondi replied, realising that that might not have been the most sensible response.

"Ho, ho, ho. Is that a confession of past misdemeanours?"

"Oh for god's sake, man, what are you on about?" Hamondi asked his face flushed with colour.

"A complaint has been made," Lamont replied.

"About me?"

"About you."

"By whom?" Hamondi asked, as his body temperature soared and his heart began to race.

"A Cisturion by the name of Alton," Blagg replied.

"Oh," Hamondi sighed.

"Oh indeed," Lamont said raising both eyebrows.

"Oh," Hamondi said once more.

There was a knock on the door.

"Yes," Blagg said.

The head of a Cisturion popped round the opening door and said, "We're ready, Legates."

"Thank you, Cisturion. We'll only be a few minutes more," Blagg answered.

"Let's get to it. What you proposed to Alton is illegal, and therefore you have committed an illegal offence," Lamont calmly stated.

"But," Hamondi began.

"There's no buts," Lamont continued.

"That's a good one," Blagg laughed.

"While we're away you should think about how we, and Alton, might be persuaded to forget all about it," Lamont suggested.

"Where are you going?" Hamondi asked.

"To war," Blagg replied, "to kill the Sods."

"Be creative and be sensible, Bishop. We'll see you in a few days and we'll expect an answer. You may go now," Lamont concluded as he and Blagg stood and left the room, leaving the door open.

It took Hamondi a few minutes to settle himself. As he went outside, he saw the last of the CISTS marching from the castle and to battle.

Camellia had been disappointed that Green seemed to lack any sort of bottle. Following her ill-advised attempt to seduce Whiskerbot she suggested to the Prime Minister that the best way of dealing with Ham's advisor was to organise a sudden and unexpected death such as constructing an apparent suicide. Green would have none of it. That wasn't what he actually said: what he did say was that he didn't want to know about it; then again that may have been the interpretation that Camellia put upon it. They were, however, still agreed that it was essential that progress be made toward a time when Gloriana Beatrice would be Queen and Camellia Regent; a time when she and Green would assume effective control of the State. If Whiskerbot continued to be an impediment then he should be 'cast out'; the conundrum came in defining exactly what 'cast out' meant.

Camellia had sent pigeons north to the nunnery (where she had lived her teenage years until her marriage) where many of the ancient arts were carefully and lovingly preserved. It took some time but she was delighted to be interrupted at her luncheon by a courtier who said that there was a strange old woman dressed in black asking for her at the main gate.

"Did she give her name?" Camellia asked.

"Indeed, Mam, she did."

"And?"

"Sister Belgravia of the Fragrant Domiciled Nasturtiumites."

"Wonderful!" Camellia shouted. "Send her up."

In the absence of a sane mother and sober father, Sister Belgravia had played a seminal influence in the development of the young Camellia. The nun had taken her name from that area of London in which she had lived and worked before taking holy orders. Camellia was one of the chosen few who knew her history, as Sister Belgravia had sought to hide the reasons for her fall from grace and subsequent entry into the ranks of the Nasturtiumites.

Sister Belgravia had never married, though she had had the pleasure of 'knowing' men (a condition that was almost obligatory in Belgravia), and had in time fallen in love (BBW) with a member of the intelligence services, one Sandy Hanny. Hanny had been closely involved in the construction of secret dossiers that had been used by the then government to legitimise their commitment to the coming war. He was of necessity a shadowy figure who moved between the Ministry for War and the 'independent' scientists who validated the intelligence gained by operatives in the field. The Cabinet had been very divided on the case for war and wanted absolute verification of the so-called 'facts'. Hanny was given this job. The most senior scientist, Professor 'Brain' Stuyvesant, was crucial to the evidence base. Hanny suspected that he had falsified his research in order to exacerbate the likelihood of conflict and set out to prove it. He discovered that Stuyvesant was a major shareholder (through a false name) of the manufacturer of the warhead delivery systems. Hanny was so worried by this that he committed the cardinal sin of talking about it to Sister Belgravia (or Sam as she was known at the time). She had advised him that he should help expose the Professor and thus help prevent a disastrous conflict.

The last time Sam saw Hanny was when she kissed him goodbye in the early hours of a Wednesday morning. He was found the next day dead on Hampstead Heath; it appeared that he had slashed his own wrists, and that prior to that he had been involved in 'cottageing' in the park. A witness was supplied. Sam was devastated; she knew two things he would never have taken his own life and he was not homosexual or bi-sexual. In due course, an inquest was held. The verdict was suicide. The newspapers (this was before the presses finally stopped rolling) made a fuss for a couple of days, but, with war looming, what did one secret agent matter?

Sister Belgravia was never the same again; it turned her from a warm loving woman into a bitter and vengeful fury. Her profession was a chemist and she decided to employ her knowledge to wreak justice upon the head of the man whom she knew in her heart had murdered her beloved Sandy: Professor 'Brain' Stuyvesant. She poisoned him. He died, but the police couldn't prove a thing even though they had every intention of continuing their investigations and so she gave up the world as she had known it, disappeared from view and joined the Nasturtiumites.

As a nun, she had continued her scientific interests and had concentrated on the history and applications of the ancient art of poisons and poisoning.

When they were finally alone, the two women embraced and then sat together in the silence of Camellia's sewing room. Sister Belgravia was dressed in the customary black of her order (the sombre tones only lifted by the white emblem of his Holiness the Bishop of England sewn above her cold heart); her small frame was made more diminutive by the bulk of her attire.

"Now, my child, what is to be done?" Sister Belgravia asked.

Camellia told her everything: all that had happened, of Ham, of Green and their plan, and the future of Whiskerbot.

When she finished her tale, Sister Belgravia asked, "How long do I have?"

"Not long, Sister. As soon as possible really."

"Does this Whiskerbot person suffer from any illnesses or persistent maladies?"

"None that I know of."

"Did you try to turn him into an ally in the usual way?" the Sister asked.

"He spurned me," Camellia replied.

"Not a wise move. Is it to be short and painless or very long and agonising?"

"Is short and agonising a possibility?"

"Anything is possible, my child," Sister Belgravia replied. "You must introduce me to him as soon as possible so that I can see the man, see the nature of his humours, and gauge his weight."

"Oh thank you, Sister," Camellia said clutching her hand.

"I think I shall stay on with you after the deed is done. I have become bored with the nunnery," Sister Belgravia said, with a smile upon her pale thin lips.

83

Una and Gilt made slow progress through the passage; Una found the going particularly hard, as with her hands locked behind her back in handcuffs she had no means of protecting herself as she fell in the dark. Gilt offered neither sympathy nor help but merely pushed her ever on. They finally emerged from a secret door hidden behind an ancient gravestone adjacent to the church. There they found Clem and Seth waiting in the shadows of early evening beneath the old yew trees.

"I thought as how you were never coming, Master," Seth said as he helped Gilt through the bramble thicket that partly covered the gravestone.

"Keep your voice down. Is everything ready?" Gilt asked in a whisper.

"It is, master," Seth replied.

Una was not pleased to see Clem. "You bastard! You betrayed us," she said.

Clem made no reply, but advanced upon her and attempted to grab at her breasts. Una spat in his face.

"Bitch," he said, slapping her already badly bruised and bloody face.

"Clem! Leave her be. There'll be time later," Gilt said. "Now back off."

"You promised her to me," Clem stated.

"Not now, you bloody fool! Come on, move. They'll be after us soon," Gilt said as he dumped Orb's robes amidst the brambles. He was now dressed in his black night combat suit, his weapons about his belt and his gun still firmly trained on Una.

Within moments of Lump's alarm call the castle was quickly searched but there was no sign of Una and Orb. In the great hall they gathered.

"Where have they gone? We must find her," Roque said.

"It'll have been that bastard, Clem. He spent years searching for secret passages. I wasn't interested; I wish I had been now," Aidonis apologised.

"Tap the walls," Marx said. "There'll be a hollow sound and then we've found it."

"They'll not be there now," Serene said.

"Where do the passages lead?" Roque asked.

"I think he said to the outer walls," Aidonis replied.

"Then that's where we must go. Use the ramparts and send more outside," Marx commanded.

As they emerged from the hall and into the open, they heard the cry," Fire! Fire! The church is on fire!"

They ran to the drawbridge and Anvil shouted, "Where's Lump."

"The Bloomers are in there," Serene shouted as she struggled to keep up with the rushing Sods.

While Clem and Seth set fire to the church Gilt lashed Una to a Sodster that he had moved from its original hiding place and placed behind the tall hedge that bounded the green lane. Una tried to cry out, but this was too much for Gilt who clubbed her across the head; she was easier to tie up in that condition. As the flames licked the mounds of dry grass and leaves that had been placed against the church doors and walls, Clem and Seth ran to where Gilt waited with the Sodster. Gilt's two helpers climbed aboard as Gilt said, "Now pedal like fuck. Stop for no man and, get her to the Hall in one piece. Now go. I'll hold 'em off."

Lump and Baby were at the church first and started to try and beat out the blaze. Flames roared, smoke billowed, and within moments the wooden beams were caught. There were sparks everywhere as they tried to release the cats before they all perished. The Bloomers inside howled in terror. It was a sound that filled all who heard it with a spine tingling dread. At the best of times, Bloomers made pretty scary noises, but this howling was of a different nature and magnitude; Bloomers weren't normally frightened of anything. More Sods arrived; water was pulled from the well and branches were torn from the yew trees to try and beat out the blaze. Finally, they opened the doors and the Bloomers poured out into the night. As they worked to retrieve the cats, Gilt made his way back toward the church. As they gathered most, but not all, of the animals together and tied their collars to ropes a shot rang out and Baby fell to the ground holding her chest. Lump knelt down beside her and cried out, "Baby! Baby, what is it?"

"That bastard, Orb, has a gun," Roque shouted in what was now silence.

"There aren't any guns," Marx said.

Serene knelt down with Lump and Baby and put her arm around the boy's shoulders.

"Miss Baby?" Lump cried.

"Kiss me, Lump," Baby murmured, and he did upon her forehead.

Another shot rang out and a Sod fell to the ground fatally wounded.

"Everybody back inside the castle!" Marx commanded.

"I'm going after Una!" Roque shouted.

"He'll kill you and you're no use to her dead," Marx replied.

"Baby?" Lump held his old friend.

"Inside!" Marx shouted once more. The Sods ran for the castle gate.

"What about Baby? She's hurt bad," Lump pleaded.

Serene felt for the pulse in Baby's wrist, put her ear to Baby's mouth, and then very gently said, "Baby's dead, Lump."

Lump started to sob and through his choking tears said," It's all my fault, all my fault."

"Come now, Lump. Let's get you away from here," Serene said as she helped him to his feet. Maggie and Ronnie rubbed their great heads upon his chest and seemed to sigh with emotion.

"I'll take her," Marx said as he lifted Baby from the ground.

As they ran, Gilt's voice rang out in the darkness, "Follow and you die!"

Then Gilt ran up the green lane, confident that none would dare follow him in the darkness. As he reached Navenby Hall he found Seth and Clem waiting for him with the Sodster. Una had regained consciousness, but was in a bad state. Gilt gave her some water.

"Why are you doing that?" Clem asked.

"I have to bring her in alive," he replied, and then said, "Quiet, I hear something. Get this thing hidden, now!"

What he heard were the sounds of CISTS running, not that he knew what they were, but he was pretty sure that Hamondi had got the message through and these men were making for the castle. He had intended to let them pass, and when they had disappeared over the brow of the hill down to the castle, begin their ride to Lindum, but then it struck him that it was foolish to waste such an opportunity.

"You stay there. Don't make a sound and keep her quiet," he told Seth and Clem.

He stood in the centre of the Grantham Road and waited. The only sound the CISTS made as they ran came from their feet. They lit their way with flaming torches. When they were but a hundred yards from him, he raised his pistol and fired a single shot in the air and shouted, "Halt! Friend ahead."

The column of CISTS stopped, and a voice called out, "Who goes there?"

"Secret Agent Gilt," he called. "I sent the Bishop to you to tell you the Sods were here."

"Prove it," Lamont called back. "Have you got a gun?"

"I have. May I approach?" Gilt asked.

"Darts at the ready, lads," Blagg whispered to the men behind him. Blowpipes were raised and darts silently inserted. "On my command, fire," he continued.

"Approach, but slowly now," Lamont instructed.

Gilt approached Lamont and held out his letter of authority from the Prime Minister with Ham's Royal Seal, "These are my credentials," he said as Lamont took them from his hand.

"Bring that torch nearer," Lamont instructed the nearest torchbearer and then read the letter that he then passed on to Blagg. They then nodded to each other and Blagg said, "Hold your fire. Well, agent Gilt, it seems you're who and what you say you are. What do you want?"

"Your names, please," Gilt asked.

"Legates Lamont and Blagg," they replied in unison.

"Esteemed Legates Lamont and Blagg, the castle is heavily fortified and, as far as I can see, you carry no means to scale its walls," Gilt observed.

"What of it? We'll make what we need. We will be victorious," Lamont replied.

"I don't doubt it for a moment," Gilt replied, thinking that these men's understanding of warfare was slight. "I just thought I could make things a little easier."

"Go on," Blagg responded.

"I have this," he said pulling Clem's plan of the castle from a pocket.

"What's that?" Blagg asked.

"A detailed map of every secret passage into and out of the castle."

"Uevera and her Sods are inside?" Lamont asked.

"Of course," Gilt lied. There was no way he was giving up his prize, and the Hamsters she was worth, to these two numbskulls.

"Do they know you've got that map?"

"No."

"How did you come by it?" Blagg asked suspiciously.

"None of your business, I'm afraid," Gilt replied.

"He asked you a civil question," Lamont said.

"I gave him a civil reply, Legate."

"We are in authority here," Lamont continued.

"Not over me, you're not. I am the Prime Minster's secret agent. I take no orders except from him," Gilt calmly stated. "You've seen my papers. Now why don't you go and get the Sods while I go about my own business?"

"Come on, Lamont," Blagg said. "Don't waste your time; he's given us the in."

"Thank you, would be polite," Gilt suggested.

"Piss off," Blagg replied and then shouted to the waiting CISTS. "On the count of three: one, two, three!"

Gilt waited and watched the column move off down the escarpment.

84

Roque couldn't sleep. The Sods had been severely shocked by the events of the previous night but Roque was doubly shocked; not only had he lost his leader but the woman he loved. Mind you, the distress caused to his friends and comrades was as intense, albeit for different reasons, as Una had not only inspired loyalty, but affection, amongst her Sods, be they the leadership or the most insignificant five year old.

Roque decided that he needed a walk to try and clear his thoughts and think through what could be done. He was riven with guilt that he had not taken his chance and gone for the gunman and taken the risk of being shot; he was not a coward but the caution Marx had urged had made him feel that he was. As he walked along behind the utmost parapet he sensed someone or something in front of him.

"Who's there?" he asked. There was no reply and so he moved closer, eyes straining in the dark, "Who's there?" he asked again and received a groan in return. It was then that he saw what lay in front of him: Lump was curled up fast asleep on the flagstones with his trusted Maggie and Ronnie asleep on each side of where he lay.

He shook his head, smiled and quietly said, "Poor Lump."

At this the cats stirred and began to growl. "Friend," Roque said.

At this Lump woke and sat up rubbing his eyes that were red raw from a night spent half awake and crying. "Comrade, I'm sorry," he said.

Roque knelt down beside him and said, "Listen, Lump. Una told you to go and leave her with Orb. You did as you were commanded. It's not your fault. I think deep down Una wanted him to be her father and it clouded her judgement."

"Do you think so?" Lump asked.

"I do. What we've got to do now is figure out how to get her back safe and sound whilst that man has a gun. We're no

236

match for guns."

"He killed Baby," Lump said and started to cry again.

"Come on, on your feet," Roque said, pulling Lump up. "Let's get some breakfast, find the others, and have a council of war."

Dawn was almost breaking as they descended the steps to the courtyard in front of the great hall. The cats began to make their terrible, barely audible, warning growl. Lump stopped, put his finger to his lips and whispered, "There's something not right."

Roque, Lump and the two cats quickly hid behind one of the adjacent flying buttresses. Lump knelt down by the cats and again whispered, "Quiet, danger, wait." The cats quietened, and Roque and Lump very carefully peered round the corner of the buttress. In the dim light they could just make out the shape of men dressed all in black moving stealthily along the inner wall to the castle's gates and drawbridge. At this moment, two Sods came round the corner carrying buckets of water for the breakfast stoves.

"Who's that?" one of them said as they neared the dark shapes. A strange blowing sound and a slight whistle immediately followed this and the two Sods fell to the ground; the CISTS had used their blowpipes.

"Raise the alarm," Roque shouted at the top of his voice, "Intruders! Enemy within!" Sod sentries took up the call, others followed suite, and soon there were the sounds of banging doors and running feet.

Lump had a different idea. He unleashed his two Bloomers and quietly said, "Enemy, kill!"

The two cats didn't need a second command. They were gone in a trice bounding and roaring toward the CISTS. Two tried to raise their blowpipes but the cats were too fast and were upon them; the cats offered no mercy but tore at the flesh of the invaders whose cries were awesome to hear. The other three ran off but the cats bounded after them and brought two down. The fifth kept running but was felled with a single blow from Marx who had run to the scene still dressed in his sack nightshirt. They were almost upon the prone body when Lump called "Stop! Heel, Maggie!

Ronnie! Heel!" For a moment the cats hesitated, but then stopped and sat next to the man whom Marx had pinned to the ground with his massive right foot.

"Now we really do have cats of war," Marx said.

"How did they get in?" Roque asked.

"The same way Orb got Una got out, I should guess," Marx replied. The man beneath his foot stirred and Marx said, "I think we'll ask this bastard how and find out what's going on."

The Bloomers growled and the man cowered at their noise.

From the ramparts above came the cry, "Enemy without!" This was followed by similar cries from all around the walls.

Wesley ran up, rubbing bleary eyes. "What's happening, Comrades?" he asked.

"Will you help Lump guard this creature? I need to see what's happening up there." Roque requested.

"My pleasure," Wesley replied taking out the long knife he had taken to carrying in his belt ever since Clem had attacked Una.

By this time, dawn had fully broken and the sight that greeted Marx and Roque was not a happy one; the castle was surrounded by the serried ranks of CISTS, their diaphanous silk skirts blowing in the breeze.

"Who the hell are they?" Roque asked.

"They aren't friends," Marx dryly observed.

A Sod stood up on the parapet and shouted, "Fuck off skirts!"

A CIST in the front rank raised his blowpipe and blew. It was only in the millisecond before it hit that they saw it in the air, but by then it was too late. The Sod fell to the ground. Marx and Roque ran to him, but he was dead; the thin dart had pierced his chest.

"Issue instructions for no-one to expose themselves to fire," Roque commanded.

"I will," Marx replied as he ran off, "and I'll get Anvil. He might be able to figure out what's killed Harry. The dart itself isn't big enough."

It hadn't taken long to persuade the surviving CIST to show them how he had entered the castle: all that had been needed was for Maggie to put her face in his, bare her teeth, and growl. All the man knew for sure was that his leaders had a map of all the secret passages that threaded through the castle. This was shocking news as they quickly realised that their walls were far from impregnable. The first thing they had to do was to secure the passage that led from the wainscoting to the outer wall.

The Leadership gathered in Aidonis' chambers to discuss, first, the task of making the castle secure and then what to do about the enemy without; the rescue of Una would have to wait until these matters had been resolved. The consensus was that someone, or a number of Sods would have to go down the passage and make the outer door secure. The CIST had told them that there was a locking bar at the outer entrance. They felt that they would need to ask for volunteers for this extremely dangerous task.

It was then that Aidonis intervened and said, "I shall go. This has all been brought about by that bastard, Clem."

They looked at each other for a moment until Roque said, "Thank you comrade. You're a brave man."

"Just guilty," he replied.

"Forget the guilt," Serene said "This is no one's fault. We are at war."

"I'll go and get changed into something more suitable," Aidonis replied without further comment.

How were they to protect themselves from further invasions? The only course seemed to be to guard everywhere that might hide a tunnel or passage. This seemed an impossible task but then Lump said, "Use as many Sods as we can spare from the walls and I'll give each and everyone a Bloomer. They'll smell them coming and then they'll raise the alarm and attack if they're told."

"That's a great idea," Marx said.

"What happens if they come in at many places at once?" Wesley asked.

Roque sighed and said, "I think it's the best we can do. Marx would you please organise the guards and, Lump, will you muster the Bloomers? Where did you put them after the fire?"

"Them that's left are in the dungeons. It's 'orrible down

there," he replied.

"Those that are left?" Serene asked.

"Yes, some escaped," he answered.

"How many?" Serene asked again.

"Just one died in the fire. There are forty two left, there were fifty five, so that makes," he faltered as he tried to work it our on his fingers.

"Twelve," Serene completed the sum, "Twelve wild Bloomers. Oh dear."

"They'll breed," Lump said.

"Feral Bloomers are not a concept to conjure with," Serene observed.

As Marx and Lump left the room, Anvil entered holding an old piece of parchment on which he had scribbled hurried notes; he looked distinctly worried.

"The poison's a cocktail of very nasty things indeed," Anvil said. "I don't know who made it or where they got the stuff, but it's a mixture of cyanide, curare, and strychnine: lethal, even in small doses."

"There's no antidote?" Serene asked.

"None. The blend makes it impossible to deal with, even if I had the right chemicals here, which I don't. There's nothing I can do," Anvil replied.

"There's lots you can do, my friend," Roque answered. "The first thing is to think how we are going to get the better of these soldiers and the next is how we find where they've taken Una and how we set her free."

Aidonis returned in what once had been described as a 'track-suit'. "I'm ready," he said.

"I don't think you should go alone," Roque replied. "It's too dangerous."

"He's not going alone," Wesley said. "I'm going with him: he shall not walk through the passage of death alone, I will be his staff and protect him, yeah even as the night follows the day, I shall. . ."

"Shut up, Wesley," Roque interrupted. "Now is not the time for a speech, but thank you, yes, you go with Aidonis. You've got a better chance together."

"Come on then, comrade," Aidonis replied. "Let's get to it."

"Aidonis, before you go, I haven't been everywhere in the castle, but is there, or was there an armoury?" Anvil asked.

"Of sorts," he replied. "There's a room in the west of the keep, but I've not been in it for years."

"Is there armour?" Anvil asked.

"There is some stuff, but I don't remember what."

"I'll look," Anvil replied.

Roque said, "Good luck, brave comrades. I'd rather you came back alive and that the passage was not secure than lose you two, understand?"

Within a few minutes the two men passed through the wainscoting and into the dark passage.

The Sodster made good time to Lindum and though it was risky they pedalled across the perilously shaky Pelham Bridge without incident. At the foot of the great hill that led to Uphill, Gilt and the two pedallers dismounted and pushed the vehicle, upon which Una lay, up the steep gradient.

The CISTS at the gate had never seen a bicycle, let alone a Sodster, and were thus more than a little agitated when Gilt demanded immediate entry. Lamont and Blagg had left Alton in management of the small holding force of CISTS that had remained in the city (this had been quite deliberate, as they felt that it would keep the pressure on Hamondi during their absence and thus ensure a sizeable heap of Hamsters). After about five minutes, in which Gilt's patience had reached rock bottom, Alton arrived. Being in sole command of the forces in the city he was feeling particularly important and in this condition he tried to mask his wonder at the sight of this strange machine and the beautiful woman who lay tied to it.

"Who the hell are you lot and what's she doing tied up on that contraption?" Alton asked.

"Secret agent PP2, Gilt's the name. That," he said pointing at Una, "is mine. Who she is, is none of your bloody business. Now let us in."

"What do you mean, secret agent?" Alton asked.

"Can I have a private word?" Gilt responded.

"Security is not a matter of privacy; it's a matter of public accountability," Alton pompously observed.

"You guys think you're something special, don't you? I had the same sort of difficulty with Lamont and Blagg."

"You've met Legates Lamont and Blagg?"

"Yes, and I have to say that their, and your, sense of self-importance gets right up my nose."

"Cists are important."

"I presume that 'cists' means something?"

"Counter Insurgency Services Troops."

"Do you know what a cist actually is?"

"A single soldier."

"A cist, spelt with a 'y' is a cavity in the body filled with abnormal matter, or should I say pus," Gilt sneered.

"Cist doesn't have a 'y' in it," Alton replied.

"Listen, son," Gilt said pulling out his letter of authority. "Read this. I presume you can read?"

"Cisturions are required to read. It's part of our training," Alton said as he took the letter and slowly read using his finger to follow the words.

"Would you find it easier if you tried it out loud?" Gilt asked.

Alton ignored the jibe and continued his slow progress through the document, and when he had finished, said, as he saluted, "Enter, Agent Gilt. How can I be of service to you?"

"That's better," Gilt replied and wondered why those 'in command' seemed to be such bloody morons. "Now, where can we lock her up? I want guards posting. An attempt may be made to rescue her. That done, you will take me and my staff to suitable accommodation."

Una lay quietly listening to this interchange; at least she now knew the identity of her abductor though it gave her little comfort. She had seen the forces that would, by now, be at the castle and she just prayed that Roque, Marx and the others would concentrate upon defence and not try and rescue her; well, at least not straight away.

BBW the city had decided that, as part of its drive to become a tourist attraction, it would convert the castle buildings into a museum. The question had been 'a museum of what?' This had absorbed the thinking of city officers and elected councillors for nearly eighteen years and after much argument they had secured funding from the Regional Assembly (long since defunct) to create the 'National Museum of Imprisonment'. Una soon found herself manacled to the wall in an extremely well designed replica of an American death row cell. Though the surveillance cameras no longer worked, the treble barred walls made the place appear incredibly secure. A little natural light seeped through a long slim slit at the top of the cell walls.

Alton left Gilt, Clem and Seth in the cell with Una.

"Well," Gilt said with a smile, "I don't think you'll be leaving here in a hurry."

"You may have captured me, but you will not defeat my Sedanistas," Una said with great confidence.

"I think that is being dealt with as we speak, my dear," Gilt replied.

As Gilt spoke, Clem moved nearer to Una, so near in fact that she could smell his breath, the condition of which seemed to deteriorate with every moment that passed.

"You two going now?" Clem asked.

"Yes, I think we'll be on our way," Gilt replied.

"You can't leave me here with him!" Una stated.

"I know," Gilt replied and turned to Seth, to whom he whispered, "would you please kill him, Seth."

"Now, master?" Seth asked.

Gilt nodded. Clem was so involved with the prospect of 'having' Una that he was still smiling as Seth's knife slit his neck from ear to ear. Blood spurted as Una screamed and Clem fell to the ground where he grabbed at his neck in a vain attempt to staunch the flow. He twitched and writhed but within a few moments was dead.

"Thank you," Gilt said, "a loathsome creature."

Una stared at her dead assailant and then looked up at Gilt and Seth and said, "Did you have to kill him?"

"Did you have a better idea? Anyway he'd served his purpose.

243

I promised him you in exchange for his map of the secret ways into that bloody castle. I lied; a gentleman would never offer up a beautiful woman to pathological scum like that."

"He gave you a map," she said in a voice full of loathing, "so that he could have sex with me?"

"Sex is a powerful motivator. Come, Seth, we must leave Una to her thoughts."

"Get him out of here," she protested.

"Why? He won't do you any harm now, will he?" Gilt replied. "I'll send someone to get him later, and then maybe we'll let you out of those things so that you can have a mite to eat." As they reached the door, he turned and said with a laugh, "Now don't go anywhere will you?"

The door slammed shut and Una couldn't help but watch the blood drain from Clem's body. The great dark pool now lapped against her bare feet. She looked down at herself and saw that she was splattered with blood but there was no way she could wipe it away.

Her thoughts moved to the comrades in the castle and what Gilt had said. "Has he made it up," she worried. "Is it true?" Then she cried, slowly at first, tears rolling down her cheeks, but then she sobbed and recognised that deep in her heart she had hoped that Gilt, or rather Orb, had been her father. Then she stopped crying and forced herself to focus on hope rather than despair.

86

Aidonis and Wesley spent some time in silence adjusting to the dark in the secret passage; truth be told, this period of waiting also helped them to quiet their jangling nerves. Before they entered they agreed that they would only talk in the slightest of whispers and, only then, if it was really necessary. They would have liked to have brought a vegetable oil lamp but thought this to be too risky. They had no knowledge of the shape or direction of the way; the captured CIST had merely followed the one in front and could not say if it ran in a straight line or not. So Wesley finally took a deep breath, tapped Aidonis on the shoulder and they set out with the musician taking the lead. Though they didn't realise it, the passing of Gilt and Una and the subsequent movements of the CISTS had reduced the amount of cobwebs quite considerably but the rubble was still a regular hazard. They moved slowly and carefully in the darkness trying to fall as quietly as possible. After some time, they turned a corner and there, some way off, a chink of light came though the slightly open outer door.

Their task was to close and lock the door but it was likely that guards were stationed at the entrance. They changed places with Wesley going to the front; he was smaller and lighter than Aidonis and they felt that if Wesley could get it shut, then Aidonis could brace himself against the door whilst Wesley found the locking bar. Now they crawled slowly, so slowly, that their progress seemed slight but gradually they came nearer to the opening. A mouse ran over Wesley's head where he lay listening; it was all he could do not to shout out; the sudden 'liveness' on his neck made him shake with terror. They both lay still and listened and gradually they made out the sound of voices talking.

"Shit!" Aidonis thought. "There are guards."

Wesley's thought was very similar but came into his mind as," Well that's really pissed on our chips."

Once more they moved forward until they were within a couple of feet of the door.

The men outside were moaning.

"What's all this bloody fucking about with passages," the first voice said.

"It gets on my tits. We're stuck here twiddling our bleeding thumbs," a second continued.

"I joined up for a fucking good fight, not all this marching miles and bloody miles and not a punch-up in sight," a third added.

"I know what you mean," the second one said.

They droned on whilst Wesley held up three fingers. Aidonis nodded in reply. Then the door opened wide and a CIST entered. The Sod and the singer lay as flat as they could.

245

"What you doing?" a voice called from outside.

"Having a slash," came the reply.

"Shy, are we?" the first voice called.

"Piss off," the man in the passage said as he started to urinate. "I'm not getting fucking thorns in my cock, I can tell you that for nothing."

He continued to empty his bladder for what seemed like a lifetime to Wesley as the liquid splashed from the floor onto his face. They used to argue that drinking your own piss was good for you, but presumably even those given to such practices would have sympathised with Wesley's circumstances. Wesley didn't know what the CIST had been drinking but his urine was most acidic. Eventually the man replaced the offending article in his jock strap, adjusted his skirt, and left the passage. Neither Aidonis nor Wesley could believe that he hadn't seen them.

This seemed like as good a moment as any and so Wesley pointed at the door, nodded and mouthed, "Now." Wesley could see the locking bar where it stood leaning against the wall. He leapt at the door shutting it with a bang whilst Aidonis jammed his full weight against it. Startled cries came from outside and a shoulder hit the door, Aidonis held his ground and within a few fumbling seconds Wesley had the locking bar fixed across the rear of the door.

The two men hugged each other and Wesley shouted, "We've done it!"

"Let's get out of here," Aidonis responded as they started to move as quickly as they could through the now total blackness. As they stumbled away an axe thudded into the door behind them.

"Oh holy shit!" Wesley cried as a second blow cut into the door. They ran, Aidonis bringing up the rear. They fell, the door began to splinter and soon a hole was made. They heard the sound of blowpipes being pushed through the opening and then the swish of darts flying through the air. They threw themselves to the ground as the darts bounced harmlessly off the uneven walls.

Wesley said, "Scream like you've been hit!"

This they did, got to their feet and started off again. It was a narrow part of the passage and Aidonis' bulk filled the way. There was that sound again. This time the darts flew into Aidonis' back and he gasped with pain and shouted, "They got me, Wesley. Keep going. I'm a dead. . ."

He didn't finish his sentence as death had come upon him; now he stood wedged almost upright, a human shield between Wesley and the darts. Wesley tried to pull him with him but the man was too big and there was no room for manoeuvre. With a heavy heart Wesley made his way through the passage and away from the danger.

Beyond the walls, Lamont and Blagg set about making their preparations for their frontal assault. The men they had despatched early had been 'tasked', as they described it, with opening the castle gates and, if there was time, the lowering of the drawbridge. When neither of these events took place, they rightly concluded that their CISTS had been killed or captured.

Lamont and Blagg gathered their Cisturions together in order that they could agree the best way of moving the assault forward. Lamont wanted to use the map to invade every passageway described there and make the assault from within. Blagg preferred a full frontal assault on the walls once they had cut down the trees, made the necessary ladders, and produced a battering ram from a tall beech tree that was beyond the perimeter of the church's graveyard. Although he had eventually been persuaded to use the secret ways in, he felt that it wasn't in the CISTS' style to behave in a subtle way.

Whilst the CISTS got on with the work of preparation, the Legates and Cisturions debated the pros and cons of each strategy. They could not agree. A newly promoted Cisturion, one Brewster Fenchel, spoke up.

"Excuse me, Legates," he began, with a certain amount of

trepidation, "but is there not a middle way?"

"Which is, Fenchel?" Lamont responded.

"Couldn't we do both things at the same time? Then we could hit them from the inside and the outside at once."

The Legates thought about it; the other Cisturions mumbled to each other, and then Blagg spoke on their behalf, "First class idea, Fenchel, first class."

"The living proof that a consultative management process works," Lamont added.

"Cisturions," Blagg continued, "Are we in agreement?"

As one, the Cisturions said, "Yes, Legates."

"Then make the preparations, and when complete, report to me and the battle will commence," Lamont concluded.

High up on the parapets, Marx and Roque watched as the woodland was destroyed. They watched as the CISTS constructed ladders and tied kindling into the makings of torches.

"What are they doing?" Roque asked.

"They are going to attack, scale the walls, hurl flames at us and Christ knows what else."

"There haven't been any more invasions through the secret ways," Roque said.

"There will be, believe me there will be. If I was running their side of it, that's what I'd do anyway."

"We'd best go and try to muster as many as we can. It'll mean women and children fighting as well. There's hundreds of them out there," Roque replied.

In all there were five hundred and eleven men, women, and children in the castle. Twenty seven children were under the age of ten and were therefore deemed unable to fight. Of the men and women, nine were aged grandparents and they were to be allocated the task of caring for the underage fighters. This meant that there were four hundred and seventy five Sods available for the battle to come. From just looking at the assembled CISTS, Anvil estimated that they were about five hundred in number and not one looked anything but very fit and able.

Lump, accompanied by Maggie and Ronnie, patrolled the

castle checking that each of his sentry Bloomers had food and water and that the Sod that attended them knew the key words of control; Lump didn't want any accidents.

Serene and Anvil eventually found the old armoury in the west of the keep and in a far dusty corner they found a pile of armour stacked up against the wall. By the light of an oil lamp they sorted the relics into what might be usable and those items that were so damaged that they were beyond adaptation. After an hour they had assembled various items: a Heaume; a Poitrel (which wasn't a lot of use being breast armour for a horse); three Tonlets; one Aketon; two almost intact suits of Maille; one Bishop's Mantle; a very large suit of French Botte Cassee; and a couple of Buckler shields.

"I'm not sure what good all this old iron is going to do us," Anvil mused.

"I'm going to find Marx," Serene replied. "He seems to know about all this ancient history."

"Well, he would, wouldn't he?" Anvil observed.

Serene found Marx and Roque in the Great Hall, anxiously pacing up and down outside the door to the passage through which Aidonis and Wesley had passed.

"We should see what's happened to them," Roque said.

But Marx shook his head and said, "We must wait."

"Comrade!" Serene interjected. "We have found some armour. We think some of it's usable."

"Do you want me to come and look?" Marx asked.

"Please," Serene replied.

"You go," Roque said with a nod. "I'll wait here, but don't be long. Something's wrong and those bastards out there could attack at any time."

"They'll come by night, you mark my words," Marx replied. "Come on, Serene, show me the way."

They found Anvil struggling to lift the Botte Cassee toward the door and the light, "Bloody hell, this thing weighs a ton," he groaned.

Marx took a sharp intake of breath and advanced to where the suit of armour lay in the dust. He lifted his broadsword (that he had acquired all those many months ago) above his head and smote the armour with all his strength. The sword bounced with a great clash of sound. Serene gasped.

"Why did you do that?" Anvil enquired, somewhat put out at Marx's treatment of his find.

Marx smiled and said, "Do you know what that is?"

"Not my field," Anvil replied.

"It's French. God knows how it ended up here. It's known as 'proof' armour, and that means it can resist any weapon, or at least any weapon that those buggers out there have got."

"Is it any use?" Serene asked. "There's more."

"I think it might just fit me," Marx answered with a smile. "Let's see what other little treasures you've found."

Before he could do this, a young Sod ran into the doorway shouting, "Come quick! Roque says as how to come quick."

When the three comrades rushed breathlessly (Anvil and Serene being some way behind Marx) into the Hall, they found Roque with his arm around the shoulders of a very distraught Wesley.

Una was unsure how long she had hung on the wall; all she knew was that the pain in her shoulders and back was now so great that she doubted that she would retain her senses.

As she swooned she heard a voice say, "Time for tea."

She opened her eyes and saw Gilt standing in front of her with a wicker basket containing what looked like some form of bread and a bowl of evil smelling soup.

"Can't have you fading away now, can we?" he said and nodded to two guards who entered the cell. "You can remove that stiff and leave it outside," he continued. As they dragged Clem's body through the door, two further CISTS released Una from her manacles, and as she collapsed to the floor, Gilt said, "Eat. You've got some visitors but they can wait until you've dined."

Despite the smell Una gulped down the thin gruel and

munched at the bread.

"Enjoy," Gilt said with a smile as he left Una alone in the cell, the door once more locked and the guards at full attention.

When he returned with the 'visitors' he found Una sitting on the stone floor as the cell was bereft of furniture.

"I shall make the introductions," Gilt said. "This is the Lord Chief Justice Hangedogge. Bishop Hamondi you already know, and this is Ruston Terbinne, the prosecuting Notary and his Clerk, Shaclokke."

This troop of defenders of the state were followed by five guards carrying five wooden chairs and within moments they were seated in front of the bars.

"You are Una Uevera?" Terbinne began.

"Who gave you permission to speak?" Hangedogge said rather gruffly.

"I, er, thought," Terbinne responded.

"You are a prosecuting notary. You are not required to think. You are required to do as you are told, or, more precisely, as I tell you. Understood?" Hangedogge said with a fierce glare.

Terbinne nodded. Shaclokke scratched away with his dip pen on the parchment roll that lay upon his knees.

"So, do you deny that you are Una Uevera?" Hangedogge asked.

"No," Una replied.

"Do you deny that you are the leader of the so called Sedanistas?" he asked.

"No," Una replied.

"Do you deny that you have committed acts of sedition and threatened the stability of the English State?"

"Whose English State?"

"Ours, of course," Hangedogge replied.

"We seek to liberate the people, the Legits, and all those whom you oppress, from your tyranny, from the oppression of Ham and your creatures in government," Una stated with considerable force.

"I think one might regard that as a confession," Hangedogge said to Terbinne, who nodded in agreement. Shaclokke scratched away.

"The trial will be blessedly short," Hangedogge said.

"I will defend myself," Una stated.

"Of course," Hangedogge replied. "There is no one else to perform the task. Yes, a very quick trial."

"And a protracted death?" Hamondi asked.

"Indeed. Sedition is the severest of crimes," Hangedogge responded.

"I will make my case in court. The people will hear," Una said defiantly.

"What people? The trial will be held in camera. You know what that means?" Hangedogge asked.

"I demand a public trial," Una said.

"No, that wouldn't be a very good idea, would it," Hangedogge responded. "We will begin when the Prime Minister arrives in the next few days. Until then, secret agent Gilt, please ensure that the prisoner is secure and kept in good health. We don't want her so weak that her execution is without excitement."

Gilt nodded as they left the room.

"You utter fucking bastard," Una said to Gilt, her face pressed against the bars of the cell.

"'fraid so," he replied. "Sleep tight."

89

Una had lost track of time (it was actually the afternoon) and whilst she tried to get some sleep Sister Belgravia was otherwise engaged.

The Sister was excited by her new role as Royal Poisonner (as she thought of herself) and she went about her preparations for the elimination of Whiskerbot with speed and a sense of professionalism not usually found amongst members of her holy order. (The Nasturtiumites were not known for their worldliness, devoted as they were to the preparation of unguents from the flowers of the plant from which their founder had taken their name, having had sight of an apparition whilst in the cottage garden of Bolsover Manor.)

Unlike Camellia, she found no reason to seek to ingratiate herself into her victim's life. The matters she had to address concerned dosage, pain and speed of death. His weight had been the easiest matter to assess; given his height, weight and age he would only need a moderate amount of the 'elixir of death' as she called her potion. Camellia had asked her what it contained but the nun had refused to divulge its contents with the response, "In God's house there are many mansions. You stay in yours and I'll be happy in mine." Camellia was not used to such forthright refusals to answer a simple question but knew that it was best not to argue.

It was Whiskerbot's habit to take tea with Ham each day late in the afternoon and such was the case on this day. Ham had a predilection for all things sweet and the royal kitchen staff had the greatest of difficulty in meeting the desire for sweetmeats. Whiskerbot, on the other hand, abhorred all things sweet (no doubt a consequence of his years spent in Seattle) and so would fill up with rather bitter oatcakes before joining the monarch for nettle tea. Sister Belgravia had discovered this habit through careful interrogation of the pastry cook on the recipes favoured by the royal household. It was this knowledge that enabled her to add the necessary ingredients to the mixing bowl in which Whiskerbot's oatcakes were made. The nun neither knew, nor cared, if any of the kitchen staff licked the bowl or kept back a few biscuits for themselves. All the better really; it would seem like a more general case of food poisoning.

As the years had progressed Whiskerbot had found the monarch to be increasingly irritable at this time of day and so prepared himself for tea with good swig of royal gin. It was a lovely mixture; he would first bite the biscuit then fill his mouth with gin and crunch the whole lot up into what he found to be the most palatable of mixtures. When the flunkey departed he took the biscuit from the pewter plate, pulled the cork from his bottle of gin, and indulged in his normal way.

As the mixture hit his stomach he gasped with amazement. "Damn good gin this," he thought as the glow in his stomach radiated throughout his body. By the time he joined Ham in the music room he was almost euphoric.

"You seem in a particularly fine mood today," Ham observed.

"Indeed, Majesty, I am." He refrained from mention of the gin or the biscuits.

Camellia and Sister Belgravia were hidden behind a moth-eaten curtain that hung behind the defunct grand-piano but with a good sight of Whiskerbot as he sat opposite the monarch.

"I thought you said this was it?" Camellia whispered.

"It is," Sister Belgravia replied in an even fainter voice.

"But he looks really happy," Camellia whispered back.

"Be patient, my child," she said placing a finger to her lips.

"Nettle tea?" Ham asked as a footman poured two cups.

"Yes plea. . . Oh I say! Oh!" Whiskerbot cried.

"What is it?" Ham asked.

"I'm on fire! I'm exploding!"

"Get him some water!" Ham commanded.

As the footman ran off, Whiskerbot cried, "My eyes are melting! My god the pain! My teeth are melting! Arghh!"

Whiskerbot changed colour; he was a radiant red that soon evolved into a bloody purple. He screamed with pain and shot up into the air and, landing on his back on the ground, continued to scream as his skin turned black. Green bile started to flow from his nose and his arse let out great, harsh, howls of gas. Bile flew from his ears. He screamed and rattled across the floor on his back as he tried to escape the searing pain that filled his body. The footman rushed in with a jug of water but halted at the sight of Whiskerbot and his screams. Ham took the jug of water and hurled it over the supine advisor and companion. As the water hit Whiskerbot's face it turned to steam and the dying man let out the most terrifying scream.

"My god! He's on fire!" Ham stated the obvious..

For a moment after the water hit, Whiskerbot turned from black to white, but in a millisecond he was black once more. He let out one final howl of agony as his bowels emptied into his breeches and he died.

Ham fainted.

Camellia turned to Sister Belgravia and said, "Most impressive, Sister."

"Just about met your requirements, I think," she replied.

The two women quietly made their escape from their hiding place, though no one would have noticed in the pandemonium that broke forth as footmen tried to wake Ham and move the Majesty from the dreadful wreck that had once been a man.

As Camellia and the nun made their way back through the castle they found kitchen staff running screaming, "Plague! Pestilence! Death!"

Sister Belgravia had been correct in her assumption that others would eat the fatal cakes and suffer a similar experience to that of Whiskerbot. She smiled and said to Camellia, "Looks like we've got a few thieves in the kitchens."

"We should go and see," Camellia replied.

"No, I shall go and offer pious help. You must go and console the Majesty, lest it has any unnecessary anxieties," the nun instructed.

It was several hours before Ham stopped shaking: it was not everyday that one saw a trusted old man die in such a manner. Camellia sat with Ham and mopped the royal brow, but all the Monarch could say was, "You should have seen it; you should have seen it. One minute he's in the very best of health and the next, oh Camellia, you should have seen it."

"I'm rather glad I didn't," she said in as shocked a way as she could manage.

Elsewhere in Hampton Court, the nun was busy trying to quieten the rumour that the Black Death had returned. Whiskerbot's unfortunate demise left a vacuum; there was no one to officially pronounce upon the events of the day so the Sister went to the Royal bedchamber to seek guidance.

Ham was not up to the task and so Camellia asked, "Shall I deal with things, your Royalness?"

Ham, of course, was only too happy to accept her kind offer.

Outside the door to the chamber she hugged Sister Belgravia and said, "It's begun."

The nun smiled but said nothing as she stared at the closed door of Ham's chambers.

90

It was a cold night and a thick frost lay upon the ground. Inside the castle walls braziers burnt as Sods and Bloomers stood at sentry duty whilst others patrolled the walls. Roque had organised the Sods into two hour 'watches' to ensure that tiredness did not weaken their defences.

The Sedanistas' council of war had spent the afternoon and early evening defining and developing a set of responsive strategies to the attack that Marx was sure would be both bloody and difficult to contain. They had assessed their strengths and weaknesses and concluded that they had a few, but important, potential advantages over their assailants: bikes; Sodsters (if they could get at them); some armour for their best fighters; the Bloomers; and most important of all, a belief in the justice of their cause. As you will know one passionate freedom fighter is worth at least three mercenaries.

There were six usable tunnels and passages into the castle (the seventh was still blocked by Aidonis' body) and at about one o'clock in the morning CISTS began to enter these dark places. They had abandoned their silk skirts and were almost invisible in the darkness, and they moved as silently as mice. There were ten CISTS in each of these squads, the Legates being unsure of what they might find as they progressed into the castle. Their plan was to attack from within, take the Sods by surprise, get the gates open and the drawbridge down as the external forces scaled the walls whilst others blew their poisonous pipes. In other words, they had taken Fenchel's advice. The only problem they had was the coordination of the attack. The Legates had studied the map and Fenchel had done the calculations as to how long it would take each squad to be ready to break forth inside the castle. They concluded that they should allow thirty-two minutes from entry to exit and that the exterior attack would commence at exactly this latter time. How was this to be achieved when there were no timepieces?

The answer was counting. Each squad was allocated a 'counter' and a further 'counter' would stand with the Legates. Two hours had been allocated to 'counter' training as it was crucial that they all counted to the same beat so that when Lamont lowered his hand the counting began.

The CISTS' ladders hit the walls of the castle at nearly the same time as the squads burst forth within the castle (which goes to show the value of training). Ten swung open the stone door in the great kitchen screaming their war cry, "Die!" Three Sods were on guard and as the door opened they picked the cauldron of boiling water from the great stove and hurled it upon the foe. On they came. A young Bloomer released from its leash rushed at the nearest CIST and embedded its teeth in his neck. As the man screamed in agony, one of the squad drove a poisoned dart into the Bloomer's neck who fell dead. One Sod fell fatally wounded whilst the two others fought hand to hand. Four CISTS broke forth from the kitchen.

Upon the battlements Roque ran as fast as he could, burdened down as he was by his suit of Maille, encouraging the Sods to push the wooden ladders back. The CISTS were good and as hands sought to push them away darts plunged into gnarled bare hands. Within a few moments, Roque found himself confronted by six men; he charged at them screaming, "Freedom!" wielding his immense broadsword. They had no chance to blow their pipes and he cut and swung amongst them until they lay dead, whilst other Sods used knives and clubs to beat back the enemy. The Sods hurled the dead bodies over the brink and down upon the climbing CISTS.

Marx stood in the centre of the keep waiting for the next wave of CISTS who would come from within. He was an even more intimidating sight than normal, clad as he was in the suit of Botte Cassee. Beneath his Heaume he wore the Bishop's Mantle and, slung across his back was a massive axe, in his hands he held his great double-handed sword. As the squad broke in from behind the stable block, the farm animals screamed in terror. Marx made not a sound from within his helmet, but he may well have growled as he ran at the enemy. Their darts bounced away as he fell upon them, cleaving and thrusting as Bloomers led by Lump attacked from the rear. There were ten bodies.

Elsewhere CISTS had broken through and were making for the great gates. Wesley, clad in Maille and Tonlet, wielding a sword in one hand and Buckler in the other, led the defence. The only way of avoiding the darts for the Sods clothed in their ordinary rags was to get as close as possible and fight hand-to-hand. The darts became hand weapons, but, as CISTS fell, Sods stole darts from their quivers; soon the enemy fell, killed by their own poison.

The struggle on the ramparts was not going well for the Sods. Despite their best efforts more and more of the CISTS climbed in over the edge. Sods died as CISTS high up in the trees that remained blew their deadly darts into the defenders. Slowly but surely the Sods were being pushed back but Roque realised that those that were inside had stopped using darts, "Could they have run out?" he wondered, and then shouted, "Sods, go down! Retreat! Go down below!"

As they obeyed his command, he defended the stair down which they fled. At its foot stood Marx shouting, "Roque, get down here!"

The CISTS pursued their quarry and for whatever reason, seeing Marx and Roque together, they hesitated and at that moment Roque shouted, "Lump! Now!"

Lump released ten Bloomers who bounded up the steps and set about the CISTS with such relish that even Lump had to look away. These CISTS had indeed run out of darts and their knives were too slow for the racing cats of war.

For the moment the gates were safe but yet more CISTS were climbing their ladders and clambering over the walls.

"Plan C!" Marx shouted.

The doors to the great hall immediately swung open and twenty Sods on bikes swept forth as Wesley and his team opened the gates and let down the drawbridge. Lump was one of the riders and behind him ran fifteen of his very best Bloomers. Maggie and Ronnie had been left to protect Anvil and Serene. The cats had groaned with displeasure when he had left them behind, but he wanted to protect his two old friends. Equally he did not want to risk the lives of Maggie and Ronnie. The majority of the surviving Sods quickly withdrew indoors, whilst Marx stood on the drawbridge as darts bounced harmlessly from his armour. Roque, Wesley and ten of the toughest Sods hid behind the portcullis walls to protect him from attack from the rear.

It was a brave, even foolhardy, counterattack but the climbers had to be stopped. The cyclists pedalled as fast as they could in the darkness close to the walls and, as they passed beneath the ladders, they swung hooks tied to ropes and pulled at the ladders whilst the Bloomers roared into the dark biting and tearing their terrified victims.

Sods struggled to keep their balance as they rode amidst the chaos. First one fell and then another, some knocked from their bikes by CISTS, others hit by darts. Bloomers began to be attacked from all sides and then, from out of the woods, there came the most blood curdling of sounds; the escaped Bloomers had heard the suffering of their relatives and they joined the fray from the rear. The first people they came upon were Lamont and Blagg (such commanders have always stood at the rear) and it has to be said that Lamont put up quite a struggle, killing at least two of the cats, whilst Blagg's eyes bulged with terror as the cats tore at his corpulent body.

Lump saw what was happening and called the retreat to the Sods while shouting, "Enemy, enemy, kill, kill!" to the Bloomers who, with blood in their mouths and upon their strange fur, now needed no further encouragement to continue with their feast. Lump pedalled as fast as he could back towards the castle, followed by the three remaining Sods.

Fenchel attempted to take command and led a large group of CISTS on a direct assault on the drawbridge. Marx cut two down as you would a stoop of corn and waded into the following CISTS, some of whom began to falter in the face of this massive man in armour. The darts continued to bounce of his body and head that was protected by the Heaume. This latter had been used mainly for jousting and had no moveable visor but only a thin eye slit which meant that he soon needed the active support of the Sods hidden behind the gates and bridge.

As Lump and the riders rode past Marx, Roque, Wesley and the others joined him.

The Sods fought harder than even Marx had made them train: they fell back, they rallied, cut and thrust at the enemy and slowly, very slowly, the enemy faltered. Lacking leadership, the remaining CISTS and their Cisturions were uncertain and no longer had heart for the fight.

"We've won!" Roque shouted as a badly wounded CIST, in one final desperate act of war, leapt from the ground, jumped upon Marx and plunged his poisoned dart through the narrow slit in Marx's Heaume and into his left eye. Roque drove his sword into the CIST'S back as Marx fell dead.

As dawn broke, the CISTS that were left moved off to leave the Sods with a famous victory, but one that had been won at great cost: Marx was dead and, of the four hundred and seventy five battle ready Sods they had started with, they were left with, two hundred and nineteen, and of those only one hundred and three were without wounds.

With a heavy heart Lump, gathered in his surviving Bloomers and returned them to their waiting ancestors Maggie and Ronnie.

91

Green had not enjoyed the journey north. Eccles Sedans were light all right, but the speed at which the Legits carried them was unnerving. The State Sedan's progress was slow and comfortable whereas the ride in an Eccles (despite the benefit of seat belts) was relentlessly jolting as the Legits tried to maintain the highest possible speed. What was more, the journey was characterised by constant stops and starts as groups of Legits were rotated to maintain rapid progress.

The Prime Minister was surprised to find that the country

beyond the Capital was in such poor condition; it was not only post-industrial but also strangely mediaeval. You probably think that he should have known this, being the PM, but times had changed and Prime Ministers were not as closely attuned to the needs of all the people as they had once been BBW.

They had taken only four and a half days to reach the Grantham Road just south of Navenby when the three Eccles came to a sudden and juddering halt.

Green leant out of the unglazed window and shouted, "What the hell's going on, Robbo?" as he had come to call Robinson.

The answer was self-evident: bedraggled CISTS were walking south.

Robinson and Travers were already out of their Eccles as Green climbed from his.

Robinson raised his hand and shouted, "Halt! That's an order. Halt!"

The CISTS kept walking; some had bitten flesh whilst others suffered from wounds inflicted with rusty weapons.

"I said halt!" Robinson repeated.

The CISTS kept walking. The lack of a reply was too much for Robinson who grabbed the nearest one to him and, as Travers helped him restrain the man, Robinson asked, "Where do you thing you're going?"

"Home," the CIST replied.

"You can't go home. You're a soldier. A Cist. We're at war," Robinson replied.

"You might be, guv, but we ain't no more."

"I am the Prime Minister. What has happened? I demand to know," Green commanded.

"Where are your Legates?" Robinson continued.

"Dead," the man replied.

"Dead?" Robinson shouted.

At this moment Cisturion Fenchel arrived and said, "Let him go. They've had enough."

"And who the hell are you?" Travers asked, finally joining in the conversation.

"I was Cisturion Fenchel, but now I'm plain Fenchel," he replied as he tried to stem the flow of blood from his groin.

Green looked down at the man's skirt and recoiled at the sight of so much blood, "What happened?" he asked.

"We fought; we lost. They fight hard and they have terrifying things."

"Bikes?"

"Bikes?" Fenchel replied. "Do you seriously think that a bike could do this?" he asked as he lifted his skirt to display his tattered gory nether regions.

"The Sods defeated you?" Travers asked.

"Got it in one. We killed a lot, but not enough. It was them creatures that done for us."

"What creatures?"

"Never seen nothing like 'em. Horrid. Teeth, ripping teeth," Fenchel gibbered in reply.

"I don't understand," Travers responded.

"But you had darts," Robinson protested.

"Poisoned darts," Travers added.

"Not a lot of use if you've run out and some fucking great ugly beast has got you in its teeth," Fenchel replied. "I'm going home," he concluded and walked off into the early morning light.

"I command you to halt!" Robinson shouted. "You're mutineers! I'll have you all court marshalled."

Green put his hand on Robinson's shoulder and said, "Listen, Robbo, I think you're fighting a lost cause. Let's get to Lindum before anything happens to Uevera."

"So much for your bloody Cists," Travers muttered.

"You can fuck off as well!" Robinson replied.

The sentries at the gate refused them entry and, as was usual, a Cisturion had to be found to authorise entry. As the only one left Uphill was Alton, he eventually came and let them through.

Green had remained in his Eccles whilst Robbo and Green had remonstrated with the guards. When they finally passed the barrier his humour was not good, "You!" he said pointing a finger at Alton, "take me to the cow that's caused all this shit!"

"I shall get secret agent Gilt, sir," he replied.

"Fuck Gilt," he replied, "I am the Prime Minister!"

"I'm sorry, sir, but I have strict orders. No one is to see the prisoner without secret service agent Gilt, sir."

"Take it easy, Prime Minister," Travers advised. "It's probably a safety thing."

"Then go and get Gilt!" Green shouted.

There was no need as Gilt had arrived behind where Green stood. "I'll show you the way, Prime Minister," he said.

Green whirled round and said, "Thank god, Gilt. At least now I've got someone sane on hand."

Travers and Robinson shrugged their shoulders and started to follow their leader.

"Where do you think you're going?" Green asked.

"Coming to see the prisoner," they both replied.

"No, you can do something you're capable of doing, something useful. Find where I'm going to stay. Find the Bishop, get me some decent food ready, and a hot bath, and a decent bottle of gin. Go on, get on with it!" he commanded as Gilt smiled at the two men's discomfort.

"So," Green said as he stood outside the bars of her cell, "you are Una Uevera."

"And you are?" she replied.

"I am the Prime Minister."

"Ah," she said with a smile, "I finally meet the lickspittle, the excrescence, the self-serving shite that's killing the people."

Green's mouth opened but no sound came forth.

"She can be quite direct," Gilt observed.

"Your days are numbered. You will be wiped from the face of the earth and justice will prevail. The Legits will be freed and we shall build a new England, an England for the people, not you lot of scumbags," Una said, wondering whether Wesley's coaching had really done her that much good.

When Green finally spoke, he said, "Shame really, you could have made a good politician, and now all you're going to be is a rather attractive cadaver. Gilt, we have work to do. We shall leave this bitch to her thoughts on her future."

92

As Green luxuriated in his bath at Hangedogge's Judge's Lodgings, prior to his breakfast, the Sods at the castle were attempting to deal with the aftermath of the previous night's battle.

Serene and Anvil had established a makeshift hospital in the banqueting hall and it was there that they sought to repair and comfort all those who had been wounded or traumatised in the fight with the CISTS. It was not long before Anvil's collection of potions and salves were nearly used up.

"It'll take me years to make all these again, years," Anvil said to Serene as he was finally able to sit down after administering treatment to so many.

"I know, but you only made them to use, not to keep," she replied.

"But what if we need more, if there are more battles?"

"Then we'd better start gathering what you need as soon as we can."

"It's not that easy," he replied.

"Come on, we can do it together," she said kissing him on the forehead. "You've not changed," she said with a smile.

"What do you mean?"

"Do you remember when we had things we used to call holidays?"

"Long ago."

"Well, we'd ship up somewhere and you just couldn't settle until you'd stocked up with bread, eggs, butter, ground coffee, yoghurt and your Pooh bear honey pot," she laughed.

"Do you think those days'll ever come again?"

"Not like they were before, no. That's not possible," she replied, "but better days will come. I can feel it."

"Not soon enough. We must find Una and get her back to safety," he said.

The same thought was passing through Roque's mind as he went about the business of trying to restore some order and safety after the previous night. All he really wanted to do was to go and save the woman he loved, but duty, his duty to the Sods he now led, had to come first. Then, and only then, could he set out to find her. He had no sense of joy over their victory; she was in danger and Marx was dead as well as many other loyal and brave Sods.

His first task had been to attend to the fallen Marx. It had taken them some time to remove the great man from his armour. Total removal had proved impossible after rigor mortis had set in and he would not damage the man further and so they had done their best. Once the Heaume was removed he was amazed to see that Marx wore a smile upon his face. It was as if he had known they had won the battle and that his bravery had been key to this. Then there was the problem of Aidonis who was still in the passageway. He had wanted to help bring him out but Wesley insisted that he went for the man who had saved his life, pointing out that Roque was too large to be able to really help.

Wesley and three Sods found the task daunting. Not only was Aidonis a bulky man, but he was also stiff as a board wedged upright where he had died. They pushed and pulled but they couldn't budge him. They emerged from the secret door to find Roque waiting for them. "How goes it?" he asked.

"He's locked solid," Wesley replied wiping the sweat from his eyes, "poor bugger."

"Perhaps we should leave him there," Roque suggested.

"No bloody way," Wesley angrily responded. "He needs a proper sending off, not left in a tunnel," he said. "Come on, let's try again," he said to his helping Sods as he disappeared into the opening once more.

Wesley had decided what they should do. The sounds of Aidonis' arms breaking made Wesley's flesh creep, but after this the dead singer fell forward, at last free from his imprisonment. With some difficulty they dragged him along the stone floor and out into the light. It was then that they saw the many poisoned darts sticking out of his back.

The large oak table was brought from the end of the great hall and Marx and Aidonis were laid side by side as good comrades should be. Marx was smiling but Aidonis' face was locked in a hideous grimace of pain and panic. This was too awful to behold and so Wesley went to the music room, and took a towel from one of the many guitar cases and placed it over the dead man's face. He then instructed four Sods to stand guard, one at each corner of the table, to honour the dead men.

Wesley then helped Roque organise groups of Sods who were given the task of removing their dead comrades from inside the castle to the nave of the church where they were laid out in ordered rows. Another detail was charged with the same task, but outside the walls.

As they carried the dead bodies away, Lump, followed by Maggie and Ronnie, searched the battlefield for anything that might be useful in the struggles to come. Near where Lamont and Blagg had been gored to death he came upon two quivers of darts. These he took to Roque who, with a nod of thanks, hung them from his belt. They then both went in search of the Sodsters; only one had been damaged and this provided a moment of pleasure for Roque. He immediately instructed other Sods to use them to gather as much dry grass, timber and kindling as they could find.

Whilst he was doing this Lump, helped by some young Sods, collected dead Bloomers and laid them out next to the Sods whom they had defended with such passion and aggression. When he had finished he sat upon a gravestone and cried. Anvil saw this and was about to comfort the boy when Maggie and Ronnie came to the lad and started to nuzzle and lick him; though it was hard to believe, these two Bloomers were not short on affection (well up to a point).

The next problem was what to do with the corpses of the CISTS. Roque suggested that they could be dumped in the moat but Serene objected saying that this would be a threat to the environment: they had to be disposed of properly. They concluded that they, too, would have to be taken to the church. The Sods given this task objected, saying that they should not lie with their comrades. Roque explained that they did not have time to dig a great pit and that, if they did, it would severely delay Una's rescue. This did the trick and the CISTS were taken to the crypt.

As evening fell, those Sods who could walk assembled in the great hall and the bodies of Marx and Aidonis were lifted upon wooden stretchers. A procession was formed with Lump at the head with the Bloomers. They were carried to the church and laid next to their fallen comrades. The procession passed through and around the nave; some cried because they had lost loved ones, some from the loss of friends, and some because they were still alive. As the last of the Sods passed out into the evening air, Wesley closed the church doors.

Wesley held up his hand and said, "We may have no religion but we do have love and respect. I have words to say, words I learnt from Aidonis. Please listen.

> We're low we're low we're very low,
> As low as low can be;
> The rich are high
> We make them so
> A miserable lot are we!
> We're low, we're low
> Our place we know,
> But not too low,
> To kill the foe, to kill the foe,
> We're free, we're free, we're free!

We're not free yet, but these comrades are. Never forget them, for they are heroes of the revolution."

The Sods stood in silence.

"Light the fires," Roque commanded, and lighted bundles of twigs were tossed through the windows. Within seconds the flames roared and the Sods moved back from the increasing heat that became so intense that the sandstone blocks began to crack. The arson begun by Gilt was finally completed.

It was time to draw breath, eat and talk, as there was much to plan. Roque was all for setting off for Lindum straight away, for that was where they were sure the man called Orb had taken Una, but Anvil's counsel prevailed and he was persuaded to delay his departure until nightfall.

93

At evensong, attended by the believers (in property and privilege) including Green and Hangedogge (Gilt had decided that another bottle of cathedral stilled gin was more up his street), Hamondi offered up prayers for the dead CISTS and the demise of Legates Lamont and Blagg. His words moved Alton, though the latter could hardly have known what Hamondi was actually thinking, which was, "Thank god those bastards are dead. I was never going to get enough Hamsters to get them off my back," and said out loud, "Amen."

"Amen," echoed the congregation.

Gilt, given his status and success in capturing Una, had also been provided with accommodation in the Judge's Lodgings. By the time Green and Hangedogge joined him in the spacious lounge prior to dinner he was more than a little worse for wear; he had concluded (rightly) that his enforced abstinence from the hard stuff over the many months of his search had reduced his capacity for imbibing large quantities of spirits (you may have noticed that some people get mellow when drunk whilst others follow a different course).

"Good evening, Gilt," Green said as he entered the room. "Will you join myself and the Judge? We need to plan the events of the next few days."

"Of course, PM," Gilt replied, "but there is one outstanding matter that you have overlooked in all the excitement."

"And what would that be?" Green said as he poured himself a gin and asked, "Judge, may I pour you one?"

"Most civil, make it a big one," the Judge replied.

"Hamsters," Gilt replied.

"Hamsters?" Green queried.

"Our contract."

"Ah yes, our contract," Green said as he passed the Judge his gin. "What of it?"

"We agreed that half the money was up front and the rest was paid on delivery." Gilt responded. "I have delivered."

"Most admirably," Hangedogge said.

"So what's the problem?" Green asked.

"I want my Hamsters," Gilt said rather gruffly.

"You shall have them," Green replied.

"I want them now."

"Don't be ridiculous Gilt. I don't carry that sort of money around with me."

"Then why didn't you say anything?" Gilt asked.

"I forgot."

"You forgot? You fucking forgot. I don't think so."

"That sort of language is not necessary," the Judge advised.

"And you can get stuffed as well," Gilt said waving a finger.

"There's no need to fall out over this. You will be paid," Green said in the soft voice he used to persuade the world that he was a decent man.

"How and when?" Gilt asked.

"When you return to London," Green responded.

"I may not be going back to London," Gilt said. "I might explore other opportunities."

"I will write you an IOU for the full amount," Green suggested.

"And I will witness it," Hangedogge added.

"You must be joking. An IOU, no way. I want Hamsters and I want them now."

"How am I going to do that?" Green asked.

"Not my problem, PM. We had a deal and you're going to stick to it."

"Was it in writing?" the Judge asked.

"A verbal contract is binding in my business," Gilt said, "even if it's not in yours."

"There's no need to be rude," Hangedogge replied, and then turned to Green and said, "I can see that someone in Gilt's line of work might be suspicious of IOU's and the like. I think we owe it to this man to treat him in a way that befits his role and function."

"Now you're talking," Gilt said as he poured himself another gin. "Thank you Judge."

Green looked completely perplexed by the Judge's remarks, but said, "Oh, of course."

"I have some reserves," Hangedogge continued, "and I'm sure Hamondi still has Hamsters in the treasury. Perhaps we should adjourn, see what we can do, and rejoin secret agent Gilt at dinner?"

"Now?" Green asked.

"Yes, now," Hangedogge replied with a big smile and a nod. "I'll get someone to bring you in some canapés, just to stave off the hunger," he said to Gilt.

"Thank you, Judge," Gilt replied.

As Hangedogge closed the sitting room door behind him, Green went to speak but the judge put a finger to his lips and drew the Prime Minister to the foot of the stairs and then led him up to the first floor landing.

"Now you can speak," Hangedogge said, "but quietly."

"What on earth were you talking about in there?" Green asked in a whisper.

"I was thinking about what we should do."

"About the money?"

"About Gilt," Hangedogge said. "Do you know which room they put him in?"

"Next to mine, I think, round the corner on the left. Why?"

"I think we should take a look at his trinkets."

As they reached the door Hangedogge said, "I'll take a look. You keep watch. That man is unpredictable."

When the judge had finished his search of Gilt's room the two men descended the back stairs and went out into the coach house at the rear of the property.

"We need to move quickly, lest our man sobers up," Hangedogge said as he laid out the contents of the pillowcase into which he had stuffed Gilt's possessions.

Within seconds the money belt, the knife belt, and, most importantly the gun were laid out before them.

Hangedogge took the still considerable sum of Hamsters from the belt and asked, "Your money?"

"Hell no, the Exchequer's," Green replied.

"Good," Hangedogge responded. "Now you go and find Alton and bring him, with as many able-bodied CISTS as he can muster, and return immediately to the lodgings. Be quick, be quiet go now."

"Me?" Green asked.

"Get moving, man. I know what I'm doing."

When Hangedogge entered the sitting room Gilt was busy eating some rather tasty starling canapés that he was washing down with yet more gin.

Looking up, Gilt said, "You weren't long, Judge. Any luck?"

"I think so," he said as he took the money from his judge's robe and placed the pile of Hamsters he had recently taken from Gilt's money belt on the occasional table on which the nearly empty plate of canapés sat. "Will this do for a start?" he asked.

"Judge, you're a man of your word. I apologise for my earlier wudeness, I mean rudeness," Gilt giggled.

"Not at all. A man under pressure sometimes acts in uncharacteristic ways. Perhaps you should count it."

"I suppose I should. Useful to know if there's any outstanding," Gilt replied, as he put down his glass and picked up the notes.

"Will you excuse me for a moment?" Hangedogge asked. "I am expecting Hamondi for dinner. Least I could do with him having put his hand in his treasury. Won't be a tick."

"No, I'll just see how many little darlings there are. Who's a pretty note then," Gilt said as he kissed a Hamster.

"Quite," the judge said as he left the room.

In the large hallway he paced up and down, a stern look upon his face, as he muttered, "For god's sake get a move on, Green." He then quietly opened the door and observed the secret agent still busily counting the notes.

After about eight minutes the front door opened and Green stood on the threshold. He entered, followed by Alton and seventeen CISTS. Hangedogge once more put a finger to his lips as the men entered the building. "Follow me," he silently mouthed as he moved to the door that he suddenly flung open.

Gilt looked up, somewhat startled as Hangedogge shouted, "Gilt! I arrest you in the name of the law!"

"What for?" Gilt asked as he rose to his feet, dumping the

notes on the chair behind him.

"Treason!" Hangedogge replied as he removed Gilt's gun from his robes.

"You bastards," Gilt shouted as he rushed forward at the judge.

A shot ran out as Hangedogge fired hitting Gilt in his left thigh. As he fell screaming to the floor, Alton and the CISTS fell upon him.

Green collapsed in a chair as Hangedogge commanded, "Lock him up!" Alton decided that it would be easier if the prisoner was unconscious and so cracked him across the head with his wooden truncheon. When Gilt had been rather roughly dragged from the room, Hangedogge said, "I think I'll have that drink now."

Having taken a good swig he sat in the chair recently vacated by Gilt and picked up the pile of Hamsters and said, "Well I haven't had so much excitement in ages."

"You're quite an extraordinary chief justice, Hangedogge," Green observed.

"Well, thank you," he replied with a smile, split the notes into two roughly equal piles, rose to his feet and handed one of the bundles of Hamsters to Green and said, "These are for us, I think."

"I'm not sure that I can take these," Green murmured.

"Keep you going for a bit, eh?"

"I'm not sure I can."

"Does anyone know that he had the money in the first place?"

"No, of course not."

"Then there is no dilemma."

"What are you going to do with him?" Green asked.

"We shall have the pleasure of a double trial and two executions, Prime Minister," the Judge replied.

"It doesn't seem very fair somehow."

Hangedogge started to laugh at this and could barely manage to say, "How in Christ's name did you ever become PM?"

Seth, hearing the commotion, came from the castle stables where he lay to see his 'master' being dragged to the jail. His look of wonder soon changed to a frown of anger. "I shall save you, Master," he said out loud.

Gilt's surprise on regaining consciousness on the floor of the cell adjacent to Una's (these replicas of American death row cells were not divided by walls but only bars to ensure that the condemned had no privacy whatsoever) had been no greater than hers when his limp and bleeding body had been dumped there.

She had sat upon the floor and waited whilst her enemy, the murderer of, Rocket, and countless others she guessed, came back to life.

His first words were, "That fucking judge shot me in the leg."

He then set about checking out the damage to his thigh; he tore a strip from his freshly laundered white shirt, spat upon it and cleaned the wound.

Without thinking Una asked, "Are you badly hurt?"

"No, it went straight through. Just a bit sore," he said despite the pain.

"Why are you here? You captured me," she said. "Is this some sort of a trick?"

"The hole in my leg is not a trick."

"Then why are you here?"

"That devious bastard Green owes me money for getting you and didn't feel like paying up."

"So they shot you?"

"Hangedogge did, and, more to the point, I've been charged with treason."

"You're joking," she said.

"Hangedogge doesn't joke."

"Well," she said, "the catcher caught. How does it feel?"

"Don't gloat; it doesn't become you. I need to get out of here."

"That makes two of us," Una stated. "Any ideas?"

"Not yet, but I'll think of something."

"It would be sensible if we cooperated, at least until we get away," Una suggested.

"I trusted Green. He is the Prime Minister, but I bet that him and the judge will have stolen the down payment they made on you by now. They've denied me my pay-off."

"My heart bleeds for you," Una said.

"They really didn't need to have me as an enemy, but they've got one now."

Though mad, Seth was not fool enough to believe that he could liberate his 'master' without some help and he was pretty certain he wasn't going to find it uphill in Lindum. "I'll find the Sods, that's what I'll do, and just hope that they don't 'do' for me before I tells 'em about the master," he said to himself, as he made his way downhill, back along High Street towards the Grantham Road.

94

There had been much discussion between Roque, Anvil, Serene, Wesley and Lump about how they should approach Una's rescue from wherever she was kept in Lindum. Lump was included in their debate because his valour, and control of the Bloomers, had made him a man in their, and his own, eyes. He also still felt guilty that he had not used his own judgement, and kept up his guard on Una.

The rescue party was to be small, comprising Roque, Lump, Maggie and Ronnie. The two humans would take a Sodster, with the cats sitting on the back, to Lindum under the cover of darkness and from there they would just have to do the best they could.

Wesley was to be left in command of the Sods and his task was to prepare them for the leaving of Somerton Castle. Anvil and Serene would go back to Navenby Hall with a small group of Sods and they would gather together as much food and goods as they could ready for the departing Sedanistas; the occupation of the castle and the subsequent battle had made supplies dangerously low.

"You won't be able to take the Sodster into town, you know," Serene warned.

"I know that!" Roque replied, much more sharply than was necessary.

"What I meant," she calmly replied, "is that there used to be some old allotments, places where the peasants were encouraged to grow their own food, on the top of South Common. That would be a good place to hide it."

"Sorry," Roque said, "bit strung up."

Serene and Anvil exchanged a glance; they had some idea of the anguish that Roque was going through.

"My uncle used to have one of those allotments," Wesley said. "Nathan Shakespeare was his name, and he grew the greatest marrows ever to grace the sunlit slopes of the Common. How he would sit and…"

"Not now, Wesley," Serene said as gently as possible.

"Apologies," Wesley replied.

"Is this uncle still alive?" Roque asked.

"Probably. He was a healthy old stick, but he'll be old."

"Will he be friendly to us?" Lump asked.

"Tell him about me, then he'll be friendly."

"Where does his live?" Roque asked.

"Shakespeare Street."

"But that's his name?" Lump queried.

"That's why he's called Nathan Shakespeare, the Nathan who lives in that Street. So there be Tom, Dick and Harry, Mildred, Susan and Etty Shakespeare as they all live in the street. It was the same in all the streets downhill," Wesley replied.

"It must be a Lindum thing," Anvil suggested, "just a bit strange."

"I'm more worried about people seeing our Maggie and Ronnie," Lump said, slightly perplexed at the direction the conversation was taking.

"Good point," Roque said. "Perhaps we should leave them behind."

"No way, Comrade," Lump said very firmly. "If we're goin' to rescue our Una we'll need 'em. Them's the best weapons we got."

"Cloaks," Serene said.

"Cloaks?" Lump asked.

"They can walk on their hind legs, can't they?" Serene asked in return.

"But not for miles," Lump replied.

"If they've got cloaks that drag on the ground, all covered up, then you and Roque can take one on each arm as if they were old folks," Serene suggested.

"I think we'd better try this first," Roque replied.

"There's some cloaks in the cupboards in our room," Anvil said. "I'll get them."

Maggie and Ronnie had always been good learners and soon mastered the technique of walking supported by Roque and Lump. The cloaks tended to fall open and so Serene sewed up the fronts all the way to eye level which meant that the Bloomers particularly strange appearance, especially their teeth, could be hidden from view.

"Has anyone ever heard the story of Little Red Riding Hood?" Anvil asked with a giggle and a smile.

Only Serene had, and she simply said, "Anvil!"

Roque and Lump were disguised as Legits, the Sodster was made ready, and then the rescuers were ready to set off under a dark sky in the dead of night.

As those that were to remain behind at the Castle made ready to see the rescuers off, Serene suddenly said, "Wait. I've been trying to remember this all day."

"We should be on our way," Roque replied.

"It'll only take a moment. They may be useful; they're in my room."

Within a few moments she had returned, slightly out of breath, carrying a linen sack on which was written 'The National Cycle Museum'. "Here," she said, offering the sack to Roque.

He took it, looked inside, looked back at Serene thinking that the old lady had finally lost it. "I don't understand, Serene. There's just lots of little oblong things."

"Lighters," she replied.

"What?" Roque asked.

"Souvenir cigarette lighters."

"I still don't understand."

She plunged her hand into the sack and pulled out a blue

one and lighted it with a roll of her thumb; the flame was bright and high. "I meant to give them to Una long ago but so much happened, I forgot."

Roque took another lighter from the sack, lighted it and smiled, "Wonderful. Instant fire. You never know, they just might come in handy."

"You're a star," Anvil said as he kissed Serene on the cheek.

They made good time and soon passed through Waddington and on through Bracebridge Heath, turning right past the old mental hospital that had been turned into swish apartments BBW and which now stood derelict and open to the sky. It was as Serene had said: there were allotments and there were also strange wooden buildings with empty openings in the walls. One of these buildings was big enough for the Sodster, and its exterior, almost entirely covered in the dense growth of a rampant clematis and attendant bind weed, provided ideal cover for the vehicle.

They had already decided that their first journey into down-hill Lindum would be without the cats; they really did have to check out the lay of the land. Maggie and Ronnie sat in the overgrown doorway and watched their young friend disappear into the night.

Roque and Lump kept to the deep shadow of the hedge as they made their way down Cannock Hill. As they neared the foot of the hill, they could just make out the shape of a figure moving toward them; as it grew ever closer they could hear the figure talking out loud.

Roque took his broadsword from where it was slung across his back and he and Lump pressed themselves deep into the hedge.

The man's voice said, "I'll save you, master. Save the master, save the master, Seth will save the master."

When the man reached their hiding place Lump and Roque jumped forth and Roque cried out, "Who goes there!" as he placed the blade of the sword across the man's neck whilst Lump grabbed him from behind.

Had they ever seen Seth then they would have recognised

him instantly but his actions had been seen by none of the Sods.

"Don't hurt me," he begged. "I'm looking for the Sods from the castle."

"What Sods?" Roque asked.

"The one's where the master stole the woman from."

"What do you know of that?" Roque demanded.

"I was there, I was there. I set fire to the church with Clem," Seth replied.

"Kill him!" Lump said.

"Don't kill me! I know where she is, but I need help."

"Where is she?" Roque demanded.

"In the castle jail. She's locked up with Master Gilt."

"In the jail? You can show us?"

"I'll show you. I'll help; must save the master."

"Who the hell is this master?" Roque asked.

"Orb he was called when you let him in, but he's a secret agent. Gilt's his name, and now they've shot him and locked him up."

"We can't trust him after what he done," Lump said.

"I'll help you. I fight good for the master; three is better than two," he pleaded.

"You come with us. Try anything and I'll kill you stone dead on the spot," Roque warned.

"Save the master, save the master," Seth mumbled away to himself as they made their way into town.

It was just after dawn when they entered the deserted Shakespeare Street; most of the terraced houses seemed to have been abandoned and had fallen into disrepair. Roque's heart sank, as he feared that Wesley's uncle would be no more, but when they reached number 34 they found the house in good condition even though the windows on the ground floor were boarded up with old wooden planks.

Roque knocked on the door with the handle of his sword. There was no reply. He knocked again. After a few moments they could hear the sound of feet slowly coming down the wooden stairs and a moment later a muffled voice said, "I'm not in."

"Nathan Shakespeare?" Lump asked.

"Who's asking?" the voice asked.

"We're friends of Wesley," Lump replied.

"Wesley?"

"Your nephew. He said you'd help us. He said to say he's never forgotten you taking him fishing in the Witham, not that you ever caught anything, he said," Lump said, his mouth close to the door.

"Wesley, you friends of Wesley?" Nathan asked.

"We are. We needs a place to be, out of sight," Lump continued.

There followed the sound of numerous bolts being shot and then the door opened and Nathan said, "Better get thee in then, hadn't thee?"

Before them stood a very old man wrapped in an ancient pink candlewick bedspread. He had a black beard of considerable volume whereas his head was entirely bald except for a single tuft of black hair that hung over his left ear. What was most extraordinary about his appearance was his size; he stood just a little over four feet tall.

"You be thinking I be small bin thee?" he asked, closing the door as his three visitors crammed into the tiny hallway.

"Well, not really," Lump said as he stared down at the old man.

"Well, you'd be right if thee was, cos I is, bin I?" Nathan replied with a smile. "Best thee follow me. I lives up the stairs, and there'n't enough room for us all down here, bin there?" he continued as he climbed the bare boards of the narrow staircase. At the top of the stairs he turned left and they followed him into one relatively large room where he said, "This be me home. Welcome to thee, bin it?"

On entering the room Lump's mouth dropped open, not because Nathan seemed to end every sentence with a question, but because the room was full of books.

"Only Mr Hammer has books, but not so many as this," Lump said.

"Aye, them be books," Seth answered, "lots of books, bin they?" he asked quite unnecessarily.

"What sort of books, Mr Shakespeare?" Lump asked.

"Them be poetry books, bin they?"

"So that's where Wesley gets it from," Roque said with a smile.

"Be just as well young Wesley didn't get his height from me, just the love of words, bin it? But you didn't bring thee here-unto for as to discuss poetry, bin thee? But don't thee be telling 'em they be here. They be burning 'em nonetheless, bin they?"

"No, we shan't do that, but we do need your help," Roque replied.

"Better sit thee down then, bin it?" Nathan replied.

As there were no chairs apart from the one on which Nathan sat, the three visitors sat on the floor, whilst Roque told of their mission and Seth explained why he had joined their quest.

When the tale had been told Nathan rose from his seat and said, "I'll be getting dressed then. I'll find out what be going on in the City, bin I? Find some help, bin I?"

Nathan's 'going out clothes', as he called them, were somewhat less surprising than the candlewick bedspread, consisting of a brown Hessian jacket and trousers, grey smock and a very battered black bowler hat. Having told them to make themselves at home, there being food in the kitchen, and warning them not to leave the house or answer the door, he set off on his errand.

95

As Nathan made his way to the foot of Steep Hill, Una and Gilt were being locked in leg irons and moved from their cells to the Castle's courtroom. This latter was empty as they were placed in the wooden dock and their chains locked to rings set in the floor. There were no seats so they had no choice but to stand and wait. After a few moments, an usher entered and shouted, "Silence in court! Silence in Court! Be upstanding for his eminence the Lord Chief Justice Hangedogge."

Hangedogge entered followed by Green, Hamondi, Robinson, Travers, and, at the rear, the prosecuting notary, Ruston Terbinne, and his brainlessly unctuous clerk, Shaclokke. Hangedogge climbed the steps to his podium and sat down. The usher shouted, "Be seated!"

"Let proceedings commence." Hangedogge began. "We are here today to hear the prosecution's case in respect of the acts of sedition perpetrated by one Una Uevera and the acts of treason committed by a man known as Gilt. How plead the defendants?"

"I suppose it would be silly to ask if there is a defence notary?" Una asked.

"Yes, prisoner Uevera, that would be silly," Hangedogge replied.

"Presumably I can defend myself against this ridiculous charge?" Gilt asked.

"That's most unlikely as there is no defence against an act of treason once proved," Hangedogge answered.

"But isn't that why we are here, to listen to the evidence, to see if the charge is true?" Gilt protested.

"Where's the jury?" Una asked.

"These are matters of the utmost importance to the state. In these circumstances, I will be both judge and jury, supported of course by the Right Reverend Bishop."

"That's bollocks," Una said.

"You're correct there, comrade," Gilt said rather too loudly for Hangedogge who scowled at him.

"Terbinne," Hangedogge said, "present the evidence."

Terbinne rose from his seat and carried a leather bound folder to the usher who, in turn, handed it to the Judge. Hangedogge opened it and read the pages slowly and carefully. The court was silent. After five or six minutes he said, "This evidence is compelling. Perhaps the Bishop would like to give a second opinion?" holding up the folder for the usher.

After a further ten minutes Hamondi said, "I agree, your eminence."

"Excuse me, when do I get to see that?" Una asked.

"You don't. The contents are a state secret," Hangedogge responded.

"This isn't justice. This is nonsense," Gilt observed. "Fucking crass nonsense!"

"You're in contempt of court. Be silent!" Hangedogge commanded as he removed a black cap from the drawer of the desk at which he sat. "I shall pass sentence. Una Uevera guilty as charged. Gilt guilty as charged. The court will consider its verdict." He paused for a moment and then said, "You are both sentenced to public execution. Given the nature and severity of your crimes, you will be taken from this place to another place and at first light on the morrow you shall be taken to another place where you will be crucified until you are dead, so help me god."

"Amen," Hamondi added.

"Usher, issue the proclamation. Tell the Crier to cry," Hangedogge commanded. "We shall have a good crowd, methinks," he added with a sinister smile.

"You're completely and utterly mad," Una shouted.

"Insane," Gilt added.

Hangedogge banged his gavel on the bench and called, "Proceedings closed."

"Be upstanding!" the usher shouted as Hangedogge descended from his high place and left the courtroom followed by the others.

By the time Nathan reached the square between the castle and the cathedral, the Crier was already ringing his bell. "Now hear thee this," he cried, "Now hear thee this."

People stopped in their tracks and listened, perhaps none as intently as Nathan. He followed the Crier as he made his way down Steep Hill and into downhill Lindum carrying his message of doom for Una and Gilt.

Una and Gilt were silent when they were returned to their cells. Execution was bad enough, public execution worse, and crucifixion was a death too terrible to contemplate. Gilt was the first to speak.

"We'll only have one chance and that'll be when they take

our chains off to put us on the cross."

"Some chance that'll be," Una replied.

"We'll have to take it."

"How will they do it? They won't nail us up, will they?" Una asked.

"Hangedogge might authorise anything. He's fucking mad."

"And you're not," Una thought as their conversation came to a halt as they heard the sounds of wood being sawn.

Nathan returned to the house in Shakespeare Street and told of the proclamation.

"We will have to be very ruthless if we are to save Una now," Roque said, when he had recovered from the shock of her forthcoming execution.

"I'll kill 'em all," Seth said as he pulled his long thin knife from where it was hidden under his tunic.

"We've got Maggie and Ronnie," Lump said, trying to be brave.

"Thee will need help. Three to free is not enough, bin it?" Nathan said.

"But that's all we have, and two cats of war," Roque replied.

"Be this the time for men and women to rise up, think thee?" Nathan asked.

"But will they? Una's nothing to them." Roque said.

"There be some like me, some who has had enough, seen enough; some might come, bin they? You do what you needs must do and I'll do what I must. I'll be there at break of day, before the sun comes up. If I be on my own, then so be it, but if I be not alone then we'll see, bin we?"

"Thank you," Lump said.

"Be there sommat that I be offering 'em?"

"Sorry?" Roque replied.

"To get 'em to help, bin it?"

"Freedom," Roque suggested.

"That's a concept, bin it? Incentives is what's needed, in it?"

"Only freedom," Roque said once more.

"Many be old and tired, bin they? Live for today for tomorrow them might be no more, bin they?"

Lump picked up the sack where it lay on the floor and offered it to Nathan with the words, "We has these."

Nathan took the bag, looked inside, and immediately started a little dance of joy on the spot. "Perfecto, bin them? Not seen the likes of them in many a year, 'as I?" he chortled. "I be going then. Wish me luck. Be needing it, woan I?"

Nathan left them alone and went out on his mission.

It was a long hard day of waiting, but when night fell Roque, Lump and Seth slipped out into the darkness and made their way back up Cannock Hill to where the Sodster and the Bloomers were hidden.

96

As Roque and Seth pedalled the Sodster down the road, Roque looked back to see if Lump and the two cloaked Bloomers were okay and then turned to Seth and said, "If anyone sees us and looks like they might sound the alarm, kill them."

"You needs not ask me," Seth replied. "You think I'm a mad 'un, and maybe as how I am, but I will save the master and your Una."

When Nathan had returned earlier Roque had asked him where they could hide the Sodster near to where the execution would take place. Nathan thought about it for a bit and said, "It'll have to be Uphill if thee be going to make a quick getaway, bin it? There be an old disused fire station just beyond The Bail. It be empty now. That be the place, bin it?"

As the Sodster approached the foot of Yarborough Hill, they saw Nathan waiting for them in the entrance to the path that led across West Common. As they approached him, two CISTS emerged from this path and saw the Sodster. Before they could say a word, Seth had leapt from the bike and slit the throat of the first man, whilst Nathan cracked the other over the head with the stout stave that he was carrying. Seth fell upon the second unconscious CIST and stabbed him through the heart.

"Bloody hell! That's enough Seth!" Roque said.

"Better dead than sorry," Seth replied. "Giss us hand; can't leave 'em here."

The two dead CISTS were tossed over the hedge and rolled down into the deep undergrowth that covered most of the common.

"Thanks," Roque said to Nathan.

"Be in for a penny as in for a pound, bin I?" he replied. "I'll show you the way, bin I?"

Roque paced up and down, anxious for action, whilst Lump talked to his Bloomers, "Now Maggie and Ronnie, I want you to be fierce. We got to save our Una and without you two we're in the shit!"

Nathan stared in wonder at the cats, "There been no need to ask 'em to be fierce, they be fierce, bin they. Thee can tell just by the lookin' at 'em, can't thee?"

"Did you manage to raise any support?" Roque asked Nathan.

"I done asked, me ducks, but thee never knows if they be coming or not, do thee?" he replied. "If they be's a comin' then they comes, and if they comes, they'll be up for a scrap, woan they? Them may be old, but that's half the point, in it? Them thinks the old be good for nothing, but me, I thinks we be good for something, something good, methinks, like a good dust up for a good cause, dun I?"

Seth cleaned his bloody knife, lest dried blood hinder its keenness.

As the first signs of light began to show, Lump re-dressed the Bloomers in their cloaks and they set off. People were already making their way to the square for the execution, but they took no notice as the four men and the two walking Bloomers joined them.

It was a cold grey dawn as Alton and his CISTS came to collect Una and Gilt from their cells.

"You just remember what I said," Gilt said to Una as their leg irons were fixed.

They shuffled from the jail and out into the fresh air.

The crowd was gathering fast. As they moved to the square, they saw the two large wooden crosses that had been made overnight and that now lay upon the ground waiting for the victims. Looking up, they saw Hangedogge, Green, Hamondi and various other dignitaries standing on a raised dais near where the crosses would be raised once the condemned had been affixed. Hangedogge had advocated nailing but Hamondi had prevailed, arguing that such a course might sent out the wrong signals; crucifying Christ didn't seem to have done a lot of good for the Romans.

The gathering crowd was hemmed in by a single row of CISTS, with Cathedral Swabs as back-up.

Roque made his way to the north side of the square and worked his way toward the front, his sword hidden beneath a sack that covered his back. Nathan and Lump led the Bloomers to the south side, whilst Seth went east. As they made their way, Lump noticed that there seemed to be rather a lot of old people immediately behind the CISTS.

As Una and Gilt approached the crosses, the crowd started to boo.

Hangedogge raised his hand and turned his thumb down in the style of a Roman emperor.

At that moment Gilt and Una's leg irons were removed. Their hands were already free. In a flash, the two condemned grabbed the irons from where they had fallen and swung them furiously at the nearest guards.

Roque screamed, "Attack!"

Lump pulled the cloaks from the Bloomers, pointed at Hangedogge and the others and shouted, "Enemy! Kill!" They needed no second bidding. The crowd cowered, as the cats roared and ran forward.

Seth leapt from the crowd and stabbed the guard with whom Gilt was struggling.

Nathan ran to Una's side and clubbed at her assailant.

Hangedogge saw the cats coming for him and took out his gun.

Old people removed lighters from their pockets and lit the CISTS' silk skirts and then fell upon them as they struggled to put out the flames; they bit, kicked and clawed. Swabs were

286